Toto Among the Murderers

Toto Among the Murderers

Sally J Morgan

JM ORIGINALS

First published in Great Britain in 2020 by JM Originals
An Imprint of John Murray (Publishers)
An Hachette UK company

1

Copyright © Sally J Morgan 2020

This novel is a work of fiction. In some cases true-life figures appear
but this is a literary device to create context and background to the fiction.
All the main characters are products of the author's imagination and
any resemblance to actual persons is entirely coincidental.

A CIP catalogue record for this title is available from the British Library

Trade Paperback ISBN 9781529300390
eBook ISBN 9781529300406

Typeset in Minion Pro 11.5/14.5 pt by Palimpsest Book Production Limited,
Falkirk, Stirlingshire

Printed and bound in Great Britain by Clays Ltd, Elcograf S.p.A.

John Murray policy is to use papers that are natural, renewable and
recyclable products and made from wood grown in sustainable forests.
The logging and manufacturing processes are expected to conform
to the environmental regulations of the country of origin.

John Murray (Publishers)
Carmelite House
50 Victoria Embankment
London EC4Y ODZ

www.johnmurraypress.co.uk

For Jess

Fred and Rose West committed a series of brutal killings beginning in 1967. They tortured victims to death in the cellar of their Gloucester home, and went undetected for more than twenty-five years.

'The murderous couple's modus operandi . . . was to drive out together in their car and offer lifts to isolated young women, sometimes suggesting that they come back to their house to sleep.'

Theodore Dalrymple, *City Journal*

1

Toto

Someone has written *fuck off* in dark red chalk across the front door. The powdery, blood-coloured residue stains my hand as I push the door open, and I'm hit by the smell of dank carpets. Daylight falls onto a spider darting out from beneath the wallpaper, scuttling off to hide in a gap in the skirting board. Fly carcases pick up in the breeze from the open door and whirl along the passage, and, as the wind whips my hair, I linger on the step, looking up and down the rubbish-strewn street. This place has the feel of danger. Us three girls will have to be on our mettle to live here, so it's probably a good thing that Hank will be staying off and on. He's hidden in his scratched, blue transit van at the moment, but I hope he'll make a display of carrying stuff into the house. It might make people think twice before they mess with us.

The other two are uncharacteristically quiet as they join me. Each of us is calculating what we think about our new neighbourhood in central Leeds.

'Jude Totton, you're a liar,' Nel whispers. 'You said this was Potternewtown.'

'That's what the landlady told us.'

She narrows her eyes at me. 'This is fucking Chapeltown.'

Jo and I pretend not to have heard and start passing boxes in through the doorway of the terraced house while a gaggle of children watch. The chalked swearwords intrigue me every time I walk past them. In the distance a police siren wails as a man in a torn jacket yells through a letterbox a few doors away. I am distracted by the look of his sleeve, which is ingrained with dirt. Abuse pours out of his mouth. 'I'm going to kill you. Sodding bitch. Let me in.'

As the gang of grimy kids circle our possessions, a little Jamaican girl in clean school clothes stops to stare at us. Her eyes meet mine as the door behind her opens and a woman in a nurse's uniform pulls her inside. I'm suddenly self-conscious about my unkempt hippy-looking hair and paint-spattered clothes. There's music in that house. Someone plays a piano laboriously while a wavering, female voice sings the chorus of a Tamla Motown love song. This is the nineteen seventies. Who sings like that these days? Sweet voice, though: mournful and out of place here. The door slams shut, leaving smells of unfamiliar spices and boiled meat hanging in the air.

When all the boxes and bags are unloaded, Hank finally unfolds his body out of the van and glares at the kids. They stop. He's a craggy collection of angles and stubble wearing an army-surplus greatcoat. Pulling himself up to his full height, he looms over them and snarls, 'Beat it, you manky little bastards.' His gnarled knees show through the worn white threads of his jeans, and the laces of his steel capped boots hang untied. 'What're you waiting for?'

I love his pantomime fierceness, but the kids think it's real.

Jo grew up on a tough council estate in Doncaster. 'Don't talk to the buggers,' she says, pushes her dyed-black hair off her face and hands him a plastic bag to carry. 'It'll only encourage them.'

She stares them down until, synchronised like a swarm, they disperse with whoops and curses towards the overgrown park at the end of the street. Running a hand over her hip to adjust her miniskirt she returns to moving things into the house. 'Bloody kids, you've got to watch those thieving little sods.'

At the back doors of Hank's van, I'm worrying whether they've nicked anything of mine. A scab on my cheekbone twinges as I search for the only things I own, my rucksack and sleeping bag.

'Move yourself a wee bit.' The laundered scent of Nel's cheesecloth blouse follows her as she reaches around me for her belongings. She pauses to re-fix the tortoiseshell combs controlling her straw-coloured hair, and notices that I'm fingering the little cut I got yesterday. 'Don't keep touching it.' Her Scottish accent seems stronger as her voice gets louder. 'Do you want it to heal or not?'

'Is it bleeding?'

'Aye. You'll need antiseptic on it.' She drags a box of books and paints from the van. Cradling it in her arms, her gaze returns to the threat written on our door, and she seems hesitant to go past it. 'Where am I headed with this? I suppose you two have already chosen the good rooms? I don't want this one looking onto the pavement. That's all I'm saying.'

Jo interjects in a no-nonsense voice, 'Jude's having that. I'm by the bathroom, and you've got the nice airy one, upstairs at the front.'

Nel blurts out, 'You *knew* this was Chapeltown, didn't you?'

'Sorry flower.' Jo busies herself with her belongings. 'We didn't want you freaking out on us.'

'This area has just about the worst reputation in Leeds.' Nel looks about her as though she can't believe we've done this. 'It's full of smackheads and prostitutes and . . . and muggers and whatever! People get murdered here.'

I get a thrill at her words. I like danger. I like to be frightened. Yes, this is the roughest part of Leeds, if not the whole of Yorkshire. It's dodgy as fuck and supposed to be full of gangs that prey on the immigrants who can't afford to live anywhere else. People get attacked all the time.

'Don't worry. It's not going to be a problem.' I swivel my rucksack up onto my shoulder. 'We'll be safe in the house and it's only a two-minute walk to the bus stop. No time for anything to happen between here and there. Stop stressing. You're always bloody worrying when there's no need.'

She glares at me, 'Well you . . . by the way . . . *you* . . . look like fucking Lady Macbeth with that red stuff all over your hands.'

'Was Lady Macbeth ginger?' I laugh, and she can't stop herself from grinning back.

She softens. 'Your hair is auburn, sweetheart. Dark auburn.'

I need a fag, but as I reach into my pocket the rucksack slumps forward awkwardly. Dumping it, I dig out a hand-rolled cigarette that tastes of tar and shredded apple. As the smoke blows away in the wind, Nel gives it a covetous glance and I take it from my mouth to place it between her lips.

'Thank you,' she says. 'You are *perfect*. Even if you are a scheming bloody trickster who's brought me to live in the deep dark woods against my better judgement.'

4

She shifts the box higher in her arms with the help of her knee. 'You stay out here whilst I take this in,' she says, 'best not to leave the van unguarded . . . and don't catch your hair on fire, lovely, it's blowing into your rollie.'

I look at my hands. Nel's right, they do look like they're covered in blood and there are streaks of it on my coat. I rub the chalked swearword off our door as a woman stares from behind red curtains in the house across the street. One of the kids is back from the park, and he's standing too close to my stuff. How long has he been there? I remember what Jo said about thieving little sods and get worried about my prized possession, my blues harmonica. I rummage through my rucksack for it. My ex-boyfriend, Michael, gave it to me when we were in second year at art school. I thought it was a weird gift at the time. But I learned to play better than anyone expected and now it's like my best friend. After my palm finds its familiar form, I buckle the bag extra tight and straighten up, reassured.

A young woman with a hard face and a chain around her ankle scoots across the road towards me. Her shoes are scuffed and, like me, she has a cut on her cheekbone. She might be my age, but her eyes are hollow and seem older than the rest of her. I'm struck by her hair, which is long and red like mine.

She says, 'Are you girls in business?'

'What?'

'Are you working girls?'

I haven't got a clue what she's talking about.

She checks me over, lingering on my paint-stained, flared jeans.

'Or are you students, or what?'

I say *yes*, even though I'm not. Jo and Nel are part way through a post-graduate teaching course at Leeds University, but I'm on the dole. It wasn't the plan but moving in with them seemed for the best after Dad threw me out in November.

The woman flicks her hair back and glowers at me. 'This is our patch. Do you get me?'

I don't get her. I realise we're being warned off but have no idea what from.

'Yeah, OK.'

'That's where we work.' She indicates the doorway she came from. 'No room for anyone else. All right?'

I nod, still trying to understand.

The woman seems satisfied that her point's been made as she nods and heads back across the road.

Hank appears at the front door, filling the frame with his lanky body. 'What was she after?'

As I throw my rucksack and sleeping bag into the passageway behind him, I relate the conversation and he grins at me sidelong.

'She wanted to find out if you was competition, flower.'

He spells it out.

'Prostitutes.'

'Wow! You're kidding.' I watch the woman with heightened interest and pay extra attention to her red-curtained house. Stepping out on to the pavement, Hank looks around the street. There's something of the guard dog in his stance, like he's sniffing the air for signs of danger.

'You want to be careful round here, I reckon. Especially after dark.'

Jo emerges from inside the house, drawn by the sound of his voice.

Her hand strokes the small of his back. 'It's cheap, love. Chapeltown is the only place we can afford a whole house.'

6

'You want to be careful coming from that bus stop at night. I'm not being funny but be careful what you wear and who you talk to.'

She pats him in the centre of his chest. 'It's all under control, petal.'

The frown he's wearing fades as he links his arms around her. 'I thought being married meant we would be living together.'

'Now listen to me, Mr Colin Hanks, this is 1973, not 1923. Things have changed. Haven't you heard of Women's Liberation? Anyway, we'll be together all the time, once I get this bastard diploma.'

'Don't call me Colin. Only me mam calls me Colin!'

Jo laughs as Hank squirms. Glancing at me, she pulls away and says affably, 'Oi, Jude Totton, get these boxes carried.'

Hank grabs me around the neck in a gentle wresting grip, like I'm his dog or little sister, which sometimes I feel like I am.

'You heard her,' he says and does a perfect impression of our old sculpture technician. 'Get them boxes inside. It's not a bloody holiday camp, is it?'

'Piss off.' I pick up the box full of plates. 'Get something carried yourself, Cowboy.' I dodge to one side as he makes as though to kick my arse.

Following the passageway, I find a cramped room that's both kitchen and lounge. The tattered red carpet is worn into holes near the doorway and has black patches like trampled tar near the chipped fireplace. There's the stale odour of neglect that student houses always have. It comes out of the walls and floors and stays forever, like sweat and gravy with a vague hint of cat's piss. Jo sets about sorting out saucepans and cutlery.

Hank's priorities are different. He props a battered record player on a low shelf near the table and pulls out an LP. Taking it carefully from its paper sleeve, he lowers it onto the turntable and swings the arm on to it. Pink Floyd's newest album, *The Dark Side of the Moon*, rasps out from under the blunt needle. He contemplates the spinning disc. It makes the room soft with something familiar.

Nel has made us all instant coffee. I settle beside her under mildewed curtains. The off-white padded chairs make strange noises when we move, like Sellotape peeling off plastic. As we sit contemplating this new place that we will soon call home, there's a crash from upstairs. Not a loud one, but one that indicates something falling over.

We all stiffen and look at the ceiling.

'Was that in my room or yours?' Nel says to Jo.

Hank shakes his head, 'Can't tell. Sounded like something heavy.'

They get up and head for the stairs.

'Stay where you are, Toto,' Nel says. 'Take care of my coffee for me.'

Nel began calling me Toto when we were flatting together as students in Sheffield. It started as a joke because of my surname and it stuck because she thinks I've got the same lack of concern for consequences as that little dog from *The Wizard of Oz*. According to her I'm always running off without warning, stealing wizards' sausages and biting witches' legs. She thinks someday one of those witches will bite me back.

Jo, Nel and I are close. Really close. At college, our painting studio overlooked the city hills in one direction, and a hospital on the other. Nel's desk was at the window under the hanging fabrics she'd made in the textiles workshop. They looked like they'd been spun by spiders, billowing like sails over the feathery watercolours on her table. At the other side of the room Jo hurled gobs of acrylic at huge canvases. Streaks of colour went undulating through the air to land with the sound of wet mud. Without even looking I could tell how well it was going according to the frequency and volume of the splats. Hank was trying to get her to marry him in those days and would come up from the sculpture workshop to visit. He smelled of sulphur and had dark-glassed goggles pushed back on his head as he brought her presents of little horses made from welding rods. She would name each of them: *Malcolm, Margery, Alfred,* and put the latest one in the pile with all the others.

For my part, I hunched in the furthest corner, labouring over small oil paintings of unlikely scenes. Fine-tipped brushes: zero, double zero, triple zero, my desk crammed with piles of soft and hard things. A palette of creamy colours; rags for blending out the brush marks; a magnifying glass. Jo is always saying that she can't understand why my paintings are so precise when I am so chaotic. The lecturers said that I was good at detail, but had a problem pulling it all together. I couldn't help myself; I was constantly diverted from the big picture by the disparate details. My tutor said the Royal College of Art would never accept me because of that. I always expected I would go there next. Took it for granted. But when they said I was no good, I lost my bottle and didn't even apply. I really thought I could stay at art school forever, so there was no plan B.

After graduation I couldn't think what to do. So I went back home to Bradford and hung around getting bored and angry. One Sunday afternoon in November I drank a bit too much of Dad's best whisky and decided to ride his Norton around the garden. I'd never driven a motorbike before, and after a few drinks that seemed like a big omission. I'd barely got on it before it reared up and took off like a bullet through our hawthorn hedge, leaving me embedded in the thorny twigs. Luckily, I'd dressed up in Dad's goggles and leather gloves because I liked the look, so I didn't lose an eye or anything. The bike went down the slope in the field behind us and ended up in a stony stream. It still ran for a while underwater, wheels spinning, everything bent, shiny paintwork scratched to buggery. When the family got back from their lunch at a country pub, I was passed out on the front drive.

There was a lot of shouting after that, and the next day I hitched up to Leeds to join Nel and Jo in their flat in Headingly. I was going to stay for the weekend, but I ended up as a permanent fixture on their settee. It was a nice neighbourhood, close to the university, and just around the corner from the Alternative School, where I volunteer. I liked the pubs and the parks, and the fact that I could walk to the dole office, but after a few months we got sick of living on top of one-another in a two-bedroom flat and needed somewhere bigger. Chapeltown is a whole bus ride further out but at least I'll have my own room.

On the floor above Nel calls to Jo. 'It's all OK in here and the bathroom. What about in yours?'

'Panic over, my suitcase fell off the bed,' Jo responds, 'everything's come out of it though. Right mess.'

I shift on the seat and gaze about me. This musty place is it now. This is where I'll live while I wait for life to happen.

Nel's face is so close to mine that I can feel her breath as she inspects the cut on my face. 'Let me see, Toto.' I wince as she strokes my cheekbone. She is pretending to be unconcerned. 'Just a wee cut – might bruise later,' she pauses and brushes it again. 'Hmm, actually that's quite deep. She must have caught you with a ring or something.'

Jo gets up to peer at it but remains unmoved. 'You'll live.'

Hank lights up with curiosity. 'Someone smack you in the mush?'

'I can't really remember . . . it was at Jeff's party last night. I was a bit out of it.'

Jo is more than happy to fill in the details. 'She started trying to shag Jeff's creepy flatmate, what's his name? Philip. That weird one what gets shitty if you call him Phil . . . always ogling your tits when he thinks you're not looking. Anyway, she passes out before anything happens. Comes around again and gets into a fight with Mira.'

I'm indignant. 'Shagging Philip' – the thought is humiliating – 'I don't remember that!'

Nel's giving me another *look*. 'Off your face, Toto,' she says quietly. 'You'd be better with a spliff. You're always nice and chilled when you're stoned, but you're like a lunatic on the booze.'

It's true. I have too much joie de vivre, too much bonhomie, too much red-headed crazy. I get the taste of it, and the feel of it, the whole upward buzz of it, and suddenly I've drunk too much. Then I can't stop.

Jo has to put her coffee down so that she can gesticulate as expansively as the tale demands. 'You passed straight out. Bang. Just like that. By the time you come around, Philip's decided he's got a better chance with Mira – and she's loving it because she's had a thing about him for ages, which is hard to believe, I know, but we've always said she's got a screw loose.

Next thing, he's got hold of her like he owns her, and they're both laughing at you because you're legless. Then, for some reason, Mira turns into a screaming banshee and tells Philip to *stop* looking at you. So, you tell her she's a silly cow.'

'Ah,' Hank says as though everything has now become clear, 'so she whacked you one.'

'But that's all I said! The woman's a fucking maniac.'

Jo gets distracted by a ladder in her tights.

'Shit, this is my last pair.' Looking at me brightly she continues, 'I thought you were going to kill her. You had her by the throat in some sort of, I don't know, judo grip or something. If Nel hadn't dragged you into the bathroom to cool off, I wouldn't have fancied that lass's chances. Like a bloody little fox terrier, aren't you?'

I'm trying to find it funny, but it isn't. 'She kicked me so hard . . . and I just lost it.'

To emphasise my point, I roll up my trouser leg. We all contemplate the bruise.

I have to admit that I lost control. It's frightening to lose it like that.

'You don't expect someone to attack you just for calling them a *silly cow*,' I say. 'I mean, what's wrong with her?'

Nel lights the spliff she's been making, and gently puts it between my lips. Jo leans forward as though telling me something profound.

'Well, the thing is, Toto, Mira's never liked you. On top of that, you were shagging her lovely Philip.'

I widen my eyes and cover my mouth with my fingers, 'I wasn't! He's disgusting.'

Nel nods. 'To be fair Jo, he was groping Toto after she'd lost consciousness. She had no idea what was happening. He, however, knew exactly what he was at. And that's not on.' Her eyes are steely. 'Actually, me and Jeff had to drag him off you, Toto. He's an arsehole.'

The top button of Jo's pink cardigan slips open, as it always seems to do, and she tries to re-button with one hand while still keeping hold of her coffee cup. Hank leans over and undoes it again.

Jo studies her coffee. 'I need sugar in this. How come you never put sugar in my coffee?'

Nel adjusts the silver bangles on her wrist, and wonders about it. 'Maybe because I don't think you should have sugar.'

'Penelope Gale, you've known me since I was eleven. You know I take three sugars.'

'Ridiculous. Ridiculous amount of sugar.'

There's a pause, then Jo says lightly, 'Mira would give me three sugars.'

And we crack up. We've all had a decent toke on the spliff, so most things seem funny.

The three of us are seated on the back steps while we wait for Hank to return with the second load from the old flat in Headingly. The backyard is small and dirty with a straggly self-seeded sycamore tree pushing up between moss-covered flagstones. We're talking about our names. Jo has been doing a project on designing family crests for teaching practice. She's traced all our surnames, and now she's telling us about them.

'OK, my name, my married name, Hanks. Let me see.' She leafs through her notebook, 'Descended from Flemish weavers. First recorded mention is *Anke de Ankinton* in Lincolnshire in 1194.'

'That is the most stupid name I've ever heard,' I say, 'Sounds like Hanky of Hankytown. I mean, are you kidding; Mr and Mrs Hanky of Hankytown? I'd keep that quiet if I were you. What about your maiden name? What does Salvin mean?'

'Old French. Traces back to the Norman Conquest.'

'So, you're aristocracy, are you?' Nel looks doubtful.

'Yes, I bloody am. The name means,' she reads, 'savage and untamed . . . and I've got a great family crest: two gold mullets.'

Nel nods sagely. 'Yes. I agree. You are completely untamed, and that crest is so appropriate for denoting savagery: two dead fish.'

'Cheeky cow. Let's find yours, Miss Gale.' Jo turns the pages again. 'Well, it seems Gale is Old English for a cheerful and roisterous person . . .'

She pauses and we slowly look Nel up and down.

'Don't know what happened there then,' Jo says, and Nel play-slaps her.

'Don't tell my dad our name is English,' Nel says. 'He'll commit suicide by kilt or something.'

'What about me?' I'm eager to know, 'Totton. What's Totton?'

'Hang on.' Jo licks her fingers and parts pages. 'All right. It says here . . . there's some disagreement about its origin. It might mean your ancestors came from the Nottinghamshire village of Toton. Or,' she goes on, 'it's from the German word meaning the dead.'

'That is ludicrous,' I say. 'Why would you wait until someone's died to give them a surname? A bit bloody redundant by then, I would have thought.'

Jo purses her mouth in agreement. 'Good point, which is why the last suggestion is the best. Read that please, Miss Gale.'

She tilts her open notebook and Nel recites in an amused

tone. 'It derives from the old English word "totte", which means Fool. Oh blimey, Toto. Fool. That's unfortunate!'

I should be insulted, but I'm not, because in the Tarot, the Fool is the best card in the Major Arcana: the innocent soul on the journey to knowledge. Jo says it's typical of me to find a positive in something as crap as having a name that means *idiot*.

Nel reaches into her patterned shoulder bag and recovers her tobacco tin. She makes a cigarette with infinite care. Withdrawing contentedly into her own thoughts, she blows smoke upwards and away like frosty breath. I sit close to her on the steps and roll cigarettes for later. Trying to get them all the same thickness, tearing one apart and starting again when it looks like I haven't rolled it tightly enough.

Jo nods at me. 'You're bloody obsessive, you, aren't you?'

It's said without malice, just an observation. I suppose I am and wonder whether that should worry me. Jo seems to have this ease with life, a readiness to laugh, to eat, to fuck. She would make an open book seem secretive. She tells us everything, even the things we don't want to know. Like the time she discovered masturbation when we were flatting together in first year. She'd been in the bath for ages, and when she came out, she was all glowing, 'You have all got to try that! That was amazing!' And then she told us how to do it.

We were awestruck. Nel's family are strict Presbyterian and I went to a convent school, so we've got a different mindset to Jo, who's never had anything to do with religion in her life. For us it wasn't that Jo had done it, or talked about it, that was so mesmerising. We were in awe of her lack of shame. Shame freaks me out so much that I pretend I don't feel it. Nel gets wracked by it. Things she won't talk about. It's all that

Presbyterian stuff. Sin is big for them and you can't confess it away like Catholics do. I think all that stuff sits inside her even though she doesn't believe in it any more.

Dark is falling and the rain has started. I love the smell of it. It reminds me of hitchhiking, and the scent of rain on roads when I'm thumbing a ride without a clue where I'll end up. I love not knowing where the hell I am. It means freedom to me, like the low-level thrill I'm getting from this new place where we live.

We go back inside to wait for Hank, who's taking longer than expected. Nothing is comfortable yet. I don't know where anything will belong.

'Come on, let's do the messages.' Nel is pulling on her coat. 'We need milk and some eggs for our tea and I'll need to get bacon for when Simon stays over, otherwise my life won't be worth living.'

Jo peers through the window into the dark, looking for Hank's van as I follow Nel outside into the street.

Rain settles like beads on Nel's fur jacket and we're careful not to walk too close to the gutters swirling with dirty water. The board outside the newsagent has this evening's headline: WOMAN ATTACKED IN POTTERNEWTOWN PARK, the park at the end of our street. As we walk past it on our way back, prostitutes are doing business in there and a couple of drunks hurl insults.

Nel suddenly links her arm through mine and leans into me. I'm not very good at being touched, it always startles me.

'Don't be scared, Toto,' she says, grinning. 'It's only affection and one day you'll get used to it.'

'I never got hugged much at home,' I say. 'It always takes me by surprise.'

'You don't know what to do with it, do you?' She pulls me closer. 'How come you can let any flirty creep put his hands all over you, but you're scared of being hugged by your best friend?'

'Are you talking about Philip?'

'I'm talking about Philip.'

I look away. 'I don't remember doing that.'

'Aye, but it's not just Philip, is it?'

I resist pulling free, even though I'm feeling judged. I care about Nel too much. I don't like her to find me wanting. She grips me tighter. She's waiting for me to say something.

'It's only sex,' I say. 'It doesn't matter. You know exactly what's going on when it's just sex. No one's trying to steal your fucking soul. When people touch other people for reasons other than sex, you don't know what they want.'

'I'm not stealing your soul through your elbow, I promise.'

I'm sheepish. 'I know I'm weird, but I can't help it.'

A straggly street cat winds around us as I unsuccessfully resist Nel's gentle clinch. The cat pauses, sheltering from the rain under the lintel of a window. Flustered, I use it as an excuse to pull away from Nel, stroking its scabby ears and looking at the mistrustful longing in its eyes. Its purr is like the scraping of a bone comb across fingernails.

'Now we've got a whole house, can we get a kitten?' I say.

Nel stoops to stroke the thin fur. 'You are such a bugger for changing the subject!'

'A kitten would be good though.'

'Haven't I got enough on my hands looking after you?'

'Bloody hell! Please Nel, I don't need looking after.'

'Well you *do*, but if you want to pretend you don't, that's fine by me.'

There's a red phone box on a corner a few streets along. I want to tell my family that I've changed address. I always try to let them know where I am. Even though they're not especially interested and probably still pissed off with me about the bike and everything, I imagine that one day they might look in my direction and say, 'Oh there you are. How lovely to see you. We've been worrying and worrying.'

The phone box smells like condensed bad breath. One of the small glass panes has been kicked in and glass crunches under my feet. The coin box is heavily dented as though it's been attacked with a hammer. Marker pen obliterates the printed instructions, and the word *Ratter* scrawls across every surface in the same black pen. A short, dirty kid is staring at me, so I turn my back and lean on the door he's pressed against. He comes around to gawk at me through another window. I turn away again, only to have him reappear at the other side. *Push off,* I mouth at him and he gives me the fingers.

The phone is ringing like a distant, intermittent purr. I've got my ten-pence piece slotted in place. When it clicks my sister says, 'Totton residence,' the way Mum likes her to.

I insert the coin. 'Hi Tess. It's me. It's Jude. I've just one ten-pence piece, so we've only got three minutes.'

'Oh wow, hi. Are you OK and everything?'

'I've moved to a new house. Is Mum there?'

She lets go of the phone, and in my mind's eye I see it dangling from the wall in the hallway. Tess's voice recedes as she goes to find our mother. 'Mum, it's Jude. She's only got ten pence.'

There's a long wait before there's a scuffling sound. My brother's not-quite-broken-voice says, 'Jude. What you doing?'

'I'm living it up, Marty.'

'When you coming home?'

'Don't know, soon maybe. How's school?'

'Rubbish. They took me off the hockey team 'cos my hair's too long. Oh, hang on, Tess wants you. Come home, OK?'

Tess's breathing is odd and short. 'Mum can't come to the phone.'

'Why not?'

'She's got a headache.'

I pause. 'How long has she had this headache?'

Tess's breathing is even more irregular. 'Um. I don't know.'

I'm sorry for my sister, she's only seventeen and my mother is always putting her in this position, 'It's OK, don't worry. Are you all right? How's things?'

'Oh, you know. A levels and everything. Saturday job's good though, Mrs Creek gave me a rise . . .'

The phone starts to bleep, and I've got no more money. 'Oh no, look, take care. Marty too, bye . . . bye.'

'Bye,' she says, and the phone goes dead.

Mum couldn't even be arsed to come to the phone.

Why did I expect anything different?

Compressing my lips, I stare at the marker-pen scribbling across the top of the coin box: *Ratter*. In a sudden burst of anger, I scratch hard with my thumbnail until it's obliterated.

2

Nel

My mother has dreams of an orderly daughter, and if I cut my hair that would splendidly realise it. I, however, draw the line at being shorn like a sheep for the sake of her delusions. My tumult of curls is what Simon likes, and he's always said he couldn't go out with a girl with hair shorter than his. More to the point, this Pre-Raphaelite tangle is the way I want it. If it were cut, I know from bitter experience that it would stand up on my head in a wall of thick blonde frizz and I would frighten tiny children and some breeds of dog from a distance of twenty paces. Why must teachers' hair be short and alarming? Isn't the fact of being a teacher alarming enough in itself?

Sometimes I have to pinch myself to make sure this is really my life now. I keep trying to make a joke of it, but lately everything sits wrong with me. I can't help feeling that everything is quietly fucked. Even though Dad is elated that I've decided to be a teacher, I've got this heaviness deep inside me.

Teaching would be a step up in the world, in my parents' opinion. More prestige even than Dad's white-collar job at the Midland Bank: a *profession*. If I'd only get a position in a good Edinburgh school and marry the headmaster, my parents could die happy. They're waiting for acres of grandchildren from a nice tidy son-in-law, although Simon is not exactly what they had in mind. Mum quite likes him, and was really happy when we got engaged, but my father finds him lacking in at least two ways. What he ideally wants from a son-in-law, it seems to me, is military-length hair. Also, Simon is fair, and my father has a theory that no man is biologically blonde. God knows where he got that from.

'It's nae natural,' he told me firmly. 'I never saw a man with blonde hair without it was dyed.'

Try as I might, there's no way that I can convince him that Si is natural. For my father, Simon is unforgivably effete. He's always imagined someone more masculine and more Scots for me, but neither of those things is at the top of my list. The stupid thing is that the two of them have more in common than they'd think. Si wants me to get a proper job to support us. He is the artist and needs to follow his vocation. Teachers make good money.

I have to finish this teaching course. I'm doing it for both of us. Simon needs me to do this. I mull this over as I walk to the pub to meet Toto.

The Juggler's Arms has been Toto's favourite pub since she arrived in Leeds. It's a poky collection of fusty rooms, full of art students, anarchists, Irish republicans, homosexuals and prostitutes. I like it well enough, but Toto is fascinated by the place. On a good day you can get a pie, a pint and a free argument, which she seems to find invigorating. It's the closest bar to the university, and a lot of us from the course gather there to compare notes and drown our sorrows at the end of the day.

Today has been testing. Teaching practice at the comprehensive school over in Beeston was like an obstacle race; the class teacher being the main hurdle. It all felt brutal and hollow. Nobody made anything that wasn't plain ugly. I was trying hard, but my hair kept coming unclipped to trail into the kids' wet paintings. Mrs Lewis's contempt radiated from the back of the classroom as I struggled to gain control.

When I got back to the university, the department secretary gave me a message from Simon. He'd phoned to say he would be up from Birmingham early and to remember to get meat in even though I'm a vegetarian. How am I going to get time to do that? I've got teaching practice and classes. The secretary laughed when she saw my expression. 'Flipping men. Devils for their meat, aren't they?'

Simon certainly is.

I'm standing at the bar when Toto finally arrives at the door. I catch her eye over a huddle of opinionated undergraduates discussing Marxism.

'I've got you a half,' I mouth at her.

Toto sidles past the arguing students to take the drink from my outstretched hand. She looks like she hasn't a care in the world. She sets off immediately to find a place to sit. Lager spilling over her hand as she walks, she nods at a table in one of the smaller side-rooms. I'm always alert around Toto when we're out. She's drawn to danger as though to a magnet. The more ferocious someone is, the more interested she becomes in them, so I'm not surprised when she makes to settle down next to a wild-haired old lady caked in makeup who looks like she's spoiling for a fight.

'Toto. No.'

'What?' she asks, all innocence, as I take her by the elbow to guide her away.

'Apart from the fact I don't want to sit with a bloody mad woman, we need a bigger table.'

'Why?'

I brush some crisps off another table and move a couple of empty tankards to clear space. 'Friday drinks. The tutors are coming and everything.'

She observes the number of seats. 'Just what I need.'

Minutes later, the old woman launches herself at a girl seated across from her, swinging and screaming and breaking glass. 'Don't look at me, you fucking stuck-up little cow!'

The old woman flails and the young woman yelps and clutches her forehead. A towering drag queen, dressed in a green velvet dress and a blonde nylon wig, leaps up from the next table and grabs the spitting woman by an arm. She's wrangled through the swiftly parting crowd and ejected onto the street. Toto is sitting still as a stone, observing every move. I'm strangely uncomfortable, as though I'm witnessing something private. I can't help feeling sorry for the old woman. It must be hard to be stared at like a circus freak in the place that's always been your local. She probably just wanted a quiet drink. Broken glass in the face, though. Jesus.

With a flourish of a gloved hand the drag queen turns back into the pub. 'That's the last fucking time, Doreen. Get the fuck out of here.'

Barely glancing up from pulling a Guinness for a scowling

young Irishman, the landlord shouts, 'Thanks, Simone. There'll be a rum and black there for you later.'

At the table, the girl sobs like a child and holds her head with both hands. Her boyfriend mops away the blood trickling through her fingers with a big chequered handkerchief. She lifts her face and he inspects the wound on her forehead all the while telling her she'll be OK. I'm coming out of my shock and considering whether I should help the girl, when Mira arrives with Philip in tow. Mira is flushed and self-conscious, her curly brown hair newly washed and thick foundation covering her acne scars. They make straight for our table and pull up seats. Toto purposefully avoids looking at them.

There's something creepy about Philip. He's cold and watchful. His arms are too thin for his sleeves. He's like an undernourished iguana on a dry grey rock, watching me and Toto when he thinks we're not looking, exactly like Jo said. Staring at our bodies. His eyes are hooded and his face expressionless. Mira keeps trying to take hold of his hand, awkwardly pulling at it when he doesn't respond, then dropping it to pick up her drink. If looks could kill, then the ones she keeps shooting at Toto should have seen her off by now. It's ridiculous. There's no way in the world that a sober Jude Totton would ever touch Philip. She's feckless when she's drunk, but actually, even an inebriated Jude Totton wouldn't fancy him. I hope there's not going to be another fight. After the incident with the glass and the old lady, there's a brittle energy in the place.

Toto has retreated, she has turned inward. Quiet and contemplative, she has stopped seeing this pub and gone elsewhere. I like that about her. I know whatever is going on in her head will be bizarre and wonderful, and tonight she'll tell me about it in the fire glow of her room in Chapeltown.

I think about my new bedroom and get anxious, as I realise I'll need to tidy up before Simon arrives. He's very particular. I'll also need to work out how to keep the bickering between him and Toto to a minimum. He's a bit full of himself now that he's doing an MA. They wind each other up almost as much as they make each other laugh. It's as though I'm constantly doing this awkward balancing act between them. Jo thinks I should sort them both out and tell them what's what. She says I'm too much of a pushover, but they're both so bloody useless at the normal things in life. If I don't care for them, who will?

When I say things like that, Jo shakes her head like I'm a lost cause. She's known me since I shifted to Sheffield when I was eleven. We were both strangers in a new school, me from Edinburgh and her from Doncaster. We were outsiders, starting the grammar school a term later than everybody else and never quite fitting in. I was weird and Scottish with frizzy blonde hair, and she was this shabby wee council-scheme kid. We were thrown together rather than choosing each other, but I really liked her. I liked the way she never cared if they laughed at her. I liked the way she never took the piss out of my accent, and the way she wouldn't change to make herself popular. Her family is dirt poor. Her father isn't good at holding down a job and he has health problems. He used to be a miner, but his lungs couldn't take the dust. That's why they moved to Sheffield. A pal got him a job as a gardener at a fancy hotel and her mum works in Woolworths on the toy counter.

Fellow students arrive in ones and twos along with Barry, one of our tutors. He looks at me, and then at a space that he seems to perceive next to me. 'Jo not coming tonight?' His foamy pint of Tetley's gets set firmly amongst the others cluttering the table.

I shake my head politely. 'No, her husband's up for the weekend.'

Barry is amiable enough. He's profusely bearded, with streaks of grey through mousey hair, a drinker's nose, and a brown corduroy jacket with leather patches on the elbows. His eyes are alert behind his glasses and, as he settles into the banquette, he fixes them on Toto.

'So, I've been meaning to have a chat with you, Jude. What do you do, young lady?' he asks. 'Were you at Sheffield with Jo and Nel, is that the story?'

Toto looks startled as she is shaken out of her reverie, glances at me as though anchoring herself, and nods silently.

He continues. 'You did painting, did you? Are you any good?'

'I don't know,' she says, and seems to be wondering about it. 'I thought I was.'

'Yes, she is,' I interject. 'She does really cool wee photorealist surreal things. She could have done post-grad, but she didn't get it together to apply in time. Sometimes you're not that organised, are you Jude?'

I don't call her Toto in front of Barry. Toto is only for people we trust.

'Is that the story?' he says. 'You didn't quite get your act together?'

'Well, I suppose it's *a* story,' she responds in that guarded way she has with people who intimidate her, swilling the last of her lager and lime and not lifting her eyes to meet his.

He laughs and doesn't seem offended by her tone. 'We're recruiting for next year. I'd take you on, if you're as good as Nel says. Have you ever thought about being a teacher?'

'She volunteers at that hippy school down the road, Barry,' Mira chips in. 'All peace and love and no rules or syllabus.'

I hear the scorn in her voice, but I don't know whether he does. He leans towards Toto with more interest.

'Does it work – all that democratic learning stuff?'

'I want it to. We're going to try. Everything should be democratic. Things should be better than they are.'

He is smiling at her in a patronising way. He looks far away for a moment, and opens his mouth wide to pour the soapy looking beer into the back of his throat. Wiping his mouth and beard with his sleeve he looks at her again. It's almost affectionate.

'You're full of romantic idealism, and that is an attractive trait in the young.'

Mira elbows into his space on the beer-wet table. 'Barry, it was so interesting today . . .' She's putting on a fake refined accent and it makes me embarrassed for her. She has a neediness that makes her try too hard at everything. 'I trialled that exercise with the kids; the one I was telling you about where they mix equal portions of colours together and add set amounts of white or black. I got this terrific response from . . .'

He appears not to have heard her and gets up abruptly to go to the bar with his empty glass. He doesn't offer to buy a round. I suppose he knows a bunch of students like us would happily drink his wallet dry. Mira is watching him with her mouth compressed and her brow furrowed.

Toto is observing Mira with a look I recognise. It's the one that means she thinks someone is an idiot. She makes the sound that usually goes with it; like a little click between her teeth. Mira notices, and I lean between them to break the exchange. I don't want another fight.

'Stop it,' I tell Toto beneath my breath.

'She's such a dick, Nel, honestly.'

'All the same. Stop it.'

There's a queue in the Ladies, Toto makes use of the only free cubicle. I'm leaning against the wall waiting my turn. When she comes out, I point to the graffito above the sink that reads *President Nixon Fucks Donald Duck.*

'Do you think he does?' she says. 'I'd say from his usual expression, it was the other way around.'

As I'm going into the vacated cubicle, Mira pushes into the room. I shoot Toto a warning glance, hoping they'll keep it civil, if only long enough for me to have a pee. I should have known that wasn't going to be possible.

I hear Mira through the door. 'Stay away from my bloody boyfriend. I can see the way you're looking at him.'

I hold my breath, waiting for the explosion. Toto's response is surprisingly calm. 'Call that a boyfriend? I wouldn't touch it with a ten-foot pole.'

The explosion comes from Mira. 'What are you even doing here? You're a ligger. You just hang around sponging off of Nel and Jo. You're too stoned or drunk to be of use to anyone most of the time. I bet you didn't even buy your own drink tonight, did you? You're such a pathetic little no-hope scrounger.'

There's a silence and I can feel Toto's anger. 'Fuck off, Mira,' she says very quietly, and her voice is strained. 'If you don't stop bloody pushing me, something's going to happen.'

I rush to straighten my clothes and get out of the cubicle to intervene. As I pull the door open, Toto is white-knuckled, standing with her back to me. Mira's face drops when she sees me. Like all bullies she's a coward at heart.

'Leave it alone,' I murmur and glare at her until she turns away.

I grab hold of Toto. 'Come on, we're going back outside. And you are not a ligger, by the way. She doesn't know you. Don't let her get to you.'

'I really bloody want to hit her, Nel. It freaks me out how much I want to hit her.'

'I know, but you're not going to.'

The tone of her voice makes me look at her carefully.

She rests herself against the grimy wall by the bar. I can see her thinking. Rummaging in her pocket she gives me a look that says, *I'm all right.* I back off a little to give her the space to regather.

'Look. Enough money for another drink,' she says, holding up a fifty-pence coin. 'Do you want one? Let this *ligger* buy you a drink.'

I shake my head. I know that's the last of the cash in her pocket. She got her dole this morning and I made her put most of it on her mantelpiece so that she wouldn't spend it all in one go. I'm about to reach for my purse when I realise something doesn't feel right; the familiar weight of my shoulder-bag isn't there.

'I've left my stuff in the Ladies because of all that rumpus,' I say. 'I'll not be a moment.'

As I'm about to go back in, I almost bump into Mira. She hands me my bag as though nothing has happened. 'I found this,' she says brightly. 'Really nice pattern. Where did you get it?'

I stare at it. I haven't really looked at it properly for a long time. She's always asking me where I got things.

'My boyfriend bought it for me. For my birthday – ages ago.'

She glances at my engagement ring, 'Simon? Your fiancé?'

I hate the word fiancé. It sounds like some kind of whipped cream dessert. I make a non-committal kind of noise.

'That's so nice of him,' Mira continues. 'Philip hasn't bought me anything like that yet. Maybe your Simon should have a word with him. Will he be coming up for a visit soon?'

My jaw feels tight. 'Yes. Probably.'

Mira is distracted by two women who slide past us into the Ladies hand in hand. One has cropped hair and a man's flannel shirt buttoned to the neck, and the other is wearing a miniskirt and high heels. Mira's eyes narrow as she watches them disappear through the door.

'I don't know why we all drink in here. It's full of weirdos like them. I mean, I know lots of folk go through a phase where they experiment, but those two' – she points at the toilet door – 'they're beyond that . . . probably living together, thinking they're in love like a real couple. Turns my stomach. At least *we're* normal, aren't we? At least we've got boyfriends.'

'Well if that's how you define normal,' I say.

I stare uncomfortably at the ground. Mira embodies all the attitudes I was surrounded by at school and at our church. It's an unwelcome reminder of the world outside our bohemian bubble.

At the bar, Toto is sitting next to a guy in a studded jacket with stubble on his face. He's big and muscular and she's flirting like a fool. Sometimes the people she's drawn to seem really dodgy. I tap her on the shoulder and turn her towards me. He mutters swearwords as he gets off the stool to stalk away.

He can't touch her. I won't let him.

And if the truth be told, neither will she. Not her heart

anyway. She keeps it wrapped up so tight that it won't even get dented.

'You're doing it again. Don't you ever think that you might be flirting with the wrong person? That you might get hurt? I mean physically hurt?'

Toto doesn't respond and doesn't seem to comprehend what I'm trying to tell her. I try again. 'Every time you go off for a night with some sodding zombie like him, or disappear on one of your bloody hitchhiking *jaunts*.' I say it as gently as I can. 'We worry about you. You know. I worry.'

She looks at me like I'm crazy. 'You don't need to worry about me. I'm not frightened of guys like him.'

'That's because you're frightened of all the wrong things, Toto.'

3

Toto

The Chapeltown Road streetlights cast pink-tinted light on Nel and I as we leave the bus stop to go home. There's fried food dropped all over the pavement and soggy chips are scattered amongst sheets of newspaper. As Nel steps to one side to avoid a fluttering page, the headline catches my eye along with the picture below it. A woman's swollen face and the words: ANOTHER ATTACK IN CHAPELTOWN. I look away, but the wind flips the paper up and drapes it around my ankle. I kick it off and it disintegrates under my foot.

We're gradually getting used to this street, finding ways not to stand out so much, but tonight Nel seems more out of place than usual. She is smartly dressed in a midi-skirt and her mother's old fur jacket after teaching practice. I wonder if she is fully aware of how miserable this course is making her; sometimes she sits on my bed without removing her coat, silent misery rolling off her in waves.

As we make our way along Hamilton Terrace, she's telling

me how much she despises the teacher she's placed with, when I become aware of another set of footsteps behind us. I turn to see a man. He has too much energy coming off him. He insinuates himself between us, walking at our pace, looking straight ahead as though we aren't there.

'Do you want to do business?' he asks tersely.

I now understand what this means, and I'm more unsettled than offended, but Nel doesn't know what he's talking about. 'What do you mean – *business*?'

Agitation shows in the way he twists himself to look at her. 'Five quid I'll give you, either one of you, or ten quid for you both, I don't mind.'

I'm about to tell him to try elsewhere, when Nel realises what he's asking for. Her Scottish accent suddenly becomes pronounced, as it always does when she gets angry. 'Fuck off, we're not prostitutes!'

'There's no need to swear. How come you swear like that if you're not a whore?'

'Don't call me a whore!'

'Why do you wear that fur jacket and them boots? Why has she got her coat so tight around her arse if she's not a whore?'

Outrage shoots through Nel and she is fearless. 'How dare you?' She's struggling to find words for this situation. 'I'm an art teacher, not a prostitute. Who the fuck do you think you're talking to?'

I've never seen her like this before. She is incandescent with anger. This is all going really badly. I keep trying to catch her attention. She might get hurt if she doesn't shut up.

I turn and look at him full on, draw his attention onto me, away from her.

'We're not on the game, OK? You've got the wrong girls. If

you want those sorts of women, they're in that house there, the one with the red light in the window. Go and bother them, because we're not interested. OK?'

Uncertain but persistent, his face is tense. 'I don't go in them places.'

His energy suddenly changes. He is smiling a hard, bright smile that puts me on my guard. We have almost reached our house now. I decide that he mustn't find out where we live. He's still walking between us, so I haven't got a way to let Nel know. She's picked up her step and I can hear the irregularity of her breathing.

He fingers something in his pocket and directs his attention to me. But not really to me. To something he's mistaken me for. I keep walking. My plan is to divert him. I'll keep him walking while Nel goes inside the house. Once she's safely in, I'll turn back and leave him standing. That way he won't clock where we live. I don't want him coming back.

In her haste to unlock the door, Nel gets her keys entangled in her pocket lining. She's focused on getting us both into the house. I think she assumes I'm right behind her. But I'm not.

I continue to walk alongside the man, who looks at me like I'm a cockroach in his sink. Over the road, at the crimson-curtained brothel, the girl with the cut on her cheek stands in the doorway, following everything we do. Her arms are crossed under her tightly encased breasts.

Pointing at him, I wave at her to come over. 'Hey, there's a customer for you here.'

He seems to come out of a daze, looks from me to her, suddenly sharp with interest. After looking him up and down, she takes a long drag on her cigarette and makes her way without haste towards him.

'You want business, love?'

'Yeah, but not here. That park, I've got me car over there.'

She contemplates him, and glances down the road as though she's considering it. Rain begins to fall heavily.

'Aye, all right,' she says without enthusiasm.

The girl doesn't have a coat on, and her cheap turquoise top is getting darker as it gets wetter. 'You'd better have the fucking cash, though. Five quid. Let me see it.'

I'm mesmerised by the transaction. He gets out a rumpled five-pound note to show her. She acknowledges it with a minimal nod and throws her wet cigarette into the gutter. He follows her to the park.

I edge back towards our house. Raindrops drip from my hair and onto my lashes. The front door suddenly opens, Nel grabs me by the wrist and pulls me in. Slamming the door, she locks it and bolts it, shaking her head speechlessly.

'What on earth were you doing?' She finally manages to speak. 'I mean, what in the name of Jesus were you thinking? You wee lunatic.'

'What do you mean?' I'm puzzled.

She widens her eyes at me. 'Why did you walk off with him like that?'

I blink in surprise. I thought she'd realise what I was doing. 'I didn't want him to know where we lived. I didn't want him coming back, and battering on our door.'

To me it's all self-evident. I follow her into my bedroom. There are two comfortable chairs, and the single bed makes a passable couch when pushed against the wall. Releasing her hair from the grips restraining it, Nel divests herself of everything that makes her look like a teacher.

'It was my plan . . . to protect us,' I say.

She struggles for words. 'How am I supposed to work that out? You disappeared down the road with some bloody sex-maniac-psycho. How does that make any sense at all!'

When she puts it like that, it's difficult to come up with an argument. 'Well, I don't know. It seemed like the right thing at the time.' I bite my lip, and add by way of information, 'You do realise, don't you, that you said the words, "How dare you!" to him?'

It stops her in her tracks. 'I did, didn't I? I have no idea where that came from.' She laughs wanly. 'I also proclaimed to the world that I was an art teacher.'

Jo, voluptuous in her silky cerise dressing gown, but spoiling the overall effect with a pair of big fluffy slippers, is attracted from the kitchen by our discussion. Hot soup swills in the inappropriately small, blue-circled bowl she's holding under her chin, as she tries to eat and walk at the same time.

'What's up with you two?'

I glance at Nel, but she doesn't respond. 'A guy out there took us for prostitutes.'

There's no surprise in Jo's face as she licks the spoon. 'Happened to me yesterday. Have you eaten or not? There's soup still there.'

Our boots and socks and coats steam in front of the gas fire. The odour of hot cotton and fur mixes with that of tomato soup. Jo makes herself comfortable in the nearest armchair, and Nel and I distribute our bodies across my bed.

'This definitely isn't Kansas,' I murmur to Nel.

'I know, Toto,' she says.

Jo smirks over her soup bowl. 'It might be bloody Munchkin Land though.'

'What do you mean?' Nel looks around the room for clues.

Jo struggles to keep the soup in the bowl as she tells us, 'I was up in my room trying to watch TV. I look outside and there's a load of kids, about ten of them, hanging off that spindly tree. They're only trying to watch my telly through the bloody window! So, I stick my head out and tell them to bugger off. This kid, he's no more than seven years old, goes: "Why? It doesn't bother you if I'm up a tree. Air's free."' She widens her eyes with indignation. '"Air's bloody free!" In the end I had to draw the curtains. I could hear them swearing at me all the way through the news.'

Nel looks thoughtful. Staring intently into the space above Jo's head, she starts to stick Rizla papers together to make a skin for a joint.

'You know what puzzles me about *The Wizard of Oz*?' she says eventually.

I shake my head. 'No?'

'Why does everyone think the Good Witch of the North is so *nice*, just because she's all smiley and posh? In my opinion she's the actual villain!'

'How can she be the baddie?' Jo says, 'She wears a puffy pink party frock and a crown!'

Nel looks at us like we're both stupid. 'She's pretending to be good! She makes Dorothy wear those ruby slippers, knowing they won't come off unless the kid's murdered! Then, *then*, she sends her off down the Yellow Brick Road to find a bloody *wizard*. She doesn't say, "Come to my house and I'll look up Child Welfare in the Yellow Pages." No, she packs this wee kiddie off into the Wild bloody Woods, in cursed shoes, while she prances around in a massive pink bubble. She's a menace, that Glinda.' She pauses like it's a revelation. 'There's no such thing as a good witch.'

Now we're all giggling and the psycho in the street is forgotten. The joint Nel's rolling is flawless as usual. Once she's put the tobacco in it, she takes Jo's lighter and heats the edge of the resin, crumbling it in a straggly line.

My mind strays to the rock concert we're all going to Sheffield for soon. Hank's mate is a stagehand at the Concert Hall and he gave him four free tickets. Hank donated the spares to me and Nel, and Simon's bought one for himself.

'Can I stay at yours and Hank's for the Roxy Music concert, Jo?'

Jo nods, 'Aye, course you can, petal.' She yawns and looks at Nel, 'What's Simon doing in the Easter holidays?'

'He doesn't really get much time off with his MA so he's staying in Birmingham. Says he's going to use the print room whilst the undergrads aren't there. He's got a lot on.'

Jo's forehead creases, 'Are you going down to Brum to be with him?'

Nel is uncomfortable. 'No, he reckons his apartment isn't big enough for us both. I'm staying with Gen over the break.'

'He's still coming for Roxy Music though?'

'Yes. He won't miss that. He'll probably arrive tonight; stay a few days and we'll go down to Sheffield together for the gig. He wants us to crash with some guy who runs a gallery.'

Jo nods slowly and says nothing.

After an awkward silence, she turns back to me. 'You know our term ends next week? You'll be miserable here on your own once we're all gone. Do you want to come and stop with me and Hank?'

I'd forgotten about the Easter holiday. Now I'm not a student, I have no sense of the rhythm of the year. I perk up at the prospect. 'That would be fab.'

'OK. Hank's picking me up from university on Tuesday evening. We might as well all go down together. Plenty of room in the back of our van.'

Nel's joint is tightly rolled and aromatic. I wait my turn to take a toke and let it untangle me. This is what I've been wanting all day. The smoke streams in and circulates through me. Makes everything funny. It all flows now. I like myself. I'm likeable. I feel safe.

'I'll try and score some more dope soon,' I say. 'Somebody at the Alternative School will have some, or else know where I can get it. Shall we all put some bread together and I'll get a quarter ounce of Acapulco Gold, or something good like that?'

Nel looks at me. 'No one deals Acapulco Gold outside America, so that's not going to work, is it lovely? Are you sure you're up to this, Toto? Last time you got ripped off and came back with a bag of mixed herbs.'

Jo chokes back laughter as she remembers it.

I can feel my colour rising. 'That was ages ago. It wasn't last time.' I'm glaring at Nel, but she's amiably dragging on the spliff as it flares and sputters.

'Then you'd better get it right this time, hadn't you?' she says and lifts her eyebrows.

I like dope and I like the buzz of buying it. A girl at college got two years just for being found with a wrap of cannabis. When you've got some in your pocket, knowing that you'll go to jail if you get searched is another sort of high. Get caught and that's your life fucked. Get away with it, and it's a bigger buzz than actually smoking it.

*

Jo has gone upstairs, I'm lying across the top of my bed, and Nel is across the bottom. The orange flickering of the gas fire illuminates the room. It casts warm moving shadows on her skin and reflects in her pupils.

'What if', she begins in a quiet voice, 'when Dorothy reaches the Deep Woods along the Yellow Brick Road, she finds more than a scarecrow and a tin man and a lion?'

She has my attention. This is a game we play.

'What if', she continues, 'there was a path of peacock feathers leading to a wee house hidden behind a hillock? What if there was a light on in that house and someone in the window?'

I take up the challenge and consider where the story will go next. 'What if Dorothy is distracted by the feathers because of her allergies, and her sneezes roll her over until she knocks into the door of the house. There's someone in the house, and Dorothy believes it must be a witch, because the whole house is made of gingerbread and candy, and those are the kinds of houses witches live in.'

'Which wicked witch would that be, Toto?' Nel hoists herself onto her elbows. 'Of the West, or of the East, or is it the Gingerbread Witch who eats children?'

'They don't know. The fear begins in the Lion, and it's contagious. He tells the Scarecrow to tell the Tin Man to tell Dorothy to tell Toto to run away. But Toto doesn't, because the edge between life and death glitters for her. Instead she knocks on the door, and it flies open and a man comes out.'

Nel's eyes widen. 'That's beautiful. Is that what you feel, though? Does the edge between life and death glitter for you, Toto?'

She searches my face. I deliberately look away. I've given away too much, and I want to take it back.

She pauses before she decides to continue with the story, as though nothing has been said. 'The man is made entirely of boiled sweets: mostly orange, but some are striped red and white, and some are mints.'

The thought of them being mints strikes me as particularly amusing. My silver bracelet rattles against my earring as I clasp my hands behind the back of my head.

'He's a humbug. He's the Candyman. He's lost his *high*, and the others tell him to come with them to the Emerald City to see the Wizard of Oz to get his *high* back. While he's thinking about whether he will or not, Toto slips in and steals his entire stash of Acapulco Gold.'

We're stoned enough to find this hilarious. It makes me laugh so much I knock my blues harp, my harmonica, into the cold remains of my instant coffee. Nel fishes it out and hands it, dripping, to me. I absent-mindedly lift it towards my mouth.

'Don't even think about playing that right now, you noisy wee bugger,' she says.

I wipe it off and put it in my coat pocket. She slips herself off the bed lightly and leaves me pondering the gas fire as she makes her way up the stairs to her room.

Alone, I watch a star through the gap in the curtains. It appears like a pinprick through indigo paper. Brighter than the bared teeth of Red Riding Hood's wolf.

The sheets wind and unwind around me as I twist and turn, trying to find stillness. Half-dreams of a man with a wolf's head, his teeth gleaming like that star. Then a dream memory of me in Nan's backyard, rolling dough in my hands outside her tiny terraced house. Turning it grey and dog shaped.

She's saying in her strong Bradford accent, 'I'll cook it, me love, but it can't be ate. Full of coal is that.'

41

Strangled by the sheet, I'm suddenly awake. The star has gone, and the sky is no longer dark. It's the moment before dawn. I don't know what woke me. My room is so close to the street, it could have been anything. Someone running past, or a door slamming, or a drunk singing.

I listen with my whole body, but hear nothing as I get dressed, still thinking about the pastry dog that Nan charred in the oven. My mother couldn't abide my dad's mum, thought she was common; but no one had as much joy in life. She was always laughing, my nan, dancing a hip-flicking rumba all around her cramped kitchen. Flour on her hands and in her hair. Then she died, and the dancing disappeared like a puff of smoke. When I walk past her house now the curtains are different, and a stranger pulls them closed when I try to peer inside. Sometimes I just stand and stare at the door, hoping it will open and Nan will be there.

In the hallway, I see what woke me up. Simon's big backpack blocks the stairs. He must have hitched up from Birmingham through the night. He's done that wherever we've lived. Turning up in the early hours, throwing stones at Nel's window until she wakes to let him in. I don't know if I'm sad or happy that he's here. He's fun, but he spoils things too. I pull the front door open and step outside.

Nobody is up but me. Even our dirty street seems spacious when it's empty. Though it's sunny, the early-morning cold bites as I walk down the street. I've borrowed Nel's scarf from the rack by the door, and her scent is comfortably familiar as I wrap it around my face to warm my nose. Through the corner-shop window the owner is visible, stacking piles of newspapers. Paperboys push them into their wide bags and adjust the weight until the straps sit easy on their shoulders.

The owner comes out and sticks a poster onto the billboard on the path.

'You're up early,' he says. 'Going to work?'

'No, just for a walk.'

He nods, but his expression implies that I've gone down in his estimation. The paperboys head out of the shop and take off in different directions. I follow one towards the main road. As I amble past closed shops, he cuts down a side street and starts shoving papers into letterboxes.

The butcher and his boy hang fresh lamb carcasses on hooks in the window and arrange sausages and kidneys in trays.

A baker piles bread rolls and loaves on her counter.

The fishmonger opens the doors and the smell makes me step to one side.

'Cheer up, ginger,' he shouts at me. 'It might never happen.'

He's swilling down the floor with a hose. Water and fish scales wash out and into the gutter. I move sharpish so as not to get it on my feet. Grinning, he turns away to cut off the water.

'Hey.' A woman's voice comes from behind me. 'Student girl.'

I turn to see the young prostitute. She is still wearing the clothes she had on yesterday, the same turquoise top and the short skirt. In her hand is a bent cigarette and she's waving it at me.

'Got a light?'

I dig into my pocket for my matches and ignite it for her.

'Thanks for the customer,' she says.

'Was he OK? He seemed a bit weird.'

I felt guilty about handing him onto her like that. Guilty about assuming she'd know how to handle him.

'I've had weirder,' she says. 'But he were acting like a prick, so I took his money and told him to sod off without giving him a thing. He were fucking furious, but Tommy come out and told him to sling his hook before he could do anything.'

'Who's Tommy?'

'Me pimp.' She looks at me like I'm stupid.

'Oh, yeah,' I say. 'Of course.'

She rubs her bare arms. She must be freezing.

'Have you been up all night?' I ask.

'Aye. Took a long time to turn enough tricks. I'm fine now, though. I'll get some breakfast soon.' She pauses, tips her head and assesses something about me. 'I'm Janice. What's your name, cock?'

'Jude. Nice to meet you.'

'Jude like the song.'

'Yes – like the song.'

'Alright, Jude. Thanks for the light, cock. Are you walking back? I'll come with you.'

I hadn't really finished my stroll, but I can't refuse her. I nod, and we turn back towards our street. She shivers as we walk and I feel sorry for her. Her make-up is smudged, there are ladders in her tights and goose pimples on her arms. I think about offering her my coat to keep warm, but the pockets are stuffed with all my precious things: keys, money, tobacco tin and my blues harp. I don't think she'd steal them, but all the same, I don't want to be apart from them. It also occurs to me that it might seem odd for a girl to make an offer like that when we don't really know each other.

'Hey,' I say as a thought comes to me. There's suspicion in her face and I feel awkward, but I carry on anyway. 'Fancy a cup of tea from somewhere?'

Her eyes reveal her surprise. 'You buying?'

'Yeah, I am. Where's the best café?'

'All the girls use the one around the corner, Stan's. The bloke's Polish, but he treats us nice, like.'

'OK,' I say, 'I think I know the one.'

I get a little surge of excitement. There was a fight in there as I went past the other day. Janice is hunched up, hugging herself as we walk. Conversation doesn't seem to come naturally to her.

'Have you always lived around here?' I ask.

'No, cock, I'm from Manchester. I had to get away from there, though. There were trouble. I come over here because I knew a lass I could stay with and I never went home.'

'Do you want to go home?'

'No. Nowt left for me in Manchester. Me mam took up with a bastard and when I come home one day, they were all gone: me mam, me sisters and brothers, everyone. Ellie next door said a van come and they all got in and went. Thought they went to Rochdale, but I never found out.'

'What, they just went without telling you?'

'Aye. Left the furniture and everything. Just scarpered. Then the trouble started.'

I can see that she doesn't want to talk about it anymore. Whatever happened it looks as though she doesn't even want to think about it.

Situated squarely on the corner, the café has STAN'S TEAS hand-painted on the glass. Netting is strung to obscure the bottom of the windows, and the draught makes it flutter as Janice leads us in. The top of the door knocks the bell above it, which jingles and bounces on its little coil.

The room is muggy with the smell of burnt fat. It's surprising how many people are in the café this early in the day. They look like they might be off-duty prostitutes and manual labourers having supper after the night shift, or breakfast before they start.

Plastic cloths cover tables occupied by women with dyed hair and blouses a size too small. In one corner a man in a donkey jacket taps a box of matches on a plate smeared with ketchup. Another, dressed in paint-stained white overalls, pushes an unfinished crust of toast away and takes out his newspaper.

They have all stopped talking, drinking and eating. Every eye is on me.

'Eh up, Janice. Who's the other redhead? Is she your sister or a new recruit or what?' The man in the donkey jacket runs his eyes over me.

'Leave her alone, Froggy. She's all right. She's one of them students across the road from us.'

Janice pulls out a chair by the window and indicates another one for me. The ashtray overflows onto the centre of the table.

'Bloody trouble-making student, is she? Going on them marches and having sit-ins and what-have-you?'

'Shut your mouth, Froggy, she's not doing nowt except having a cup of tea. Tell Stanislav what you want, love, he'll bring it over.' She directs herself to the tall man behind the counter. 'I'll have tea – two sugars, Stan.'

He looks at me and wipes a cup with his white apron. 'What about you?'

That is the kind of accent I've only heard in Second World War films.

'Coffee: milk, no sugar,' I tell him.

One of the women leans towards the triangular tin ashtray, tapping it with a cigarette between her yellowed fingers, traces of pink lipstick on its tip. She nudges the woman next to her and nods at Janice.

'Tommy Strangman were after you this morning, Jan. Did you know? He were tamping, weren't he, Rose?'

'He can go fuck himself,' Janice murmurs.

Rose, whose grey roots are growing out under bleached hair, clatters her cup down, 'You be careful, lass. He'll give you more than a nick on the cheek if you keep pissing him off. Am I right, Renie?'

'She's right.' Renie inspects her fingernails. 'He's got a bloody short fuse has that one. And he's quick as all buggery with that blade. Likes to use it too.'

Janice fleetingly touches the little scar on her face. 'Aye, well. I'm just fucked off is all.' She looks hard at me as though she wants to ask something, wriggles slightly in her seat and leans forward. 'Will you buy me a bacon butty?'

I check to see how much money I've got. 'Yes, OK.'

'Stan, give us a bacon sandwich, cock.' She looks at me, 'You having one or what?'

I shake my head because I haven't enough to buy two. 'I'll get something at home.'

The sandwich and drinks come. The women are still watching me. The bloke in the donkey jacket stares me out as he leaves.

'Don't take no notice of Froggy,' Janice says. 'He's all mouth and trousers. Works for the Parks, sweeping and that. You should have one of these butties.'

'Is he one of your customers?' I lift the net curtain to follow him lumbering away. He's ugly and dirty and I can't imagine having sex with him. For me sex is for pleasure, it's light entertainment. The thought of doing it with someone unattractive, even for a lot of money, makes me grimace. I think of Philip all over my unconscious body.

Janice reads my face. 'Haven't you never done it for money?'

I shake my head. 'When I go hitch-hiking, lorry drivers are always offering. But I only sleep with people I fancy, and nobody I fancy has ever offered me cash.'

It occurs to me that she might be insulted, but she carries on eating thoughtfully. After she swallows a big mouthful of bread and bacon, she nods. 'Aye well, happen you've never had to. I'm glad for you. First time I did it, it was me Uncle Danny. I were twelve and he give me a doll. One of them Barbie ones. Still in its box and everything. He didn't buy it. He nicked it. It were the most beautiful-est thing I ever had. She had a silver dress and a little crown. Didn't have it long though. Me mam chucked it out for spite. Next time he give me some sweets. I been doing business ever since. It's normal for me, cock. It's what I do. Don't mean nothing to me.'

She looks behind me as the bell above the door jingles. 'Oh shit,' she says.

'Where the fuck've you been, cunt?' The voice belongs to a thickset man in his forties, hair slicked back like Elvis, wearing a shoestring tie and a fistful of gold rings. Just the bulk of him is intimidating. His face is big and flabby, and his knuckles have indecipherable letters tattooed across them in scrappy blue.

Janice pales. 'I've got the fucking money, Tommy. I've been fucking working, that's where I've been.' She brings out a handful of notes and coins and puts them on the table.

He scoops all the cash up and shoves it in his pocket. 'You're lucky: lucky I don't batter you, you ugly little fucker. Only reason I don't is you'd make even less brass than you do now.'

He notices me for the first time. I sit perfectly still and let him look me over. He starts with my tits, comes up to my face and scowls critically. 'Who the fuck are you?'

I shake my head. 'No one, I'm just in having a coffee.'

'She's one of them students from across the road.'

He makes a dismissive movement of his head and turns away. 'Fucking students. Who gives a shit about students?'

Back inside my room I slip into bed. I always sleep better in daylight. My bones are chilled, and the blankets are warm. I keep thinking about Janice.

I think about what I saw. Tucked through the pimp's belt was a sleek pearl handle, silver hilt and finger guard; a stiletto blade folded tightly inside.

Tommy's flick knife. The one that cut her.

4

Nel

Shadows shift across my wall. This room still feels new to me even though we've been here nearly a month. The bed doesn't yet know my body, and Simon and I don't really fit in it together. He's asleep but I've been awake ever since he arrived. The curtains are partially open, and I can see cloud like a solid bank of granite as dawn breaks.

At least the freckles across his back are familiar. He scratches his face in his sleep. He's as beautiful as a girl, blond hair spread across the pillow. Dead to the world and immovable. I prop myself on one elbow to look at him properly: his perfect mouth and his long lashes, the gold cross around his neck, his pierced ear like an Elizabethan dandy. He has me trapped in this bed unless I climb over him, so I lay back and contemplate the shadows again.

Toto's door creaks open below. The front door bangs shut.

She's out there now. Prowling. Checking out the streets. I wonder how different this place is when everyone is still in bed? I should have known she wouldn't be able to resist exploring a place with Chapeltown's reputation. Always pushing her luck. She's filled with such joyful craziness, and although I'll never admit this to her, I admire her insane bravery. She knows how to be alive.

Whenever we talk about it, she laughs at me. She says it's not her who's brave and reckless; it's me who's scared of life. But I don't think that's true. I've seen her pushing things to the limit so many times. If she isn't reckless then I don't know who is.

There's a granite tor out on the moors in Derbyshire called Windgather Rocks. Our drawing lecturer took us out there on a class trip to draw it. It was so windy that day. Most of us huddled under boulders, trying not to get smashed in the face by our drawing boards.

The crag towered above us and when I looked up, Toto was lying out on the wind at an angle. Her whole body rested on the powerful upward draft, red hair streaming behind her, arms outstretched like a crucifix. Nothing holding her up but moving air. The wind had only to drop for one second and she would fall down that rock face headfirst. No one could survive that. I didn't dare shout out. All I could do was watch until she finally took a step back, standing upright and safe. I think I heard her laughing. I wonder if she's out there laughing like that somewhere right now.

I push out my arms and the flats of both my hands to discover the proximity of the walls above and beside me. My fingers run over the embossed flowers of the wallpaper, find a rip, linger then move on. I listen to milk bottles tumbling over and the footsteps of someone running down the street. For a moment, I wonder if it's Toto but she doesn't run like that. Her boot heels click. This is a heavy footfall. Like a man.

My throat is dry. I wish I'd remembered a glass of water. I want to get up. But all I can do is press my head into Simon's shoulder. His skin is sweet-smelling, and his muscles are hard like clay. If I lie against him like this, and think very deeply about it, maybe I'll find a way to love him more. The way he wants to be loved. Simon is volatile. If you don't hold his fragility with the exact amount of tenderness, he can turn like an untamed tomcat. Weakness and cruelty sit so close together in some people: in men like my father.

Maybe that's why Simon and I are together. Is it that I can't be rid of my dad?

My fucking father.

I think about the boiled heart.

When I got back from school that day, there was a strange smell in the house. Something unfamiliar being cooked in the kitchen. My mother was hunched over the stove. She didn't turn around, didn't say anything when I greeted her. There was a chopping board beside her, and the remains of carrots, onions and what could have been parsnips scattered over it. A pot bubbled on the hob, and sour steam filled the room. There were sweat marks beneath my mother's arms, a ring of salt on the outer edge, her hair sticking to her neck, and her head was bowed, bobbing in time to the stirring of the pot. Not looking up. No intention of looking up.

I withdrew quietly. Treading as softly as possible, I went upstairs to my bedroom. I took off my school uniform, put on my skirt and jumper, replaced shoes with slippers, and came down later when called to dinner. My mother's voice was agitated as she called from the bottom of the stairs. The sour smell was still there, sweetly overlaid with carrot and onion, but cloying too, dark and unpleasant in its intensity.

My father, in his neat work suit, sat at one end of the table. My mother was at the other, and I sat in the middle, head lowered. Instead of serving the food onto plates in the kitchen, as she usually did, my mother brought in a lidded saucepan, and placed it on a mat in the middle of the dining-room table alongside a dish of mixed vegetables. She glared at my father over the top of the pan. He reached for his embroidered napkin and tucked it under his collar, watching her all the time without a word.

When the lid was taken off the pot a smell rolled out that caught the back of the throat and made all three of us turn our heads away. In the pan, submerged in a thin, beige liquid, was a gristly lump of meat threaded with purple tinged tubes and yellow lard.

My father reeled back with undisguised disgust. 'What in the name of all that's holy is that?'

This appeared to be the moment my mother was waiting for. She stood up so quickly that her chair fell over and came around the table at him so fast that he also stood up and backed away. Her face was pink and patchy. She glistened and sweated in a way that I'd never seen in this normally restrained woman.

'It's heart. It's offal. It's cheap, and tough, and you have to boil it to tenderise it and cry onion tears into it to sweeten it, and this is what you've brought me to. This. You lying-so-and-so. You ruddy, scheming, lying so-and-so. You bloody, bloody jackass. You liar.'

I held my breath and kept as still as I possibly could, hands on the top of the table. I'd never heard her swear in my whole life, not even anything as innocuous as *bloody*. My parents were face to face now. He was as white as the tablecloth; she was as crimson as the cotton serviette lying by her plate.

'Pull yourself together, woman. What the hell is wrong with you?'

'Ye ken! Bloody, bloody liar that ye are.' She fell into the broad brogue of the streets where she grew up. 'How can ye go to that kirk on a Sunday, how can you look that minister in the face? Ye ken what's wrong with me!'

He flinched and looked at me sidelong. 'Penelope, away to the kitchen, bring your mother a glass of water. She's no well.'

I pushed my chair back, but my mother turned on me. 'Don't move. Do not move. I'm warning you.' She directed her attention back to the man in front of her. 'Don't tell me I'm no well. I'm better than I've ever been. Don't tell our lassie I'm no well. You're the one. It's you. I'll tell her, shall I? I'll tell Penelope what a bloody, bloody liar her father is?'

'Ach, Margaret,' he said in a low voice. 'Maggie, please, Maggie.'

The use of the affectionate form of her name infuriated her further, and she pressed towards him.

He took a small step back, tripping on the edge of the rug, reaching to steady himself on the Welsh dresser. Turning his body in a swift and seamless movement, he hit her hard across the face.

The shock, that all three of us seemed to share, emptied my lungs and made me grip the table as my mother crumpled momentarily and let out a wail. He made as though to catch her, his eyes wide, like rabbits' are when they know there's an owl near the hutch. She pushed him away, forceful and angry, but he grabbed her forearms and held her still.

'Stop it. Stop it, Margaret. I had to do that. You were hysterical.' He looked at me as he said that, not at my mother. Then he said it again with more confidence, as though if he said it enough times it would make it true, as though he could convince himself. 'I had to do that, didn't I? Completely hysterical.'

Mum pulled her arms out of his grip so hard that his fingers were left holding nothing but the air. She moved so close to him that he had to lean back so as not to touch her nose with his.

'No, Douglas, I wasn't hysterical. You were.'

He said nothing then. Nothing at all. Finally turning away from her unflinching stare, he sat at the head of the table again and gathered himself. He turned his attention to me.

'Eat it. Your mother cooked it, so eat it. Where's your manners?'

My mother left the room as he cut up the heart, which had become cold and stringy, and served me a portion. I looked at it on my plate. Gristle, sinew and tubes on a pile of vegetables, swimming in a grainy liquid in which little globules of fat were forming. I knew I had to eat it because my father was obsessed with children eating what was put in front of them. I was never allowed to leave food. For a moment, I simply watched his face. He struggled to force down mouthfuls of the indigestible organ that his wife had hardened with salt, and heated with pepper, and stewed with bitter herbs that I could not identify from the smell. It might be parsley, or rosemary, or perhaps marigolds or buttercup roots.

'Eat it,' my father said again, his face strained and spots of gravy visible on the napkin under his chin. 'It's not too bad if you don't think about it.'

Simon shifts in his sleep. I place my hand very softly on his chest to feel the beat beneath it and stare at the window, not seeing anything that's out there. Just seeing a man eating a boiled heart.

5

Toto

Simon's voice is a deep rumble. Sounds not words. Nel's is softer and slower. The floor makes unfamiliar creaks as they move around upstairs. Nel will come down to make him a cup of tea soon. He'll wait for it upstairs, calling down for it in his whiniest voice if he thinks she's not being quick enough. I stick my feet into my jeans and try not to let his presence spoil my day.

Sometimes Simon is the best laugh, but mostly he's a total pain in the arse. When Nel and he got together I couldn't believe she'd chosen such an insubstantial bit of froth as him. I was quietly happy when he decided they shouldn't cohabit. He said his bedsit was most suitable for his needs, but too small for two. It was in an attic in Whetheridge Common, where a number of our tutors lived, so he could ambush them on the way to college. He didn't want her cramping his style, was my opinion, but I've never told her that. The bastard keeps her on her toes by turning up unexpectedly at our place at all hours, as if he thinks she's up to something. My ex, Michael, says he's too fucking full of himself and even though I don't want to be his, or anyone's girlfriend any more, Michael and I still see eye-to-eye when it comes to Simon.

The front door thuds open and heavy feet tread their way to the kitchen. I guess it's Hank and find him at the small Formica table, spreading a newspaper across the speckled grey-and-white surface.

He looks up and gestures at the kettle. 'Just boiled.'

I search out my special mug. His face softens as I put it on the table to spoon in granules of instant coffee.

'Still got that, then.' He twists it to look at my enamel-paint poppies. 'You had it at Circle Road, when me and Jo first knew you.'

I tip in milk followed by hot water and nod. 'Wherever this mug and my harmonica are, that's where I live.'

'I used to think it was funny that you think about things like that, but actually it's kind of sweet.'

He smooths out the newspaper and returns to reading it as I drag out a rickety chair and set myself next to him. We fall into comfortable silence. Through the cracked glass in the back door I consider the spindly tree in our yard. The kids have climbed it so much in their determination to view Jo's telly that most of its branches are splintered and the bark has been scraped off in long tatters.

Hank coughs a little and rumples the paper. 'Have you seen this?' He points at an article on the second page. 'Another hitch-hiker's disappeared. Look' – he swivels the paper towards me – 'Jennifer Curtis-Pope, this one's called, last seen getting into a car on the M1. There's too much of this going on. It reminds me of that American case last year. Remember it? All them girls in

California. Tortured and strangled. And that bloke they've just caught over there. Raped them and cut their heads off.'

He catches my eye.

'That's America. This isn't America,' I say.

He gives a sigh. 'I think you've got some kind of death wish sometimes, Toto. It's some kind of bloody Russian roulette you play when you take off on your hitching jaunts to random places for no reason at all. There's girls gone missing *here*, in England. Like this one.' He taps the newsprint emphatically.

I sip my coffee and evade his glance. I love hitchhiking. I call it *jaunting*. Now everyone who knows me calls it that too. Some of them think it's brave and funny, others think it's stupid and irresponsible.

Hank's still observing me.

'You know I know how to kill, don't you?' I lean towards him with a wild smile.

He rears back in pretend alarm. 'Is that right, Toto?'

'I'm serious,' I say. 'When I was six, my dad taught me the hand-to-hand defence he learned in the Air Force.'

'You're fucking kidding!'

'I'm not kidding. He was air crew. If they got shot down in enemy territory, they had to escape without leaving witnesses. All he knew was how to incapacitate and kill, so that's what he taught me. I could break your fingers in one move, and I can gouge out an eye like nobody's business. If I chop you in the temple with the side of my hand – you're dead, pal.'

'Fuck off.' I can see he's not sure if I'm lying.

'No, honestly. This kid used to chase me home from school with a stick. Dad said, "Don't run – face him down." And he showed me how to fight, right? Kind of like a cross between jujitsu and karate. Next time that boy fucked with me, I stood my ground. I *knew* I could take him. Stopped him dead in his tracks without lifting a finger.'

'That was against a kid, Toto. This is different.'

'All right. Come at me then.'

'Don't be stupid.' He straightens his newspaper.

'Come on, try to grab me.' I get up, plant my feet wide and raise my palms as though in surrender.

He sighs, feigns disinterest, then leaps to his feet and seizes me. My forearm smashes down on his wrist and I twist away from his fingers. He yelps, clutches his arm and steps back.

'Fucking hell!' His eyes are wide with surprise and admiration.

I'm triumphant, but don't press it. I change the subject. 'Are you going back to Sheffield today?'

It takes him a moment or two to compose himself. Shaking the pain out of his arm one more time he checks the clock. 'Yes, I've got a night shift later, and things to pick up. Jo doesn't like that telly. Thinks it's too small. I'm getting a better one from a pal at work.'

I've finished my coffee and I'm thinking about another one. I absently put a granule on my finger and lick it without thinking. The bitterness makes me wince, but I quite like it. I do it again.

'Will you see Michael and Sid and everyone?' My eyes glaze a bit as I think about old times. 'God, I miss those guys. It'll be great to hang around with them again when we go down. Are you going to catch up with them before that?'

'I might do,' he ponders. 'I don't know, though. They're always around that poncey couple. You know, he's that lecturer at the art school, taught theory to all you painting students, and she's American. I can't stand them.'

'You mean Hugo Reynard and his wife, Callie?'

He nods and I shrug at him. 'They're OK,' I say lightly. 'They can be quite entertaining.'

Hank shrugs back. 'Not my kind of people, Toto.'

There's footfall on the stairs and, in a few moments, Jo appears, fully dressed, ready for teaching practice. She's overheard our conversation.

'That Hugo Reynard wants to get in your knickers. He always has. Even when we were students, he used to smarm all over you in his seminars. One of those chosen few he used to invite round to his house for his "special" parties.'

She makes little quotation marks in the air around the word 'special'.

I wave a dismissive hand. 'He fancies everyone. He was after Nel until she told him to fuck off.'

'Aye, but Nel hates them both. She says the wife *really* fancies you.' Jo widens her eyes and assesses my reaction.

'Callie? Well, she might a bit. She's always going on about being bisexual – as though I'm supposed to think it's really outrageous or something.'

'She had that thing with Lauren, didn't she?'

'They've both had "things" with loads of people.'

Jo gets herself a mug and looks expectantly at Hank, 'Is there tea made?'

He pushes the pot towards her. 'Might need topping up.'

'Would you go with her?' Jo's attention returns to me.

I yawn, remembering Callie Reynard's red lipstick and her exotic-smelling perfume, 'I don't know. Maybe . . . if I was in the right mood.'

Jo makes no effort to fill her mug, so Hank obliges by pouring in brackish liquid. She grimaces and adds water from the kettle.

'Anyway, young Toto, what are you doing up this early? You never usually surface until lunchtime.'

I stretch and yawn. 'I got woken up when Simon arrived.'

Hank nods, 'I heard him as well. Banging about in the bathroom.'

'Budge up,' Jo sits between us, putting her tea down on the page Hank is reading. He murmurs a protest so she removes it. There's a wet ring left on the print, and the ink smudges as she tries to wipe it off with her finger.

'Sorry, flower.'

'I give up.' He folds the paper away.

She grabs it and spreads it open again. I like the way they are with each other. They can have jokes without talking. He sips his tea as she scans the front page.

Jo points at a story about an attack in a Leeds park. 'Did you see that? It was on the news last night. I was talking to that girl across the street, the one with the little scar. You know, the one who's on the game?'

I nod. 'Janice?'

'Aye, Janice. She's all right, that Janice. I like her. Anyway,' Jo continues, 'she said the word is it was a prostitute got beaten with a metal bar. I mean really smashed up. She says they're all freaked out because there's been a few girls attacked lately. All of them prostitutes – all around these streets. Chapeltown, Harehills and that.'

Hank's face is full of concern. 'For fuck's sake, Jo. You're freaking me out now.'

'We're not prostitutes, are we? These girls were attacked while they were doing business.'

Hank alternates his gaze between the two of us. 'You both think you're indestructible, don't you? I was just trying to explain to Toto that her jaunting might get her killed, and now you're being all blasé about this crap.'

Jo frowns as though he's being illogical. 'That's different. *She*' – she points at me – 'is bloody mad. No argument. But *I've* never been groped by a slimy bloke in a Vauxhall Viva who ejected me halfway down the motorway.'

'He didn't throw me out.' I laugh at the memory, 'I dropped his wallet from the window. Then I flagged down a motorbike while he was running around searching for it. Stupid bastard's probably still looking for his money somewhere along the M1. I mean, don't knock hitching! I ended up on a beach in Cornwall that time. A week hanging out with a fire-eater and a juggler. It was bloody brilliant. Believe me, when it comes to jaunting, I'm the best.'

Hank sighs, 'Well, just be bloody careful, that's all I'm saying.'

I'm thinking about cornflakes, but I say, 'Hank, you worry too much. We're going to be all right. Listen, I can't afford to travel any other way, can I? And besides there's nothing better than living off my wits like that.' Jo is looking at me like I've confirmed her earlier assessment of my sanity, but I don't care. 'It's so cool. That time when I ended up in Cornwall, these two glorious freaks turned up out of nowhere in a campervan painted like a Japanese dragon. He had a plaited beard and blew fire out of the window, and she was shouting, "C'mon we're going to St Ives, we need company." They gave me the spare bed in the van, and I collected money while she juggled anything she could find, from pop bottles to cuttlefish, and he blew flames from his nostrils. It was incredible. I'm never going to stop doing it.'

'You're a one-off, you are,' he says. 'There's no point in trying to dissuade you from anything.'

He turns his consideration to his wife. 'I'll drop you off if you want. I've got time.'

He looks at me again. 'Anywhere you want to be? Apart from a beach in Cornwall, of course.'

I shake my head. 'Not in this rain.'

When they've gone, I check the weather out of the window. Above the wet roofs a burnt-sienna sky rumbles with far off thunder. I'm considering going down to the Alternative School today, just to hang out and try to score some dope. I like it there.

I got involved by accident. One afternoon I was wandering amongst the wreckage of houses that the council flattened to make way for a motorway. The demolition went on for miles and one of the few things left standing was an old church, moored in an ocean of rubble like some forgotten ship.

The doors were open, and strains of the Velvet Underground could be heard. I thought there must be people like me in there, so I tentatively poked my head inside. It was full of life. People with long hair and pierced ears were cleaning floors. They told me they were setting up a school as a *collective* with no rules and no hierarchy. I joined up right then, and I go there most days now.

Our full name is the *Alternative School Collective*. No one gets paid and we don't have a chain of command or anything. Maria, Jacko and Bandana Jim are the most organised and, of the three of them, Maria is the strongest. It isn't acceptable to say so, but she is the leader. We look to her for solutions and she gives us direction. Each morning we decide on the day's activities, and everyone, including the kids, has a vote. Maria gave us *ground rules* about not interrupting the person with the speaking stick, but apart from that we can all do what we want. Ground rules are different to rules apparently, but I've never discovered in what way.

Once, the police turned up and demanded to know who was in charge. When we didn't respond they looked around the room and decided Jacko was the boss, possibly because he looked like the oldest male. As they took him outside for questioning, Maria was disdainful.

'They don't understand what anarchism is. It literally means to be without a Head.' As she watched them interrogating him through the window, her contempt deepened. 'I suppose it's not surprising that the pigs can't grasp a truly democratic situation.'

She pulled the curtain shut as though the very sight of them offended her. 'Well, they've just anointed Jacko as our leader, so that will just be dandy. Votes of confidence all round. Hail to Jacko.'

Maria and Jacko have totally different takes on the world: Jacko's lot are *drop outs*. They obey nobody's rules and think life is about 'being natural'. Most of them live in a condemned house nearby called the Squat, where there are no private spaces, no electricity, no gas, no rules – and they're out of their heads on dope the whole time.

On the other hand, Maria and her anarchists want to over-throw capitalism and won't have a bar of the magical-mystical stuff that the drop outs are into. They reside at the Rectory next to the school and live like an order of monks and nuns, ruled by loads of committees and rosters.

It's ironic that we all look the same to outsiders, just a homo-geneous gang of long-haired hippies, because the Squat and the Rectory are chalk and cheese. I'm fascinated by both factions.

A few of us shift between the two groups, not quite sure where we belong. My friend Denny is like that; she lives with the anarchists *and* she does mystical stuff like the Tarot. She's like me, trying out everything to see what it feels like.

If I'm honest, what I love most about the Alternative School is the building itself. That's really why I go there so much. The church reminds me of the deserted places I went looking for when I was a child. Abandoned houses felt safe to me. I secreted myself in their ruins, hidden from my raging red-headed father and my mother who could conjure blizzards from the tiniest snowflake. Mum is 'officer class' and she married down when she chose my working-class father. He's a charming self-made man, who manages a carpet factory and covets pearl cufflinks. As a couple they spare themselves no luxury, their plush-carpeted bedroom has designer curtains and wardrobes bursting with new clothes. It's always as warm as a sauna. But life for their children is different. There's no carpet in my sister's bedroom. My brother's light switch has never worked and his clothes don't fit. My window got shattered in one of my father's rages and was never mended. It's stuck together with carpet tape and some-times, when it's really cold, snow comes in through the gaps.

In my parents' house the children always fended for them-selves and it was better not to be there. From as early as I can remember, I crept off to derelict places at every opportunity. I used to imagine that each place was my home. There were beds with perished sheets and tables set with abandoned tea-time crockery. I was Goldilocks in a home owned by dead bears. Snail trails on mouldered carpets, and moss growing in saucers. Things crumbled in my hands, but I was never afraid. A Norman keep on the edge of some woods behind our house was my favourite. There were damselflies trapped inside and house martins came swooping in though the arches to catch them, filling the space with frantic wings – then gone.

Once, at the Old Church, we concealed someone under the floorboards. He was scarred and head-shaven, with missing teeth. Jacko and some of the other men got into a huddle. Tools were brought out and boards levered up. When the police came that evening, they walked right over the top of his hiding place. It was thrilling to witness, knowing what I knew, imagining what he must feel like down there in the dark.

After he left, I crept into the space just to see what it was like. It felt like a grave.

It's stopped raining and in the sky through our kitchen window a rainbow forms. Faint at first, then vibrant, now fading again. It makes me think about the bluebirds flying beyond the rainbow in *The Wizard of Oz*. I wonder about them. All I can see in my mind is a blue-inked tattoo with a forked tail and swooping wings.

I'm far away, looking at the inside of my wrist and imagining a tattoo there, when I notice Nel at the door in her nightdress. She heads for the sink without speaking, takes an empty glass from the draining board, fills it with water and downs it in long gulps.

'Do you think that bluebirds exist?' I ask her.

She looks at me quizzically, refills the glass, drinks it down in one go. 'Yes,' she says at last, 'just like kingfishers are real. Bluebirds are American things, so that's like being mythical, but I can't really imagine why you ever thought kingfishers were make-believe.'

'Well, I've never seen one, that's all.'

'Doesn't mean they're not real.' Without asking whether I want any, she puts bread enough for two under the grill. 'Why don't you get out the butter and the marmalade and stuff, lovely?'

I find the raspberry jam and the Golden Shred and the tub of margarine that we all, for some reason, refer to as butter. She watches the bread, waiting for the right moment to turn each slice. I return to surveying the sky and the pools of water drying on the sloping outhouse roof.

'I might get a bluebird tattoo. What do you think? On my wrist.'

We both observe the spot I'm thinking about. She cocks her head. Gently, she lifts my hair back and reveals the place where the low-cut neck of my T-shirt sits off my shoulder. She lays her hand on a spot below the nape of my neck. 'Or how about here?'

I feel the trace of her fingers after they've gone.

'Yes. There would be nice,' she says, 'Really gorgeous, blues and reds against your skin.'

'Big or small?'

'Quite small.' Her attention is suddenly drawn back to the toast. 'Oh shit.' She flips the slices out with her fingertips, shaking both hands to rid them of the sudden heat. 'I'll be glad when Hank brings that toaster like he promised. D'you want jam or marmalade?'

'I'll do it.' I take the knife off her and butter each piece. I know she'll want marmalade. She always does. I do raspberry jam for myself.

'Aren't you taking Simon his tea?' I ask.

Nel shakes her head expressionlessly. 'He's gone back to sleep.'

She watches me as I eat. 'This morning,' she says, 'I woke up thinking about the time my mum forced me and my dad to eat a heart.'

I splutter. 'I don't want to visualise that at breakfast.'

She laughs, 'Really? I can't imagine why not.'

'Your mother is such a prosaic kind of woman,' I say. 'It seems such a stormy and poetic thing for her to do. Honestly, it makes me worry when I see her. Whenever we're around at your house and she's making us sandwiches I worry she might put someone's heart in them.'

Nel's mum and dad have a semi-detached house full of Scottish memorabilia, and a fridge that's always full. She used to take me there for food when we were short of money. They tolerated me, but I never thought they liked me. Nel says it's because of my ears. Only gypsies and Catholics have pierced ears according to her dad.

She gets more bread and puts it under the grill. 'My mother doesn't have the imagination to be prosaic. You overestimate her. She's a Presbyterian, for crying out loud!'

'Maybe your mother has religion as a substitute for imagination.'

Nel laughs. 'And *your* mother has what?'

I ponder that. 'Manners,' I say definitively, 'and a big hollow where her heart should be.'

'Did she rip it out to feed it to you?'

I pause before answering. 'No.'

I've gone back to a place that I don't want to remember. I'm standing on a stool beneath the turquoise doors of our kitchen cabinet. Mum is outside sleeping on a sun-drenched lawn. The baby is crying in a pram by the backdoor, light falling full on to his tiny pink face. His eyes are screwed shut and his fine dark hair is wet with sweat. I'm six years old and my little sister Tess is three. She's hungry and I need to feed her. There's a tin of Irish stew. The opener makes jagged edges.

68

I ignite the gas with the fourth match and stir with a metal spoon. When the smell from the steaming saucepan tells me it's ready, we share it silently from one dish as my baby brother keeps wailing in the porch. Suddenly my mother's eyes are on me. A flash of pain across my face. Looking at her pink-painted toenails from where I lie on the lino. My burning cheek against cold floor. My eye closing as it swells.

Her voice. 'Who said you could?'

Who said I could?

I refocus on Nel as she plays with the butter with the tip of her knife, making swirls along its edge.

She glances up at me, 'Was it your mum who wanted you to go to a convent school? Your dad doesn't seem the type. He's so . . . not that type of person.'

'Correct. He left school at fourteen and never gave a toss what school anyone went to. Mum was the one who was keen on a private education.'

'Why?'

'She's from an army family. They send their kids to boarding schools. She thinks that's normal. In the end, Dad gave in and agreed to the local convent. That was only because it was really cheap and a bit shit. Bloody horrible.'

'You're not even Catholic.'

'Well, my nan was, but Dad lapsed and Mum's Anglican. I was a Protestant day girl in a Catholic boarding school. When I was eleven, Sister St Wilgefortis told me there was no way I would ever go to Heaven, no matter what I did.'

Nel grins. 'I love being prematurely damned. We're such fun, aren't we? Nothing left to lose, so there's a kind of liberty in that. Luckily there's no God, otherwise we'd really be in the shit.'

I rinse my red mug at the sink. As the hot water touches the glaze, it slowly splits into two pieces in my hand, like it's decided to die. For a moment I'm flummoxed and consider trying to glue it back together, but the break is so perfectly symmetrical, and right through its centre. My mug-that-means-home is gone. All I have now is my harmonica.

'Shit. Look at that. My mug just split down the middle. That's God's judgement on me for not being a Catholic, that is.'

'Don't fret, lovely, I'll buy you a new one.' She gives me a sad look, like an old friend has died.

The smell of toast pervades the room and she bends to inspect it. 'I love that story though,' she says as she retrieves each slice very carefully. 'When that nun tried to drag you into the school chapel for Mass. And you gripped the door-frame shouting, "I am not a Catholic," while your sister was clamped onto your coat, screaming, "She is *not* a Catholic."'

'I was frightened of the Host. They said it was the real body and blood of Christ.'

Nel widens her eyes in mock horror and puts on an accent like her mother's. 'Jude Totton, ye cannae just go around eating Jesus willy-nilly.'

'It freaked me out. Eating *real* Jesus. I didn't even want to eat fake Jesus.'

'Nobody should eat any sort of Jesus. I think you're suffering from deep theological confusion.' Nel falls into deep thought. 'Have you ever thought about *North*?'

The crackle of toast in my mouth slows my reply. 'Why would I do that in particular?'

Nel pushes her thick blond hair back with one hand, wrapping it to lie on her shoulder.

'I was thinking about it, this morning,' she says. 'I was thinking about Magnetic North.'

'Magnetic North?'

'Yes.'

'What about it?'

'Well. There are two kinds of North it seems. A *true* one and a *magnetic* one.'

'OK. Where's this going?'

'Well, I was thinking that the magnetic one was probably the truer one; the one that draws things to it. I like the idea of True North being a wandering thing, trying to find itself. I like the idea of it being a magnet that everything points to, but which can't find a place to settle.'

'If I was a compass,' I say, 'I would always be looking for that kind of North. It would be my fixed point. I would follow it anywhere.'

We smile conspiratorially.

Feet thudding down the stairs make Nel suddenly attentive. She jumps to re-boil the kettle, grabs a mug and throws a teabag into it.

Simon is wearing Nel's dressing gown, the one patterned with red chrysanthemums that I bought for her from a charity shop on Ecclesall Road. It's delicate and shows his body off. I'm glad he seems to have his underpants on.

'Sit down, my love. I'll get your tea. Do you want toast?' Nel is feeling around for milk in the fridge.

He plonks himself down in the nearest chair and grunts. 'Just tea.'

'Oh, good morning, Jude,' I say in my best theatrical voice,

'How are *you* this morning? Well thank you very much for asking, Simon. I couldn't be better. How are you?'

'Fuck sake, Toto. I've only just woken up.'

I laugh at him. 'You're the only person I know who's grumpier than me in the morning.'

'You're still here, then,' he says. 'On and on like a cracked record. Can't a man get any peace?'

'Well,' I say, 'A *man* could, but you're hardly what anyone would call a man.'

He laughs. 'I'm prettier than you, Totton.'

'I know. That's a problem for both of us. I hear you've got David Bowie completely panicked. He's jealous of your bangle.'

He holds it out. 'Seriously, it's a cracker isn't it? I got it made by this chick in the jewellery department.'

'Doing the MA like you?' I say.

Nel slips a mug of tea into his hand, which he accepts without acknowledgement. 'Yeah. She was an undergrad at Brighton.' He rolls the bangle on his arm and admires it. 'Really fucking talented.' He looks over at Nel. 'Where's my toast?'

'Oh, sorry, I thought . . .'

'Thought what?'

'Thought you said you didn't want any.'

'Why would I say that?'

She looks crestfallen, and I can see her rewinding the conversation in her mind. He simply stares at her. 'Oh, OK.' She flusters, 'Sorry. Never mind. I got it wrong. I'll do it now.'

His mouth curls. 'Good.'

I push my uneaten toast at him. 'Have mine. She made *me* loads. And *you*, by the way, told her you didn't want any. So, stop being a prick Simon Duffy.'

'Don't Toto, please.' Nel has her back to us. She's fumbling to put bread under the grill.

Simon gives me the same flat stare that he just gave her. 'No, I said I wanted toast. You're just backing her up, like you always do.'

'You're being a prick,' I say, and his knuckles tighten into an unconscious fist. We stare each other out until I break the silence. 'Anyway. Are you still coming to that Roxy Music concert with us? Nel said you'd got a ticket.'

He sips his tea, wiping it off his moustache before speaking. 'Yeah, there's always a spare bed for me at Viktor and Genevieve's. I like old Vik. He helped me a lot when I was applying for the MA. He fucking loves my drawings. Mind you I *was* the only one who turned up for his life classes. Poor lonely old fucker.'

'*I went,*' Nel says plaintively. 'I always went.'

'Oh. Yes. You did. I forgot about you. But you were never there, Totton.'

'Why would I be? It was too early and there was too much charcoal. Hate charcoal.'

Nel has finished buttering Simon's toast. She puts it carefully in front of him on a floral side plate. He glances at it briefly.

'I didn't know we were definitely staying at Gen's,' she says with her brow furrowed. 'You said something about that gallery owner, I thought.'

Simon takes an uninterested bite of the toast. 'No, I didn't. I told you over the phone. Vik and Gen's place. We're going straight there. Remember?'

I can see that she doesn't. But she nods. As though to rid herself of troubling thoughts, she turns to me, changing the

73

subject. 'I've got a seminar at college. If you're going to the Alternative School, we could get the bus into town together.'

'Right,' I say. 'Let's do that then. I might see if I can score some hash from Denny while I'm at it. Jo's given me money towards some. Do you want in as well? If you give me four quid, we'll be able to get a twelve-quid deal.'

Nel turns to Simon. 'What do you reckon about the hash, Si?'

'Yeah, you might as well. You can never have too much dope.'

She goes to her bag where it lies on a chair and draws out some pound notes. 'I'm in.' Handing me the money she says, 'Can you afford this, Toto? Have you got enough to live on until next dole day?'

I shrug. 'I've still got that fiver from pawning those rings.'

Nel looks pained. 'That's such a rip-off. They were worth a lot more than that.'

To me, there doesn't seem a lot to discuss. 'I needed money.'

Simon laughs. 'Ha, you could always sell your body around here. Somebody would offer you a quid, I'm sure.'

Nel scowls at him. 'That's not even funny.'

'You're so fucking hilarious, Simon.' I don't rise to his bait. 'Why don't you try your luck out there? You look bloody gorgeous in that dressing gown. Add a little bit of lipstick and you'd probably make a tenner.'

6

Toto

At the Alternative School, Bandana Jim is kneeling on the steps and puzzling about his electric drill. I lower myself onto the cold stone next to him and inspect it. 'Has it got clogged up or something?'

'Don't know,' he says without breaking concentration. He has powder through his hair and the same fine particles are all over the green bandana that serves as his facemask. The asbestos panels he's working on are propped up inside the open church doors, ready to be installed as fireproofing. Holes need to be made in the board lying at his feet, but the fault in the drill is holding him up. His kerchief hangs loose around his neck and he adjusts it as he finally looks up to acknowledge me.

'Have you seen Denny?' I ask, and he nods towards the back of the church hall.

'She's with Maria. They're making a soup or something.'

*

High on the wall, an ornate board displays the number of the final hymn ever sung here and the vaulted hall, with its battered remnants of choir stalls, resonates as I move through it. As I near the kitchen, the smell of stewed food wafts out of the door and through the dusty air.

Amongst the trestle tables and folding chairs, Denny is standing with her Tarot pack held in one hand. Beside her, Maria is chopping carrots and putting them into an oversized pot on the stove. She has delicate features and a quick mind. Denny is clever too, but less capable, and often too stoned to reveal anything of her brain.

I can't help thinking that Maria's very neat for an anarchist. Wearing a toffee-coloured cardigan with raspberry-fool patterns, she's as tidy as someone who still lives with their parents. She smells of soap, which is not what Denny and I smell of. We smell of all sorts of smoke, and that's one of the reasons I like Denny so much. We all observe the boiling pot. The stew foams around some indeterminate meat.

'What's in it?' I ask.

Maria tosses in a handful of chopped carrots. 'Things they were throwing away at the market.'

Picking up a small knife, Denny seems intensely interested in the stew, as though she'd asked the question, not me. 'Yeah, but what?'

Maria sighs. 'You were there when we got it all, Denny. There's neck of mutton, bits of beef, a pork bone. Carrots, onions, cabbage, potatoes, swede.'

That's pretty much everything they're slicing up. Except Denny isn't. She's got that knife in her hand, but she's just looking.

'Where's Rosa?' I ask.

Denny thinks for a moment. 'Susie's got her. She's taken her to the park. We found a pushchair on the dump. Rosa fits in it and everything. Really good score. Susie painted it red.'

Maria studies her. 'Did you give her the breakfast I left out?'

Two-year-old Rosa, named after the Polish revolutionary, Rosa Luxemburg, is Denny's daughter, but it's Maria who keeps her fed and clean.

A scrap of potato peel has attached itself to Denny's cuff. She thinks hard and decides someone *must* have fed her. 'Susie did,' she says unconvincingly.

I see a flash of annoyance in Maria. A darkening of her eyes so quick you might miss it. She turns her attention from Denny to me, putting a lid on the stew with a sharp bang.

'I was meaning to ask you: have you three settled into your new place?'

Nel and Jo sometimes drop by after classes to collect me for a drink or to go home together. Maria was surprised by our move to Chapeltown from Headingly.

'Any more threats on your door?' she asks casually.

Denny gets animated. 'I got chased out of Chapeltown once. I was trying to score some dope. This guy got heavy with me, and two really hard-looking chicks called me a fucking lesbian because of my hair and came after me. Barely got out alive.'

'It's a good job she's an excellent runner.' Maria is smiling.

'I don't go down there anymore,' Denny says. 'I wouldn't live there.'

I shrug. 'It's not that bad. We needed somewhere cheap and it's a nice house. We're quite safe.'

'Well, I hope you're right,' Maria says. 'Life is dangerous enough without courting trouble. In my experience there are plenty of people who'll hurt you when you least expect it. No need to go looking for it by living in places like that. The Hunted shouldn't dance with the Hunter, that's my philosophy.'

Two of the older kids, Kipper and Alfie, barge in carrying a tightly rolled tent under each arm. 'Look what we got for the camping trip!' They throw the tents, still in their packaging, on the floor.

Maria cleans her hands and peers around Denny's shoulder as they both inspect them, her hand resting gently on the other girl's waist. 'Where are these from?'

The boys look at each other shiftily. 'Found them.'

Denny flicks the price tags. 'Found them in the super-market?'

They're dramatically indignant, but Maria cuts them off. 'You stole them.' She is decisive. 'OK, they've got to go back.'

Kipper, who has a ragged homemade haircut, is affronted. 'We're not taking them back. It were fucking hard getting them, and anyway, like Jacko says, *property is theft*.'

Maria and Denny exchange glances, and Maria draws herself up to her full height. Even so, she's only minimally taller than Kipper. 'Jacko didn't mean that the minute you see property you should steal it. Come on. We're taking them back.'

The younger boy, Alfie, fingers a livid rash on the side of his face, looking depressed. 'It don't matter,' he mutters. 'I don't want them anyway.'

Maria remains calm and bright. 'What we don't need is the police coming here and getting us closed down. That's what we *don't* need. So that's why we're taking these back.'

Denny joins in. 'She's right, we'll all get busted, and it's just not cool.'

Kipper looks morose and Alfie directs a series of small, frustrated kicks at a table leg.

78

At the back door, Maria has a tent in her arms. She glares at them until they pick up the others and follow her onto the street.

'Turn the stew off in about an hour,' she shouts over their heads.

Once the door closes, Denny considers for a moment and turns off the gas under the pan. When she sees my expression, she explains, 'I won't remember, and the place will burn down.'

If anyone else had said it, it would be a joke, but that's not Denny's kind of joke.

'Do you want to come down to the Squat?' She covers her eyes from the light and squints at me. 'There's nothing going on here and I need some dope. Jacko's usually got some.'

'Cool. Yes. I need some too. I was going to ask you anyway.'

Maria's phrase, *the Hunted shouldn't dance with the Hunter,* sticks in my mind as Denny walks alongside me talking about the dark things she believes in. I don't think she's trying to shock me. She says, in a matter of fact way, that she doesn't believe there is such a thing as *wrong*, or such a thing as *right*. She believes everything that *is,* is right. No matter what it is. Everything that happens is meant to happen.

'What . . . even Hitler?'

She turns towards me with a distant look. She's only mildly interested in me right now though. I seem to be as transparent as a sheet of clear plastic to her.

'If it happened, then it was meant to.' For a split second, she looks straight into my eyes and asks, 'Have you read any Jung?'

'Yes.'

'You've read about Abraxas then: the god that combines both good and evil?'

'Yes.'

'Well, there you are, it's like in the Tarot: God and the Devil all in one. It's all "right" and it's all "wrong".'

She pushes her hair off her face and considers me for a moment. I hesitate because I don't agree.

'Yeah,' I say, 'but what about choices? How do you make choices if nothing is wrong and nothing is right?'

'I don't know. All I know is sometimes there are no choices – there's just *being*.' She sees that she has to explain more. 'Like in that picture of the Fool in the Major Arcana, you know? With the rose in his hand and the dog at his heels. The white dog . . .'

She trails off. I wait for the end of the sentence.

Finally, she grins.

'That little dog looks so fucking happy. Wouldn't you rather just be the fucking little white dog?'

She makes me laugh. I *am* the fucking little white dog.

Denny drifts into silence, and walks watching her feet until we come to the one of the few rows of houses still standing in a landscape of broken bricks and weeds. Only six of them. Some are boarded up. One of them has the door open, and a naked child is half-inside, half-outside. He is around three years old and has an unwrapped tampon, which he is poised to push up his bum.

Denny bends down to talk to him. 'Zack, man, don't do that.'

From inside a female voice echoes her. 'Zack, Zack, don't do that. What are you doing?'

He stops and looks up blithely. 'Being Mummy.'

'Well,' the voice continues, 'don't be Mummy like that. Be Mummy by eating this apple.'

He drops the tampon on the step and goes in to grab the fruit.

I take in the chaotic surroundings of the Squat. Blankets and pillows thrown everywhere. A guy with a forked beard is passed out next to a sleeping woman who has a guinea pig clambering over her legs. By the far window, a couple of teenage girls layer stuff that looks like mud and stinks like cabbage on their hair. An older woman in a peasant blouse and a long skirt made from sari material is sitting at a kitchen table using the same mud to paint patterns on the back of her hands. She puts down the grass stem she's been using like a brush, nods at Denny and looks at me, waiting for an introduction.

'She's Jude. She's OK.'

'Hello Jude, I'm Shirley.' She notices me looking at the mud. 'It's Henna. It makes your hair this amazing colour, almost as good as yours,' she indicates her own thick rust-coloured hair, 'and you can paint patterns like tattoos on yourself.'

The designs on the skin of her hands look like brown lace gloves.

Denny pulls out two gloss-painted chairs for us as Shirley pours scented liquid from a teapot into cups without handles. They are exquisite blue-and-white ceramic, but too hot to drink from.

Shirley seems to see my uncertainty. 'It's hibiscus tea.'

'Yeah, it's good, you'll like it.' Denny is looking around, slightly distracted. 'Is Jacko here? I thought he'd be here.'

'You just missed him.'

'Oh. We wanted to score.'

'He won't be long. Stay and eat. We've got enough. When he gets back he'll sort you out.'

We smoke a few spliffs and people come and go. The sun moves across the sky and breezes send thistledown and flies in through the door. Thin paper posters of Indian gods and Cuban revolutionaries flutter against their restraining drawing pins.

I delve into my pocket for my harmonica, put it to my mouth and begin to draw the blues out of it. Cupping my hands around the sounds. Sucking in the long bending notes in G. More voices singing. Feet and hands drumming beats, incense burning, thick and sensuous. This is what it is to be stoned. This is why being stoned is the best thing in the world. I lie on my back to contemplate the colours of cheap glass rotating on a mobile hanging over a candle. They look like the most exquisite of flowers. If I could just stay stoned, I wouldn't have to worry about anything. I smoke more dope. Play my harp more. Sink into myself.

By the time Jacko arrives it's been dark for hours and we've eaten some kind of vegetarian curry cooked on a fire in the ruins of the backyard. We're lying around talking about good and bad, and who is trustworthy in this world and who is not, and whether there's a god or a devil and whether there are ghosts and whether you can tell the future and whether mescaline is more mystical than acid.

The fire dies down and the night gets cooler. We wander indoors and Jacko settles down to roll a spliff. Denny looks at him blearily and tries to remember what she wanted from him. It comes to her in a rush. 'Jacko. Man. We want to score. Have you got some?'

'No, but my dealer over in Hyde Park said he's getting some tomorrow.'

He blinks at me through his thin lashes and rubs little flakes of scurf off his chin. The kids clamber all over him and he lets them, adjusting his body slightly to their weight and velocity as they climb and settle and move between his knees and shoulders.

'Crash here,' he says, 'and I'll take you both over in the morning.'

Denny is troubled in a way that I can't quite understand. Maybe she feels she should go home because of Rosa, but she knows that Maria and Susie will look after her. They always do. I'm stoned, but Denny's completely gone. She's so stoned she's blocked. I don't think either of us can make it home. I didn't pay any attention to how we got here.

Lying on my back on the uncomfortable, bead-covered cushions, I'm mesmerised by one of the posters of a blue-bodied god in layers of lotus petals. If you wait long enough for life to happen, surely it will? The petals will unfold, and you'll see beneath them. Then you'll understand what the blue god is saying, and you'll know what things mean.

Shirley gives me a sour-smelling army surplus sleeping bag and I crawl into it. There are people wrapped in bedding, in pairs and singly, all over the floor. Children sleep in nooks and crannies. Candles burn in jars because there's no electricity. Strings of smoke trail across the ceiling.

I fall into sleep on the uncomfortable floorboards to constant soft human sounds, like an imagined sea in the distance, or wind in trees too small to be of any consequence.

7

Toto

Denny sits up in a sleeping bag not too far away. She's rubbing the back of her neck, lifting her knotted hair as she takes in where she is. From a chair next to her, Jacko reaches down and strokes the top of her head affectionately, like a little scratch through the parting of her hair.

'Morning gorgeous,' he says quietly.

I stretch and yawn. A champagne-coloured gerbil with spindly legs hops across my chest, and clambers into a sleeping bag containing two people. Only the tops of their heads are visible as it burrows inside. Shirley is at the sink running water into an old kettle as a shadowed man in the doorway pulls on a russet hand-knitted sweater. I hear the breaking of sticks and the chopping of wood. The smell of fire-smoke drifts in from outside.

'Come on,' Jacko says, 'let's eat, then go and get that dope.'

*

Zipping up his battered leather jacket Jacko is keeping up a smart pace. Denny matches him step for step. He's not tall, but he walks briskly. Staying abreast of them makes me pant. We cross a new highway and travel through underpasses and unfamiliar streets, deep into Hyde Park.

The house we arrive at is unremarkable from the outside, but inside everything's black. The walls are painted black, the windows are blacked out and all the furniture is black. Black velvet chairs. Black and gold woven rugs. In one room, there's a professional music system with a light show running and there are egg cartons stuck on all the walls and ceiling as sound dampeners. Jacko pushes through heavy curtains to a smaller room where a guy lounges on a chair. He's wearing tinted thin-rimmed John Lennon glasses, and his moustache curves around his mouth.

'Hey Jacko, what can I do you for?'

'Has that charge arrived yet?'

The dealer leans back. 'Yes. I've got some really nice stuff just in. I've got acid too if you want it, some speed and some quality mescaline.'

Jacko turns to me. 'Do you want acid?'

I shake my head.

'Smack?' the dealer says. 'Do you want coke? I've got both.'

I recoil. 'Do I look like a fucking smack-head? That crap is for losers. I just want some hash. Shit, man, what's the matter with you?'

The dealer fingers his gold necklace. 'Jesus!' He rolls his eyes. 'Your chick's a fiery redhead alright, Jacko. Seems you like them feisty!'

'She's not my fucking chick.'

'Ha!' says the dealer. 'Whatever you say.'

Jacko is angry. 'Shut your mouth, Oz.'

'Oh, he's still with *you*, then?' the dealer says to Denny. 'Or both of you?'

'Nobody's with anybody,' she says too emphatically.

Jacko intervenes, 'I said shut your mouth, Oz. Just get the shit.'

'I'll have some acid as well,' Denny says, as though nothing's happened.

The dealer pulls himself laboriously out of his chair and picks up a cardboard box which he takes over to a small table. There's a set of miniature scales next to some sharp knives.

'How much do you want?'

'What can I get for twelve quid?' I finger the money in my pocket.

He pulls out a tin-foiled block the size and shape of a store-bought ginger cake. Unwrapped, its treacly stickiness is stamped with a palm tree.

'What kind is it?'

'It's Afghan Black. Really oily. Class stuff. Twelve quid will get you that much.' The tip of his knife marks it out on the block.

'Deal,' I say.

He portions it with the precision of an alchemist. When cut it's like black fudge with a greenish brown centre. He wraps it neatly in tin foil, delves into a cigar box and retrieves a miniature pre-rolled joint.

'And here's a little something extra, compliments of the house.'

I feel very pleased with myself. This is not mixed herbs, nor is it a bit of Oxo cube, it's proper, grown-up cannabis that could knock your head off just with its smell. I put it carefully into my pocket and let it drop right down to the bottom.

*

On the way back to the Alternative School, Jacko indicates the miles of weeds all around us. 'You should see those in flower come August. Rosebay willow herb, just acres of pink. They say if you pick it, you'll cause a thunderstorm.' He touches Denny with a little tap on her upper arm. 'So, don't you even think about touching them, tiger. You cause enough thunderstorms without even trying.'

She looks puzzled, scanning his face for clues before realising it's a joke.

He puts his arm around her and hugs her to his side as they walk. 'You've got to do what you feel. Always. That's what's important.' He tilts his head at me. 'That's right, isn't it, Jude?'

I make a sound of assent, but to be honest I'm not sure. That would mean you understood what you felt, and I never do. Denny seems both comfortable and uncomfortable in his clasp. Her head falls onto his shoulder, but her body remains stiff as they walk, slightly out of step, across the cobbles.

We fall into silence, Jacko laying his arm over Denny's shoulder, but as we approach the school, he unhooks himself and hangs back. As we get through the door, Denny stops short.

Maria is at the back of the hall, stock-still and furious. She discards the broom she's holding and walks straight towards Denny.

'Where the hell were you?'

Denny blanches. 'I was at the Squat.'

'With Jacko?'

'Jacko was there . . .'

The meaning of it hangs between them. Something said. Something unsaid. Maria inhales. She's trying to control the

87

expression on her face, holding her mouth tightly shut, exhaling slowly whilst looking at the floor.

Finally, she looks up. 'You promised me.'

Denny looks miserable and shamed. There's a long pause, then Maria says, 'What about Rosa? Did you think about Rosa? She cried all night.'

'It was my fault.' I interject, trying to help Denny out. 'She took me to get some dope.'

Maria turns to me. '*She's* the one who chose. You make choices, then you live with them. Like a bloody grown-up.' She glares at Denny and repeats, 'Like a bloody grown-up.'

Denny puts her fingertips gently on Maria's wrist. 'I'm really sorry.'

I turn away because I have enough sense to know I should be embarrassed.

'I'd better go,' I mumble and head for the door.

Jacko is in the porch. Making sure that he's out of their line of sight.

'I'm staying out of this one. Man, she gets uptight!'

'I've never seen her like that before.'

'That's nothing. When she goes, she goes. Denny walks right into it every time though. She doesn't see it coming.'

'Is Maria angry because of Rosa?'

He looks as though he's working out how to respond. 'Something like that.'

As I leave, I look over my shoulder and see Denny watching Maria's retreating back.

It doesn't take long to get to the university. I climb up the stairs to the Students' Common Room, which is ostentatiously contemporary, full of cherry-coloured Perspex fixtures and Scandinavian furniture. The lime and aubergine abstractions on the wallpaper are overpowering. It's impossible to sit comfortably in this furniture: the chair tips me back too far and the wooden arms are at the wrong height. But it's peaceful and is a good place to wait for Nel and Jo to finish their lectures.

I distract myself by reading all the things on the student noticeboard. Handwritten advertisements for flat shares, announcements from the Chess Society, and a missing-persons poster from the Yorkshire Police that gets my attention. It's a grey-and-white photograph of a girl about my age with dark make-up around her eyes. Her long and loose hairstyle is the mark of a student. I know lots of girls like her. What's happened to her? Maybe she just legged it because she couldn't stand things anymore. Perhaps she just doesn't want to be found. I don't dwell on any other options. I don't want to think about it.

It's coming up to afternoon tea-break and one of the girls from the teaching course is already negotiating the sputtering coffee machine. She nods at me in recognition and patiently goes back to watching the machine dispensing liquid into a skin-thin plastic beaker. There comes the sudden din of a lecture hall emptying into the corridor. Footsteps and conversations resound as students arrive en masse, pushing through the door and settling into animated groups around the room.

'Last lecture of the term done then!' Jo dumps her course paperwork on the low coffee table. 'Hello you dirty stop-out.'

Nel is not far behind. When she sees me, her look of delight is quickly displaced by a scowl.

'Where did you disappear to?' she says.

89

'Sorry, sorry, sorry.'

Sunshine floods through the window. I think about light like this falling onto the unfinished embroidery in Nel's bedroom. I see the paperbacks and their green-grey covers on her floor. I think about my copy of *Mrs Dalloway* that's lying on her floor right now. I think about Clarissa Dalloway looking at the clock on her wall every day at precisely the same time, as though only one hour existed for eternity. I want more than one repeating hour in my life. I'm not going to live by a bloody timetable. If I want to be a dirty stop-out, I will. I think of Clarissa Dalloway kissing Sally Seaton only once and never doing it again. I think of opportunities never taken.

'You are so bloody selfish, Totton.'

Denny and Maria flit into my mind. I can't look at her. Jesus. I hope I'm not as irritating to Nel as Denny is to Maria. I couldn't bear that.

'Honestly, I am really sorry.'

Nel isn't listening to my apologies. 'You didn't even let us know!'

'I got too stoned. I couldn't help it. What was I supposed to do? Send you a homing pigeon, or ring the phone box on the corner? I'm sorry.'

Jo laughs. 'Stop trying to mother her, Nel. She's not going to change, are you flower? You know she's always been like this.'

'I'm not trying to mother her. I just thought she was fucking dead. That's all. I was awake all fucking night thinking she was dead.'

'She's not though, is she? She went out on the town, and now she's back, only slightly the worse for wear.'

Nel gathers herself. 'You'd better go home and get your stuff. Hank's picking us up here at six-thirty. If you're not here, we're going without you. It's the last day of term. Did you forget we were going to Sheffield?'

'Is it today?' I get to my feet uncertainly. 'I thought it was next week.'

'Yes, Jude. Today.'

Jo pulls a wry face. 'Better get going, kid, you've pissed her off.'

'I got the dope though,' I say, small-voiced, in the hope it might prove conciliatory.

Nel suddenly softens, as though against her better judgement. 'You are a bloody lost cause, Toto. Go and get your stuff. Simon's probably already on his way here.'

Back at the house, I pick up T-shirts from the floor and sniff them before throwing them in a pile of dirty washing. I think I hear a knock on the door. I wait, listen, but there's nothing more, so I carry on packing. Those shirts really are too stale. Surely there's a clean one somewhere. As I open my small cupboard next to the fireplace, clothes tumble out and I'm happy to find at least one clean pair of pants and socks. I stuff them into my wide-striped shoulder bag; I also chuck in the travelling toothbrush that I take everywhere.

There comes another, louder, knock. Then another. I pull back the curtain to peer outside. It's Janice from across the road. Her head hung; her arms tight across her middle.

When I open the door, she raises her worn face to me. 'Alright, Jude cock, can I come in?'

I hesitate because I've got to get my shit together and go. But she looks so vulnerable. It throws me off guard. She rubs her naked arms and shivers.

'Yeah, sure,' I say, against my better judgement. She closes the door behind her as I lead the way into my room.

'I just need a little bit of peace and quiet,' she says. 'I've had a fucking row with Tommy, and I can't be over there for a while. Do you mind?'

'What did you have a row about?'

As she lowers herself into a chair, she looks as though she's wondering whether it's worth telling. She scans my room, noting my paints and books and the pictures cut out of art magazines stuck to my wall.

'Owt and nowt, Jude cock. Nothing you need to know about.'

She still seems cold and I realise that I've never seen her in a coat or jacket. I wonder if she owns one. There are the faint remains of old bruises on her arms, a scab on her knee.

Watching me ignite the gas fire without a word, she sinks deeper into her chair as though it was the softest, most comfortable thing in the world. The flames burst like blue buds along the ceramic element and the smell of coal tar lingers until the fire burns yellow.

'Have you got any orange squash, or owt? I'm parched.'

I make it strong and sweet and she drinks it in one go, licking all of it off her lips and wiping her mouth with the back of her wrist.

'You're all right, you are,' she says, returning the glass to me with a smile that was probably once beautiful, but now has a blackened tooth to the side of her incisor. 'I'm so fucking tired, cock. Just let me stay awhile.'

I don't ask her if she wants a sandwich, I just decide to get her one. I've got some ham, and I know Nel has bread that'll be stale soon. Janice looks like she needs something so badly, and all I can think to give her is food.

Once in the kitchen I rummage through the cupboards to see what else I can find. Jo has left a tomato that's going wrinkled and orange. It slices messily on top of my last piece of ham. I finish it off with a scrape of salad cream.

Janice is surprised when I present her with the sandwich and another glass of squash. 'Thanks,' she says, as though she's not sure whether this is a trick and begins to eat it a small bite at a time. She's as hungry as she was thirsty, consuming it without speaking, concentrating on every morsel. Every so often she looks around her, like a cat stealing from a plate.

'You've got it nice in here. Only you sleeps in this room? You don't share, like?'

'Just me. The others come and sit in here sometimes – because of the fire.'

'Nice and warm,' she says. 'We don't have a heater in our room. There's four of us and only the two beds. We keep each other warm,' she looks away, as though she has a secret. 'I've never had a room on me own. I've always wanted that. It would be nice . . . you've got yours nice.'

I try to imagine her life. But I can't.

'Have you got a boyfriend?' She's still working through the sandwich, balancing it over the plate.

People always ask that, and it continually surprises me because it's not a thing I think about. 'I did have, but I chucked him.'

'Batter you, did he?' she says as though it would be perfectly normal.

'No.' The thought of Michael doing that to anyone is unimaginable. 'He was just . . . well . . . he really annoyed me. He kept doing stupid things. And he said I couldn't take a joke. Only according to him, every shitty thing he did was just a joke. It's OK now though. We're friends. He makes me laugh even if he is irritating sometimes.'

'If he didn't batter you, then he probably weren't that bad.' She drains her glass and concentrates on eating all the individual crumbs from her plate. 'I'm not bothered about lads. I'd rather be with a lass. Me and Babs look after each other. You got to, when you're on the game, otherwise you got nothing. I'd do anything for Babs. She'll be making sure Tommy calms down before I get back. She's a good 'un that lass is.'

I tilt my head to consider what she's just said. It's normal to her, loving another girl.

'Have you ever been with a lass?' she asks matter-of-factly. I stop to wonder whether she's coming on to me, but I can see she isn't.

'I've played about with it, but nothing serious. I think I go both ways.'

'Aye,' she says, 'I think everyone goes both ways.'

I'm slightly taken aback by her ease with the subject. She talks as though everyone thinks like that. In the circles I move in, it's become a fashionable sign of bohemian freedom, but old taboos are still strong. Nel can barely talk about it in any way at all. She has all that Old Testament brimstone in her background.

The food has perked Janice up. She gathers up her empty glass and clutches it with both hands like Oliver Twist.

'Do you want more squash?' I ask.

'Have you got some to spare?'

In the kitchen, the clock tells me that I've still got plenty of time to get back to the university to meet up with the others. Nevertheless, I make up my mind to give her this squash then tell her I've got to go.

The thick orange liquid becomes paler as the tap water swirls through it. It doesn't quite smell like proper fruit. The bottle belongs to Jo, and I've used more than I anticipated. I'd better buy her a new one.

Janice has fallen asleep in the chair. Her head lolling into her shoulder, her lips slightly parted, her palms open in her lap. Every so often there is the faintest sound of a snore and her chest rises and falls in slow rhythm. I can't bring myself to wake her up, she seems so peaceful. She looks like a child.

I put a blanket over her and drink the too-sweet squash myself, a sip at a time. Janice needs to sleep, and I'm going to let her for a while, but not too long. I need to go soon. I settle on the bed to wait for her to rouse. My eyelids droop. I didn't get much sleep on the floor at the Squat, and now it's crept up on me. The bed is really comfortable. The room is warm. Just close my eyes for a minute.

I'm woken by Janice yelling in her dreams. I sit bolt upright to stare at her as she wakes herself up with another shout and throws the blanket off as though it's a trap. She looks around blearily, and I can tell that she can't quite work out where she is.

'Who's stolen everything?' she says.

Her eyes begin to focus, and they settle on me, 'Oh, 'ey up, Jude. Must have dropped off. Sorry, queen.' She gets up and rubs her face. 'Fuck, look at the time, it's half-past seven. Better get back over there. Thanks for the sandwich and that.'

Half-past seven. I've missed my lift to Sheffield by an hour. They will all be angry with me, especially Nel. I rub my hands across my face in frustration.

What to do now? I don't like hitching after nightfall. It gets too cold, and drivers have a hard time seeing you. I could be out there for hours and never get a ride. If I get up early enough in the morning, I can still be at Jo and Hank's by lunchtime.

I watch from the doorway as Janice makes for the brothel across the road. Before she gets there, the door opens and Tommy emerges, blocking the entrance with his whole body. In the street light his eyes are nothing but shadow. He has his thumbs in his waistband and I can't help but look. Look to see if the knife is still stuck in his belt like a stick of pearl. It's too far away to see, but I know it's there. She does too. She stops short. Watchful and wary. I wait. He steps to one side. She scrambles through the door. He steps in and slams it.

8

Nel

The coloured glass panels in Gen and Vik's front door are loose behind their grime, and the paint is peeling. A broken flowerpot nestles in a stand at the back of the porch and dried leaves cover the floor tiles. Simon delicately kicks old shards of ceramic aside as he presses the brass doorbell. I'm not really paying much attention because I'm still annoyed with Toto.

'Hope they're in.' Simon is focused on the door. 'I did tell Vik we were coming. I suppose they could be round at Hugo's though.'

Hugo Reynard is a lecturer who owns a townhouse a few streets away in this trendy neighbourhood. It's Simon's favourite part of town. He once had a bedsit close by and I know he fancies himself owning one of these well-appointed properties. I can see the ambition in his face as he waits, studying every detail of the brickwork. For my part I don't care much about the area's trendiness, but I've got a soft spot for the big park at its centre. It's connected to the town green belt and was our favourite late-night route home when we were undergrads. Toto and I spent many a night lying in its grass on our way back from clubbing, or after Hugo's famous gatherings. Everyone loved those parties except me. I used to get so pissed off with all the posturing and fakeness, what with everyone trying to out-shock one another and pretending to be more interesting than they were. Toto and the others still like to hang out there, but I find Hugo and his wife Callie unbearably pretentious.

Genevieve is more my kind of person, she flatted with me and Toto before Viktor seduced her. These days she runs a fabrics business, selling her own designs from a showroom at the front of her workshop. She's open and bright, and everyone likes her. Viktor is not quite so accessible. He taught us drawing and was famous for outbursts of passion about Picasso and Käthe Kollwitz interspersed with long brooding silences. I never could see much point in him, but he has Gen's heart, so there must be something going on in there.

Simon presses the bell again, and Viktor shouts from inside, 'The door's open, just come in for Christ's sake!'

We meet Genevieve scurrying towards us in the passage. 'Bloody hell Vik, it could be anyone. Don't just tell them to come in.'

When she sees us, she stops and squeals in delight. 'Viktor, it's Nel and Si!'

'Yes, it's only us, lovely. I like your new hairstyle,' I say.

Her wiry, brown hair is cut short and complements the clothes of her own design. She primps it. 'Suits me, don't you think?'

Viktor waves from behind her. A roll-up protrudes from beneath his moustache and sheds ash down his shirt. He's bald-headed, but athletic for his age, which must be over forty. When he left his first wife for Genevieve it caused a glorious

98

scandal at college. His wife stormed in and slapped him in the Life Room in the middle of class.

As we come into the hallway, Vik avoids my gaze. He's never quite comfortable around women and I'm not sure if he's ever looked me straight in the eye. His response to Simon's a different matter. He grabs him in a bear hug and they whack each other on the back in a growling display of male camaraderie.

Viktor glances at Gen like he's been vindicated. 'I knew it was them. I knew they were coming.'

'So did I, but *anyone* could have been ringing that bell.'

We follow Gen through to what was once the lounge. It has great natural light, so Viktor turned it into his studio. Jars of pencils and grubby erasers balance on most available surfaces. He's been drawing something on a man-sized piece of paper pinned to an equally large board. We circumnavigate it to the big kitchen-diner. Genevieve's textiles vie with Viktor's drawings for wall space. Her fabrics are full of elegant petal shapes in subtle colours, while Vik's massive charcoal rendition of a stormy landscape looms over the sideboard.

'I like the new drawing, Vik,' Simon says, throwing his backpack down.

Viktor grunts, but his eyes shine.

Gen's more concerned with me. 'You all right, Nel? Good trip down with Jo and Hank?'

'It would've been' – I lower my bag to the floor – 'but we waited for Toto for bloody ages and she never turned up. God knows where she's got to. I could kill her, honestly.'

'She'll have got tied up in something, forgotten the time.' Gen knows Toto almost as well as I do. 'She'll hitch down like she usually does. She'll be all right, so don't worry. Shall I hang up your coat, Nel?'

99

'No,' Simon says. 'What room have you put us in? She'll take it up there out of the way.'

I was taking my fur jacket off, but now I pull it back on as Gen points in the direction of the stairs.

'The room next to Sid's is all ready for you. You've stayed in it before.'

Viktor and Genevieve have lodgers. Toto's ex, Michael, has a room in the loft. Sid is in a box room on the second floor. Lauren is also in the attic, but she has a separate kitchenette and comes and goes with a rhythm all her own.

'Come on.' Simon grabs his bag and makes for the stairs. 'Let's get sorted.'

Gen gives me a crushing hug. 'I'll get some food ready. Then you and me can talk while those two get all boring about drawing.'

Enormous poppy heads pattern the counterpane fashioned from one of Gen's fabrics. The matching red pillows have two white towels folded on top of them, and the window is propped open.

Simon inspects himself from various angles in the mirror, concentrating on his pink shirt, then on his tight, black-velveteen flares. He's dissatisfied and strips them all off, using his shirt to wipe under his armpits. He delves into his rucksack, bringing out a glossy purple shirt with a ruff like a buccaneer, and silver drainpipe jeans that prove to be even tighter than the first pair.

'How do I look?' He displays himself confidently and I give him the approval he's looking for. He nods in satisfaction, his eyes back on his reflection.

'Are you going to change?' He wears a critical expression as he scrutinises me.

'Do I need to?'

'Yes. You look frumpy dressed like that.'

He's playing with that bangle again. Silly wee smile on his face. He catches me looking at him and his eyes narrow. 'Get changed for fuck sake.' He pokes his knuckled finger into my ribs. 'Come on, hurry up.'

He approves of the long skirt and lacy blouse he picked out for me. I follow as he leads the way downstairs, running down the steps as he always does.

Gen pours us each a lager, and Viktor fumbles with some lettuce in a bowl. 'Will you two eat spaghetti? I can do a meat sauce for us and a tomato one for you, Nel. Would that be OK?'

'Bloody vegetarian! She's a pain in the arse, isn't she, Vik?' Simon hooks a proprietary arm around my neck.

After we've eaten, Simon and Vik go to look at the new drawings in the studio. I've never wondered what they talk about when they take the whisky bottle and two glasses and retire in there. The murmur of their banter is familiar. It's the routine that Simon likes. For some reason though, tonight I find myself thinking that they're talking about me. It unnerves me so much that I down my lager in one go. Gen gets another can from the fridge.

'They're set in there for the night,' she says. 'Si looks like he's having a ball in Birmingham. He's done well, hasn't he?'

'He's talented. You can't deny that.' I try to look enthusiastic, but it feels like I'm grimacing.

'Are you all right? You seem a bit down.'

I take another long draft from my glass before responding. 'I'm struggling with this teaching stuff, to tell you the truth. I honestly don't know if I can stand it for much longer. Si says I've got to stick at it because the money will help us after he graduates. He doesn't want to get a job straight away. He says he'll need time to build up his portfolio and get an art dealer or a lecturing position. My parents want me to finish the course and be a teacher. Everyone wants me to do it, but I'm finding it hard.'

'What do *you* want to do?'

'God knows, Gen.'

She is silent as she ponders something. 'You should come with me to my workshop tomorrow, have a look at the loom and the silkscreen set-up. You could even have a go if you want.'

Her offer makes me so unexpectedly happy. Si and Vik chunter away in the other room as I hug myself high across my chest 'Really? Jesus. I'd love to.'

She fills my glass again. 'You know you're always welcome to use the workshop.'

Her expression changes to one of curiosity. 'What's that mark on your arm?'

My eyes widen, 'Where?'

'Where your sleeve has pulled up.' She gets up and points to it more closely.

'Oh,' I say. 'I knocked into the corner of a shelf at college.'

Simon appears from the other room, clutching his empty glass. 'The Scotch has run dry. Vik says there's another bottle under the sink. "That's a bloody funny place to keep your booze," I said, and he said it's because thieves wouldn't ever think of looking there. Do you get robbed much, Gen?'

She is at the sink, delving far into the cupboard. 'No! He's just eccentric.'

'Ha,' Simon is gleeful. 'There's no one in this whole wide world like old Viktor.'

9

Toto

I once saw a greenfinch tied by its leg to a stall at a country market. It jerked on the twine like my heart is jumping right now.

I feel like that finch has settled in my chest and it's testing its wings before it flies. The motorway is just beyond the brow of the hill and I quicken my pace towards it. I'm on my way to Sheffield. Happy because I'm on the road again. I need to thumb a ride like other people need a fix. Some people ride motorbikes too fast, others jump from aeroplanes. My preferred game is much more dangerous. It's played with men in small cars who hide girls under leaves on the top of moors and deep in the woods.

The cars on the motorway are a river of metal, a flow of shining paintwork. Along the edge of the slip road, singly or in pairs, are other hitchers. Some have pieces of cardboard with the names of towns in hand-drawn letters. One of them is a khaki-uniformed soldier, but most of them have long hair and flared jeans.

'Been here long?' I ask a couple who are wearing backpacks and look like students.

'Not long,' he says. The arm of a jade-coloured shirt escapes from the top of his stuffed rucksack. 'Already seen three people picked up.'

I stick out my thumb in the direction of travel. I don't waste energy like a beginner by waggling it about. I catch the drivers' eyes and dare them not to stop.

Soon the queue of hitchers reduces. A truck picks up the soldier. A woman stops for a girl who clutches her billowing skirt as she wriggles into the front seat. The couple climb into the cab of an articulated lorry, and the girl waves at me as they pass.

Eventually the only people left are a guy with a sign for London, and two girls standing near the beginning of the slip road. A dilapidated Ford Zephyr pulls up next to them. The girls negotiate briefly and get in. The car comes slowly down the hard shoulder toward me. Rust-spotted white, with a bent bumper, and the right-hand-side headlight has been wedged in, so the connecting wires are visible. As it rolls to a halt, I take a careful look at the two men in the front.

'Going far?' the passenger asks.

'Sheffield.'

'Easy. We can do that.'

They seem OK, but I've got this set of rules designed to keep me out of harm when I hitch. I prefer to ride in trucks, because they are big and obvious. They can't park in unusual places without being noticed, and also the drivers have schedules to keep. But this is a car, and when it comes to cars I'll only get in if:

I'm not the only one being picked up.

I can get out quickly.

Men don't outnumber me.

The driver doesn't scare me.

Persuaded by the fact that there are two other girls on board, I climb into the back. We are crushed together in the beat-up saloon. I can feel the warmth of the nearest girl's arm through my sleeve. Odours of cheap aftershave lotion, cigarette smoke, and male sweat fill the car. The driver watches me through the mirror. As he flicks a Benson and Hedges cigarette from its gold packet to his lips, his attention slips over me and on to the other two girls.

'Which bit of Barnsley was it?'

'Town centre. You know – where the shops are.'

It never occurred to me they were only going that far.

The second girl has a shrill and irritating voice. 'Aye, but you can drop us off on the slip road if you want.'

Looking at them in the mirror, as though he's measuring something up, he says, 'No, you're all right, we'll take you into town.'

He scrutinises me again. Intent. Still sizing me up. 'Is that all right with you, hippy girl?'

I don't like the way he said that.

'Doesn't bother me. It's a stone's throw from there to Sheffield.'

He gives his companion a brief glance, and I don't like that either. The other one turns around, stares me full in the face. Not much in his eyes. Not much expression.

'Yeah,' the driver says. 'No trouble, they're both on the way to Nottingham. No trouble. That's where we're going. Easy.'

I survey the landscape as we pass piles of coal and crushed cars in wrecker's yards. I'm conscious of the driver; the thickness of his shoulders and the size of his hands on the steering wheel. I study the back of the other one's head. The oil in his hair and the dandruff on his corduroy jacket remind me of Jacko. I think about the Rectory and why I could never live there. Endless rules and committees. Then I think about the Squat. No privacy, no boundaries, all that forced intimacy. I couldn't live like that either. I'd rather live like this: on the road, belonging nowhere and following the direction of my outstretched thumb. Testing life's edges.

A verge of celandine flowers stretches into the distance. Acre after acre of them. I remember Nel and I standing knee-deep in them on Knaresborough's riverbank. Fields of yellow flowers shivering in ripples of wind. She and I exchanged a single glance as we shared the same thoughts. Sulphur seas full of tiny starfish-like flowers formed between our minds.

Now I sit with my eyes hooded, listening to the sounds of the badly sprung car as we creak and bounce southwards.

When we reach Barnsley, the traffic is dangerous, so I jump out on to the pavement to let the girls leave. They giggle and make off down the street, whilst I think about whether I want to get back in. The driver gives me just one enquiring look.

'Hop in love, we need to be going.'

I think about my rules and know that I'm going to break them. I spin the chamber of an imaginary gun.

'OK.'

I get back in and slam the door shut.

It traps my coat.

*

They head out of town, but after a while, I realise that something isn't right. This isn't the way to Sheffield. I look at the roads and don't recognise them. 'Which way are we going?'

'The back way, love,' the driver says.

This is wrong. I lean forward. 'We've missed the turn off.'

The driver glances at me and I don't like the way he smiles as if he knows something I don't.

Pushing myself back in the seat, I say it again. 'We've missed the turn off.'

The other guy is staring out of the window too deliberately. The driver gives a light laugh. 'Have we? Have we missed the turn off?' He looks about with exaggerated concern. 'Yes, I think you're right. I think we have.' He nudges his companion. 'We've missed the fucking turn off.'

Where are we? These are country roads and unfamiliar fields and trees. The spires in the distance aren't ones I recognise.

The driver turns as he steers. 'Do I look like a soldier?'

Taken aback by the question, I examine him carefully in the mirror, noting the set of his mouth and the coldness of his eyes. I decide not to say anything. His attention moves back and forth from the road to my face.

'I were a Para. Parachute Regiment, best bloody regiment in the British Army. He were too,' he motions at his sidekick. 'We were there at Bloody Sunday.'

My body freezes. I remember seeing it on TV. I was home from college for Christmas. My parents had got their first colour television. They had turned the colour dial up so far that everything vibrated in impossible hues. On the news, a Belfast priest held a white handkerchief spattered in blood as a flag of truce. Real blood in unreal colour.

Catholic men and women dead on the ground.

'We shot the fuckers,' he says. 'I took one of them out myself. They were shooting at us from the rooftops, from windows. Those bastards on the streets, they all said they didn't have guns, but they did, I fucking know they did.'

He looks at me through the mirror. 'We could rape you if we wanted. It would be easy.'

I decide to pretend he's joking. So I laugh. Yes, he could. I laugh as though I'm certain he never would. There is something like disappointment in his face. The other one shifts uncomfortably, turns and looks me over.

My mind races. They mean it.

Two men. Two soldiers. Self-defence lessons from your dad can't cover this.

I move to the middle and push my head into the space between them. 'Have you got any sisters?'

The passenger's eyes widen. So he does. He has a sister.

'You remind me of my brother. What's your sister called?'

'Jill,' he murmurs.

I study the driver. He's unmoved.

As we drive through a leafy hamlet, I tell him about my brother, about my Nan, about family Christmases and Sunday lunches. He says nothing, just looks straight ahead.

My mouth dries. I should jump and run. I think they came out today to find a girl to rape. They meant to do it all along. I place myself in the centre of the back seat, so that I can lean between them as I talk. Getting close. Making myself human. The car slows at an intersection. I edge my hand along the worn leather seat, feeling its cracked surface until my fingers find the door. All my senses slow and intensify.

I find the handle and grip it.

There is a clunk, and air rushes in.

108

I throw myself out, my hand protects my face.

I roll onto my shoulder and scramble to my feet.

Now I'm running down a country lane, twisting and turning like a hare, breath tearing my chest like saw strokes through wood. Behind me the car has stopped. I look back once, only once. The passenger has jumped out. The driver has one foot out of the door. My head is clear as I run. I just need to get back to where there are people. I can hear the sound of my feet on the gritty road and the alarm calls of thrushes. I run past a closed pub. Slow. Stop. Hands on my knees. Gasping. I've scraped the heel of my hand. Bruised my shoulder.

I've been blown off course and have no idea where I am.

It's a picturesque hamlet, too clean and manicured for anyone to live here. Tiny cottages line the side of the road. Some are crumbling brick with low eaves and wonky windows. Others are white wattle and daub, their wooden beams exposed at angles under thatched roofs. It's eerily quiet. I step over to a bus stop to look at the timetable, but it's illegible. On the other side of the road is an ivy-covered Georgian building and the sign swinging above the door says HARRISON AND SONS, GROCERS.

Steps go down to basement level and the temperature drops. A man in a brown shop coat watches from behind the counter. His shelves are packed with goods from floor to ceiling and his presentation of tins and jars is impeccable. Meticulously aligned labels and lids and a finger's breadth between each of them. On the counter lies a partially sliced baked ham and a block of strong-smelling cheddar.

He closes the drawer of his till. 'What are you after?'

I scan his goods and point to a packet of cigarette papers.

Through the high small windows adjoining the street, I see the tyres of the Zephyr cruise slowly past. They are hunting me, but I'm hidden in a shop smelling of cheese and smoky ham fat. The shopkeeper looks me over. He wants me to get out of his shop.

'Is there a bus from here to . . . '

He finishes my sentence, as I hoped he would. 'Nottingham?'

'Yes.'

'In about half an hour. The bus stops over the road.'

As I take my change, I thank him as graciously as I can. He's not concerned about my manners. All he can see is a dirty hippy.

Out in the daylight I lick the scrape on my hand, particles of grit in the wound.

The hunters have gone. Not even a whiff of sulphur left to betray that they were ever here.

I am alive.

I exhale, file the soldiers' faces and that car carefully in the back of my mind.

As I'm about to cross the road, a pastel-pink convertible draws up alongside me, its canvas roof folded down. A middle-aged woman, in pink-framed glasses with small upward wings, looks hard at me as she pulls up the handbrake.

The graze on my hand stings and I rub my palm against my jeans.

Getting out of the car, she slowly removes a pair of string-backed driving gloves. 'What happened to you?'

It takes a while to I find the words. 'I kind of fell out of a car. Well, jumped. These guys driving . . . they freaked me out. I was hitchhiking.'

'Freaked. You. Out.' She repeats these words as though I'm

not even speaking English. 'Don't you know hitchhiking isn't safe for a girl on her own? Hasn't anyone ever told you that?'

What would a woman in a salmon-pink two-piece suit with a brooch on her lapel know about anything? Two men wanted to rape me. I can't look at her. I feel a tic in the corner of my mouth that I struggle to control.

'Are you all right?' She puts her hand on my shoulder. 'Did you get hurt?'

There's something about her that reminds me of Mrs North, my history teacher at the convent. She had the same way of looking at me, as though I was a strange but harmless feral creature.

'Nothing happened. They just freaked me, that's all.'

'Where are you going?'

'I'm trying to get to Sheffield.'

'How old are you?'

I'm not all that surprised by the question. I look younger than I am. Sometimes that works well for me, but sometimes it's a pain, 'Twenty-one,' I say.

It's clear that she doesn't believe me. 'You must be the same age as my daughter. First year at university.' She glances at the paint spatters on my jeans. 'Art school, by the look of you. You'd better get in. I'll take you to Sheffield.'

'Oh.' I'm taken aback by her generosity. 'Are you sure?'

'I haven't got anything on this afternoon, and, to be honest, I'd feel terrible letting you wander around by yourself. Go on. Get in.'

She searches through her handbag in a slightly distracted way. 'I'll just pop in here,' she inclines her head towards the shop. 'Won't be long. Turn on the radio if you want.'

The interior of her car is spotless. A scented pine tree made of flat cardboard hangs from the driver's mirror. There are no cigarette packets on the floor, no finger marks on the dashboard. The tension in my shoulders subsides. When she gets back, she hands me a can of limeade and a sausage roll in a white paper bag.

'So, Miss Twenty-One, do your parents know you hitchhike?'

I play with the lip of the bag. There's no point in trying to convince her I'm not her daughter.

'Yes, but they don't particularly approve.' That's a lie, I've no idea what they think. I change the subject. 'So, I'm in Nottinghamshire?'

'You're not much of a hitchhiker, are you?' She puts the car into gear, 'No, you're in Derbyshire. On the border.'

'I got blown off-course. Got taken the wrong way.'

'By an ill wind? What sort of tornado blew you off-course then, young lady?'

'Not a tornado, an old Ford Zephyr.'

She gets the reference. 'Very good,' she says. 'I like that: Zephyr, the god of the west wind.'

That makes me ask whether she's a teacher or a librarian.

'I'm married,' she says.

As we drive through flat fields towards the M1, she tells me she lives on a farm with children and hounds. Not a small farm: a big farm with a manager employed to run it. She has people who clean for her. This information makes me look at her more carefully. I've never met anyone with servants before.

'Eat that sausage roll,' she says, 'and drink that pop. You look like you need it.'

I do both, trying not to get bits of pastry all over the immaculate interior.

'What's your name, Miss Twenty-One?'

'Jude.'

'Judy?'

'No, Jude. My dad got it off the cover of *Jude the Obscure*.' She thinks I'm joking, but I'm not.

'Yes,' she says. 'There's definitely something obscure about you, abstruse even.'

I look away. 'I know what *abstruse* means,' I say softly, 'and *recondite* and *arcane*. I've got my A level English.'

'Hmmm,' she says, slowing around a bend towards a cross-roads. 'And did you read dictionaries for a hobby as a child?'

I don't tell her so, but I did. The one my nan gave me. The stairway in her little council house was stacked up the sides with books that must have been there since my father was a boy.

'You're not like your dad,' Nan used to say. 'Our Bobby would never sit and read like you do. You take after me.'

I move my attention from the hedgerows to the Pink Lady. 'Yes, I read a lot when I was little,' I say with a hint of self-mockery. 'Now I know *way* too much.'

She glances at me. 'Is Sheffield home?'

'No, I'm going to visit friends. I come from Bradford.'

'Ah yes,' she says. 'Bradford.'

The peppery taste of the sausage roll lingers as I sip my limeade. It's flat, but soothingly sweet. We listen to *Woman's Hour* on the car radio and withdraw into silence.

The soldiers become smaller things in my mind, miniatures of themselves. The fear has turned into exhilaration. I beat them, I won.

I'm fucking bulletproof.

10

Toto

There's no response to my insistent knocking at Jo and Hank's door. They've gone to the concert already. I must have missed them by half an hour at the most. The night is still early, so I make another plan. A discarded cigarette packet from the pavement flattens out well enough for me to write in biro:

Hi Jo and Hank. I got here! Had a terrible time hitching – I'll tell you about it when I see you. I'm going to Hugo and Callie Reynard's to try and get a bed for the night. I'll call around again, or maybe see you at the Lamb and Flag for a beer tomorrow or sometime. Tell Nel I'm OK and I'm sorry. Tell her to come to the pub too. Sorry. Love, Toto.

I push it through their letterbox and set off from their scruffy inner-city neighbourhood for the more upmarket locality of Whetheridge Common. I'm confident that I'll be welcome at the Reynards. Hugo was one of the trendier lecturers at college; his wife Callie is exotic because she's American, or maybe Canadian, and it's always been cool to be seen hanging out with them. I'm a willing member of the coterie of ex-students they've collected. We breeze in and out of their house drinking their booze and eating their food. The deal is that we amuse them and decorate their furniture with our young bodies. In return, they introduce us to hard liquors, foreign cuisines and sexual attitudes we've never encountered outside fiction. They believe they're exploiting us, and we believe we're exploiting them.

As I reach their door, I become less confident. My clothes are a bit wrecked from the fall on the road, oil-stained and torn. I press the bell and wait for a figure to materialise behind the rose-coloured panels.

Hugo opens the door with a gin and tonic in his hand and his shirt neck open. 'Well, well, well.' He smiles knowingly and calls, 'Callie, Jude's here.'

His wife appears behind him in a red cocktail dress. Wearing the self-assured smile of a film star, Callie has the presence of someone who knows exactly how striking they are. She is a charismatic, if slightly intimidating woman in her late twenties, taller than Hugo by about an inch. Her perfectly applied crimson lipstick enhances my feeling of inferiority as her hazel eyes look me up and down.

'Well, bring her in, Hugo,' she says. 'Don't leave her out in the cold.'

She smooths her dress over her hips and flicks her blonde braid across her shoulder. I can't help thinking they make an uneven but attractive couple.

Hugo stands to one side and indicates the way with a wave of his ice-laced gin.

In the lounge, standing next to their over-stuffed couch, Callie's pouring me a drink.

'I'm assuming a Campari cocktail,' she says. 'A negroni?'

I nod, not because I'm a seasoned cocktail drinker, but because I'll drink anything she offers me.

She observes me archly. 'You *can* take your coat off, you know?'

Stepping across their newly stripped oak floorboards, I hang my coat on a hook in their hallway.

She indicates my feet. 'Boots too.'

Ice cubes clink as they hit the bottom of a tumbler, followed by the successive sharp odours of Blue Sapphire gin, Cinzano Rosso vermouth and Campari. She cuts a slice of orange and deftly adorns the glass. The drink is a beautiful red, like thin blood, like pomegranate, like a carnelian in front of the sun. It has dark scents of bitter herbs and raw alcohol.

'Can I stay tonight, Callie? I'm kind of stuck.'

She's standing close as she puts the drink in my hand. 'Of course, the guest room's free, and there's always space in my bed if you get lonely.'

The last part of the sentence is normal banter: mock seduction interspersed with innuendo. She touches my hand for just a little too long as she gives me the glass.

The zip on my red boot sticks. I set my drink down and wrestle with it as I sit on the smaller of their two settees, determined to make the most of everything on offer here.

The aroma of garlic-laden cooking comes from their kitchen. They're talking quietly, and pans clank as they move things from stove top to table.

This world is clean and cream-coloured. The floors are smooth, the tasteful white throw on the back of the chair is smooth. The Victorian ceiling rose is perfect above the perfect cream light shade. I close my eyes. My muscles start to unstiffen.

Hugo enters, carrying olives in a ceramic bowl and a little plate of crackers with cheese. Fuck, I hate olives.

'Good timing,' he says. 'Genevieve and Viktor, and Michael and Lauren are coming for dinner, possibly Sid too.'

'They're not going to Roxy Music tonight, then?'

He looks as though he doesn't know what I'm talking about and puts some jazz on the stereo: John Coltrane's *Blue Train*. The sound spreads out like perfume through the house, easing me, slowing my heart. As Hugo turns in my direction, he sweeps his hair back. His pale-brown eyes settle on me. He is meticulously shaven and for a second his easy confidence reminds me of my father in one of his rare good moods; all casual bonhomie and glib charm.

He indicates the olives. 'Genevieve and Viktor brought these from Tuscany. They're the real thing. None of your bottled rubbish.'

He proffers the bowl. I've got to take one. Slippery and brown and pungent. I'd never seen an olive, or an aubergine or even a green pepper until I met the Reynards. I don't really like any of them.

To me olive is not a flavour. It's an oral assault. Nevertheless, I eat it, trying to look like I have them every day.

'Can I use your bath, Hugo? I'm a mess.'

He observes me in a way that I don't like. Maybe I'm ashamed of my sweaty state, maybe I don't like the way he lingers a little too long on my breasts.

I'm always on my guard with Hugo. I make up my mind not to tell him too much about what happened today. The best thing to do with this man is entertain him.

'I got lost on the motorway,' I say. 'Completely lost!'

'Are you serious?' He laughs. 'How does anyone get lost on a motorway?'

I laugh too, shrugging as though I can't understand it. 'I must have offended the God of the Highway. Condemned to wander for ninety years for my transgressions. I have no sense of direction.'

That works, it amuses him and whilst he's laughing his eyes are closed and I don't have to worry about what he's looking at.

He lowers himself beside me on the couch and offers me another olive, which I refuse. 'No, honestly, I really need a bath.'

Callie has returned. Her attention flicks between us as she wipes her hands with a tea towel. 'I need you in the kitchen, Hugo. You know I hate chopping onions.'

He gets up and puts the olives on the coffee table. 'Yes, of course. By the way, Jude would like to have a bath.'

They exchange a different kind of glance.

Callie raises an eyebrow. 'Really, how delightful.' She reaches out and touches the top of my arm with one finger, whilst sipping her cocktail. 'A bath or a shower? We've got both.'

'I'd love to soak in a tub.' I look at my road-scraped clothes, remember the sweatiness of my T-shirt and consider another of my needs she could fulfil. 'You couldn't wash my clothes for me, could you?'

Her mouth hardens for the briefest of moments. She weighs something up and looks me directly in the eye for far too long. I lower my head. Her expression changes and she gets a different kind of smile, crooked, as though she's decided something. Turning towards the stairs, she holds her hand out to me. 'Come on, let's sort you out.'

I finish my negroni, which makes me slightly light-headed. Pushing a couple of cheese crackers swiftly into my mouth, I follow her upstairs.

Her perfume is a warm trail of amber.

'And how did you get into such a state, may I ask?' she says over her shoulder.

I shrug, trying to think of a good lie, but not finding one quickly enough. 'I was on a bit of a jaunt, and it didn't go too well. I got chased by soldiers, but I saw them off.'

She looks as though she's trying to make sense of what I've just said and leads me by the hand into the room across their landing. I usually sleep in the attic, which has enough space for about four of us to crash in, but it seems that tonight I will be sleeping here in the guest bedroom.

The white, metal-framed bed has a quilt in a cotton cover instead of normal sheets and blankets. She says it's called a duvet. There is no carpet on the stripped wooden floor. Two wardrobes, side by side, stand opposite the curtained window. Like the bed, the wardrobes have been hand painted in textured white emulsion. I have never seen this kind of decor anywhere else. I imagine it's based on rustic France, but I've never been there.

I look at Callie, then the bed, and pretend that I haven't. She opens one of the wardrobes.

'Now,' she says thoughtfully. 'I get a chance to dress you exactly as I want. Isn't that going to be fun?'

Her expression tells me to trust her, and she chooses a long lace frock with a low neckline and slightly flared sleeves. It's like she's giving me sweets.

I'm intrigued by the dress. I would never choose anything like this for myself. It's soft and girly and white. I try to imagine myself in it. I think it will show off my body in a way I'm not used to. I'd like to know what that feels like.

'What about underwear?' She asks and lets her gaze wander from my face to my breasts and then further, to my crotch.

I blush. 'I can't borrow your underwear! I've got my own in my bag.'

She ignores my plea and seems to be assessing my body size. 'My bras will be too big, but you don't really need one.'

'Are you saying my tits are too small?'

'No, I'm saying that they're pert enough not to need support.'

We hold each other's eyes for a moment.

'I've got panties that will fit you.' She laughs at the look on my face. 'They are brand new and unused, and you can keep them.'

In the tiled bathroom, steam dampens my hair. After swilling my hand through the clear water to test the temperature, I step into the claw-footed bath. It's still too hot, so I stand for a while to let my legs and feet adjust to the heat.

It is a very self-conscious bathroom. It's like a film set, full of props. There's a bone-handled cut-throat razor and an old-fashioned shaving brush on the lip of the hand basin. I lean out to pick up the razor. Testing its edge with my thumb, I think about what could be done with a blade like this. It reminds me of Tommy's flick knife with its elegant handle. It occurs to me how theatrical I must look, standing naked in the bath with a razor in my hand. I put it back and sink into deep water that comes up to my armpits.

The mellow notes of Dave Brubeck's 'Take Five' drifts up the stairs.

Callie comes in carrying a perfumed candle and puts it on the windowsill without a word.

I don't try to cover myself up. I don't want anyone to accuse me of being uptight, or inhibited. She discreetly picks up my clothes and casts me a veiled smile.

'People will be here soon, so don't be too long.'

I don't move my head, but my eyes follow her as she leaves.

I wonder if she knows I'm looking.

Her footsteps on the stairs recede. I'm alone. I close my eyes and lie back in the hot water. I imagine I look like Millais' *Ophelia* with my hair spread out on the surface of the water, hands floating.

When I open my eyes, Hugo is leaning in the doorway watching me. I've never liked the way he suddenly appears and examines your body whenever he wants to. There are moments when he's got something of a thin wolf about him that makes me careful. A cold acquisitiveness. A fleeting expression of cruelty.

I have his measure though. He's just a lame old dog fox. I know how to handle him.

'You don't even know you're beautiful, do you?' he murmurs.

'That's because I'm not.'

'I beg to differ.'

I look straight at him and sing, very softly, a sly songline of fox lust. I call him *Reynardine*.

'What's that from?'

121

'Fairport Convention's setting of a very old ballad, Mr Reynard. A song just for you.'

He shakes his head at me, like I'm too clever for my own good, and pushes his weight off the doorjamb. Turning away, he says, 'Don't stay there all night.'

Gen and Vik arrive first. 'Jude!' Gen exclaims and hugs me firmly, 'How are you, Toto? She pauses to give me a look that I can't quite interpret. 'Nel's at the Roxy Music thing. She was expecting you.'

'I know. I messed everything up . . . all got out of hand.'

She leans back and looks at the long white dress I'm wearing, with its flimsy lace insets. 'That's Callie's. You look great in it though.'

Callie's voice comes from behind me. 'Doesn't she just? I'd like to keep her here and dress her up every day.'

As the other three arrive one by one, conversations become intense and competitive. Lauren and Sid are my old comrades from art school, as is my ex, Michael. They lounge on various bits of furniture, loose-limbed and barefoot. Lauren has perennial ennui and isn't talking much, but she never does unless she's stoned. Her silence is part of her allure.

'How come you're all not at the concert tonight?' I ask.

'No money, and no one who'll get us free tickets.' Michael raises an eyebrow as he speaks, and I'm instantly irritated with him, like in the old days.

He and Sid sit on the smaller couch within touching distance of each other. Michael's long chestnut hair frames his angular cheekbones, and impressive beard. He fingers the mother-of-pearl buttons of the ironed shirt he wears like a tunic over his trousers. He is long-bodied and a gold chain adorns his ankle.

Sid is small and dark and constantly watching Michael. His skin-tight, striped V-neck sweater sits on top of a thin burgundy shirt with puffed sleeves. He looks like a Jacobean fop. His trousers mould around his crotch a little too snugly, and he has an ultra-fashionable feather-cut hairstyle almost identical to Lauren's. It's odd how alike they are sometimes. Their body types are so similar you could take them for twins. Sid is not silent like her though: he makes bubbly, hilarious conversation and can find a smart riposte for anything.

In the lounge, Callie and Hugo hold court as everyone satellites around them. Lauren rolls her eyes at me from the other side of the room and starts to make a joint. Callie watches her with something close to dislike.

The dining table has been brought out from its usual place in the window alcove, and its oaken leaves have been extended to accommodate eight diners. There's a projector on a pot stand behind one of the couches, and it casts a film high onto the wall.

Cabaret has been running for some time. We've discussed how the opening shots reference German Expressionist paintings, and how clever the undercurrent of threat and fascism is. We cheered the scene where the suave aristocrat, Maximilian, seduces both Sally Bowles and Brian Roberts.

'This bit! This bit now!'

Michael points at the screen and nudges me as Brian and Sally begin the famous scene where they reveal to each other that they've both been sleeping with Maximilian.

Michael's not the only one who's been waiting for it. We all chorus the lines along with them, whooping in delight at the climax.

After Hugo rewinds to replay the bit where Joel Gray appears as the Kit Kat Club Master of Ceremonies singing 'Willkommen'. Michael says, 'Now that's androgyny, that's what I'm talking about. I'd love to be that androgynous.'

Viktor responds. 'Well why have you got that fucking beard then?'

Michael is indignant. 'I don't mean looking like a girl. I mean having that kind of air about you of simultaneous masculinity and femininity. Like David Bowie as Ziggy Stardust, or Mick Jagger in *Performance*, or' – he searches around the room – 'Lauren, or even you Jude.'

I didn't know I had any kind of air, especially not in this dress.

Sid gets to his feet to spread his arms in ostentatious display. 'Everyone will notice he didn't include me. That's because I'm not androgynous . . . I just look exactly like a girl.'

'Yes,' Lauren says dryly. 'You're a more feminine version of me.'

We are instructed to take our places at the table. The first course is a fondue, which I've never had before. Callie and Hugo are excited about it because it's the first time they've had it out of its box. It's a weird orange bowl-thing, with a burner underneath it, which goes on the table. It's filled with hot cheese sauce. There's a pile of bread cubes, and long thin forks for dipping them in the molten Gruyere. A bowl of salad accompanies it, full of things like walnuts and magenta leaves I don't recognise. I'm sitting here like a princess in Callie's low-cut dress. Every so often someone flirts with me or feeds me, gives me something to drink or a cigarette.

'Chianti?'

Well, why fucking not.

'Did Gen and Viktor bring that back from Italy too?'

'No, that was us, 'Hugo says. 'We got a case when we went to Sienna. Stuck it in the back of the Citroen and bounced it all the way to Calais.'

'I've never been to Sienna.' I'm getting drunk. 'But I *have* been to Rome.'

'Have you, now?' Callie says.

I'm struck by the shape of her eyes. And their colour. Ochre-flecked with Indian yellow. Why have I never noticed that before? 'Yes, with my school when I was thirteen. Me, twenty other girls and three nuns.'

'Hmm,' says Sid. 'I bloody love nuns.'

Michael is very drunk. He laughs uncontrollably. 'Nuns!' he says, as though that explains everything.

I give him a withering look and continue the story. 'We went to the Vatican, we had an audience with the Pope, and I climbed about a hundred steps on my knees to look at some saint's mummified finger in a fucking box.'

Genevieve stubs out her cigarette and leans forward. 'An actual audience with the Pope?'

'Well, me and about seven hundred other people in St Peter's Basilica. The whole affair was bizarre, but do you know what was really weird though?'

They all wait to hear.

'There was a guy who spent the whole time touching up Sister Mary Rose. He had his hand inside her habit touching her tit. I mean, he was touching up a nun . . . in front of the bloody Pope. The *Pope*! And she was transfixed, like a rabbit in the headlights. She didn't move a muscle the whole time.'

'The Second Coming!' Hugo says.

Viktor retorts, 'Probably not. Probably her first coming!'

He rolls his cigarette in his fingers, surprised at his own wit.

Michael suddenly sits erect and observes me intently. 'Did you just say you had an affair with the Pope?'

'Audience, not affair!' Three people say at once, and Lauren laughs her strange little barking laugh.

'Yes, Michael. Yes. I had an affair with the Pope. You dickhead!'

'Sorry,' he slurs. 'No, sorry, misheard.'

I look at his glazed eyes and the melted Gruyere cheese stuck in his beard. I can't believe I once thought I was in love with him.

'Fuck,' he says. 'This fucking cheese thing's hard to do.' He glances apologetically at Callie. 'I think I drank those cocktail things too fast.'

Sid wipes him down solicitously. The wisecracking has stopped for a moment. Sid has been in love with Michael since forever, but Michael only wants the unattainable, hence neither of us was what he was after. Sid and I once slept together for mutual comfort. In between our labouring, unsuccessful attempts to achieve orgasm, we talked endlessly about the complexities of Michael.

The remains of the boeuf bourguignon lie in a casserole dish on the table. There's more wine and I'm drinking it because of its colour. Deep, deep red. I am drunk. Definitely drunk. Hugo has replaced *Cabaret* with *Performance*, and the projector rattles and whirs behind me. Mick Jagger, Anita Pallenberg and Michèle Breton are intertwined with each other on the wall. I'm in the heady and dangerous phase of intoxication.

Hugo is trying to explain to me the difference between a sybarite and a hedonist. Michael suddenly says, 'Lauren, would you kiss another woman?'

She looks at him in the bored and wry way that only Lauren can. 'Of course I would.'

She and I exchange the quickest of knowing glances. We both know she's kissed a woman before. We both know she's kissed me.

'Jude?' Michael can't help himself, he's going to dare us.

Sid gets there first. 'Come on, let's see it. Girls kissing!'

I smirk at Lauren. We are drunk and giddy and fearless. We lean across the table and kiss, full on, to the applause of the room. A kiss is a kiss, and I like it. She draws back looking me straight in the eyes, and we laugh triumphantly. I remember how much I used to like kissing her, how stoned we were and how much fun it was.

Callie isn't applauding like everyone else. I don't feel quite right. It's really hard to focus on the film. Mick Jagger is dancing with a tube of light, and things are distorting. I stand suddenly and unsteadily and try to make my way to the toilet without falling over.

I'm throwing up Chianti, Campari, Cinzano, Blue Sapphire. Someone stoops behind me, gathers up my hair, holds it away from the bowl. I look up momentarily. It's Callie.

'It's OK, just let it go, baby, just let it go.'

It's so humiliating that it makes me cry. I sit on the cold, tiled floor, brushing away tears with my sleeve. I hear her leaving, but she reappears with a glass and fills it with water. She's different, softer and quieter.

'Come on, swill your mouth out,' she says.

I do.

'Stand up.'

She washes my face, neck and hands softly with a soapy flannel. 'Better?'

I nod feebly, sad and ashamed. She makes me look at her and laughs affectionately. 'What am I going to do with you?'

I totter slightly and grab her arm. 'I think I need to lie down.'

Unbraided, Callie's hair is longer and blonder, wheat coloured like Nel's. She pulls my dress over my head and steps out of hers. Kissing my neck, she grips my hair and bites my ear until it hurts. She smells of herbs and alcohol and I make no resistance as she lays me on the bed. She fucks me so much more tenderly than anyone ever has before. Her eyes hold mine until I can't bear it anymore. I fight these sensations, struggling as though my body has its own separate existence. Nothing in my life has ever been as intense as this.

After I come, my astonishment amuses her. 'It's all right, Bluebird,' she murmurs gently, 'I've got you now.'

Hugo stands in the doorway, silent, unmoving. I look for jealousy, but don't find it.

Callie gives him a long wide smile. He returns it and leaves.

She cradles me for a moment, and kisses me again. 'OK baby, Mama Bear and Papa Bear are going to have some grown-up time together. You get some sleep and I'll be back.'

As she leaves the room, streetlight touches her body. She

is more graceful naked than clothed, more beautiful than I had thought.

In their bedroom across the hallway, they are making love.

Lying in soft pillows I'm too tired and drunk, too confused and aroused to sleep. The trees rustle outside the window. A vixen screams.

I drift in and out of shallow sleep. Callie returns, slipping under the covers and drawing me to her. Her touch is as delicate as the first time. She takes me again, shows me how she wants me to take her, and takes me for a third time. A thrush in the park begins the dawn chorus. I am emptied. I'm concentrating on the soft touch of her lips as she kisses my forehead. Can't open my eyes. I curl up in her embrace, my back against her belly, her breasts against my shoulders, her lips against my ear.

11

Toto

My brow feels like it has an iron band tightening around it. Piercing light comes through the window. I lift my head and look around. A jug of water and tumbler of freshly squeezed juice sit on a tray. People are moving in rooms below. Domestic sounds and the chattering of Radio Four come from the kitchen.

I need to drink.

The juice goes down in one go, followed by two glasses of water, but they make no impression on my hangover. The jug is empty, so I stumble to the bathroom to get more. There's a new toothbrush placed obviously on the basin. After using it, I wander naked back to bed to lie face down on top of the covers. As I do, someone downstairs turns the radio a notch higher to listen to the news.

The newscaster is talking about that girl who disappeared hitching to Derby. The one Hank showed me in the papers: a student with long dark hair. Jennifer somebody. I sink into

130

unconsciousness as a female voice intones, *It's not like our Jenny. She never goes off without telling us. Something must have happened.*

I resurface to the sound of a bath running, and the feel of a soft hand brushing down my back and across my behind, finishing in a gentle pat.

'Wake up, Bluebird.'

There's the sweet smell of rosemary in Callie's hair, and the taste of mint as her mouth finds mine. I feel inexplicably vulnerable. I'm not used to still feeling something for someone when the night's ended and the morning has come.

'You found the toothbrush.' She kisses me with quiet purpose. Whispering, so I feel her lips on my ear, she tells me slowly. 'First I'm going to fuck you, then I'm going to bathe you, then I'm going to feed you.'

We make love on the edge of the bed. Afterwards I lie underneath her on the floor. My hair twists across my face and my lungs heave. She brings her hand up from my crotch and rests it on my breast. She leans over me, and I push back my hair so I can see her. I can feel her smile on my skin.

At her table, in clothes that aren't my own, I look at a plate of toasted brown bread spread with unsalted butter and chunky marmalade. Callie is at the stove in her dressing gown, brewing coffee in a glass percolator. It bubbles intermittently, filling the room with its peaty smell. I am awash with unfamiliarity. Every time I look at her, my body responds. She has plaited

her hair again and her neck is exposed. It's difficult to understand how I never noticed her beauty until now.

'Eat your toast, I don't want you fading away on me.'

I obey.

'Is the coffee too strong for you?'

I consider the question. The instant stuff I usually drink
doesn't taste like this at all.

'It's just strange.'

Everything is strange right now.

'So many new tastes in so short a span,' she says knowingly.
'*Real* coffee being the least of them.'

There's no one here but us. She holds my hand across the
table.

'Do you want to stay for a while?' she says, rubbing my wrist
gently with her thumb. Her eyes are questioning. I have hardly
spoken a word to her since she first kissed me. I have this
peculiar feeling of being fictitious, like I'm in a film, or someone
has made me up. How am I supposed to respond? Life is full
of rules, but most people forget to tell me what they are. How
am I supposed to know what I want?

'What about Hugo?' I ask, scrutinising her carefully. She's
looking as though she's working out what to tell me.

'We have an open marriage, everyone knows that. It's no
secret Hugo does his thing and I do mine. We love one another,
but we don't tie each other down.' She pauses as though to
read my response. 'I'd like you to stay for a while. It won't be
a problem with Hugo.'

I try to weigh up what this all means. At least one of my
friends has already had a liaison with Callie, and I consider
whether I should follow suit. One-night stands have always

been simpler. I can get my head around them. Being one of Callie's flings is something else altogether.

But I think I will stay for a while.

Callie has left me alone. I'm curled up on the couch in a kimono, drinking a cup of the instant coffee I found in the back of a cupboard. As I listen to the Velvet Underground, I peruse the Reynards' book collection.

Earlier she told me Hugo's gone away for a few days, so we can have the place to ourselves. She implied he has an arrangement of his own with someone else. I couldn't help trying to work out who that might be, but I didn't push it.

The emptiness of the house reminds me that I don't really belong here. I feel a bit like a robber, only I'm not stealing *things*: I'm stealing their whole home.

Hugo and Callie's collections of records and film reels are compartmentalised on wooden shelves the length of the wall. I've been coming to this house long enough to know that they keep their music separate. Hugo's records are mostly contemporary jazz. Hers are more cosmopolitan: Leonard Cohen, Jacques Brel and Edith Piaf. Next to the turntable is *Com Que Voz* by Amalia Rodrigues, who sings in Portuguese. The emotion catches me in my chest even though I don't understand the lyrics. Callie played it twice this morning and, unlike me, she understands the words. I'm intimidated by her cleverness.

It must be late afternoon by now. I can't be bothered to find a clock. I wonder whether I should get dressed properly or just spend the day in this thin, blue robe. Wrapping it around myself, I continue to explore the house. My bare feet pad across the polished floors, across Turkish rugs, up and down carpeted stairs. I take in the David Hockney prints and wooden ornaments from somewhere in Africa.

This, I say to myself, is my reward for surviving. This is what you get when you outwit danger. Risk everything and you win.

I pick a book and lie on the couch again. It's called *By Grand Central Station I Sat Down and Wept,* and I've chosen it because the title is a poem in itself. It feels exactly the right weight in my hand. I'm flat on my back, with one leg bent, reading and eating an apple, when I hear a key turning in the front door.

It's her. Something in my body wakes to her presence like a school of tiny fish darting through shallow water. Even before I see her, my breathing has altered.

Her lipstick perfectly applied, she struggles into the room carrying bags emblazoned with posh-looking logos.

'Look what I bought you, Bluebird. Presents, things to make you as stylish as you should be.'

She shows me the new clothes: three fine-cotton blouses; a pair of bell-bottomed jeans; a floor-length peasant skirt; smart trousers; and a selection of pants and T-shirts. They are all in various subtle shades of blue, because she has decided blue is my colour.

I feel awkward. 'Fuck, Callie, I don't know whether you should . . .' I'm silent. Grateful. Humiliated. Confused.

'Your old clothes are falling apart. They're only good for throwing away.'

'I can sew them up. That's what I do.'

'I don't think so. I've already put them in the bin.'

I'm shocked. 'You threw my clothes away?'

She's surprised at the question. 'I'm sorry. Were you really that attached to a filthy pair of ripped jeans and a few worn-out T-shirts?'

'Not attached exactly . . . but they were mine.'

'Darling. These are better.' There's exasperation in her tone. To her, this is of no consequence, merely a practical matter that makes sense.

I acquiesce. She's right. They are better. When I see myself in the mirror, I have to admit that I look good. She adjusts the blouse to enhance my minimal cleavage and runs her hand appreciatively over my hip and the outside of my leg.

'That is a lovely fit, and those colours bring out the blue of your eyes.' She kisses me quickly. 'Come on, we have to cook. I need to keep your energy up.'

She has slipped a chef's apron over my head to keep my new clothes clean and has me chopping shallots and fresh herbs from her garden. She has plaited my hair into a braid not dissimilar to her own. As she's showing me how to make an omelette properly, I catch my reflection in the darkening window. It stops me for a moment.

Who is this clean, blue girl?

She's made me smooth, made me regular. Hardly me at all. I don't dislike what I see; it's simply another unfamiliar thing to get used to.

'What's this flavour? The herb I chopped?' Its green colour tints my fingers.

'Russian tarragon. Do you like it?'

'Yeah, it's kind of . . . creamy.'

'Good with mushrooms too. Listen, I was thinking: shall we drive over to Manchester tomorrow? We can have a day out without worrying about things.'

'Without people seeing us, you mean?'

That was too critical. I didn't mean to be, but now it's out there.

She stops and looks at me warily. 'Yes, I suppose so.'

'That's OK with me. I'm yours to do with what you will.'

Again, words trip from my mouth with a facetious edge.

She busies herself with something inconsequential on the table. 'If you don't want to, we don't have to.'

I need to reassure her. I put my arms around her waist and insinuate my body against hers.

She regards me carefully, as though she can't get my measure.

'I do want to, I do.' I try my best to soothe her. 'I'd like to go to Manchester. I've only been there once, for a Joni Mitchell concert. I was out of my head the whole time.'

Her guard lowers a little. Slowly, she removes my hands from her waist to hold me by my wrists. Folding my arms behind my back, she clasps me tightly to her.

'You know, when I first met you,' she says in a low threatening voice, 'I thought you were the most intolerable little shit. You were backchatting Hugo in a Film Society seminar, just asking for a good hard slap. A smart-ass little hippy chick.'

My lips part flirtatiously. 'Yeah, but a clever smart-arse little hippy chick, you've got to admit.'

She gives me the sharp slap on the backside she clearly feels I've needed for the past four years. Even though it stings, I'm laughing. I flirt, because flirting is what I do best. I'm not sure if I have any other skills.

She releases me in order to take a sip from her glass of wine, and refills mine. 'Drink it slowly. We don't want a re-run of last night's spewing marathon.'

I have no idea how not to drink too much. Under normal

136

circumstances my general rule is to drink until it's gone. I take one of the cigarettes from the box on the table. I falter as I recognise the brand. Benson and Hedges. The memory of the driver of the white Zephyr, with a cigarette between his lips, crashes into my brain. The memory of running from rapists.

'What's wrong?' Callie asks.

We make ourselves comfortable on the couch, and as I drink more, I tell her about the soldiers. She plays with my hair, listening quietly and absently running my necklace chain through her fingers as I finish the tale. She's thoughtful and doesn't respond immediately.

'You're crazy,' she says finally, 'Aren't you frightened about what could happen to you? Especially with all these disappearances going on.'

Fear is the armature that underpins my life. Fear is the ribcage, the bone structure, the blood pulse that, if I wake in the night, I can hear underneath everything. Fear is the only constant I know. The only way I know how to deal with it is to embrace it and survive.

I look up at her and say, in a matter of fact way, 'I'm frightened of everything, which makes me frightened of nothing.'

'What does that mean?' She scrutinises me. Perhaps she thinks I'm being a smart-arse little hippy chick again. Her fingers gently wind and unwind a strand of my hair. She waits for my response with an air of patient enquiry.

'People think I've got a death wish, but I haven't. I've just always wanted to find the point where fear becomes so big it transforms into something else . . . because then you're free of it, aren't you? It's not fear anymore.'

Callie wrinkles her brow in bafflement. 'A fear so big that it becomes something else,' she murmurs as though reciting a clue from a crossword puzzle. 'What is it, if it's not fear anymore?'

'I don't know. Maybe freedom.' I trail off. 'Oh, I don't know,' I say lamely. 'I can't explain it. Nel always tells me I'm frightened of the wrong things, but actually, I'm frightened of everything, so anything I do has to be a negotiation with my fear.'

'Are you frightened right now?'

'I told you, I'm always frightened.'

And in that moment, I open myself to my fear that she's going to hurt me. I look up into her eyes and am completely overtaken by fear.

'Sweetheart,' she says barely audibly. She manoeuvres her body so she can cradle me with the most extraordinary tenderness.

'Don't, I'll cry.'

'You can. It's OK to cry.'

And I do.

12

Nel

The neighbour shuts her door with a clunk as I stand on the Reynards' doorstep. 'Another one,' she says to herself, glancing at me through narrowed eyes. 'The goings-on in that house ought to be against the law. Free Love they call it. I call it disgusting.'

'Good morning,' I say in my best teacher's voice.

'Don't *good morning* me if you're going in there. Women with women, men with men and everything in between.'

Adjusting her wicker shopping basket, she pointedly turns her back and sets off towards Ecclesall Road.

I'm not sure how happy I am that she associates me with the *goings-on* in this house.

I press the doorbell. I need to see if Toto's OK. The Easter break is almost over and I've hardly seen her in the four weeks since she arrived. Twice to be precise. Once at the pub, and once at Gen's. That Reynard woman was with her both times, and we couldn't talk properly. When they came to the pub, she didn't even have time to get her coat off before Callie dragged her back out, and at Gen's she was leaving as I was coming in. We literally just waved at one another. Simon says I should leave her alone and mind my own business, but his nose is out of joint just because my attention's on someone other than him.

I ring again, long and hard. Maybe they're in bed, hoping I'll go away.

The squalling of birds draws my attention to the park behind me. Starlings are hunting down a kestrel. They swoop and scream as a mob, driving the solitary predator into the trees. It prompts a memory of my impromptu visit to Toto's family home last summer. I was over in Bradford to see my auntie and thought I'd drop in. Starlings settled and resettled in the trees all around her house and I remember the sound of thousands of feathers from hundreds of wings each time they rose into the air.

Trying to avoid the overgrown hawthorn hedge, I had to push past her dad's vintage motorbikes on the driveway. The house was a shabby, four-bedroom villa with art deco mouldings and roughcast white walls. So much more imposing than my parent's home, but in such disrepair.

Toto's sister, Tessa, answered the door, peeping at me like a fearful wee mouse. A boy, who turned out to be her brother Marty, stared from the living-room door in his ill-fitting school uniform. Toto would do anything for her sister and brother. I'm an only child and have always craved the connection that siblings seem to share. These three had developed their own way of communicating. Silently, with looks and nods and raising of eyebrows. It was one of the ways they dealt with their parents. Toto told me that silence never provoked them, but most other things did.

When Toto came down the stairs and saw me, she was both delighted and mortified. She didn't want me to see the state the house was in, so I was ushered straight through it and into the back garden. It wasn't much better. Their rose-bushed borders were so tangled that I thought they must house a comatose princess. I remember rotting flowers and Toto's laughter at the thought of Sleeping Beauty in her flowerbed.

I'm so absorbed by the memory that I don't notice the door open. When I turn around, Callie Reynard is looking at me.

'Yes?'

Every time Callie and I come across each other, she acts as though we've never met. It's irritating. We've had so many conversations, I've even been a guest in her house, but it's like I don't exist. When I complained about it to Lauren, she said it was because I treat Callie Reynard like *she* doesn't exist. I know she exists – I just don't think she's very interesting.

'Is Jude here?' I match her coldness. 'Can you tell her it's Nel?'

'Wait there' – she partially closes the door – 'I'll get her.'

I take a small step back. 'OK.'

She rethinks, 'No, actually, what am I saying? Come in.' She raises her voice in the direction of the stairs, 'Jude, your friend Nel is here for you.'

I hear Toto before I see her.

'Hey, you.' She appears at the top of the stairs and stoops to see me better.

'Hey lovely!' That glorious sun-in-a-thunderstorm smile of hers improves my mood immediately.

'Hang on,' she says. 'I'll get some clothes on and come down.'

'Why don't you wait in the living room?' Callie indicates

the door to the lounge before returning upstairs. 'Make yourself at home.'

I'm carefully polite. 'Thanks, I will.'

When Toto appears in the doorway, I feel like my jaw is going to crack from smiling at her. To my amazement, the girl-who-hates-hugging hugs me. She's scented like vanilla and I don't want ever to release her.

I step back to look at her. She seems wrong. She's wearing clothes that I've never seen before. I don't like them.

Reading my expression, she becomes sheepish. 'Callie bought them for me.'

'Callie Reynard bought you clothes?'

'Yes.' She's embarrassed. 'I know, I know, but honest to god. You should have seen the state of me after hitchhiking. She says blue is my colour.'

Who the hell is Callie Reynard to decide that Toto has a colour?

'Blue's not your colour. Green is. Look at your hair, for Christ's sake. Green's your colour.' I quieten my voice, remembering that Callie is close by. 'What's the story with you and her anyway? Michael said she practically threw you over her shoulder and carried you off to her boudoir . . . apparently you were *drunk*. Now there's a surprise.'

'Be nice, Nel, I like her.'

'She's a bit of a wanker, though, isn't she?'

Toto looks around us as though I've spoken too loudly. 'She's different when you get to know her,' she says in a whisper. 'She's clever and sophisticated and really good at sex. Don't screw up your face like that!'

'I just don't like her. I'm sorry, but I don't.'

'She's kind too. She's been kind to me.'

That takes me by surprise, as does the vulnerability I see in Toto's face. 'Has she?'

'Yes.' She drops her head and stares at her hands.

I get this overwhelming feeling that I want to cry.

'Is this serious then?'

'Bloody hell, I don't know.' Toto recovers her composure. 'I mean, I'm having a pretty fantastic time, but I don't know if I'd call it *serious*. She's taken me to see *Twelfth Night*, and we went to this really posh restaurant. I ate fresh salmon. I've never had that before. It's all kind of exciting actually, and hardly ever *serious* at all.'

'What's fresh salmon like? Is it better than the tinned stuff?'

'Hmm. It wasn't as nice as I thought it was going to be. Pretty bland really.'

'All right, Toto, you keep having fun. I hope she doesn't break your little clockwork heart, that's all.'

She pulls a face that indicates she thinks that unlikely, just as Callie Reynard coughs loudly from somewhere else in the house. I'm certain it's not a real cough. It seems designed to remind us that she's here.

'Toto,' I say, 'can we go for a walk or something?'

'OK.' She's unexpectedly decisive. 'Let's go. I'm starving. Fancy breakfast at the Banners Café?'

'Well, I hate to tell you, but it's already lunchtime and I've had breakfast, but aye, I really want to get out of here.'

As we approach the Banners Café, a woman covered in splashes of cooking fat comes out to reset the sandwich board that's fallen over in the swirling wind. She looks disappointed when we decide to go in, and when we choose a table near the counter she looms over us with a pad and pencil.

'Yes?' she says shortly. 'What will you have?'

Her hair is covered in so much hairspray that it looks solid. Toto is trying not to stare. She fiddles with the tomato-shaped ketchup dispenser and the chrome sugar-shaker, moving them about like big chess pieces over the ring marks from countless ages of cups. After long thought, and without looking directly at the woman's hairdo, she orders beans and chips and I opt for coffee and a chocolate eclair.

'Did you see her head?' Toto leans across the table and whispers as the waitress retires to the kitchen. 'You could crack an egg on it. It's amazing what you can achieve with hairspray. I used it on a papier-mâché mask once, went hard as a rock. I just don't think anyone should spray it on their head.'

I shield my mouth and whisper. 'She smells of sulphur too. Do you think she's on day release from hell?'

'That's an interesting thought: a portal to hell on Banner's Cross Road.'

Our laughter doesn't last long. My thoughts keep getting stuck on Callie Reynard.

Toto is watching me like she's trying to assess something. 'What's wrong, Nel?'

She knows what's wrong. I can feel that I'm scowling. I don't want to, but I can't help it.

'Do I really need to say it?'

She winces and turns her cheek as though she can tell what's coming.

Everything comes tumbling out of my mouth. 'You should have come to Roxy Music. Hank went to all that trouble to get you a ticket and you just wasted it. It was great, too.' I sound stilted, even to myself. 'Well no, actually it wasn't great. I was too near the speakers. Nearly deafened me; my ears were ringing when we got back to Gen's. And you said you'd meet us at the Lamb and Flag, but you never turned up, then when you *did* come, you hardly even talked to me. And where's that dope we paid you for?'

'Shit,' she says. 'I'm sorry. I forgot. It's in my bag.' She rummages, 'Here, a piece for you and one for Jo.'

'OK, slip them under the table. I'll be seeing her later.'

We touch hands briefly as she conveys the tiny silver-foil packages to me. When she looks at me, I have the strangest sensation of drowning. When did she ever give a fuck about posh restaurants and fresh bloody salmon? I don't like her in that blue. It isn't her bloody colour.

'You've gone all pale.' She furrows her brow. 'Are you poorly? What's the matter?'

I can't tell her, because I don't know.

Outside the Reynards' house we loiter, reluctant to part. On the common across the road, a little girl in a pushchair sobs in shudders. Her greasy-haired mother shakes the pram until her knuckles go white. 'Shut up,' she rages, 'or I'll give you something to cry about.'

Sitting on Callie's wall, we become absorbed in watching a couple of gaunt men who have unexpectedly set on one another at the edge of the woods.

'Junkies,' Toto says. 'There's a few of them living in that bit of the woods where the paths don't go. I nearly fell over their camp when I was exploring the other day. They've got tents made out of tarpaulins, big dogs and everything. It's quite cool; you have to admire the way they fly under the radar. Look at them though; they're smashed, completely out of it.'

One of the men is holding a teenage girl by her elbow as he swings to punch the other guy in the face. Ripping herself away, the girl runs for the road. As he turns his head to watch her, the other man knocks him to the ground.

I gasp and stand up. 'Are they all right?'

Toto has hold of my coat, 'Don't get into it. The girl's OK, that's the main thing. Look at her run.'

I'm troubled. Every part of me wants to chase after the teenager. Make her safe. If I could save the whole fucking world I would. It all needs bloody saving as far as I can see. I feel like crying and I don't know why.

I just don't know anything today.

Trying to pull myself together, I wonder whether my period is due. If Simon were here, he would call me an irrational pre-menstrual woman. He would laugh in that patronising way of his and rub the top of my head. I try to calculate where I am in my cycle, then give up. I can never work it out. I always used to worry about periods and getting pregnant, but since they put the contraceptive pill on prescription everything has changed. It's all up to me now. There can't be any more accidents because Simon forgets to wear a jonnie. He can't do that to me again. All that turmoil ending up in unexpected blood down my leg at a bus stop and a baby never born. Not that he cared that much. In fact, he seemed very proud that he'd managed to impregnate me. Asked me to marry him and bought me a ring like a brown pebble that my mother tried her best to admire.

'Aye, well it's a wee bit strange to look at, but it's lovely you're to be wed. I was giving up hope of it. You're twenty-two, hen. The clock is ticking.'

I fiddle with the ring, and Toto notices. 'Shit piece of jewellery really,' she says, 'He could have tried a bit harder if he was going to be a pillar of society and ask for your hand in marriage.'

'Don't be so rude. It's what you're supposed to do. Get engaged, get married. Be in love. We're in love.'

'If you say so, Nel. I think that's all crap, but if that's what you want.'

'What's crap? Getting married or being in love with Simon?'

'That's for you to work out.' Her eyes darken.

I study her sharply. She is hunched, almost petulant.

There are things here that neither of us wants to say.

Readjusting my bag on my shoulder, I compose myself. 'All right, best be off. I'll wander over to Jo and Hanks. We're going to the White Hart to meet Michael later.'

'Sid not coming?'

'No. He's seeing someone, so he's a bit busy apparently. Why don't you come?'

She kicks at a bit of fallen branch, 'We're going out tonight, and anyway, I'm barred from the Hart. The landlord accused me of being *on pot* because I was laughing too much.'

'That bloke with the big plastic-looking glasses? Looks like Elton John?'

'Yeah, him. I wasn't even stoned. I was just happy.'

'He's gone now. There's a new landlord and he's much nicer. Why don't you come along on Monday? It's Jo's birthday, Simon's up for the week and we're going to have a celebratory drink for her.'

Toto stops smiling. 'Simon's up? Where is he then? I thought he was too busy to leave Birmingham.'

'He's having a wee break. Right this minute he's meeting with the printmaking tutors, showing them slides of his work, trying to get some teaching next term.'

I ignore her sour expression and continue. 'Look, if you can't come tonight, at least come for Jo's birthday. If Callie will let you out, that is.'

She gives me a playful push. 'Shut up.'

I push back. 'No, *you* shut up.'

As we're messing around, Callie Reynard appears at the upstairs window of her house behind us.

Toto stops dead, all laughter gone. 'I'd better get back in. I've stayed out longer than I meant to.'

She backs off, but I make her hug me. She's her usual awkward unhuggable self, but there's something more; both of us know Callie is watching us. I can feel Toto's discomfort, but I'm bloody-minded about the whole thing. I won't let go.

'Will you come to the pub on Monday?'

She is already through the gate, waving. 'I'll try. Promise.'

13

Toto

There's music playing, something Spanish that I don't know. I dawdle in the hallway, slowly hanging up my coat, brushing it down and adjusting its folds. I think about how to approach things. My best friend Nel is out there, walking away from me across the park, her hair blowing about and her coat done up tight. And my lover is upstairs avoiding my presence.

It's such a pain in the arse that they don't like each other. You'd have to be blind to miss the fact that Callie thinks Nel is a snotty little bitch, and Nel thinks Callie is a stuck-up cow. When they're together it's like I'm walking over a whole floor of eggshells. There isn't any substitute for those absurd and beautiful conversations that I can have with Nel, and while I don't seem to laugh much with Callie, she makes up for it in other ways that I'm not ready to lose yet.

As I go up the stairs, I can hear scrubbing noises and there's a faint smell of bleach. I find Callie in the bathroom in rubber gloves, cleaning the shower.

'Ah,' she says, 'you decided to come back. I'd almost given up on you.'

She's giving me that suspicious look that I'm getting accustomed to. Every time I stray too far from her side, she becomes insecure and I have to reassure her. It's quite sweet in a way, to see her so vulnerable when everyone else thinks she's full of confidence.

'I didn't know where you were,' she scrubs at an invisible mark on the glass. 'You go out at lunchtime, and you don't come back until now.'

'Well, if you keep me in bed all morning, I'm bound to want breakfast at lunch.'

She stops scrubbing quite so hard.

I reach down and stroke her neck.

I don't really care if we go out for dinner. I could easily stay in these rumpled sheets, even if they are sticking to my back. My eyelids are heavy. I bury my head into Callie's scent on the pillow and it's like a drug.

She's wrapped in a towel in the doorway. 'You'd better get a shower, Bluebird, you're quite unpresentable as you are.'

She calls me Bluebird, but I don't have a pet name for her. What would I call her? She's older than me, and it seems rude even to consider it. I don't call her darling, or sweetheart, or even Callie very much. I try not to call her anything. Even using her name seems presumptuous.

Water is running. 'Shower's on. Come on darling, we haven't got much time.'

Callie's pulling out various bits of fashionable apparel and scrutinising herself in the full-length mirror. Trying different combinations, standing at different angles. I linger in the warm bed to watch her. It takes a massive effort for me to drag myself into the shower. The hot water is a shock, but the expensive soap is silky and perfumed. Callie watches me as I lather myself. Her eyes follow my shape upwards at a leisurely pace. She has a smile of self-satisfaction, as if I meet a standard that indicates something about her, not me.

In the bedroom, she has lain out the clothes she wants to dress me in. These garments are all hers. Smart evening wear. A cherry cocktail dress, a pair of sheer tights. As I tentatively pick up the frock, she is searching for something else in the smallest wardrobe.

'My shoes won't fit you,' she says eventually, slightly defeated. 'I need to get you some decent ones. Your knee boots will be all right tonight though. Make you look rather trendy. Good colour with the dress.'

I don't really like all this dressing up in her clothes, but I also don't want to look out of place in a posh restaurant. It would be churlish to embarrass her, so I make an effort, even though I squirm inside.

'Callie?'

She's located a slimline scarlet jacket, which she holds up against me. 'Mmm?'

'How do you feel about me going out to the pub on Monday night? It's Jo's birthday.'

'Jo?'

'My friend, Jo.'

'The one with the dyed black hair and the miniskirts?'

'Yes, it's her birthday.'

She gets out a different jacket, blue this time. 'No,' she says to herself, after thinking about it, 'the first one is better. Monday? You want to go out on Monday?'

'You could come too.'

She makes me slip my arms into the scarlet jacket. 'That one. Yes, that's the one. You look lovely.'

'Do you want to?'

'Well, actually, it kind of suits me if you go on your own. I thought I'd see Hugo on Monday. We need to sort a few things out. Probably best if you're not here while we do.' She pulls my collar into place and brushes down my arms. 'Will that girl be there?'

'Who, Nel?'

'Yes, the one you saw today.'

Something tells me to play it down.

'There'll be lots of people.'

14

Nel

Gen's workshop is beautiful, in an airy building by a stream in a new industrial estate. There's a showroom at the front and lengths of her fabrics are displayed in the window. It smells of inks, and miniscule floating fibres catch the sunlight as they escape the handloom set up at the back. A young man I haven't seen in my previous visits is carefully positioning a silk-screen frame on a ream of linen laid along a bench. His long brown hair is tied back, and I think I recognise him from somewhere.

'Hi,' he says in greeting and returns to his meticulous labours, lining the screen up, ready to print another block of stylised flowers onto the fabric.

'This is Nick.' Gen throws her bag on a desk by the window and sets herself into the swivel chair. The desk is covered in paperwork, almost hiding a typewriter and adding machine. 'Good to have him back after the break. We'd never get this done otherwise. Big order from Dogwoods.'

'Is that the furniture company in Priorsdale? The one that does all that handmade stuff?' I ask.

She nods. 'They've got a new top-end line coming out and they like my stuff. I've got another place in Derbyshire interested too, they do curtains.'

She picks up a roll of printed material and shows it to me. 'Do you like it? It's runner beans, the flowers, that is.'

'It's superb,' I say quietly. 'That dark orange against the green. Fabulous.'

Nick pours ink from a container into a jug, adds the thickener and stirs it in with a spatula. 'Yeah. People are loving it. We can hardly keep up with it, can we, Gen?'

Genevieve nods thoughtfully. 'We're OK for now. Chugging along nicely.'

Nick is pleasant company; he likes to chat as he works. 'I hear you were at Roxy Music. Would have loved to have gone.'

I am absorbed in watching him pouring the beautiful creamy colour along the top of the screen before he squeegees it through the fine mesh. 'That's a shame,' I say. 'We had a spare ticket. Our friend didn't turn up.'

He laughs knowingly as he wipes the squeegee's rubber blade. 'Was that Jude Totton?'

'You know her?'

'I was the year below you guys when you were at college. I used to see you around with her all the time, but you were never as wasted as she was.'

'I thought I recognised you,' I say apologetically.

He picks up the screen and lays it carefully next to the block of orange that he's just completed. 'How's Jude getting on?'

'She's the same.'

Simon comes in from the yard. He'd wanted a cigarette and

it's a fire risk in the workshop. He looks at Nick with curiosity and has no problem recognising him. 'You're that second year, aren't you? The one that does the big minimalist silk screens?'

Nick looks flattered. 'Third year now.'

Si gives him a comradely smile. 'Getting ready for your final show? Your work is really fucking nice, man. Really fucking nice.' He turns to Gen without missing a beat. 'Great place you've got here, and your prints aren't bad for a textile designer.'

Gen pushes him gently in the shoulder. 'Shut your mouth, bloody Fine Artist.'

He wanders around, picking things up to look at them, peering into cupboards and inspecting equipment.

'This chick I'm sharing with in Birmingham, she's a jeweller – really fucking talented – her dad's going to set her up with a workshop in Brighton. He reckons little businesses like this are the way to go for designers. I think it could work for printmakers too, but you've got to have the start-up money, haven't you?'

He stretches out his arm for Gen to look at his bangle. 'This is one of hers. Her name's Trish Markham. *Really* talented, I'm not kidding. If you ever expand this into a design shop, her stuff would be great here.'

I watch his eyes. A chill runs through me.

He doesn't have to tell me. I know.

He's sleeping with that girl.

Gen frowns at me. 'Are you all right? Are the ink fumes getting to you?'

I give a laugh that sounds forced even to me. 'I just need a smoke. You carry on. I'll pop outside.'

Simon is unconcerned. 'I'd better get going. I'm meeting Bruce and Wally at college. I've almost convinced them to

155

bring me back to do some workshops. I've got some more ideas I want to run by them. Bought a bottle of Scotch.' He flashes a small flask of whisky out of his jacket pocket. 'Bribery is always the best way.'

As we leave the workshop, Nick and Genevieve are searching for a particular weight of material in a supply catalogue. I observe Simon. His eyes are bright, his body inflated with confidence. He looks like someone I don't know. It's like a thread has broken between us.

My eye rests on the bangle that he keeps touching, rotating around his wrist. Elegant spirals of silver. Made with love.

'OK,' he says. 'I'll see you later, back at Vik's place.'

He barely looks at me. Then he's gone.

It's a slow but dulling realisation: we're not a couple, and I don't love him. He hasn't been mine, and I haven't been his, for some time.

In the snug at the back of the White Hart, the jukebox plays 'You're so Vain'. I've done everything I can think of to get myself into a better mood for Jo's birthday drinks. I've put on sparkly glad rags, the plum-coloured lipstick that Simon doesn't like, and the burnt-umber eye shadow that makes me look like a vampire. I've smiled like a fool at everyone. I'm sat here on this leather banquette next to Simon as though everything is fine in our world. Across the table Toto lounges next to Michael while he inspects the David Bowie album he bought for Jo's birthday.

At the bar Hank leans in to give some money to the barmaid. He pauses to nod at Lauren who is perched on top of the upright piano. She never seems to sit on chairs, or anything at ground level if she can help it. 'You all right for a drink Lauren?'

'I'm fine, thanks, Hank.' She raises her full glass in salute.

Jo scrutinises Lauren, while arranging her birthday cards on the marble-topped table. 'You're going to get us thrown out, sitting up there like that, flower. Toto got barred just for laughing. Famous, that is.'

'I know. I was there. We were both barred.' Lauren says and makes herself more comfortable.

'Last time I ever have the temerity to laugh in a pub,' Toto interjects, as Hank places an exotic looking drink in front of Jo.

'Happy birthday, Mrs Salvin-Hanks. Get that down you.'

'What *is* that?' Michael examines it suspiciously. 'It looks like custard.'

Jo inspects the toothpick-skewered glacé cherry in her Snowball. 'Advocaat and lemonade. I drink it on my birthday. Only time I do. It's a tradition in our family.'

'Do you actually like it?' Michael's mouth turns down.

'No, not really.' She looks as though she's surprised herself. They laugh, and she takes a huge swallow, trying to get it down as quickly as possible. When she's finished, she widens her mouth, sticking out her tongue in disgust.

Toto waves a pound note at her. 'Do you want a drink? One that you actually like?'

'Don't mind if I do. Cider please, flower.'

'Anybody else?' Toto looks around with bravado.

Michael empties his glass. 'I'll have another, seeing as Simon fucking *I'm-doing-an-MA* Duffy never offered. You'll be getting a nice big grant to do that, eh Simon? Even if it is only second-division Birmingham and not the Royal College or the Slade.'

I wince. That hits home. Simon falters and he throws the toothpick into Michael's empty glass as he says, 'You're lucky I even lower myself to talk to you. Jealous, mate. You're just jealous. Anyway, get your own you tight fucker. Jude hasn't got two pennies to rub together.'

Michael takes the toothpick out of his glass and drops it in the ashtray. 'No, pal. Time you bought a round I reckon.'

'Oi!' says Jo, 'Pack it in, Michael. It's my birthday.'

Toto's face has gone a colour to match her red hair.

'I said *I'm* buying a round, Simon. Keep out of it.' She turns to Michael, 'Is it a half of bitter or what?'

'You've gone red.' Michael says.

'Yes, I know.'

Michael laughs, 'Happy to help you spend your money, Toto. Yes, a half of Sheaf's would be appreciated.'

She looks mollified and shoots me a glance, proud and fragile all at once. You can see it when her armour slips like this, when she thinks she's revealed too much.

'Right,' she mumbles. 'Half of bitter and a cider.'

She makes her way to the bar, regaining her composure with a straightening of her back. I remember the first day we met. I'd never seen anyone quite like her. We were new students in the Life Room getting a speech from the Dean. Toto was in her red T-shirt and hipster flares, slouched on a table with her back against the wall. A mass of auburn hair and the solemn countenance of a rebel. She intrigued me. After a moment, I realised that I was staring and turned away. When I looked back, she was gazing right at me, blue eyes unblinking.

We sought each other out and started talking. I felt like I'd always known her. We talked about everything: went to the pub and talked about books; walked through the park and talked about life; sat up all night in my room talking about the people we'd loved, the people we hadn't, and the people who'd never loved us.

That's when I first saw it, that look. The slip of her armour, just for a second. When she talked about her mother her eyes dulled. She was like someone grasping at empty air as they fall through space. Something between us locked into place like pieces of a well-made jigsaw, and that feeling has never gone away for me. It frightens me, but it's always there, and right now, while everything seems so wrong with Simon, it's weirdly reassuring to know that at least this hasn't changed.

Lauren clambers down from the top of the piano and pushes in between me and Michael on the banquette. Simon budges along grudgingly as I move up to accommodate her.

'What's that bangle, Si?' Lauren leans across me to grab his wrist and look at it. 'That's fucking gorgeous. Where did you get it?'

I wish she hadn't noticed it, but I'm not surprised. It's not his usual style. He normally has a collection of thin hoops covered in coloured enamel rattling on his wrists. He likes to play with them, sliding them up and down and over each other. All he has on his arms now is this one exquisitely sculpted bangle.

He smiles at the bangle and then at Lauren, like he's really pleased she's spotted it. 'Yeah, this chick made it. If you want one, I'll tell her. She makes fantastic stuff. Talented as fuck.'

I feel sick. I pick up my glass and drink in gulps. I need to get away from him.

'Right. Anyone want anything from the bar?' I push past Simon.

'Careful!' he says, 'that's my foot.'

Toto's still at the counter, waiting as the barmaid pours the drinks. She looks at me like she thinks there's something wrong but can't work out what. My shoulders are hunched high, my head low. She stares at me so intently that I want to hide.

'What's up?' she says very quietly.

'What do you mean?'

'I don't know. You don't seem right. Are you OK?'

'I'm just out of sorts. Simon's being a prick, and *you* didn't help.'

'Me?'

'All that disappearing, and not turning up when you say you will, and then fucking getting into this ridiculous thing with that Reynard woman.'

I know I'm being unreasonable, but I can't seem to stop myself.

'I like Callie,' Toto says plaintively. 'C'mon, Nel, don't be mean.'

I don't seem able to back off. 'Well, don't complain to me when it all goes pear-shaped.'

She sighs with her head tilted on one side as she works out how to respond. 'You won't lose me, you know. You're my best one. I'm just having fun. That's all.'

I feel a bit happier when she says that, but I'm not sure I really believe her. This doesn't seem to be like all those other brief liaisons in her life.

I'm scared by the moment of quiet contentment I saw in her when she said Callie's name.

15

Toto

On the way back from the White Hart, Lauren looks up at a shooting star and says, 'Come on, let's get stoned in the park, like we used to.'

Making *oops* noises as she loses her footing, she slithers down the grass slope to a copse of willow trees and I stumble after her. Our eyes adapt to the dark while we get comfortable on the trunk of a fallen tree and Lauren grins at me, as though she's been wanting to say something all evening.

'So, Callie fucking Reynard! Wow,' she laughs wryly. 'Hope you know what you're into, girlie. She's fun at first, then it gets heavy. She is so bloody possessive.'

I shrug, trying to be as cool as she always is.

We each search the other's face.

I don't want to ask Lauren about Callie, because I don't want to know. Then suddenly I do want to know.

'Did you fall for her?'

She wavers for a second. 'Fuck, Toto. You know I never do. Are you? Falling for her that is?'

My silence is too long.

Lauren takes a brass pillbox out of her pocket and places it on the trunk between us to make a joint. As she roasts a piece of cannabis on the end of a pin, we consider the things we'll reveal and the things we won't.

She speaks first. 'I bet she calls you Bluebird, doesn't she?'

I glance at her in surprise. My pet name might not be as special as I'd once thought.

'I'll also bet', she says, 'that you haven't had a spliff the whole time you've been there.'

I'm awkward about the fact that Lauren has trodden the same path I'm now on, but I'm hungry for information.

'Did she throw your clothes away too?' I ask.

She lets loose a small laugh. 'God, no. I'm a much tougher deal than you are, puppy.'

I don't doubt that. Not for one minute.

We smoke the joint carefully, watchful for police cars up on the road.

'Hope you're being an obedient little doggie, Toto.'

'Stop taking the piss.'

She removes the spliff from between my fingers and puts it in my mouth. 'Don't be so bloody touchy. You need to go off for one of your hitching jaunts, loosen you up. Look at the stars, you maniac, they're amazing.'

We slide off the log to stretch out in the cold grass watching the sky.

Lauren takes the last toke of the joint, burning it right down to the roach before stubbing it. 'You know, if you get fucked off with not smoking dope around her, look in the bathroom cabinet. You'll find the stash of Happy Juice I forgot to take with me when we finished. Help yourself.'

'Happy Juice?'

'Yeah, Demerol. Liquid painkiller. It's the bright-pink stuff hidden at the back. I must have left at least two bottles.'

'What does it do?'

'First it makes you shrink, and then it makes you grow. Then you fall down a rabbit-hole and have conversations with fat caterpillars.' She amuses herself with that thought for a few moments before continuing. 'No, it's cool stuff: like a cross between acid and speed. Drink about a quarter of a bottle, that'll be enough to just take the edge off reality for about four hours. Too much and it's a heavy trip.'

'Thanks.' I perk up. 'A little bit of unreality might come in handy.'

Lauren lays back, her hands interlaced behind her head, 'Look at that,' she whispers. 'The sky's fucking melting.'

It is. I'm hypnotised by the meteorite shower. Stars that appear and disappear like those little lights that swim inside your eyes if you've sneezed too hard. We lie in silence for a long time watching them burn up in fevers.

Lauren stirs after a while. 'My back's all wet from the ground. I'm going back to sit on that log.'

'Yeah,' I mumble, and look around for my lighter and tobacco. Lauren pulls herself up onto her elbows. 'Hey, guess what. I forgot to tell you,' she says. 'I've got a bloody job. No kidding. At the Sheffield City Museum. A trainee. They're teaching me how to restore old paintings and stuff. It's fucking brilliant, one of those Training Opportunities Scheme things. It's for eighteen months and at the end of it I might get taken on full-time. I start the week after next.'

'What sort of things will you do?' I'm animated by the thought of that kind of employment. Another meteor falls and burns out at the horizon as we sit ourselves down on the log again.

'It's all about the varnishes and the oils and the pigments. All that stuff you're always going on about from those old books you've got.'

She carries on telling me about the boss, and the tea room, and the other trainees, until she stops short and laughs. 'Jesus. I never thought I'd have a job. I'm not even sure how much I want one.'

We lapse into silence and I can't help wondering what might have happened if I hadn't moved away to Leeds. Maybe it would have been me in that job, not her.

Scanning the horizon, looking for the last of the comet shower, Lauren pushes her short hair back with one hand and stretches. She gives me a sly sideways look, like she wants to tell me something. 'Has Hugo tried to take you to the cottage yet?'

'I've hardly seen him. Callie says he's staying out there. With someone I think.'

'Probably.'

'Have you been there?'

She nods. 'Callie used to take me. It's her place really. She bought it with her family money. It's out in Foxdale, not far at all. Hugo goes there a lot.' She brushes off a leaf sticking to the palm of her hand. 'Always with someone special. Always going for long trips to the moors in his car.'

In the grass beside us I notice the skeleton of a mouse – its curved ribs no bigger than fish hooks. I don't want to be taken to a cottage. I don't want to know who has been. I don't want to know about places on moors that you have to reach by car. Those kinds of places freak me out. I think there are dead children under all the lumps and bumps of gorse bushes and heather.

I'm stoned and it's just after midnight when I get back to Callie's. She doesn't like me having a key, but she's allowed it for tonight. I use it with difficulty. It's stiff like it's cut wrong or the mechanism needs oiling. I have to push it in and out a few times before it works.

The smell of Hugo's aftershave is a jolt. There's jazz playing, and murmuring conversation in the living room. There are bits of grass on my coat. I remove it slowly, giving myself time to think. As I brush it off, I compose myself, take a breath, and hang it up.

'Hi,' I call.

'Is that you, sweetheart?' Callie replies.

After a significant interval, she emerges. Her lipstick is smudged. Hugo sidles around her, tucking in his shirt and straightening his jacket.

'Well, hullo, Jude Totton,' he says, 'I trust you've had a good night out on the town.'

'I have, Hugo Reynard,' I retort. 'I trust your evening has also been enjoyable.'

Callie smiles differently for him than she does for me. She performs it. 'You see Hugo, she's still every inch the smart-ass little hippy chick.'

'I can see that. And looking very lovely in that blue.'

'Goes with the hair, don't you think?'

They scrutinise me with conspiratorial approval.

I feel like I'm a new car they own.

'Doesn't Callie have an eye for the sartorial, Jude? She chose this one for me.' He smooths his tight-fitting paisley shirt for inspection. 'She has quite the knack.'

'Yes,' I murmur, 'it's *one* of the things she's good at.'

Callie positions herself behind me to regard Hugo, linking both arms around my waist and resting her cheek against my hair. Traces of his cologne come through her perfume as she nestles into me.

'Don't we make a lovely couple?' Her tone is coquettish.

His lip curves. 'Can I join in?'

I know I'm glaring. I'm not up for anything with him. I feel the shake of her head as she lifts her chin from my shoulder.

'This one's all mine. No sharing.' There's a forced lightness in her tone, but I can tell she means business. 'You two don't get to fuck each other. She doesn't even get to so much as flirt with you, or anyone else for that matter,' she continues. 'She's off limits.'

He's suddenly less affable. 'As I said earlier, I've got my own affairs to deal with.' He looks at Callie coldly. 'I'll leave you two to yourselves for a while.'

Callie's demeanour changes. She steps away from me and grabs his lapel. 'Why can't you tell me who it is?'

Hugo detaches himself and pushes her arm away roughly. 'You don't need to know everything, Callie. That's not part of the agreement.'

She stares hard at him and I can't tell what she's thinking. Her breathing is heavy.

I take her hand. 'Leave it,' I say very quietly. 'Let him go.'

Hugo's face is rigid with things not said. Callie mirrors him.

As he leaves, he says, 'I'll be back for more clothes. Maybe tomorrow.'

In the bedroom she's different from usual. All pretence of gentleness gone. Biting hard, digging in her nails, holding me down too forcefully. And what she wants me to do to her freaks me out. She wants me to tie her up. Bind her by the wrists so it hurts.

'Is this what Hugo does?' I say, fingering the silk scarves that she's lain on the pillow. They are soft in my hands.

She rolls onto her belly. 'Choke me with a scarf. Pull it tight. Kneel on my back. Fucking hurt me.'

The scarf finds its own voice between my fingers. Like it wants to do it. It's a siren song, a black flood inside me that longs to know everything this dark world can show me.

I rear up and back away. This is nowhere that I want to go. This is nothing I could ever do.

But she does.

They do.

'I *asked* you . . . is this what he does?'

She twists to look at me across her shoulder. She says nothing, but I know it is.

In the bathroom, the pink cough mixture is exactly where Lauren said it would be. I drink straight from the squat bottle until I think I've swallowed enough.

Slamming the door, I'm out on the streets. Empty. No cars or people. I'm full of anger and confusion. She wants me to fuck her like he does. She wants to lie with her face away from me. She wants me to be Hugo.

And Hugo likes to choke her.

As I'm walking, I think about the feel of silk stretched taut across my palms. I think about the strength it takes to cut off air from the lungs. I think about silk stretched tight around a neck and the moment that the light snaps into dark.

16

Nel

As the evening has worn on the silence between me and Simon has become heavier, his look more dismissive. It's like being far out on a windless sea, with your boat slowly sinking from a wee insidious, unfindable leak. I don't love him, I don't even like him. And it's pretty clear that he doesn't like me either.

He made a phone call earlier. Just out of my hearing. Out of the blue he has to get back to Birmingham. Something urgent, but not quite describable. When I asked what it was, he waved his hand and his eyes darted to the side. 'Just stuff,' he said.

He's packing his things up to leave early in the morning. He's not laughing and talking loudly anymore. He's quiet. Strained, even. Not looking at me. Not talking.

'Si?'

'What?' He rolls up a shirt.

'Tell me about the bangle.'

'Tell you about the bangle? What the fuck are you on?'

His reaction is out of all proportion. He throws down the shirt and looks at me fiercely.

I stay calm and try to keep my voice steady. 'You're seeing someone. I know you are. The girl who made that bangle. What's her name? Trish. The *really fucking talented* one.'

He stares at me. Silent. Thinking things that I don't want him to say.

I shake my head. 'You know what, though? I don't give a shit anymore. We're over. Go and be with her. I'm finished with you.'

His face goes taut and red. 'You're fucking finished with me?'

He doesn't shout, he hisses, and kicks his bag so hard that all his possessions burst out of it. 'Who the *fuck* do you think you are?'

A panic starts in the pit of my stomach.

He grabs my throat and pushes me backward, fingers pinching the breath out of me. 'I'm finishing with *you*, you fucking stupid bitch. I only came up here to do you the courtesy of dumping you face to face. Give you a nice time before I leave you. Then *you* suddenly decide that you're dumping *me*? Are you kidding me!'

He folds his hand so that the finger knuckles are like a solid wedge and stabs it into my ribs. Intense, focussed pain. He draws back and searches my face for submission, then does the same to the tops of my arms. Does it in all the places he knows. He is an expert.

I roll up. Silent. Endure it. Offer him my shoulders and back to protect the ribs already pock-marked with bruises. Bruise upon bruise. As usual there is no screaming. No shouting. Sudden silent violence. Gen and Viktor talking calmly downstairs, Sid listening to the radio in his room, Michael coughing in the stairwell.

I'm face down on the floor as Simon steps over me and heads to the adjoining bathroom. I roll onto my hands and knees and drag myself onto the bed. I am tender with pain. I can see the bruises on the tops of my thighs, feel the ones on my ribs, arms and back. It's worse where they sit on top of the older ones. I can barely remember when there were no bruises.

He comes back from the bathroom to collect his razor; he always shaves before he goes to bed as well as in the morning. He's meticulous about the contour of his beard. He likes it sharp as a pencil line drawn with a ruler. I stare up at him feeling empty. He looks straight back.

'This is what we're telling people, OK? I dumped you because of Trish. That's the truth anyway, isn't it? That's what you'll tell them.'

It's not a question. It's a statement. It's a command that he expects to have obeyed.

I shake my head. 'I don't care Simon. As long as I'm shot of you, you can say what you like.'

He's thinking about hitting me again. I know the look. Fear makes me cower, but I still manage to say, 'If you touch me, I'll yell out loud, and I'll show them. This time I will.'

That infuriates him. He steps in as close as he can. 'You keep your fucking mouth shut.'

All I can look at is the safety razor he's wagging in my face. It's made of dull white plastic and is a ridiculous weapon. This is what he's reduced to and he can't frighten me anymore.

'Do you really want Viktor to know what you've done to

me?' I say, just above my breath. 'Do you think Gen would stay quiet about that? She'd tell all of those lecturers you're trying so hard to impress. Everyone would know, Simon. Your name would be mud. Touch me one more time and I'll tell them.'

His expression says he knows I'm as good as my word.

'And stop waving that stupid plastic razor at me, you look like a half-wit.'

He turns his attention to the thing in his hand and seems to understand how absurd he appears. It stings his pride and inflames his anger, but I know he won't have the balls to hit me again.

In one last masquerade of power, he throws down the razor and grabs me by the hair to make me look at him. 'You remember this. You brought all of this on yourself. You always provoke me. I'm sick to death of your selfishness, your whining. Your fucking hysteria. No one would blame me if they knew what I had to put up with . . . and give me the fucking engagement ring. It's mine.'

I tear it off my finger and sling it across the floor. 'Fuck you, Simon.'

We watch it scudder to a halt beneath the window. He releases me and scrambles over the varnished floorboards to scoop it up. Opening the window, he lobs the bauble out with all his might. His satisfaction is laughable.

He returns to the bathroom, banging the door shut. Pulling myself over to the window, I open it wider for air. Coldness is like clarity. I'm not crying. I don't even want to. He is what he always has been. He's never going to change. What he's been doing to me is humiliating, and I don't want anyone to know, but if I have to, I'll tell the fucking world. Tomorrow he will go, and I'll never see him again. I only have to endure him until then.

He says I'm hysterical.

Whenever a woman protests a man's behaviour, she's called hysterical. Like my father with my mother. How the sweet Jesus did I end up picking a man like Dad? A weak man, a cruel, spineless man like my dad. There's something in Simon's voice. Something in his hands I never saw before. I recognise it now. Simon wearing my father's face, holding dead things in his fists. My father with a tiny body in his hand. I remember it all. I was nine, dressed in a woollen coat with a velvet collar. White cotton gloves on, ready to go to Sunday school. Daffodils drooped in a vase on the kitchen sill whilst upstairs my mother was making beds.

Through the kitchen window I saw the shed door being jostled outward. My dad came out with a strange expression on his face. His starched shirtsleeves were pinned tidily below his elbows by springy metal garters, and I wondered what he was doing in the shed on a Sunday. He never did his gardening on a Sunday.

I'd made a bed for Blackie in a box next to the mower. She was going to have puppies soon. I couldn't keep them, I knew that, but I wanted to see them before they got given away. I liked puppies. I'd always wanted one. I used to sit by myself in the airing cupboard singing, *How much is that doggie in the window, the one with the waggledy tail?* I would sing it so quietly that I barely heard it myself, all the while warming myself on the water cylinder in the darkness.

My father was shaking his hands, as though to rid them of

something as he headed down the steps to the kitchen. He looked at me, glassily, and pulled a tin bucket out from under the sink.

'Stay here,' he said, pushing past me into the hallway. 'Maggie,' he stood on the swirling patterns of the carpet and called up the stairs, 'why is Penelope still here?'

My mother's disembodied voice came from a bedroom. 'Hasn't she gone? Penelope, why've you no gone?'

I fingered my plaited pigtails, each one constricted with a brown rubber band. 'I'm going *now*.' The electric clock above the kitchen table told me I was right. 'Nine o'clock. I always go at nine o'clock.'

My father was filling the pail in the sink. I remember him flinging his arm out towards me in alarm. Fear made me scuttle away. Standing on the front step staring down at my smart white school sandals. I didn't close the door. Something was not right. I didn't know what it was.

'There's eight of the damned wee things.'

'No need to swear, Douglas,' my mother replied. 'Deal with it. No mess please.'

Through the open doors of the silent house, I could hear the bucket swilling as my father carried it from the sink. I wavered. I had to go back and look.

When I got to the shed, I could hear high-pitched squealing and there was scuffling and splashing. At first, I could only see my father's back and hear his heavy breathing as he crouched on one knee. Behind him, Blackie whimpered on a stained blanket. I stepped to one side to see better. My father stood up, a dead white puppy, hanging dripping in one hand.

*

Tight-mouthed, Simon comes back into the room. He throws the bedspread onto the floor and gestures his head towards it before climbing into bed to face away from me.

I kneel and pull the bedspread around my shoulders. I would rather sleep on the floor than lie with him even one more night.

I sing in my head as I stretch out on these boards trying to find some comfort, feeling the bruises forming.

17

Toto

After leaving Callie's house, I crash through Whetheridge Common with my head full of unexpected rage. Lauren's magical tincture melted my brain like she promised. Except I'm not happy. It was supposed to unsharpen my reality, but it's done the opposite.

I strip off my boots and socks to wade along a stream, following its stone bed through the deep woods in my bare feet. The freezing water refocuses me. I've been wandering for hours. Wondering what to do and where to go. The effects of the cough mixture are lessening. I'm not sure, but I don't think I'm hallucinating anymore.

I hear the junkies fighting and shouting in their tarpaulin camp and the glow in the sky tells me they've got a fire going. It roars like it's out of control and sparks fly over the trees, but I'm full of such turmoil that I don't care if they burn the world down. I keep thinking about the things Callie did tonight. She bit my thigh till it bled. It hurt so much that it made me want to hurt her in equal measure. I held a scarf in my hands and nearly choked her. I wanted to do it. I'm chewing the inside of my cheek as I watch the space between the horizon and the stars, hoping for an army of owls to erupt from the woods to suffocate the city in feathers and murdered mice. Is this shame that I'm feeling?

I keep walking along the stream until it meets a path that forms a bridge. This is the way through the town green belt that'll get me to the motorway. If I keep going, I could just hitch back to Leeds for a day or two. Get my brain straight. Tomorrow's signing-on day at the dole office anyway, so instead of letting Callie drive me, I could get there under my own steam. I'm sick of asking permission. Fuck that. She's told me what her rules are. Well these are mine. I do what I want.

Wiping my feet dry with my coat, I put my boots back on as my teeth chatter. If any fucker out here wants to kill me, just let him try. I'm surprised because I'm crying. Thinking about Hugo and silk scarfs and people who say they love you but don't. I'm pulling on armour. Pushing everything away. Trying to turn myself from the white dog in the tarot card into something smarter: a fox or a wolf, or even a black-furred bear. I need to toughen up.

I make up my mind. I'm going to hitch back to Chapeltown. Even though the missing girl they talked about on the radio still hasn't been found, I'll be fine because I always am.

Reality seems to be stabilising. Time is settling down and the sweating has stopped.

On the slip road to the motorway as day breaks, I refuse the first lift because the travelling salesman looks sleazy. The next vehicle to stop is a cement mixer and I accept the ride because the concrete will have to get to its destination before it sets and the lorry won't be able to wander off course for other agendas. The driver is balding, with bags under his eyes, and he says he needs company to keep him awake for the last part of his run. I have to punch him in the arm at least four times before we get to Leeds. It is fun to feel the vehicle begin to drift as his head droops, and satisfying to see him jump bolt upright after each of my blows.

'Thank you,' he says every time.

The fridge in our kitchen judders to life like an abruptly woken animal. It contains a half-full bottle of sour milk, which I pour down the sink. I'll need to go to the corner shop. There's nothing here to eat, but at least I've got money to buy something after queueing up at the Employment Exchange. I really hate signing on. Today the clerk looked at me like I was shit, pushing six pounds and fifty pence under the grill and overseeing my signature like he was a skinny bespectacled Mr Bumble and I was Oliver fucking Twist.

Some of the others from the Alternative School were signing on too, including Denny. She looked rough, like she'd been out on the town for days. When I asked what was up, she shook her head and her voice was croaky. Apparently, there was trouble whilst I was away. The kids burned down the pet hutches. Luckily, Bandana Jim saw the fire before it spread and they managed to extinguish it, but Denny said Maria was really cut up about it. Then she asked if I was coming back to the school soon, and I had to think before I answered. I like playing with the kids and making them laugh, but what

actual use am I to them? I said something like, 'Yeah, probably.'
Denny shrugged and mentioned a party tonight, over in
Headingly somewhere. I'm tempted to go with her. There's
always free booze at parties.

I'd like to get trashed.

That thought makes me realise that I think like a pauper.
It really rattles me. For the first time, I worry that my life
might always be like this, that when these boots wear out, I
won't be able to afford new ones.

Fuck. Will I always be living in shit rooms in the shit parts
of shit cities?

I throw that thought off, because at least I've got cash now.
That's the great thing about dole day: for about three hours I
feel as though I could buy anything in the world. All I want
at this moment, however, is a carton of milk. I check that
there's enough coffee in the jar and then take myself off to
the shop. It's late morning and the streets are quiet. Most of
the prostitutes and drug dealers are sleeping now. Even the
stray dogs look relaxed, as though they know that the stone
throwers, kickers and stick wielders aren't about.

The bloke in the shop gives me a nod of recognition. 'All
right love? Me and Mrs Patel was wondering where you was,
wasn't we, Priya? Haven't seen you for a while.'

His wife adjusts her sari. 'Missed you coming in for your
pint of milk with your nice polite smile.'

I pick up a container of milk and put the money on the
counter. 'Nice to see you again.' I lift the cardboard carton and
wave it at them as I leave. 'Best milk in Chapeltown.'

She laughs, but he looks puzzled.

*

On the way past the brothel, the door opens and one of the girls sweeps dust out onto the pavement. Another slips out behind her and shakes a rug. Janice is carrying an armful of cardboard as she heads for the dustbin.

'Eh up, Jude!'

'All right Janice?'

She stuffs the rubbish into the metal bin and tries to shove the lid on. It balances on top of the protruding cardboard. 'I'm not too bad, queen. How's yourself? Have you been away or what?'

She takes out two cigarettes, lights both, and gives me one. 'I owe you. You was a good friend that time.'

We sit on the kerb in front of my house and smoke as though we've never had a fag before. Her lip is healing, like it's been split. She looks at me sidelong and leans in as though to tell me a secret.

'I don't want to say nowt, but if you're not careful someone's going to break into your place. It don't look like there's no one there. I'm telling you, if you're going to go off like that, you need to leave a light on in the passage. Put a radio on in the kitchen or something. I've already warned a couple of lads off. They're only scared because they think I'm telling them from Tommy. But that won't last.'

As I'm reaching out my keys to go back inside, I notice Tommy coming out of the brothel. He stops to look for something in his pocket and his eye catches mine when he looks up. He stares at me for a moment before casting his gaze to Janice, then back to me again. She doesn't notice him; she's concentrating on taking a long draw on her cigarette. He seems lost in thought as he goes back inside.

Janice sits on the dirty kerb looking up at me, weighing

something up. 'Will you be around for a while, queen? I might have summat for you.'

I nod. 'Yeah, I'll be here most of the day I reckon.'

She heaves herself upright and brushes the back of her tight skirt down. 'All right. I'll be back over in a minute.'

'I'll get the kettle on.' I say.

She scurries across the street with her head down.

It isn't long before she's back, knocking on the front door in a series of rapid taps. She pushes past me in a rush and heads straight for the kitchen.

'Are you OK?' I follow close behind.

Pulling out one of the chairs, she sets herself heavily at the table, breathless and a bit pink in the face. 'Sit down Jude, cock. I've got you a present.'

I try to imagine what it might be as I hand her a mug of tea. She stares at me until I draw out the chair next to her and comply. Her hands are shaking as she reaches into her bra to draw out a folded envelope, which she lays down directly in front of me. Whatever is in it, is small. The envelope seems to have no substance.

'Go on,' she says. 'It's for you.'

I look at her face, trying to work out what it could possibly be. She nods at the envelope again, so I pick it up and unfold it. A white tablet slips out. It's speed.

'Where's this from?'

Janice looks all around her as though even in this small kitchen, someone might overhear her. 'Tommy sells them to the punters and in the nightclubs up town. I know where he stores it, and I've been pinching a few to sell for myself. There's a lot of young lads around here who love this stuff.'

She is glassy-eyed, and her face is still red from excitement.

'It's for you. For nowt. You was really kind to me that time.'

I stare at the amphetamine tab sitting in my palm. I don't know how to tell her, but after last night's pink-medicine trip, I'm in no mood for speed. Not that I've ever liked it that much: it makes me anxious, and then unbelievably depressed, like I'm the most stupid person who ever lived. Janice looks so happy though. Her eyes are shining like she's given me a birthday present.

I simulate an expression of gratitude. 'Wow, thank you.'

'Students like drugs, don't they? I knew you'd like it.' She has stopped trembling and takes a quick mouthful of tea. As I shove the tab in my pocket, she nods at me as though I've replied to her. She seems to be talking herself into feeling safe about it. 'He don't know. He's got so much fucking stuff he don't even know what he's got. Don't worry about me, Jude, cock. I've always been quicker than he has.'

I look at the scar on her cheek and her broken lip and wonder if that's true.

After she leaves. I put the tab of speed on the fireplace. I won't be wanting it. I consider the option of hitching back to Sheffield today. I don't like the thought of somebody breaking in while I'm here on my own. After what Janice told me, I'll be awake all night holding a kitchen knife if I stay. Maybe I should go over to the Alternative School. Denny and Maria would let me crash at the rectory. I could go back to Sheffield in the morning.

I drink the rest of the milk, scrunch up the carton and throw it in the bin. After switching on the hall light and the kitchen radio, I get a change of underwear and a few other bits and pieces and set off through the backyard, reasoning that if no one sees me go out the front door, they might not know that I've left. On the way out, I notice that the window to the kitchen doesn't latch properly. There's nothing I can do about that now.

Down the narrow alley behind our house, kids run in and out of the tiny yards that back onto it from either side. An old man brings his bin outside his gate and tuts at the mess all around us.

'Look at that,' he says. 'This ginnel is a bloody disgrace. Never seen an alleyway as bad. Some bugger's dumped another mattress. We'll have all them bloody prossies doing the dirty on them. There's enough used jonnies around here at it is.' He scowls at a spunk-filled condom tied in a knot next to his foot. 'Used to be a nice place. Church-going.'

I nod a kind of neutral agreement and he looks at me more closely. 'It's no place for a lass like you round here.' He shuffles his bin into position. 'No place for anybody.'

I cut through to the street, looking back towards our house as I cross the road. Tommy stands outside the brothel with his legs planted wide. He has a cigar stub in his mouth and he's looking at the driver of a shiny black Vauxhall parked at the kerbside. The man in the car puts a wad of money into Tommy's hands. A group of skinny teenage boys, wearing clothes that don't fit, scrutinise the pimp surreptitiously. He knows, but he doesn't care. No one's going to steal from him, no one's going to snitch. He counts the money ostentatiously and looks around with satisfaction as he puts it into his inside pocket.

18

Nel

Simon hops into the passenger seat of the Citroen, never once looking back. He's all forced laughter and loud good-byes, eager to be on his way, slapping the dashboard in his impatience. Viktor sits beside him, a picture of bewildered discomfort. He occupies himself by opening the glovebox, pushing the contents around as though he fears something important is missing.

The last thing I hear Simon say is, 'OK, Viktor my man, get me to that motorway.'

Gen clenches my hand in hers as the car turns the corner. 'Are you all right?' she whispers as we head back into the house.

I don't know what to tell her.

She has no idea, as she ushers me inside, that her palm is pressing on the most tender part of my body. He's gone. Relief and bewilderment come in turns. He was as pretty as a girl when we first met. Delicate hands. Gentle eyes. The opposite of what I see in him now. When did wanting him turn into fearing him? Why did I stay when he's given me nothing but spite for so long? Each feeling draws back and hits me again and again like an incoming tide.

I have this need to walk. I can't stop. Around the common the birds are flocking. A *murmuration of starlings*. Their wings mutter patterns of panic. Rising out of the trees as a billowing configuration of moving black dots, rising and dispersing in the early cold. They seem unreal, or perhaps it's me that isn't real. The flock is as distant from the world as I feel right now. It wheels as though fearful, each bird is lost and clinging to the one beside it. An anxious sound like Chinese whispers – *we're lost, who knows the way?* No one. No one knows the way.

Yesterday somebody thought they owned me, but today I belong only to myself. Nothing's the same. There's no purpose in the things I did before. No point in the teaching course I was taking for Simon's benefit. All my reasons are gone. I feel like a moth inside a pupa, everything melting and reforming into a new, unknown version of me.

My head is spinning, and I have to hold on to something to steady myself. Grabbing the back of a park bench and slowing my breathing, I search for some kind of stability. I pick up a twig, hang on to its solidity and put it in my pocket: something constant; something real. I won't disintegrate.

The outer edge of Whetheridge Common is an anchor. Everything on it is orderly. The benches are painted in stolid green gloss, the flowerbeds are planted with French marigolds. All the tracks are well swept and the rubbish buckets are fixed at appropriate intervals. I'll walk around its edges while I try to find a stable place inside me.

Mum and Dad are surprised to see me. On the television in the corner of their ornament-cluttered sitting room, comedians exchange double-entendres to the sound of canned laughter as they both wait for me to speak. I've never made a habit of showing them my feelings, and I don't start now.

Concentrating on the electric fire in the mock-brick fireplace, I tell them, in a very level voice, 'I've finished with Simon and I'm packing in the teaching course.'

Wee lines form around Mum's mouth. She's embroidering a place mat with field mice and flowers. The needle between her thumb and forefinger flashes as she turns to Dad to gauge his reaction.

A flush creeps up his neck. 'What do you mean? Just because that big nancy boy's gone aff and left ye, it disnae mean ye gie up on a good career. Use your damn brains.'

Mum finds her voice. 'Your father's right, Penelope.'

'I don't want to be a teacher.' I try to stay calm, 'Can I not make you understand that? I barely like adults, never mind hordes of kids. How does it make any sense for a person like me to do a job like that? I know it's what you wanted for me, but I've tried it. And I hate it.'

Dad props himself up on the arms of his chair. 'Thinking only of yourself as usual, never a thought for how your parents feel.'

I close my eyes. Words splutter out of me. 'I'm not doing that any more. I'm not bloody doing things just to keep you two happy. Nothing I do ever makes you two sodding happy, anyway!'

'Don't you swear at your mother.'

'I'm not swearing at my mother. I'm swearing at you, and you might as well get used to it, because it's likely I'll do it again.'

My father's face gets pinker as he throws his television glasses down and heaves himself up to shout at Mum. 'D'ye see? That's how she talks to me. Is that how y've brought her up. To speak to me like that?'

The slammed door reverberates behind him.

'Look, you've upset him!'

'He needs upsetting.'

Mum returns to her needlework as though nothing's happened, which is the way she deals with things when they get too difficult. She pulls a mustard-coloured thread from its skein and squints to thread her needle. 'Will I make your room up, hen?'

She's struggling to get the silk through the eye. Why is there never enough light in here? Why can they not just open the curtains? Every time I return to this house it's like being strangled. But now I've told them, I can just leave and start breathing.

I drain my cup. 'No, I'll get myself off to Jo's and leave you be.'

'Will you no stay for your tea? Don't worry about your father, he'll calm down soon enough.'

I survey the clutter of ceramic Scottie dogs and tartan place mats, and all the while my father makes his presence felt by banging cupboard doors in the kitchen. I remember a boiled heart, and a drowned puppy, and shake my head.

'No. I'll be on my way.'

It's a long bus ride to Jo and Hank's place. As I arrive, Jo's dad emerges out of their door, buttoning up his grey gaberdine mackintosh. 'Ey up, Penelope, love.' He steps back to avoid me. 'I nearly bumped right into you.'

'Hullo, Mr Salvin.' I sound like the child I was when I first met him. 'How are you?'

Hank bobs his head around the door. 'Is that you, Nel?'

Mr Salvin unfolds his flat cap and wiggles it about until it's snug on his balding head. 'We've just popped in to see our lass and the lad. Taking the new dog for a walk.'

'Come on in.' Hank attempts to usher me in at the same moment that Jo's mum endeavours to get out.

'Oops,' she says cheerfully. 'Don't mind me. I'll soon be out of your way.'

Even in her bulky woollen coat, she doesn't prove much of an obstacle. She's a petite woman who looks like the Queen in a hat like an upturned chrysanthemum. Tugging on its lead behind her is an unwilling miniature poodle.

'In't he lovely?' She leans down to pat him. 'We got him from the Dog's Home not long ago. Just brung him round to show our Joanne. He's lovely, in't he, Joanne?'

'Aye, he is. If that's what you like.'

Mrs Salvin has a proud smile, 'Our Joanne's house is getting so nice, don't you think, Penelope? It's lovely in't it? Nobody could have a lovelier house than what our Joanne's got.'

'Aye,' says Jo's dad. 'They've done right well have these two.'

Their living room comes straight off the street, with only a doormat to mark the transition. A small fireplace has a bucket of coals next to it, and the couch is set under the window opposite the sizable colour television.

'Is that new?' I nod at it as I hang my coat on the back of the door.

'Had a lot of overtime this last month. Thought we might as well get a colour one.' Hank makes himself comfortable on the two-seater sofa, 'Got a phone now too.' He points proudly in the direction of the sideboard. 'What d'you reckon? Looks like something out of *Lost in Space*.'

It does. The angular red handpiece sits over the rotary dial and it's a thin and mean-looking piece of modern design.

'Very nice.' I wipe my hand across my face.

'You're looking a bit peaky, petal.' Jo observes me closely. 'Are you all right?'

'Aye,' I say in an offhand manner. 'I'm fine. Really, really fine.'

'Really, *really* fine?' Jo lifts her chin and narrows her eyes.

I can't work out how to tell her. It's all too big. I need a bit more time.

'Ach, I'm sorry. Bit of a headache.'

'You've got a headache! I've had me Mam here all afternoon with that little dog. Don't know what was worse, the talking or the yapping.'

I settle myself down on the sofa, 'Your mum's not so bad.'

'Aye,' says Jo. 'I know.'

'Are you stopping for tea?' Hank enquires, 'We was thinking of having fish and chips.'

I breathe in, like a sigh in reverse. 'Go on then. Why not?'

'That's it,' he says. 'Stay the night too, if you want. The bed's made upstairs.'

He has no idea how much that means to me right now.

He looks puzzled when I say, 'Fuck yes. Thank you, Hank.'

*

We take the carry-out meal onto their wee patio and perch around a cast-iron pub table with matching chairs. The smell of hot tar wafts into the yard from over a high steel fence.

'What's behind there?' I indicate the wall with a tilt of my head.

Jo barely looks up. 'Roadworks Department. They're there all hours. Ian next door says it gets even worse later in the year.'

Unlike me, Jo's an extrovert. She talks easily to people and they happily chat back. She judges no one and nothing ever phases her. Joanne Salvin-Hanks has always known what she wants in life, and that's chiefly not to be poor and never to have to worry about money for the gas meter.

Bundling chips into a slice of white bread, she pushes it into her mouth, as Hank struggles with the oversized piece of hake burning his lips. Catching his eye, she laughs and it's the same laugh she had when we first met. Despite her dyed hair, her turquoise eyeshadow and her coral lipstick, I still see her the way she was when we were eleven. She doesn't alter. She is always solidly herself. Today that's what I need. I'm hanging on to it.

'Is it just me, or is it getting colder?' Hank gathers up the paper and polystyrene trays that the fish and chips came in and we move inside.

'So, when are you going back up to Leeds?' I ask Jo as she flicks on the kettle. Looking across at Hank, she calculates. 'Well, there's no rush, is there. I know term's started, but we haven't got any lectures or anything this term, just essays, so Sunday probably. Hank'll be taking me up. You'll be wanting a lift, won't you . . . for that job interview you've up there?'

I look at her blankly.

She prompts me. 'At that girls' school in Headingly.'

I'd forgotten about that. I never even replied to the letter.

Jo is busy looking for teabags as she speaks. 'I'm falling all over myself, trying to get ready for that one in Attercliffe. I know it's a rough school, but God, I hope I get it. It would be perfect, being so close to where Hank works.'

I stare at her from their couch.

'What's up, flower?' she murmurs, 'You look peculiar.'

It's time to do it. Time to tell them. I take a deep breath, then run at it, like jumping into a swimming pool. 'Simon's got another girl. I've chucked him.'

I can't bring myself to look at them. I stare at the floor and wait for the silence to end. When I look up, Jo is slowly shaking her head from side to side. 'Well, I never liked him. I never said owt, but he's too bloody full of himself, and he's horrible to you sometimes. The way he talks. You're well shot.'

Hank goes quietly to the fridge, brings out a bottle of cider and pours a glass for me. 'Get that down you. Don't waste anymore time thinking about that poncey little shit. He's not worth it.'

'Cheers to that.' I raise a toast and we clink glasses full of sweet fizzing alcohol. 'So, are you sure it's OK if I stay over? It feels weird at Gen's. Simon's gone, but Viktor is such a big mate of his. I feel wrong being there. And I can't stand being at my mum and dad's. I'm sorry.'

'Course you can. You can stay anytime you want. You know that. Drink that cider and watch *Coronation Street* with us on our new TV.'

19

Toto

'Jude!' Denny throws the door to the Rectory wide open, 'What's going on?'

'I've got drink.' I hoist a six-pack of cheap lager high, like a trophy. 'I thought we could go to that party tonight.'

She steps back, giving me space to enter. I manoeuvre around a stack of bagged groceries to slip my coat off. 'Can I crash here after?'

'Sure.' Her expression changes as my clothes are revealed. 'What the fuck are you wearing?'

The garments Callie bought are the worse for wear after my night in the woods but, even dishevelled, they're clearly not my usual style. I get self-conscious, worried I look like some kind of uptight office clerk on her way to a Saturday night disco at the Locarno.

'Did you have those on when I saw you at the dole office?'

'Yes . . . under my coat.'

'You look weird in those, man. I don't like to say, but you do.'

'I know. Do you want this lager or not?'

'Fuck, yeah. Help me carry this shopping through, will you? Maria's in the kitchen.'

Maria is pinning notices on a corkboard covered in hand-printed notices and political posters. She greets me cheerily, but focuses disapprovingly on the booze. 'Starting already?'

Denny tugs on the ring pull. 'Yeah, me and Jude are ready to rock and roll.'

'Want one?' I offer a can to Maria.

'I don't really drink.'

It feels like a reprimand. I take too big a gulp from my can to hide my embarrassment. Froth prickles the inside of my nose. I can't keep the fizzy liquid contained in my mouth. Wiping foam off my chin with the back of my hand, I look around. 'Nice set-up.'

They're very organised. Stickers punctuate a wall calendar. The gold star on every Friday highlights the importance of the HOUSE MEETING, and a marker-pen notice directs that ALL MILK BOTTLES MUST BE RINSED AND PLACED IN THE CRATE.

I help Denny by handing her groceries as she loads the shopping into overhead cupboards. 'How many people live here, again?'

'Ten,' Maria says. 'I mean, not everyone volunteers at the school, like we do, but there are plenty of rooms. It's free . . . and we've known each other a long time, so . . .'

'Were you up at the university together?'

'Yes, we all met at the Anarchist Society.'

A stainless steel pot makes bubbling noises on the stove.

'Who's cooking tonight?' Maria lifts the lid and Denny takes a cursory glance at one of the rotas.

'Bandana Jim.' Denny opens a cupboard to look for alternatives. 'There's some baked beans,' she says. 'We could always have those. Do you want some, Jude?'

The gassy lager is filling me up. 'No, I'm not hungry.' I drain my can and look around for a bin to put it in.

'OK,' Maria says to Denny, 'I'll go up and check on your daughter. Why don't you take Jude into the drawing room? It's more comfortable in there. You can relax. Light a fire or something.'

'It's really warm today, Maria.'

'Fires are always nice.'

They have a weird little stand-off until Denny agrees.

After Maria goes upstairs, I point at the rotas and rosters on the wall and whisper in fear of being overheard. 'Are you on any of these committees? There are thousands of them!'

Denny furrows her brow. 'Um . . . I think I was once, but I always forgot to go.'

I'm going to laugh. I push it down. 'Was it the Christmas Decoration Committee? There must be a Christmas Decoration Committee, surely.'

'Don't let Maria hear you say that. She can't cope with people taking the piss.'

'I'm asking *you*. Was it the Christmas Decoration Committee or did you decide Christmas was a bourgeois, individualist, capitalist festival and scrap it? Come on, confess, you know you can tell me.'

We are choking with suppressed laughter, watching the door in case Maria returns.

As Denny lights the fire in the drawing room as instructed, I notice that they've got a phone. It occupies a small table along with a notebook and a coin tin. I think about Callie. I wonder if I should ring her, tell her where I am? Shit, it's only one night and I'll probably be back by tomorrow evening. She'll be fine. Let her dance to my tune for a change.

'Do you fancy a joint?' I perch on the edge of an armchair by the hearth. 'I'll skin up if you want.'

Denny nods as though I've offered her something as ordinary as a digestive biscuit, opens her pack of cards and shuffles.

'Come and do tarot with me.'

She lays out the cards across the table in the shape of a cross and mumbles automatically. *'This behind you, this before you, this above you, this below you.'*

'Are you doing a reading for yourself?'

'Yes. As a warm-up.'

'Don't read for me,' I say. 'I don't want to know the future.'

I remember my convent school and learning biblical texts from the Book of Leviticus. Our form teacher, Sister John the Apostle, wrote *A fortune-teller shall be stoned to death* on the board and seemed to be looking straight at me as she placed the chalk back on her desk.

I smile to myself. *Stoned to death.* Sounds good to me.

Listening to cards being turned, I skin up the spliff. I'm pleased with how well I've crafted it and get comfortable, lying back in my chair to smoke.

My foot knocks into a tattered paperback of Greek mythology as I stretch. I pick it up and turn it in my hands. It's called the *Oresteia* and I vaguely remember it as a bloodthirsty story of family murder. It falls open where the spine has cracked. Drawing deep on the joint, I read about Agamemnon who sacrificed his eldest daughter to get a fair wind for war. Somebody has scribbled indecipherable things in the margins. *Brutal and insufferable*, are the only words that are clear.

'Jude?' Denny is looking at me expectantly. She must have asked me something. I study her face, searching for clues.

She indicates the tarot cards, 'What's your *significator*? Queen of Cups or Page of Cups?'

I'm emphatic. 'Look, I don't want a reading. I don't believe in it for all that, and anyway, even if I did, I wouldn't want to know.'

She nods. 'I don't either. It's something to do. I like the pictures.' She goes ahead and deals anyway.

The first card is the Tower. It predicts catastrophe. A flaming grey turret sits on the pinnacle of a bleak mountain. Lightning strikes a roof shaped like a golden papal crown. Two figures plummet towards the ground. One is a man with a crimson cloak. The other is a fair woman in red shoes. Flames follow them on their descent into ice-filled chasms.

Denny flips the card in the hope I haven't seen it.

I scowl at her. 'I've got the Tower, for fuck sake.'

She looks guilty, as though she personally made that happen. 'Look, it doesn't mean anything. They're just archetypes, aren't they? They don't tell the future or anything. I don't think so. I mean I do it, but I don't really believe it. I think they tell us about what's inside ourselves. That kind of thing.'

I'm not sure what she's talking about. I don't want to know what's inside me. The Tower is a really bad card, that's the point right now. I take a long pull on the joint before handing it over to her.

Denny quickly reveals the next card. It's the World. In the centre of an oval laurel wreath, a partially naked woman is dancing. Her hair is the crude yellow used in every card in this pack. She is draped in a swirling cloth that covers her belly and crotch and she is carrying a baton in each hand. Bare feet step lightly. Four disembodied heads sit in each corner, the symbols of the Evangelists: Matthew the Angel, Mark the Lion, Luke the Bull and John the Eagle.

'That's a good one.' Denny is happier about this card than the last one. 'It says here, look, in the instruction book . . .'

She tries to make me read it, but I won't, so she recites: 'Reward, completion, cosmic consciousness; also change, travel.'

I don't want to engage with her on this anymore. I concentrate on a passage in the *Oresteia*, 'That bastard Agamemnon, what a shit! He has his own daughter's throat cut so they can go to war!'

Brutalised girls everywhere you look.

Denny is still focused on the cards. 'What?' she says eventually, trying to catch up with my change of direction. 'Oh yeah, Iphigenia.'

'It says here she was hoist by her ankles like a goat.'

She goes into deep thought and falls silent.

'Hung her from her feet and gagged her to still her screams as they cut her throat.' I pause for emphasis. 'Her *own* father hangs her upside-down and slits her throat. Sacrifices her so he can kidnap a woman who chose to leave him.'

She continues laying out the cards. 'No, you've got that wrong, Helen wasn't *his* girlfriend, she was his brother's. It was all about her uncle and her aunty.'

'It's just as bad. Maybe it's worse. His daughter's an expendable good. Jesus, you wouldn't treat your dog like that!'

Denny looks up from the Tarot. 'What do you expect?'

She becomes engrossed in the cards again.

At the sound of a drawer opening behind us I turn to see Maria rifling through it. She pulls out a bottle of what looks like aspirin and the drawer judders and sticks as she shuts it, making the contents clatter like change in a till.

'The world runs on the random acts of cruel men,' she murmurs. 'Always has, always will.' She glances up and frowns at the window that is very slightly open. 'What's the point of a fire if you leave the window open, Denny?'

There are streams of cobwebs blowing inwards from the edge of the frame. Some of them have clumped together like a net curtain. It reminds me of Miss Haversham's wedding dress, rotting with her wedding feast, gnawed by the teeth of mice. I imagine a horde of rodents with tiny incisors flashing like wet bone. Maria slides the window shut.

'Rosa's not well.' She looks hard at Denny. 'How long have we had this junior aspirin?'

'No idea.' Denny doesn't shift her attention from the reading.

Maria returns upstairs and more cards are exposed as Denny lays my future out across the tablecloth. First, the Hanged Man dangles by one leg from a tree like Iphigenia.

Next, a black-armoured skeleton cuts a swathe across its card. Death leads a procession under a white rose on a black banner and everything falls before him. He tramples kings, bishops, men, women and children beneath the hooves of his horse.

A passage from the Bible comes into my head:

And I looked, and beheld a pale horse: and his name that sat on him was Death.

Out of a thunderous summer sky each of the Riders of the

Apocalypse is idling through the clouds on horses of different colours: a white stallion, a red mare, a black charger, and the pale horse ridden by Death.

But I'm thinking about the red one that I learnt about in a dark room under the embittered eye of a nun:

And there went out another horse that was red: and power was given to him that sat thereon to take peace from the earth, and that they should kill one another: and there was given unto him a great sword . . . and the sun became black as sackcloth of hair, and the moon became as blood.

Closing my eyes, I see the horse and its rider, red with blood; they've ridden through blood, they're soaked in blood. He wears a cloak of children's skins, and the horse is led on a rein by a witch with tiny red eyes. They are walking through a field of hanging corpses. Golden girls hung by a leg, throats gaping.

There's nothing to hide behind.

Death is random and rides a pale horse.

Cruelty is relentless and rides a red horse.

Back upstairs Maria is crooning to Rosa. The sound of her feet on the boards above are a rhythm to go with her lullaby. Denny looks up as though seeing through the ceiling, the trace of a gentle smile on her lips.

I take the end of the joint back and draw on it again, 'Denny? Can I ask you something?'

'You can *ask.*'

'Why do you live here and not the Squat? I mean, the Squat seems more like your kind of place.'

'It's more comfortable here. Maria's here.'

'Are you with Maria? I mean, are you a couple?'

She says nothing. Her mouth twists and the gentleness disappears. She looks sad and stubborn all at once.

I continue. 'Look, I've kind of worked out that Rosa is Jacko's kid. Am I being stupid, but Maria keeps saying things? Is she in love with you?'

Denny suddenly laughs a bitter, quick laugh. 'Maria doesn't love me. She loves Rosa.'

'But what about you? Do you love Maria?'

The question confuses her, she thinks hard. 'I *need* Maria.' She scowls and gets to her feet. 'Come on let's go and eat something. It's too fucking hot in here now with that fire and the window closed. No matter what time of the year it is, Maria always thinks we should have a fucking fire.'

Once in the kitchen, we stop talking as Maria returns carrying Rosa. The two-year-old's face is flushed and she's glassy-eyed. When she sees Denny, she murmurs and points before burying her head under Maria's chin.

'What's wrong, baby?' Maria says. 'Have you got a cold?'

Rosa's small left hand is behind her ear, stroking her own neck. Maria puts her gently into a highchair by the table and gets her some blackcurrant juice.

The toddler pushes the beaker away slowly, as though she knows it will fall over if she does it more energetically.

Maria strokes Rosa's clammy head. 'Your child has the flu.'

'Has she?' Denny puts her baked-bean stained plate in the sink. 'So, will you stay with her then?'

'Well, you're not going to, are you? So, I suppose it has to be me.'

Denny swills the crockery under running water. 'I want to go to this party tonight. That's OK, isn't it?'

For a moment, Maria contemplates her, then in an apparent change of mood, she laughs. 'Yes, it is. Who could stop you anyway?'

Lifting Rosa out of the chair, Maria dances her around the room, crooning softly as the child rubs her own ear, and then her own hair. Leaning back, Rosa is transfixed by the light bulb overhead.

Denny softly sings 'Bella Ciao', an Italian anti-fascist song, as we walk. She played it on a thick, crackling record just before we left. She sings as though I'm not here, as though no one is here; not loud but intense.

'What does it mean?'

She looks at me for a moment. 'Goodbye beautiful girl, goodbye, goodbye, goodbye.'

The streetlights have come on. I didn't want to wear my coat to a party, so I've borrowed one of Denny's old leather jackets. She has three of them, in various states of disintegration. I'm wearing her least favourite. It smells like the inside of a wardrobe, but I like the anarchist star painted in cracked enamel across the back. It looks out of place with the rest of my blue outfit, but I don't care. We have shared two joints and all the lagers. I'm thinking about hardly anything at all.

As we come around a corner the cloying smell of beer escapes through the doors of a rough-looking pub. There's a car parked up on the pavement. A white Ford Zephyr with a bent front bumper and exposed wires around the headlight. I stop short.

Denny says, 'What's up?'

'This car.'

'What about it?'

I dig into my pocket for the remains of an old tobacco wrapper, rip up small pieces of foil and poke them carefully into the lock, prodding them deeper with my fingernail. 'Their key is going to push this into the mechanism and jam it. It will be fucked, and they'll never know how or why.'

She bends down to admire my handiwork. 'Why this car?'

I meticulously wedge in the remainder of the foil. 'When I was hitching, two bastards took me off into the backwoods to try to rape me.'

She draws in her breath and turns her gaze from me, to the vehicle, and back to me again.

'In this Zephyr?'

I nod at the rusty paintwork. 'I couldn't mistake it. They're ex-soldiers. They were in Northern Ireland and shot people on Bloody Sunday.'

She widens her eyes and walks around the car inspecting it.

'You're sure?'

'Yes.'

'They shot people on Bloody Sunday and were going to rape you?'

'I ran for it when they stopped at a junction.' I show her the traces of scrapes on my hand. They've healed over, like biro lines. 'I did that on the road when I rolled out.'

She darts into a garden and comes back with two big stones, one for each of us.

'Come on,' she says, and nods at the car. 'Forget bloody *subtle* . . .'

So, I do. I totally forget *subtle*, and we shatter the headlights, then the side windows. I pull out a jacket from the seat and grind it into a pool of oil in the gutter. Denny smashes the rear lights and the mirrors. With exultant whoops, we simultaneously throw both stones through the windscreen. We do it all so fast, it's like we've been choreographed.

Then we run. It's the second time I've run from that car, but now I'm laughing, I trip and roll in mud, and rip the knee of my smart blue trousers, covering them with dirt.

Getting to my feet, I turn back to see the driver coming out of the pub with his mate behind him. I wait long enough to enjoy the dismay on his face. We dive under low boughs in the adjoining municipal gardens to become invisible. His shouts of rage bounce off trees as he discovers his jacket is torn, and his un-openable car is full of shattered windscreen.

Denny and I run full tilt and she sings another anarchist song at the top of her voice, the Spanish Civil War one that Jim taught the kids at the school, the one they sing at the police whenever they see them. But now Denny changes the words:

> *Ay compañero, Ay compañero.*
> *We're going to fuck the fucking 'Paras',*
> *They're the ones who rape and pillage.*

We duck under branches, tripping, and get up again breathless.

We sing to each other,

> *Smash the Nazis and the Fascists*
> *Ay compañero, Ay compañero.*

By the time we reach the party we are panting, giddy and muddy. The front door of the house stands ajar and light falls onto the stone stoop. This is Jeff's house. Mira's creepy boyfriend, Philip, and a couple of other students that Denny knows live here too. They have a lot of parties.

People lean against the iron railings or sprawl out on the steep steps drinking beer from paper cups. No one looks too closely at us as we move past the room where music is pulsing and on to the kitchen with its table stacked with cheap booze.

Denny grabs two cans of lager, hands me one and rips hers open.

'Tuborg,' she says, reading the label meditatively, 'I like Tuborg – Danish or something. I wonder if Kierkegaard drank Tuborg?'

'Who?'

She looks at me like she can't credit that I've never heard of him. 'Danish philosopher, believed in the moral supremacy of the individual's conscience. Jung named a neurosis after him, and thought he was a twat for saying animals didn't feel fear.'

'Oh,' I say, and incline my head sagely, as though that made perfect sense. I keep forgetting she went to a proper university, not an art school.

She takes a long, satisfied pull on her can and nods to herself. *Anxiety is the dizziness of freedom.*

'What?'

'Kierkegaard said that. He also said, *Life is not a problem to be solved, but a reality to be experienced.*'

'Fuck sake, Denny, how do you remember this stuff? You're drunk and stoned, and you still remember this stuff.'

'I'm only stoned. I'm not quite drunk yet.'

I go back to the pile of booze, divide a six-pack of lager in two and give her half. Someone is watching me. It's that wanker Philip, standing alone next to the fridge at the other side of the room with a bottle in his hand. He's such a fucking snake.

Denny and I open cans of lager one after another. I drink mine far too quickly. It makes me belch, and that makes me laugh. Then I drink cider. Next, I drink something pinkish-brownish-red from a salad bowl. People are talking all around me, and I'm glad Philip has disappeared back into the crowd.

There are so many people here. Rooms full of music and flashing lights. Heat from bodies, and the smell of booze and dope. Someone grabs my hand and leads me towards the dancing. Trying to lip-read his animated conversation. Giving up and just dancing.

The music is pumping through my whole body. The Rolling Stones pounding out 'Street Fighting Man'. Sweat all around me. The nutmeg smell of men, the cinnamon smell of women. Sweat in my eyes and I'm still dancing. Dancing for the feel of it in my arms, my legs, my belly, my swirling brain. I don't dance like they do in those stupid films that are supposed to be about us; caricatures of so-called hippies made up by middle-aged men in suits. Hippies don't fucking exist, they've been made up to look like us, invented to disempower what we really are. I'm not a *hippy*. I'm a long-haired, drug-taking, risk-chasing, fucking *freak* who wants to blow up the world and make it start again. I throw the hot and heavy jacket off and liberate my body from its constriction. First, I dance up close with a thin boy wearing blue eyeliner and then even closer to a curvy girl in a spangled dress. I don't care who's looking at me, or how they're looking at me. All I care about is what I feel right now. The intensity of being alive stuns me. It's so incomprehensible. So fucking unbelievably beautiful. And that edge. That drop off into death and oblivion is what makes those colours so visceral and these sounds so over-whelming. That edge between Life and Death, the one that glitters and pulses with pure adrenaline. The edge that keeps me dancing.

Starting to spin, I push my way out of the room to look for another drink. I get distracted by the pattern on the wallpaper and try to merge with the wall of the corridor. Another spliff turns up in my hand. I prop myself between the stairs and a telephone table and smoke it until it's gone.

Voices float lightly from the surrounding conversations. The sounds make me open my eyes, which have become bleary with dope and booze. I try to get myself up from what I now realise is the floor.

I can't . . . I can't quite get up.

I'm wasted.

The music keeps thudding, distorting like rubber bands that won't keep shape. The floor is unsteady. I roll onto my hands and knees and study the fibres of the carpet. It is fasci-nating. It has things in it. Little beads of something, flakes of cork from wine bottles and the tiniest scraps of paper in the world. It also smells bad. What I really need is to lie down somewhere and sleep for a while. Get sober. Once I've done that, I'll be able to sort myself out. I manoeuvre myself to the stairs, which I ascend on all fours. At the landing, I pull myself up to standing position assisted by the wall. Looking around, I make out that all the bedrooms on this floor are full. In the nearest one, the light bulb is wrapped in coloured cellophane; it makes the air seem thick, like it's full of red wine. Someone's teeth flash. Is that Philip? A head obscures the face. A boy, with his face made up in white foundation, lowers his kohl covered eyelids as he licks a Rizla paper. Cannabis is roasted over a lighter's flame. The smell of patchouli oil. A woman laughs, and a man says, 'No, quick, pick it up, it'll get lost under the bed.'

There are too many people for such a small room. I need to lie down.

I try another door. Coats are piled on a single bed and two white bodies are entwined amongst them. I see her knees and the inside of her thighs.

'Sorry.' They don't hear me. 'Sorry.' Pressing my forefinger against my lips, I retreat to find a set of stairs leading upwards. At the top there's a small, empty bedroom. Curtains billow in the breeze through a sash window. I wait for my eyes to adjust to the low light. There's a smell of socks and an unkempt bed stands next to an impressive stereo system. The only orderly thing in the room is a stack of pristine albums.

I lie down on the bed, face first.

I fall and fall.

At first, it's just greyness. Stepping in black pitch bogs. Worms as big as sea snakes have eyes unfurling like roses. Apple-sweet odour of death. Under my foot a face bobs up like a stepping-stone, then another one. I'm trying to climb onto an island, but I keep slipping backwards. The water smells like old brass. I'm held fast, I'll never get out of this. Clouds of ammonia. Dead girls sink until there's nothing but an ear, a cheek, a sightless eye. Sounds crash out of the trees. Branches are torn off by winds. I walk through spear-blade leaves and broken bones. I break into a sprint. I run and run, over ground that splits and bucks. Stopping to gulp in air I see my reflection in the tar-black water. My body has white puppy fur over breasts and arms. I have a face that is narrowing. Auburn ears with blackened tips. Pain in my jaw as my teeth grow sharper. There is a sound behind me like the growling of a bear. The clatter of the witch's monkeys as they fly down through the trees.

The sense of someone being too close makes me turn onto my back. Philip is staring at me. He's so near my face I have to turn away from the stink of his breath: beer, cheese, unbrushed teeth. Eyes so insipid they're hardly blue at all. His face has too many edges.

'Jude,' he says. 'What are you doing in my bed?'

'Oh, is it yours? Sorry I was just . . . I needed somewhere to crash.'

His mouth is a sneer. 'You're in my bed.'

'On it . . . *on* your bed.'

'Don't you remember the last time you and I got cosied up like this?'

I narrow my eyes at him. 'I'm not getting cosy with you. I've never got cosy with you.'

He leans too close. I thrust at his shoulder trying to push him away. He doesn't move.

'Get out of my way. I'm going back downstairs.' I shove him again but now he pushes me so hard that I fall backward onto the mattress.

'Stay where you are, bitch. We've got unfinished business. And now you're in my bed.'

'*On* it, dickhead.'

He takes his shoes off. Jeans. Underpants.

I draw back in alarm. 'What are you doing?'

'What I'd really like is if you cried. So why don't you do that? Why don't you cry? I'd really fucking like it if you cried.'

208

He rips the button of my trousers open and pulls down the zip. Now I'm not drunk anymore. He's on top of me, naked from the waist down. He's torn my clothes. He pushes my pants to one side.

I scrabble and twist. Teeth bared. All I can see is red light bursting in my skull.

I punch him in the mouth with as much force as I can.

He rears back in surprise.

I say, 'No. *You* cry, you fucker.' Childhood defence lessons are ingrained in my body as reflexes. I grab two of his fingers in one hand, and two in the other. I wrench them apart and backward. He yelps and arches his spine.

'Do you feel that? Do you feel that?' I hear myself shouting. 'I'm breaking your fingers, you prick, and what *I'd* really like, would be if *you* cried.'

The pain drops him on his knees.

I haven't broken his fingers yet, but I will.

He's squealing like a little pig. If he moves, I will break every tiny bone in each of his fucking hands. I'm filled with a storm. I think of dead girls hanging by their heels and of running from soldiers in cars.

I increase the pressure on his finger-joints.

His eyes falter from hatred, to uncertainty, to fear.

Sounds of people in the garden below remind me I'm not alone. 'Shall I call for help? How do you think that would go down? You with your pants off, flashing your tiny John Thomas, and me breaking your fingers while you squawk like a little fucking baby?'

'No,' he's whimpering, 'don't.'

'Shut the fuck up.' I adjust my grip to make it firmer.

He writhes, trying to relieve the pressure on his hand.

I'm fighting demons. My father never taught me to swim or ride a bike, but he taught me how to kill a man with precision. All I need to do is press my fingers into his windpipe or smash the edge of my palm against his temple, and this fucking prick will be dead.

I pull his fingers further back. They make cracking sounds. There are tears in his eyes. His mouth twists. 'I'm sorry.'

'You're not fucking sorry. You're just beaten.'

I struggle with the rage inside me. He looks scrawny and ridiculous, gasping for air. Helpless like a goldfish on the carpet.

'Don't,' he croaks.

'Shut your bloody mouth. You're nothing. If two soldiers couldn't take me, what the fuck made you think you could?'

He's kneeling on the floor nursing his fingers as I slam the door. I stand at the head of the stairs. I'm a drunken Boadicea, raising her arms in triumph after a night burning Rome to the ground.

20

Toto

In the early hours, I wake on a settee covered with a blanket. There's the remains of a fire glowing and I blink as I look around the room. It must be Denny and Maria's place. My mouth feels like someone's emptied a vacuum cleaner into it. Rubbing my face, I vaguely recollect a party, but there's no memory of how I got here. My discomfort makes me wonder if I might still be fully clothed. The twisted, strangled feeling is down to the fact that I'm still wearing everything, including Denny's leather jacket.

The light goes on, and before I quite register what's happening, Maria is tugging gently on my sleeve. 'Just checking that you're OK. If you're as drunk as Denny is, I want to be sure you're not going to choke on your own vomit.' Maria puts a glass of water on the floor beside me. 'I had to get one for Denny, so I thought you might need one too.'

I struggle to sit up and, as I do, she removes the jacket and tugs off my boots. Before I know it, she's stripped me down to my underwear and got me back under the blanket with the glass of water in my hand. She must do this a lot with Denny.

Once she's satisfied that I'm sorted out, she sits cross-legged on the carpet.

'How are you, now?' She says it kindly, as though talking to a child. 'Do you always get as drunk as this? Or is tonight a special occasion?'

I don't really take in anything she's said. The liquid is what I'm focused on. I swallow it without pausing for breath. My throat rehydrates as radically as one of those Japanese paper flowers that expand into lilies in a glass of water. Slowly, her words permeate my brain. That's not a question I want to answer.

'Jude, I just need to say this – don't try and be like Denny. That girl is a train wreck. I love her, but she's a train wreck. She's got no direction, no purpose. And I'm sorry to say this, but you're getting more and more like her. That's not going to work out well for you. You need to think hard about what you're doing, Jude. If you believe in our school, be reliable. Turn up when you say you're going to. Do the things you promised.'

She looks at me with her clear eyes. 'See, I don't mind if you don't want to do it. Just choose something that has meaning for you. If it's art, then do that. Do *something*, have a purpose, but don't choose Denny as your role model for Christ's sake.'

There's a long silence as I take that in. Before she gets to her feet to go back to the kitchen, she pats my hand. 'I just needed to say that.'

Since I met Denny and Maria, I've decided that I'm an anarchist like them. I've read the books that they lent me, some of which are on the shelves in this room: Proudhon, Bakunin and Rudolph Rocker. As I lie here I wonder, for the first time, whether I am seeing something different in all this than they do. I like the idealism and libertarianism of it all. But maybe Maria sees it as something you have to practise: a workplan rather than a schema of interesting possibilities.

She has hit a nerve.

Don't be like Denny.

I listen to the careful sounds of Maria making her way upstairs to the bed that she and Denny share. The creaking of bedsprings tells me she must be slipping in beside my drunken friend. My head aches. I think for a moment about how Denny treats Maria. Am I doing that to Callie? I took off without a word of explanation. I got up out of that bed where she lay with a fine silk scarf around her neck, put on my things and ran for it. I could have talked to her. I could have told her what freaked me. But no. I panicked, like I always do when I'm frightened, and legged it.

I put my clothes back on as quietly as I can, swap Denny's jacket for my coat, and creep out of the house. I'm going to break one of my hitchhiking rules. I'm going to go back to Callie in the dark. Tail between my legs like a muddy little mongrel.

Within three hours, I'm making my way along the pathway in Whetheridge Common back to Callie's house.

I walked through the green belt after being dropped off in town. It was an easy ride to Sheffield. I kept a stolid lorry driver company, making him laugh at the antics of a pair of boxing hares we passed on the embankment. He shared his flask of coffee with me and wanted no more than my company. The common is peaceful at this time of day and greenfinches flock across the path ahead. The stream under the arched footbridge runs over loose pebbles. I stop to watch as a kingfisher dives out of a holly tree and into the water like a sapphire bolt. Who would have thought they would be so small? No bigger than a sparrow but gaudier than a sultan's bride in a book of fairy tales. It breaks out of the stream with a fish in its beak and flies into the prickly leaves of the holly, gone as abruptly as it appeared.

No one, anywhere, is up yet, or that's how it feels. I take the opportunity to find a quiet spot away from the road to play my blues harp for a while. Callie doesn't like the blues, so I usually make my music out the back, or in the park, but never within earshot of her. The more I play, the more remorse I feel for running out on her.

I search for a peace offering. In a neighbour's garden purple flowers weigh down a lilac tree. I climb over the wall to steal them. It's not as easy as I expected. The struggle with the thickness of the woody stems is epic. I swear at icy drops of falling dew as a blackbird calls out in alarm. The few sprigs I retrieve aren't as impressive as I'd hoped.

Getting back in the quiet hours of morning and having no key tests my burglary skills. I unhook a window propped open in the downstairs toilet and wriggle through, landing on the toilet seat with the bunch of lilac held high so as not to damage it.

Once in the kitchen, I creep around, making breakfast for Callie, trying to be as quiet as I can, opening drawers and cupboards in slow motion.

Upstairs, Callie slumbers in a sprawl, her mouth shaping

words. Shifting in her sleep, she reaches across the bed, patting the sheets with her flattened palm and widespread fingers. Who is she searching for, me or Hugo? As though aware of somebody's presence, she suddenly stiffens and opens her eyes blearily.

'Hullo my bluebird, what's happening here?'

'Stole flowers for you and made you breakfast.'

She's more touched than I expected. Pulling herself up in the bed, she brushes back her hair and looks at the bouquet with delight.

'You came back.' Her eyes are soft and uncertain.

I put the tray next to her and perch on the edge of the bed. 'I'm sorry I didn't tell you I was going. I went to sign on.'

There's nothing I want to tell her about the anger and confusion that sent me off. 'Look,' I point at the jar on the tray. 'I found the French jam.'

She eyes the toast appreciatively, but before taking a bite, she asks, 'How did you get in? You haven't got a key, have you?'

'You left the toilet window off the latch. I'm a proper little housebreaker, I am.'

She laughs and looks disapproving, all at once.

'Hey,' I say, 'do you know what? I saw a kingfisher in the park. Tiny. Orange and gold and blue. I used to think they were mythical.'

'What a strange little bluebird you are. It's hard to make sense of you sometimes.'

The lilac blossoms are silhouetted on the windowsill. She gazes at the clumsy bouquet, far away in thought.

'Do you know about the meaning of flowers?' she asks.

'Do flowers have meaning?'

*

215

She goes away to return with a cloth-covered book called *The Language of Flowers*. Slipping back into bed, she hands me the book.

'Look up *Lilac*,' she says as I leaf through its age-spotted pages. 'What does it say?'

I read aloud. '*First Love.*'

'Am I the first woman you've slept with?' She preens, as though anticipating my answer.

I pause because it won't be the answer she wants. 'No.'

In an instant Callie's face becomes cold. Inspecting me so intensely that I turn my head away, she takes my chin and twists my face back towards her.

'Was it that girl you're always with, the quiet one who came around the other day? What's her name?'

She knows her name. I'm full of indignation. 'Do you mean Nel?'

'Yes.'

'No, I never have.'

'But you'd like to.'

I brush off her hand. Even clothed, I'm exposed. 'Fuck sake, Callie. She's just my friend.'

I turn towards the door, but she grabs my wrist. 'Don't you dare do a runner on me again, young lady.'

'Well stop talking about Nel like that then.'

'You love her though, right?'

'Fuck off, Callie. Don't. Keep your mouth shut about Nel.'

'Do you love me more?'

I can't make my mind up whether she's joking or not. I think she is. She's smiling, but icy. Suddenly she's kissing me.

'Say you love me more,' she whispers, slipping her hand inside my blouse.

'I love you more,' I say, because I want to go where she's taking me.

The art nouveau clock in the front room chimes twelve for midday. Callie's waiting for the frosted varnish that I applied to her fingernails, to dry. She blows on them. 'Beautifully done,' she says and gets up from the settee, waving her hands gently to speed the drying process. 'You have a delicate touch with a brush.'

'I went to art school for a long time to get that skill.' I get up off my knees.

She doesn't seem to hear me, suddenly distracted by something that's drawn her attention through the window. 'There's a tradesman's van in Hugo's parking space.'

'Really?' I say, distracted by a drip of frosted-turquoise varnish and frightened about what it might do to her soft furnishings. I screw the top onto the bottle and put it gingerly on her fashion periodical.

'He's just sitting there reading a newspaper as though he owns the place.' She shakes her nails dry in a more agitated manner. 'It's a private parking space.'

It occurs to me that it could be Hank. He doesn't like the Reynards, so it would be just like him to park there and wait for me to notice. I drag the curtain further open to get a look. My hunch is right. His van is like an old friend. I recognise every dent in its shabby blue paintwork. Hank, completely engrossed in the *Guardian*, is lounging across the front seats like he's been there for a while.

'Oh.' I sound unexpectedly happy. I glance at Callie to gauge her reaction.

'Is it someone you know?' Her expression implies she thinks I'm going to lie.

'Yes, it is.'

'Does he mend fridges or something.'

I push the curtain across, deliberately obscuring her view. 'He's at the steelworks.'

'Oh, a *steelworker*,' she says, 'I don't think I've ever met anybody who does that sort of thing.'

'For fuck sake, Callie.'

'I'm sorry?' She dips her chin as though she hasn't heard me right.

I'm fed up with this snobbery shit from her. I don't want her talking about Hank like that. She doesn't know anything about him.

'OK,' I say, with an air of finality. 'I'm going out for a while.'

'What do you mean?'

'I'm going to spend time with my friends.'

She says something that I can't quite hear as I shut the door behind me.

'Ey up, Toto, flower.' Hank folds his newspaper and throws it into the back of the van as I jump into the passenger seat. 'I thought if I sat there long enough, you'd turn up. Jo's sent me over to get you. Where's your boots?'

He peers down at my bare feet and I realise that I was in such a rush to get out of the house that I've forgotten to put them on.

'Oh bugger,' I say. 'Never mind. Michael does it all the time. It can't be that bad.'

'Aye, we'll only be going to our place for us dinner. You'll be fine. You do eat *dinner*, don't you? Or is it *lunch,* now that you're in with the posh crowd?'

'Oh, shut up Hank. Stop talking bollocks!'

'Are you having a good time with her ladyship in there, or what?'

'I am. I know you don't like her, but right now I'm having a fucking good time.'

'All right then, Toto. Keep having fun. Can't argue with that. Listen, we've got Nel at our place. She's upset, like, and we thought you might cheer her up.'

I search his face in alarm, 'What's wrong with her?'

'She's finished with Simon, but don't ask me about it. Let her tell you.'

The revelation shocks me. 'Shit, is she OK?'

Hank glances at me. 'She's decided not to carry on with the teaching too.'

Jo draws me in through the front door and nods over her shoulder towards Nel, who's sitting hunched on their settee, brittle and diminished.

'She's not in a good way. It's that bastard Simon. She won't admit it, but she's in a state.'

'Don't talk about me as though I'm not here,' Nel says. 'I can hear you. I'm all right.'

'She's not all right,' Jo says firmly to me, then turns to Nel. 'You're not all right, so don't pretend.'

'Hey, you,' I say softly and head to the settee to sit beside her.

Nel frowns briefly, trying to be tough. 'Don't touch me,' she says. 'I know you hate being touched.'

'Yeah, but if *I* touch *you*, that's different. That's allowed.'

'Wee idiot,' she laughs, and pushes me gently with her fingers, but as soon as I put my hand on her shoulder, her lip quivers and her forehead falls against my neck. It starts small, like the sound of a kitten mewling. Before I know it, I'm folding her into me like she's a child, like I'm trying to absorb her.

'I'm sorry,' she weeps harder. I rub her back, pressing my face tight against her head.

'Don't be sorry. Just tell me what the fucker did to you.'

'He's shacked up with the girl who made that fucking bangle, so I dumped him. That's it.' She disengages herself and wipes her face quickly and harshly. 'I'm fine. I'm fine. I'm fucking glad it's over to be honest.'

I observe her carefully. That isn't all of it. I can tell by her expression there's something else.

She widens her eyes with a shake of her head. 'Don't, Toto. Please don't look at me like that. I just can't talk about it.'

I back off, because it's what she wants.

Hank beckons her over to the table, where there are four plates of salad. 'Come on, have some cider, forget that tosser.'

Nel is subdued. Jo, Hank and I say nothing: surreptitiously watching her, furtively looking at each other. Trying not to let her see that we're monitoring her. Topping up her drink. Passing her salt and salad cream. Being met each time with a tiny shake of the head. She just keeps drinking the cider.

After a while she gets out of her chair unsteadily. 'I'm going to the bathroom. Won't be long.'

But she is long.

We've cleared away and washed up, and she's not back.

Jo wipes the sink. 'Go up and see if she's all right, Toto. She'll tell you. You're the only one she ever talks to properly.

She seemed OK when she first got here, didn't she, Hank? She was all upbeat about packing in the teaching and happy she was shot of his nibs. Then she started to get all brooding, like.'

After I knock on the door a few times, Nel says in a small voice, 'It's not locked.'

She's sitting in the empty, iron bath, fully clothed with tears on her face. I lay one hand over hers on the enamel rim and gingerly give her some toilet paper for the tear on the end of her nose. She uses it quickly, then pulls both sleeves down to cover her fingertips.

I say, 'That fucker Simon isn't worth crying about. You know that, don't you?'

Rocking herself slightly, she says, 'I wasn't thinking about him to be honest. I was thinking about my bloody father. Remember I told you he drowned those puppies? How can you drown puppies, Toto? How can you just take them and drown them in a bloody bucket? Eight wee white puppies.'

I lean over the side of the bath and stroke her shoulder. 'I think you're a bit drunk. You hardly ever get drunk. But when you do, you always cry.'

'It's the cider in the middle of the day.' She says and rubs her eyes. 'Hank keeps giving me cider.'

She seems to become very small. 'Can I show you something? But don't tell the others.'

'What?'

She shifts awkwardly in the empty bath. Lifting her blouse, she shows me a pattern of blue marks across her torso.

There's a red explosion inside my head. 'Did he do that? Did Simon do that?'

She makes the smallest up and down movement of her head.

I'm on my feet. I can hardly get the words out, 'I'll fucking
. . . I'll kill him.'

She reaches up and grabs my wrist. 'No Toto, don't get all
worked up.'

'Nel, those bruises! Look' – I lift her blouse again – 'they're
all fucking over you. Fuck's sake Nel, look at them.'

She takes the toilet paper I gave her for her tears and wipes
away mine. 'Stop it. Soppy bugger,' she says so gently. 'I'm all
right. Look, I'm not crying about it, so why are you? Come
on you. I've got you. Stop your grieting.'

Little sobs choke me, 'But I can't bear that he did that to
you. I swear . . . I'll—'

She grips my hand. 'Listen to me, Toto, don't do anything.
Promise me. There's no point. I don't want anyone to know.
It's done. It's never happening again.'

'Why the fuck did you stay with him? How long has he
been doing this, for Christ's sake?'

Her face falls like I'm blaming her. 'I didn't know how not
to be with him.' She twists her fingers in her long hair and
holds it across her mouth, hiding her lips like a gag. 'When
it starts, you think it's a one-off. You think maybe you did
something. And then it's all the time and it's normal. And you
don't know how to stop. You don't know how to stop anything.
You look at the door, but somehow you can't go through
it. I'm so fucking angry with myself, Toto.' Her eyes mist
up again. 'So angry and ashamed that I didn't know how to
end it.'

21

Toto

There are letters for Hugo stacked behind the clock on the mantlepiece. No letters for me. It's not my home. I take off my coat and throw it across the back of the settee, feeling out of sorts and not able to settle. Callie poses self-consciously by the bookshelf with a negroni in her hand. It isn't her first cocktail of the day. It's no more than five o'clock, but her eyes are heavy, and the flush of alcohol isn't flattering.

Images of Nel's bruises fill my mind and I can't let them go. Even knowing she'll be safe with Jo and Hank, it was hard to leave her there, hard to come back here and carry on as though nothing's happened. I'm trying to get my head around it. I can't believe Nel blames herself for all the things that bastard Simon did to her. I want to go hunting for him like some kind of rampaging lunatic. But I made a promise and I don't break my promises to Nel. Not on purpose, anyway.

Callie disrupts my train of thought 'Did you have fun with

your strapping steelworker?' she asks with forced nonchalance, swirling the ice in her glass with too much energy.

'He's not a strapping steelworker.' I rub my brow, controlling my irritation. 'He was in my year at college. You've met him before, at Genevieve's house. And he's married to my friend. There's nothing going on between us.'

Callie pauses as though she's trying to place him. 'Oh,' she says, 'is he with that girl with the miniskirts? The one who—'

'Look,' I say, 'today's been shit if you must know. Nel's split up with her boyfriend.'

Before I can say more, she wanders over to stare into the street with an air of boredom. It's obvious that there's no point in talking about this stuff with her. She's not interested in what happens to my friends. That's not what we do. I should have remembered that.

I turn my focus to her drink instead. 'Can I have one of those?'

That seems to cheer her up. 'Of course. I'll teach you how to make one.'

'Ow.' I'm distracted by a twinge in my left foot and I throw myself down on the sofa to examine it.

'What's wrong?' Callie lowers herself onto her knees in front of me. She deposits her cocktail on the coffee table and takes a tissue from a box beside it. She holds it to my lips.

Spit,' she orders, and I do. She tends to my foot with deep focus.

'Little piece of something stuck in there. Hang on. Nearly got it.'

The sharp pain makes me gasp and I crane to see what she's holding.

'Practically nothing,' she says, 'a splinter of glass. If you must go out without footwear, you need to be more careful about where you tread. Come on, time for a negroni lesson. Stopped hurting?'

'I suppose so . . . Nearly, anyway.'

'Right. When you've got this mastered, you'll be making them for both of us.'

Once I've mixed two negronis, and drunk them both very quickly, we decide that I'm not too bad at making this drink. After the third one, everything is going more slowly than it should. It's probably best if I don't try to stand up. I attempt to make conversation as though I'm sober.

'What did you do while I was out?'

Callie strokes my hair, and I lean into her hand like a cat. She doesn't answer straight away. 'I did a few things in town. Ran a few errands.'

The next morning there's a scab on the sole of my foot. I pull on clean socks and search for my boots in all the places I usually dump them. By the bed. At the front door. In the kitchen. Under the table. On the backdoor step. Next to the sofa.

I can't find them anywhere, and I start to panic. What if Callie's thrown them away? When I look up, she's watching me, her face pensive.

'What have you lost?' she says quietly.

'My boots.'

'What do you need them for?'

'I was going to go out.'

'Why do you need to do that?'

'I just need to find my boots.'

She doesn't seem to be listening. 'Hmm,' she says twisting a strand of her hair around her finger.

'Callie, what have you done with them?'

She is not speaking. I'm not sure if she's angry or sad or both.

'I want my boots,' I say after the silence has stretched beyond tolerance.

'I've taken your boots to be re-soled,' she says with forced lightness.

'But I haven't got anything else for my feet. What am I supposed to do without shoes?'

'It'll just be a few days.'

'But I need them.'

'I've told you; they're being repaired. Just a few days.'

While we're sitting on the sofa, we hear the front door closing and footsteps in the hallway. It can only be Hugo. Callie glances at me in alarm. We watch the living room door and wait for his appearance, but he doesn't come in to greet us. I get a glimpse of him passing and hear the sound of his brisk tread up the stairs. Callie looks thrown, but breathes deeply and gathers herself, brushing non-existent dust from her lap as though readying herself for something.

'Stay exactly where you are,' she instructs.

I'm awkward in an unbuttoned blouse and a pair of panties. I start to get up, but she points at me, in warning. 'Just stay right here. This is between me and Hugo.'

I don't know what else to do but obey her.

'Hu?' she calls as she goes into the hall. 'Hello darling. Staying long?'

Buttoning my blouse, I listen as she mounts the stairs. A muffled conversation begins in the bedroom as I retrieve my trousers from beside the sofa and pull them on. In an effort to distract myself, I study my reflection in the mirror. The new thick, gold hoops in my ears remind me that I miss the delicate silver rings Callie removed and put in her pocket for a memento. I focus on the little cut that has become a scar on my cheekbone. The conversation on the floor above goes on, but I can only hear intonation. Her anger followed by his laughter. Questions and answers. Cadence and inflection.

It's gone quiet. Sounds of a bed creaking. Moaning.

They're fucking.

I don't know what I feel about that.

I don't know what I feel.

Things knocked over. Muffled talking again. According to her rules, I'm not allowed to flirt. But she can fuck him practically in front of me. I don't know if this is fucking cool at all.

I can't bear to listen, so I flee into the garden. My knees get wet as I kneel on the lawn to make a daisy chain. Trying to keep my imagination off Callie and her husband.

My lover and her husband.

Pushing down my feelings.

Fingers trembling.

A slug undulates over the flowerbed nearby. It's the colour of alabaster. Stalk eyes recoil from contact with plant stems. Slime all over the flowers. I stop plaiting the daisies to watch it negotiating the lawn's edge. Lengthening and shortening, dirt sticking to its rippling edges, it looks as full of melancholy as I am of rage. A wound grows in the flesh of a leaf as it feeds.

The French windows open behind me, and someone steps outside. I look up hopefully, but it's Hugo. He's wearing a newly laundered shirt and his cologne travels ahead of him, sharp and pine-scented. In his hand is a glass of orange juice, which he proffers.

'Come inside, it's all OK.'

I get to my feet. He acts as though everything is ordinary. I have no sodding idea what ordinary is anymore.

'You actually think I want your fucking orange juice?'

He laughs. 'You don't usually mind taking my food and drink.'

We look at each other in silence.

He is slight: a slight man in every way. There is no weight or depth to him. He is as insubstantial as powdered chalk.

'Jude, there's no problem here. Callie and I have an arrangement about this kind of thing. I know she's told you that.'

He pauses for a long time, considering me. There is something so irritatingly self-satisfied about him. He puts the unwanted drink on the flowerbed's brick edging and looks at me as though I'm a resistant student in one of his interminable theory seminars.

'She has to let you go home at some point, though, doesn't she?' He says it as though it's a joke. 'She knows she does, otherwise it's *kidnapping.*'

His voice gets quieter. 'You need to go soon, Jude. You can come back, of course . . . to visit.'

As I go into the house he says, 'I'm not suggesting that you stay away for ever. Come and go as you please.'

He waits for a reply.

228

Fuck him with his plans and permissions, I don't answer to him, I'll go when I'm good and ready and not a moment before.

He takes my arm, turns me towards him. I don't respond. His mouth hardens and his right hand darts upwards.

Holding me by the throat he whispers, 'Are you ambivalent to everything, Jude Totton, is that what your problem is?'

As I look into his eyes, I remember what Callie wanted me to do that night when I ran back to Leeds, the thing *he* does to her.

He likes to choke women. I see it in him now.

Fucking look at him; thinking about choking me.

I'm cold with rage. I stare him down.

'Fuck you, Hugo Reynard.'

He falters, and his hand falls away from my neck.

In the kitchen Callie is dishevelled and her eyes are pink. She glances at each of us quickly, lowers the gas under the espresso and reaches out a hand to me. I go awkwardly to her side and slip my hand into hers. She kisses me on the mouth and fleetingly checks Hugo's reaction.

Unmoved, he picks up an apple from the wooden fruit bowl and bites a chunk out of it. As though remembering something, he pats his pocket and says, 'Shit, nearly left my wallet in my other trousers.'

He leaps back up the stairs two at a time.

I follow Callie as she moves quickly to the front room. She motions me to the window and points at their Citroen parked outside.

'Who's in the car?'

I peer through the gap in the curtains. There's someone in the front passenger seat, but I can't make them out. Someone slender. Looks like a girl. It suddenly occurs to me it could be Lauren.

Callie is watching my face, her back to the wall like she doesn't want to be seen from outside. 'Who is it?'

'I can't see, Callie. Honest to god. I can't see.'

As we hear Hugo bounding back down the stairs, she sits on the couch in an attempt to compose herself. He stops briefly at the door to wave his wallet. 'I don't think I'll have that coffee, got to move it. See you later.'

The door slams shut. Callie goes back to the window and watches his car as it moves away up the road.

22

Toto

It's been a week since Nel showed me her bruises. Callie is crashing things around in the kitchen. She isn't happy that I've been ringing Nel every day at Jo's, but she's going to have to put up with it. I'm at the bottom of the stairs listening to the ringtone, playing with the torn fragment of paper that has Hank and Jo's number on it. When Jo picks up, I lay the scrap on the phone table, take the whole telephone set in my hands and climb three steps up the staircase to sit down. It's ridiculous, but I feel like I'm hiding behind the bannisters.

'Hiya. How's Nel today?'

Jo lowers her voice as though concerned about being overheard. 'She's putting on a brave face. You know what she's like. I'll go and get her.'

As I'm waiting, Callie hovers nearby. I glance pointedly at her and turn my back.

'Hey, you,' Nel says softly.

'Hey, you. Are you alright today?'

'Aye, I suppose so, lovely.' Her voice doesn't seem to have any volume anymore, 'It's still all a bit strange, but it's getting better. I'll be fine. I'll be looking for a part-time job soon. Get on with my life.'

Callie edges past me up the stairs. 'Sorry, Bluebird, I need to get something.'

I don't believe her. I don't trust that she won't listen in on the line in the master bedroom, so I change the subject just in case.

'Will you be staying in Sheffield a bit longer?'

'I'll be around for a while. Gen wants me to go and stay with her; she feels bad about all the shit that happened at her house. I'll probably go there this weekend.'

'But what about Simon? He's there all the time.'

'Gen says she'll make sure we don't overlap.'

Callie comes slowly back down the stairs, checking that the pictures are hung straight as she descends. I shuffle to one side and look up at her. 'Can you get past?'

She gives a slight nod and concentrates hard on where to put her feet.

'Hey, lovely,' I say to Nel. 'I think I need to go, but maybe we could catch up again soon?'

'That would be great. Don't fret, you. I'm OK.'

After we finish talking, I go to the kitchen for a glass of water. As I stand next to the sink drinking from a beaker, Callie looks at me.

'Is there something wrong, Callie?'

She shakes her head. 'No. I was checking the fridge. We're getting low on things. I might have to pop out for groceries. Do you want to come or stay here?'

I look down at my feet. 'I'll have to stay here. Will my boots be ready yet?'

'If I get a chance, I'll check, but it's the other end of town.'

I'm going stir crazy. It's been days since I last had my boots and it's just me and Callie non-stop. Being unshod is becoming a problem. At first it wasn't so bad, but my soles have got more and more sore. Every time I venture outside, I get another nick or bruise. I wish she would just go and get the bloody things.

She gathers her belongings. After putting on a tailored leather jacket and admiring herself in the mirror, she collects her keys from the phone table. As the front door shuts behind her, I realise with quiet exultation that this is the perfect time to ring Nel back to talk properly. I settle myself back on the stair, but the scrap of paper with Jo's number has disappeared. I check my pockets and search around on the floor. But it's gone.

Callie's absence is liberating. It comes over me, like a fever, that if I don't spend time with other people, I'll lose my mind. So, I make my way around to Genevieve and Viktor's place barefoot. It's good that it's only a few streets away, because my feet react to every tiny pebble and shard of wood beneath them and I'm hobbling by the time I get there.

Genevieve lets me in. 'How are you, Toto? It feels like it's been ages since you came around. Are you all right? It's crap, isn't it, about Nel?'

'Yes, I saw her at Jo's and she's pretty upset,' I say carefully, trying to assess how much Gen actually knows. Nel doesn't want me to talk about the violence. So I won't.

'Vik says Simon will probably come to his senses soon. He thinks his head's been turned but he'll get over it.' Lifting her eyes to mine, she looks at me searchingly. Maybe she's wondering how much *I'm* aware of. 'I don't know,' she adds quietly. 'Might be a blessing in disguise.'

In the kitchen, Michael sits at the table drinking from a jug of lime cordial and propping his bare feet on a chair. He's wearing cricket whites belted with a tie, and a collarless dress-shirt rolled to expose his forearms.

'Hiya. Long time no see. Nice of Mrs Reynard to let you out to see your friends.'

He notices my feet. He hasn't worn shoes since we were in first year. It gets him thrown out of pubs and abused in shops, but he doesn't care. The soles of his feet have become tough as leather, whereas mine are soft and tender.

'You need to harden those up, Jude.' He uses my name as though it is an indication of stupidity, like he used to at the end of our days as a couple. 'Use surgical spirit. Wipe it on like guitarists do with their fingertips.'

'It's not a permanent thing, *Michael.*' I use his name like a weapon. 'I don't need Callie's permission for anything. It's just that, today, I don't have anything to wear on my feet.'

They both wait for me to tell them why.

But I say nothing.

Eventually Genevieve fills in the long gap in the conversation. 'How is it that you are shoe-free?'

I must seem shifty. They know me too well.

'Callie's getting my boots repaired. They're at the cobblers.'

Genevieve and Michael raise their eyebrows at one another in a way that makes me suspicious. Once again, I find myself wondering what they do and don't know.

Genevieve leans towards me. 'Toto. Don't you have any other shoes?'

'Genevieve. You know I don't. Not here.'

Michael interjects. 'So, Callie bought you new blue clothes, that time, but no new blue shoes.'

I react fiercely. He brings out my terrier temper. He always has.

'I didn't fucking want her to buy me anything, OK? I'm not fucking *Sally Bowles*. This is not *Cabaret*, OK. Fuck you, Michael. Fuck you.' I stand up to go.

Genevieve grabs my arm and sits me back down again. 'All we're interested in is the lack of shoes. No one said you were Sally Bowles.'

'He implied. He fucking implied.'

'No, he didn't. And stop saying "fucking" so loudly; the neighbours think we're bad enough already.'

Michael leans towards me with a grin and misquotes *Cabaret*.

'*Fuck Max.*'

I don't want to laugh, but he makes me, so I kick him.

He leans back cheerfully. 'So, when do you get your boots back?'

Genevieve pours me a tumbler of cordial and waits for my response. I shrug, 'When they're fixed, that's all I know.'

I can tell they're uncomfortable, but they're not ready to say anything negative about Callie.

The silence is broken by the sound of Sid coming in through the front door. After calling out to ascertain our location, he joins us.

Settling himself in a chair next to me, he nods at my feet. 'So, it's true.'

'What's true?'

'The rumour that Callie's holding you prisoner by stealing your boots.'

He waits for my response.

My temper flashes. 'What bloody rumour?'

He looks like he's spoken out of turn and bites his lip as Genevieve signals at him with a widening of the eyes I wasn't supposed to see.

'We've already gone over the shoes thing,' Michael says absently. He picks up one of Viktor's newer albums and peruses the sleeve. He's one of those people who like to recite the facts about a band, and to discuss the minor production details at length. He also gets bored very quickly.

'So, Sid, you're gracing us with your presence these days?' Genevieve's tone is teasing, but she's eyeing him pointedly.

Sid ignores her comment and gives me a soft punch in the arm. 'How are you, Toto?'

'Off my leash.'

He laughs. 'Me too.'

Sid scratches his neck, his eyes darting backwards and forwards between everyone. All I can think about is my boots.

A desperate idea rises in me. 'Gen, I need to borrow some shoes. Have you got any?'

Genevieve compares her feet with mine. She can assess anything to do with clothing at a glance.

'Mine will be too big, or I would,' she says sadly. 'You might be the same size as Lauren though. Let's ask her when she gets in.'

Michael rotates a pear slowly in his fingers. He scowls at me before breaking its green skin with his teeth. I watch it getting pulped as he speaks. It's fascinating and repulsive all at once. A juice bubble forms in the corner of his mouth.

'It's no bloody big deal,' he says. 'Stay with Callie until you get your boots back, then leg it.' He considers me. 'Or are you having too much of a good time being a plaything?'

Even though I know there's no malice in it. Even though I know Michael thinks and speaks in reverse order. Even though I know there's some truth in the accusation, or maybe because of it, my blood runs hot and I'm on my feet again.

'You are such a prick,' I say hoarsely.

Sid hugs me from behind and laughs in my ear. 'There's nothing wrong with being a plaything. Cool it, puppy. You're getting all bitey.'

I pull away from him. Genevieve gives Michael a light slap around the head, and he, as usual, looks bewildered. Sid moves away from me, rubbing my back as he does.

Tiny birds move from tree to tree as I look through the window. A tortoiseshell cat is poised on a whitewashed brick wall, chittering at them. Craning its neck, it yawns to disguise its frustration as they rise too high to catch. I gather myself, pressing my dirty feet into the floorboards.

Sid's shoes are muddy, and there are dirt stains on the bottom of his wide maroon trousers. He sees me looking and gives me an embarrassed smile. He's being shifty. I've never seen him like this before. I've never seen him muddy either.

'Have you been out in the countryside or something?' I ask as I return to the table.

He hangs his head. 'Oh, I just went for a walk out in the Peaks this morning. Stayed overnight with someone.'

'Anyone I know?'

He looks away. 'Just a guy I work with at the bookshop. No one you've met.'

Genevieve puts a big plate of sandwiches on the table as Michael leans back on his chair and stretches. His belly button is revealed through the parting of his shirt and trousers. He's thinking deeply about something else. 'Did any of you ever eat worms when you were kids?'

The question stops us all in our tracks.

I nod. 'Yes, actually I did.'

Michael isn't surprised. Genevieve's expression hasn't changed. Sid looks like he's still trying to remember whether he has or not.

'Come on then. Spill the beans.' Michael waits for me to regale him with my worm eating experience.

I screw up my face in an effort to bring it to mind. 'It was before my sister was born, so I must have been about two and a half or something. I remember being in a corner of the garden and finding some old slates, and I used one as a chopping board and one as a knife. Just cutting up these worms,' I pause thoughtfully, 'and just, well . . . eating them.'

Sid sets himself astride a chair. 'Did they taste of dirt?'

I shake my head. 'I can't remember the actual flavour. They were all pinkish and purpley, like the inside of someone's mouth, and I liked them enough to eat more than one. My mum freaked out. I didn't realise they were disgusting until she told me so.'

Sid is fascinated. 'Have you eaten any recently?'

'Not that I know of.'

Genevieve scrutinises her tomato and cheese sandwich with waning enthusiasm. 'So, tell me, Michael, what was it about these sandwiches, which I lovingly prepared for you all, that made you think about eating worms?'

He blinks in surprise. 'Oh, nothing to do with your sandwiches. It just came into my head.'

'Well, get it out of your head.'

Sid is still thinking. 'What about slugs? Who's eaten them?'

'Sid, stop it!' Genevieve pushes her plate away. A figure moves past the window and a few seconds later Lauren comes in.

'Lauren, have you ever eaten a worm or a slug?' Sid asks before she can even discard her canvas shoulder bag.

She looks perplexed. 'Is that some kind of euphemism?'

'No, we're doing a survey.'

She helps herself to a sandwich. 'Definitely never a slug,' she says. 'Not sure about worms. Accidentally ate a big beetle in a salad once. Well, technically it would have been half a beetle.'

'What kind of beetle?'

'No idea. It was pale green all over and tasted like sulphur.'

'Would you all kindly stop talking about eating invertebrates!' Genevieve looks at her food with something close to despair.

Lauren hasn't heard her. I can see she's thinking about other invertebrates she might have eaten. She says, 'Toto, do you think there were any insects in that big bag of grass we ate when we were in third year?'

I snigger at the memory.

Genevieve looks at us both in bewilderment. 'You ate grass?'

I nudge her. 'Don't you remember?'

'No.'

'We had that record player in the kitchen, the one that used to get police messages sometimes? When we lived at 46 Circle Road. Remember?'

Genevieve looks like she has some recollection of it but can't see the relevance.

I continue. 'Me and Lauren were in the flat one lunch time,

and this police message comes over the record player: *Car twelve, go to number 46*. And Lauren completely lost her cool, which was funny in itself. She thought the police were raiding us. She ran around, found everybody's stash, and threw it all down the toilet. Acid, mescaline, speed, cannabis, everything.'

Lauren nods. 'I did. I *did* do that' – she pauses for effect – 'and we had this big jar of weed someone had posted to me through the mail . . . from fucking *Nigeria*. It was full of seeds and woody bits, and yes, probably beetles and worms and stuff. Anyway, I threw it all in the tomato soup I was heating up and the both of us ate it all, so the police wouldn't find it.'

Sid says, 'And did the police come?'

'No,' she says.

'Nothing came,' I add. 'Not even a taxi.'

Sid ponders for a moment. 'That would have been embarrassing, throwing other people's stashes away and the police not even having the grace to turn up.'

I agree. 'Yes. Try telling someone that you've flushed their dope down the toilet because the record player told you to. They weren't happy.'

Lauren covers her mouth, unable to speak for laughing. She recovers her voice and continues. 'And we went up to college that afternoon, so stoned we were tripping. Toto was seeing dwarfs with goblin faces everywhere.'

'They were *horrible*,' I interrupt.

She coughs with laughter and waves her hands. 'I was convinced there were blue lines coming out of the sky and following us like wires. We had bits of twig and seed stuck in our teeth and kept falling asleep in unexpected places.'

We're both laughing at the recollection of it, and so are the others, when someone comes in through the French windows.

I look up to see Callie and stop laughing abruptly. Everyone else stops too, and she is awkwardly aware of it as she searches for a seat.

'Oh, Gen, you're not on your own.' She places her cigarettes and lighter on the table and scans our faces. 'I thought I'd drop by for a chat. Did I interrupt something?'

After a moment's hesitation, Genevieve pushes a chair towards her. 'No, of course not: just Jude and Lauren entertaining us with stories about eating insects and getting smashed because of imaginary police messages on their stereo. Tea?'

Callie nods and eyes Lauren and me with distrust. Lauren stares straight back and Callie's face hardens. I wonder whether I look guilty, because for some reason, I feel it.

'Not really insects,' I say lamely. 'Annelids and molluscs to be exact.'

Michael shrugs in disagreement. 'To be fair there *was* a sulphur-tasting beetle mentioned.'

'Annelid?' Callie says flatly, like I'm being a smart-arse little hippy chick again. 'Would that be a worm?'

I nod uncomfortably, but the fact she has demonstrated her superior knowledge to the rest of the room makes her relax a little. She drags a cigarette out of its packet. Sid reaches over and takes one for himself.

Callie lights them both with her small mother-of-pearl lighter. 'A worm: a thing which is both male and female simultaneously,' she says archly.

'Yes,' says Sid, 'and also tastes delicious if you're two and a half years old. Eh, Toto?'

Michael picks up the lighter and plays with it absently, flicking it into flame over and over again. Callie retrieves it without a word, picks up her Gauloise cigarettes and puts them back in her handbag. Her attention falls to my feet, which I self-consciously slip underneath my chair.

Michael observes Callie with a stillness I recognise as the precursor to him saying something far too candid. The LP on the stereo spins and clicks, waiting to be stopped.

'Michael, put another record on,' I say too brightly.

He perks up at that and reaches down to leaf through the stack of albums on the floor. He picks one out. 'Do you like Captain Beefheart, Callie? *Trout Mask Replica*. Fucking amazing album.'

She gives a shake of her head. 'Don't really know it.'

He carefully pulls the album out of its sleeve. 'He is a genius. Just the weirdest, most creative, bloody amazing guy.'

Putting the disc on the turntable, he swings the arm back until it clicks. The record begins to spin. Lowering the needle onto the second track, he sits on his haunches next to the speakers. 'This one is so fucking out there.'

He's playing the 'The Dust Blows Forward N' the Dust Blows Back' and Beefheart chants a song about a dandelion moon and red-diamond lice.

Lauren keeps saying, 'Fucking love this one. Fucking *love* it.'

Callie busies herself in her handbag, bringing things out and putting them back in again. She's slightly bemused but trying to hide it.

Michael pores over the record cover. A man in a tall hat holds a fish's head like a mask in front of his face. He reminds me of a cantankerous pilgrim father.

Michael strokes one side of his chestnut beard and looks in Callie's direction. 'Such a bloody lunatic, this guy. When he made this album, he took his band off to this shack and treated them like crap. Made them practice for fourteen hours straight a day, screaming at them until they cried. Wouldn't feed them.' He pauses as if considering something and says casually, 'Took away their shoes.'

Callie's mouth tightens. Lauren coughs to cover a laugh as Michael glances quickly at Callie, whose face is now icy, and turns back to the record cover, all innocence. 'Don't you love the names of these musicians: *The Mascara Snake, Antennae Jimmy.*'

Sid tries to pretend nothing has happened, 'Frank Zappa was the producer, wasn't he? Can you imagine those two together?'

Callie stubs her cigarette out on the stained saucer ashtray. Beside the open French windows, Genevieve carries two cups of tea. She catches Callie's eye and indicates the exterior.

'Got a minute for a chat?'

Callie retrieves the cigarettes and lighter from her bag. 'Sure.'

As she follows Genevieve onto the patio, I kick Michael. He laughs at me, low and mischievous.

Genevieve closes the doors behind her, so the garden sounds are cut off.

I'm angry. 'Have you got any idea what kind of shit you've stirred up for me?'

'Cool it, Jude. She needs to get her sense of humour sorted. She needs to give you your fucking boots back too.'

I sidle to the window where I can see Genevieve and Callie conversing intently. 'What do you think they're talking about?'

Sid is at my side, also trying to listen.

Lauren shakes her head. 'You, of course. I told you she'd get heavy. She always does.'

Sid quietly pushes open the window enough for us to hear what they're saying. His eyes glint at me, as he whispers, 'I can't miss this, Toto.'

Through the rustling of the laburnum tree Genevieve's saying, 'She can't stay forever, can she? Can she, Cal? I mean to say. . . it's getting a bit obvious. There's even talk up at college.'

I can only see the back of Callie's head, but by the set of her shoulders I can tell she's furious. Arm extended; she flicks her cigarette with a thumbnail.

'Jesus Christ, Gen, you too?' She is full of fire. 'All of those guys up there are screwing the students and the life models and the departmental secretaries, but if one of the women gets a piece of the action, there's hell to pay. I mean, even the female lecturers have to work to different rules from the guys. Look at Susan Rilsdon in the textile department. She actually married the student she was seeing, but she nearly got fired for it. Same thing with Celia Needham in ceramics.'

Genevieve puts down her tea to wave her hands in denial. 'Look, it's none of my business.'

'You're damn right it's none of your business. Not when your Viktor spends all that time in the Peaks with Hugo, shagging god knows which students in our—' She stops, her voice filled with indignation. 'No not *our*. . . *my* cottage. *My fucking cottage*. Not when you're screwing Michael and thinking no one knows. You're damn right it's none of your business.'

The shock makes me shut the window. I turn to look at the others.

They've all heard what she said.

Wide-eyed, I whisper-shout at Michael. 'Are you really?'

'What?'

'Fucking Genevieve?'

'Not seriously, only now and again.'

Lauren gets up. 'Callie takes things too far. That's what she does every time. She shouldn't have said that. Genevieve keeps out of everybody's face. She was only trying to help. That's not even true about Vik either, well not any more.'

Michael reties his belt and puts another Captain Beefheart record onto the turntable. *Safe as Milk* begins to play.

Sid quietly brushes the dirt from his trousers. I remember he mentioned walking in the Peaks.

I stare at him until he returns my gaze.

I say at last. 'Are you shagging Hugo?'

He smiles wanly. 'Yeah.'

I look at the other two. 'And is everybody really talking about me and Callie up at college? Is it like general fucking knowledge, is everyone calling me a "plaything"?'

Michael shrugs. 'Well, kind of.'

I stare at the three of them, feeling a wave of nausea. 'So, everyone is fucking everyone. Sid's fucking Hugo, Michael's fucking Genevieve, I'm fucking Callie. That's all genders and persuasions covered. So, nothing's real, nothing's true, and nothing's special. What about you, Lauren? I'd hate you to get missed out.'

She is calm and thoughtful. 'Well, I've already had all of them, except Genevieve . . . *and* each of you three as well, by the way.'

I laugh bitterly. 'We think we're living in some French film, but we're not: we're in bloody Sheffield.'

They look at me blankly. I am the object of gossip in a provincial art school, I'm being held captive, without access to my boots, by a woman who is giving me the best sex ever, but whom I may not actually like.

Forlornly, I roll my wrist and feel the coldness of my silver identity bracelet. I have a growing sense of unease at the predicament I'm in. I can't stay much longer, like some kind of pet, with no shoes and no money. I *do* have to go. I have to go back to Leeds and rejoin my real life. I don't even recognise myself in these fucking blue clothes.

Callie pushes open the French windows, her eyes like flint. She picks up her bag without looking at the others, 'Come on Jude, we're going.'

On the record player Captain Beefheart is singing about yellow brick roads and girls made of sunshine.

Callie waits. Her jaw is set, and strands of straw-coloured hair escape from her braid. I hesitate for a moment, but she darts a glare at me. I step in her direction, leaving the others watching me with scarcely hidden amusement.

Beefheart keeps on singing about yellow bricks, telling me to walk without looking back.

My feet sting as I struggle to keep up with Callie. She unlocks her front door with an angry twist of the key. Walking in ahead of me, she throws her bag on the kitchen table. I'm uncertain about where to place myself, or what to do. I hover behind her as she grabs a cloth and wipes the already impeccable worktop.

'Shall I make you an Earl Grey?' I ask in a futile act of conciliation as I pick up the kettle.

She won't look at me. 'Don't you think I've had enough bloody tea already?' she says, throwing the cloth in the sink.

I put the kettle down, feeling tongue-tied and miserable.

'I'm sorry,' I say, though I don't know what I'm sorry for. 'Do you want wine? Shall I get you wine?'

She gets herself a cigarette but doesn't offer me one. I hug myself and stare at my stained feet. She notices them too. 'Your feet are filthy. Could you do me the courtesy of washing them before you trail around my house ruining my carpets?'

I go upstairs, relieved to leave her anger behind in the kitchen.

Balancing on a small white towel in the bathroom, I manoeuvre my left foot into the hand basin, hopping precariously as I try to find equilibrium. Using her expensive soap, I scrub the grimy sole of my foot. The water turns murky. Bits of grit and grass stick to the soap. Swapping feet, I splash dirty water on the spotless floor, and the towel gets muddy streaks on it. My feet don't seem any cleaner, just wetter. I wash them again and the grime spreads further.

When I've finished, the towel is ingrained with dirt. The hems of my trousers are soaked. Her elegant soap is misshapen. Grey water has reached the far corners of the tiled walls. Still my feet aren't clean enough. I despair of myself. I don't belong here. I toy with hiding in the bathroom for the rest of the evening because I can't bear the iciness spreading through the house, but I can't do that. This isn't a party in a student house where you can hide by locking the bathroom door. Perhaps I've been in here too long already.

At the spare bedroom window, I peer out. Dusk has come and gone, leaving me looking through my own reflection into a void.

There is a photo album on the bed that I pulled from a

drawer when I was looking for somewhere to put my laundered clothes. Callie moves noisily below, while I sit in silence up here. I turn on the bedside lamp to study the grainy black-and-white photographs. In one, a baby is propped on a blanket in a landscape of pine trees. In another, four blonde girls wearing mittens and berets stand under snow-capped mountains. One of them must be Callie, but I can't tell which. They look so similar. The pictures of her parents are faded.

They don't smile much.

There's another photo which I'm sure is her. Aged about ten, she has skinny arms, and her legs are all knees and grazes. She wears a pair of shorts and a cotton top with buttons shaped like flowers. Her teeth are controlled by metal dental braces. I look at the happy girl in the photograph. I think about the woman she has grown into.

Claustrophobia tightens like a tourniquet. Maybe I should just forget about ever getting those boots back and leg it in my bare feet. Except I love my dark-red boots; they make me just a little bit taller, and just a little bit cooler, and a little bit leaner and more mean-looking than I really am.

There's an Edith Piaf record playing in the room below. Perhaps Callie's mood has lightened. Maybe I'll risk it.

As I prepare to go downstairs, my attention is drawn to the wardrobes along the back wall, both tightly shut, oval mirrors on the doors. A thought occurs to me. Callie has shoes in them. Maybe she'll have some old walking shoes good enough to keep but too ugly for daily wear. Her feet are bigger than mine, but if I took a pair of Hugo's thick socks as well, I could wear hers if I really needed to.

And I do need to.

I open the smallest of the cupboards. It is full of last season's dresses and a couple of only slightly dated coats and, yes, there are shoes in a pile on the floor. Most of them are high-heeled and pointed. I rummage through them, pushing the hem of an old maxi-coat aside to get a clearer look. I move some battered boxes to one side.

Then I stop.

Hidden at the back, stuffed in a carrier bag, are my boots.

They are repaired and polished, their deep red leather now oiled and supple, and the soles new and unsullied. There is a small white ticket on one of them bearing the name of the cobbler, and a handwritten note in careful, old-fashioned fountain pen.

'Mrs Hugo Reynard. Pick up Friday 4th May, before midday.'

That was a week ago.

When Callie sees me in the kitchen doorway, holding my boots, her face falls. I shake my head at her, trying to understand. She looks ashamed, and then uncertain and then defensive.

'You've had them back for a week.'

She can't look at me. 'I know. I was going to give them to you.'

'When? When were you going to give them to me?'

She is silent.

I put them on the counter. 'I've been in bloody bare feet. I've been stuck here not able to go anywhere. I've got cuts on my fucking feet, Callie.'

'Christ, Bluebird, it was only a few days. I put them in the cupboard and forgot.'

'I'm not your fucking bluebird, OK. You didn't forget. I've been asking you about them every bloody day.'

Her head dips suddenly like a small child; like the girl in the photograph.

She takes off her apron and looks at me. 'I didn't want you to go. I knew you would, once you had your boots.'

'That's fucking *mad*, Callie. Do you know how freaking *insane* that is?'

Suddenly I don't see her as that much older than me, for all her apparent sophistication and haughty superiority, she's probably not even thirty yet. She crumples up her apron and drops it on a chair, like it's a skin being shed.

'Callie. This is all just too . . . I feel like I'm going to suffocate. I've got to go.'

'I'm not ready for that.'

'Yeah, but I am.'

She leans against the sink, arms folded, looking past me. At last she focuses on me,

'You really are a little shit, aren't you?'

'Am I? I don't think I am.'

She hardens. The look in her eyes tells me that she thinks I should be more grateful, 'I give you everything you want, don't I? All I want in return is that you stay around.'

'What . . . until Hugo decides he's had enough of his current fling?'

Callie looks shocked, and turns away.

'Don't,' I say, 'Don't pretend that this matters to you.' I feel tears prickling but suppress them until my throat aches with it.

'I care about you,' she says.

It's stilted and I don't believe it. 'No. You don't. All you care about is you and Hugo. You and he have this fucking open-marriage thing, but according to *your* rules *I* can't sleep with anybody. I can't even flirt with anyone. But *you*, however, can screw Mr High and Mighty Fucking Reynard anytime he turns up. I just don't think that's cool any more.'

I look at her long and hard and she looks straight back. I don't care what she says. I know that it's Hugo who matters to her; it's Hugo she loves. She takes lovers to deal with the fact that he has no idea how to be faithful, that he has no intention of being monogamous, that he lives to follow his dick. She takes lovers to give herself some kind of dignity, to have some semblance of control. She takes lovers to try and be on an equal footing with him, to have someone in the house when he's not there.

I put my boots on the floor and lower myself into one of the chairs.

'I'm going to go, Callie.'

Briefly brushing her hand across her mouth, she says, 'Yes.' She seems resigned.

'I'm sorry,' I say.

The meal she has made is sitting in pans. Picking up the apron, she ties it on again.

'We should eat. No point in wasting it.'

There isn't any bitterness in her voice. She exudes sadness, like a minor grief, like the death of a pet. I feel wretched, but relieved. She gets up briefly to change the record to cover our silence. It's a quiet, jazz instrumental, one I would have associated more with Hugo than with her.

'I'll take you up in the car tomorrow, if you'd like . . . to Leeds.'

'No, I don't want you to do that.'

'I'm not letting you hitch, not with all these murders and disappearances going on.'

I haven't been taking much notice of the news, but obviously Callie has.

She serves up the starter, which I have recently learned is called an artichoke.

I push the strange looking vegetable around the plate with the tip of my knife. 'I hitch all the time. I'll be all right.'

'Don't you know how to eat the heart?' she unfolds her napkin.

I look up at her in surprise. 'Eat a heart?'

'That artichoke heart?'

I stare at her, confounded.

She takes my expression as an indication of my ignorance about artichokes. 'You take each petal, dip it in the mayonnaise, and bite out the pulp.'

Bite out the pulp from the petals of a heart.

I observe her in a slightly horrified way, which she takes as further proof of my lack of confidence in dealing with artichokes. She gets up and shows me how to eat it, leaning close to me. I smell the mix of her perfume, deodorant and perspiration.

Pulling a petal off she bites the tender flesh away, leaving behind the flaxy shell. 'Do that with all the outer ones. As you get closer to the centre there will be smaller, tenderer leaves. You eat those whole, apart from the tips. Be careful of them because they're sharp. Nip them off with your teeth. Next there's a layer of fibres that protects the core. You have to scrape that away very carefully, because they can stick in your throat. Finally, you get to the heart itself. Eat it whole with your fingers.'

There's artichokes and mayonnaise on her breath. I'm still not able to speak after my lesson in consuming a heart.

She returns to her seat and spreads her napkin over her

knees. 'Now about the hitching. If you won't let me drive you, what about a coach ticket? Seriously, haven't you been following the news? Hitchhikers get *murdered*. Everyone seems to know that except you. That girl *still* hasn't turned up. God knows what awful thing has happened to her.' She pauses. 'So many murders, Jude. One was only a few miles from here – that student teacher they found strangled at Bolsover. Nobody ever got caught for that. He's still out there for Christ's sake! And that other girl who'd hitched up from London and got found dead over in Knutsford.'

'I know, I remember them.'

I fall into silence. I recall them very well. The student was Barbara Mayo. The other was Jackie Ansell-Lamb. I read everything about those murders when they happened. We talked about it all the time at college because they were found so close to Sheffield. Each was last seen getting into a saloon car and found strangled with a ligature. Left dead in lay-bys.

That's where I got my hitch-hiking rules from. That's why I only go in lorries, or in cars that have women or children in them. It's the reason I won't get into little saloon cars with men who want to take me out to the Derbyshire moors.

'*Take a coach*, for God's sake.'

I shake my head and tentatively suck the flesh from one of my heart petals.

'I hate coaches. I'm not going in a coach. I might not even go straight to Leeds, actually. I might go jaunting, I need to clear my head for a while.'

Later I follow her upstairs to bed. We lie apart. Backs turned. As I drift into sleep, I see her eating the petals of my heart, sucking the pulp out and discarding the casing. The air is hot and still, and I kick off the sheets.

During the night I wake, and she is pressed into my back, her arms around me. I struggle for a moment with the sense of being constricted, as I feel the tightness of her grip. I carefully take hold of her hands where they clasp my upper belly, and gently prise them apart.

She responds by letting go completely and rolling away.

Why does the dark seem so complete tonight? I can't stand lying next to Callie any more. Her arm trails out of the bed and she is snoring like something hard has stuck in her throat. The petals of my heart?

I'm angry with myself for being such a fool. This is what you get for letting someone in. All I can feel right now is disappointed anger.

I need to clear my head of all this crap. I need to hit the road. I need to jaunt. I can't face another conversation or discussion. As Callie's snoring deepens, I quietly get up and dress, throw things into my bag and creep out of the house. I need to go right now.

Hitch to anywhere.

Just get gone.

23

Toto

It was a surprise to be dropped at Leicester Forrest East Services. I couldn't have been listening properly when I climbed into the cab of the furniture van. I thought the driver said he was going north, but he's taken me south. I've never hitched from Leicester before and I'm not familiar with the layout of this service station. It's like a tarmac and concrete village with a complex of buildings, huge storage tanks and different parking areas for private cars and commercial vehicles. It's hard to work out where to get a lift from.

The man in mechanic's overalls outside the petrol station is thoughtful when I ask him for the best spot to thumb a ride to Leeds.

'You're on the wrong side of the motorway. Everything over here is going southwards, so that won't be any good. Either go to the bridge right over there' – he points vaguely beyond the buildings – 'or maybe you should just go down the service road and onto the roundabout. The road goes to both the north and south intersections. I think it does anyway. That's probably the most direct route to take.'

It's a longer walk than I imagined and there are hardly any vehicles. I've never hitched on a slip road that was so quiet. Hitching has been a nightmare today. It's like I've lost my sense of direction.

I end up at a kind of overgrown traffic island, with nothing around but fields. It's peaceful and just for now the quiet and solitude is appealing as I didn't get much sleep last night. I sit on my haunches against a fence post amongst dandelions and Welsh poppies, listening to the occasional ticking of a grass-hopper. There's barely enough movement in the air to lift pollen from the flowers. It's so quiet that when I make a skinny rollie, the rasp of my fingers is audible against the thin leaf of paper. As the tip of my tongue wets its gummed edge, two young men come bursting out of the field behind me. It's so sudden that my fight or flight instinct propels me to my feet, and the unfinished rollie sheds its contents onto the ground.

The youths tumble through the fence, feet tangled in wheat and wire. Chaff comes up in clouds.

One of them stumbles upright and sees me. 'What the fuck!'

I am as much of a surprise to them as they are to me. For a moment they dart about indecisively, as though they're thinking about running back into the crops. Then they stop. The squarer and more ginger one turns his back on me, clasping his head with both hands, panting.

All I can see for miles around are fields. I ask them, 'Where the hell did you come from?'

They gawp at me, unable to summon an answer. The taller one, who has shaggy brown hair and a smooth boyish face, pulls himself to his full height.

'That way,' he says, motioning at the field behind him. He seems aware his answer is absurd, but he has no other to offer.

I scowl. 'You freaked me out. I just . . . shit . . .' I trail off as I gather the threads of tobacco clinging to the bottom of my trousers.

'You've got burn,' he murmurs wistfully.

'I've got what?'

'Tobacco.'

We size each other up. Something about the way they're dressed is odd: identically, in pale denim jackets over nylon shirts and heavy dungarees. I find it unlikely that one person would choose to dress like that, let alone two. They're unshaven and creased, covered in plant debris, but oddly clean at the same time. I try to weigh the situation up. I can't think of anything else to do but introduce myself.

'I'm Jude,' I say to the taller one. 'What do they call you?'

This causes him concern. He carefully considers his answer. I'm not part of whatever plan they're working to. It's like he doesn't want to tell me anything, but he doesn't know how not to.

'Lenny,' he says eventually, and his tone implies it's self-evident. I carefully piece my rollie back together. I like the look of him. He runs his eye over my body. Our eyes meet again in an interested kind of way. If we were in a nightclub, we'd be dancing by now.

'And him?'

The other one has angled his body away from me and is unwilling to acknowledge my presence. He kicks the grass gently with the back of his heel. Dandelion clocks break apart and float away, low to the ground.

'He's Mawkin,' Lenny says after a long pause, as if there were other options but they all eluded him.

His companion closes his eyes with a groan and slides down a fence post until he's sitting amongst the weeds like a denim potato sack. 'Stop fucking talking, Lenny, you prick.'

Lenny looks hurt by this rather than offended. Then exasperated. 'What's she going to do, Mawkin? You miserable, fucking arsehole, we're miles from fucking anywhere. She'll get a lift, or we'll get a lift, and we'll all be long gone.'

Still agitated, and with his hands anchored in his armpits, he turns his attention back to me.

'Is that a real name?' I ask of the square, gingery boy. 'Mawkin?'

Lenny answers for him, 'It's his surname, me duck. He likes it better.'

Me duck. That's a Nottingham expression.

I lower myself onto the ground, putting Lenny between myself and the sun. I like his spare body, his mid-blue eyes, and the way his brown hair stops just short of being curly. There's a fresh man smell about him, like aniseed. When he's not appreciating my hips, he stares at the cigarette resting between my fingers.

'Two's up?'

'What?'

'Share your smoke?'

For the first time, Mawkin looks at me with interest. His gaze moves over me until it finds the cigarette, and there it stays. Still he says nothing.

I pull out my precious tobacco tin and throw it to Lenny. 'Nah, roll your own, him too.'

Before he opens it, another thought occurs to him and he

cocks his head like a dog. 'Got any shit in here? I could kill a spliff.'

I smile but say nothing. My dope is safely in my pocket.

He gives a good-natured shrug and opens the tin to take out a paper and enough tobacco for a smoke. Before he returns it, he says, 'Cool tin.' He thumbs the gouache and varnish poppy field on the lid. 'It's nice.'

After flipping his smoke to catch it between his lips, he scrunches the outsides of his pockets in search of a lighter. We share my next-to-last match, our heads coming close together over the flame.

Pinching his cigarette between thumb and forefinger, he draws it deep, taking all the smoke in and holding it. His face relaxes into contentment, and he throws the tin into Mawkin's waiting hands.

They have dry straw in their hair. Mawkin's clothes are covered in flecks of it, as though he's rolled or slept in hay. His face is troubled, and he's hunched like the weight of the world is on his shoulders.

'So, who's after you?' I ask Lenny.

'Eh?'

'Are you running away from prison or something?'

Lenny's eyes widen. He abruptly brushes a fly away from his face.

'No, shit, no. It was— I mean, we're at a training institution. It's a new . . . a Young Offenders Training Institution.'

He tries to slur the word *offenders*, but I've heard it.

'You mean borstal?'

'It's not called that.'

A heavy bumblebee appears. It's as loud as a motorbike. Taking a flight line between us, it shoots off like a rocket over the fields and our eyes follow it. The interruption gives Lenny time to settle.

I look at him. 'I'm not going to grass you up. I don't do shit like that.'

My voice is low and disarming, it soothes him.

Mawkin has lain in the longest weeds he can find and is dropping asleep. Even as he slips into unconsciousness his face remains troubled. His mouth falls open. His hands uncurl and his cigarette falls onto the ground beside him. Agile as a cat, Lenny crawls over to him and steals it.

We sit next to each other and lapse into quiet.

It occurs to me I should be scared of them. They're escaped criminals.

'What are you in for?'

'Mawkin's a burglar. He robs houses and shops and things. He can open anything. He can make keys out of wire . . . got exams and everything.'

'Exams in burglary?'

'No! City and Guilds and that.'

He glances across at the frowning man boy now fast asleep. There's respect in his eyes. He leans back to feel the sun on his face. He's forgotten I asked him a question, so I ask again.

'What about you? What did you do?'

His face is untroubled. 'Taking and driving away.'

'Stealing a car?'

'Cars.' He emphasises the 's' at the end. 'I fucking love cars. If I see a car I've got to sit in that driver's seat and push the pedal to the floor.' His voice is low and excited. 'I can't help it. I've got to.'

He's far away now, remembering all the cars he's had.

'Once there was this bloody Triumph Spitfire, sitting there.

Door open. Keys left. I jumps in, turns the ignition and I'm gone! I'm onto the M1. I'm doing a ton. The cops are chasing me, but I'm over the fucking county line giving them the fingers. Dumped it, wired a Cortina and I'm back in time for the pub.'

I gather dandelions from amongst the dry foliage. The stalks are stiff and woody. I'm finding it more finicky to make them into a chain than I would with daisies.

'Why didn't you steal a getaway car?' I ask, searching for another flower.

'What, *now*, you mean?'

I nod.

He picks a dandelion and gives it to me for the chain. He hunts around for more, clearing the grass away from the roots and picking them low to the ground. 'Weren't no cars where we come from. We come all the way here through fields and farmland. Followed the hedges. Mawkin don't reckon we've got that far. Reckons we're still quite close to the unit, but that's his plan. He thinks they won't be looking close. Reckons they'll think we're far away by now, because we've been gone awhile.'

'How long?'

'Two days. Slept in a hedge, then in a barn. Ate stuff he put away from dinner and breakfast and that. Raw potatoes we dug up. There were leaves too, some weed called fat hen, that's what he called it. He knows about that stuff. Reads books and everything. Got water out of a trough. Washed in it too. He's funny like that, got to be clean. Fucking knackered now though.'

As if to illustrate his point, Mawkin stirs and stretches in his sleep. The movement of his leg hitches up his trouser to reveal the top of his boot and the pallid skin of his calf.

The grasshoppers come in all sizes and colours. They leap onto my fingers and crawl on the back of my hands. A stately brown one treading over a zebra-striped infant. Olive brown, shifting to melon green, along the length of a spiny little leg. They get in the way as I plait my flower chain.

'Did they chase you?'

Lenny's hair slips across his forehead. He is absorbed in his search for dandelions. He lies on his belly parting the grass carefully. Screwing up his face, he looks at the sun as though it were a clock.

'No. Mawkin planned it all like. We sloped off from the work-detail. They thought we was going back to the milking shed, but we legged it. He was going to do it by his sen, but I knew he were up to something and I just followed him. His grandad's sick in Derby. He wants to see him.'

He strips a plant stalk into fine lengths that curl into tiny springs.

'They'll work out where you're going,' I say. Another grasshopper has materialised on my hand.

'I know, I just want a pint and a shag with me bird before they catch me again.'

He darts me a look that's both exultant and sad.

'What's she called, your bird?'

'Lizzie. Have you got a lad?'

'I did have but we argued too much.'

I put the dandelion chain on his head like a diadem. He grabs my wrist gently with one hand, and holds the back of my neck with the other. Before I know it, his mouth is pressed into mine. I like the taste of him. I respond. Our breathing gets heavier. This is the best way I can think of to get Callie from my mind. Meaningless sex. Move on. Move on and forget

262

it. I retreat into the taller undergrowth in the dip of the field ditch, and he crawls after me. Soon we are fucking among the foxgloves and dock leaves.

Mawkin sleeps on, murmuring and occasionally twitching like a dreaming dog. Not a car comes by. Afterwards, we doze in the dry grass, too weary to care about the hardness of the ground and the sharp stones pressing into our skin. He rests his spent head in the curve of my hip, momentarily content with life. Some men roll away and never look at you after sex, but Lenny is naturally affectionate. He strokes the length of my arm and fingers the silver identity bracelet on my wrist.

'*Toto*,' he reads. 'You said you was Jude.'

'Toto's my nickname. Why do they call you Lenny? Is it short for Leonard or something?'

'No, it's what they called me down our street since I were a nipper . . . like Lenny the Lion – you know, that puppet what that chap makes talk on TV, what's his name, you know, Terry Hall? Because of me hair, I were all shaggy like a little lion.'

He's still all shaggy like a little lion. Soft and open like a girl, but long and lean like a man.

I nod at the crown of flowers, still intact if slightly crushed, 'And now you're a dandy lion . . .'

He doesn't get the pun. He moves his fingers with care as he buttons his shirt.

Mawkin awakens, stretches his leg like it's cramping, and sits looking about him with suspicion.

'Christ, I'm thirsty.' He focuses on Lenny and his floral crown. 'What are you? A fucking hippy now?'

I shake my head. 'No, he's a lion. A dandy lion, King of Beasts.'

I shoot a knowing glance at Lenny, which he returns.

Mawkin intercepts it and understands. It annoys him. It seems to confirm his suspicion that Lenny can't be trusted to get his priorities right.

'We call dandelions "piss-a-bed" where I come from. You'll be peeing your pants in the night.'

'I haven't had enough to drink to piss anything, pal.'

Pointing at the flower chain hanging from Lenny's long fingers, Mawkin is contemptuous. 'That's not even dandelions. That's catsear.'

Lenny inspects the flowers as though affronted. 'What the fuck's catsear?'

His companion sneers a little, as if that was exactly the response he was expecting. He avoids looking at me. I think he believes if he ignores me long enough, I'll disappear.

'Looks like dandelion, but isn't,' he says. 'Look it up, you ignorant twat. I bet you've never spent a day in a library in your fucking life.'

Lenny takes the accusation in his stride. 'No, I never fucking have. Been in plenty of pubs though, and what I need now is a bloody beer.'

The stubble on his chin is sparse, and he scratches it fast and hard like a dog. He's had the fuck, now he needs the ale. Mawkin brushes dry grass from his trousers. Straw falls from his hair like he's some kind of disintegrating scarecrow. He finally allows me a look that acknowledges my existence, and pulls an empty, flattened milk carton out of his pocket.

'Hold on, I'll be back.'

I'm surprised at his agility as he jumps back into the field and runs off at speed. Hedges soon hide him, and we can't see him anymore. Lenny seems vulnerable, unsure whether he's been deserted.

I punch him playfully on the arm. 'Gone to get you that beer?'

'Gone for a piss, more like.'

He dismantles the chain and puts one flower in his pocket as a memento. He discovers something else in the pocket.

'There it is!' He pulls out a lilac-coloured plastic lighter. 'I thought I'd lost that.'

He tests it. The flint grinds and a little flame flickers briefly. He hesitates and holds it out. 'It's no use to me without tobacco. Swap you for another snout.'

He has no forward planning. None of the *deferred gratification* I learned about in O-level sociology. Not only that, but he's already forgotten the cigarette he stole from Mawkin.

I say, 'But that lighter might come in handy later.'

'I need a fag now.' He waves the lighter at me expectantly, his other hand held out for my tobacco tin.

I accept the lighter, momentarily touched by his gesture. He knows I would have given him a cigarette anyway. For some reason he wants an excuse to give it to me. It's one of those transparent disposable ones, half-full of fuel. As I fumble to put it in my pocket, my harmonica falls out. He snatches it before I can grab it, and playfully elbows my hand away as he blows into it. The noise is raucous. He laughs at me and I laugh at him; he gives it back.

I play a short blues riff.

'You're good at that for a girl, aren't you?'

Mawkin returns. The previously flattened milk carton is now back in its normal shape and full of water. His hair and shoulders are wet. He delicately offers the carton first to Lenny and then to me, careful not to spill it.

'Where did you get it?' I ask dubiously.

He motions at a copse in the distance. 'Can't you hear that? That kind of hissing noise?' The water is clear, so I take the risk and drink it.

We lift our heads. I'm not sure at first, but then, yes, a noise I had taken for distant traffic surfaces as the hiss of water.

'One of them irrigation sprayers in a field over there. Clean and wet, it's all you want.'

Once we've had a drink, the question of food arises. Mawkin nods at the pile of flowers that was once a crown. 'If those *was* dandelions, we could eat them.' He looks around his feet and points at a rosette of serrated leaves. 'Now, *them's* dandelion. They'll do.'

He crouches and with a tool beaten out of a tea spoon, digs them out wholesale, handing some to me and the rest to Lenny.

I look at them lying in my hands, roots and all. 'What am I supposed to do?'

'Eat everything except the stems.'

So I do. Peppery at first, followed by bitter, I mean *really* bitter.

'It's food, it's not poisonous,' he says, reading the look on my face. 'My grandad used to give us this when I was a kid. Lived on a farm. Not his farm, like, he only worked there. Loads of stuff you can eat off the land.'

He regards Lenny, who's still morosely staring at the greenery in his hands. 'Bloody eat it, lad, it's all there is until someone picks us up.'

Lenny looks around bleakly. 'Do you know what? We could fucking die here before anyone picks us up.'

And I think, yes, we could. There's been nothing much passing for hours. The odd disinterested delivery van and one or two cars have rolled past at intervals, never giving any sign of even having seen us. I hear the traffic rumbling on the M1, but can't help agreeing with Lenny.

'We *could* croak it here, marooned,' I mutter.

Mawkin seems to think that too. His demeanour has changed towards me, as though he's taken responsibility for me as well as Lenny. He looks at my shoulder bag.

'What have you got? Food, money, or nowt but that tobacco?'

He seems to be asking out of concern. It makes me realise I really don't have much at all. He reads my face and makes a huffing noise. 'Useless, like him. All he fucking brought was a stick of deodorant and a lighter.'

'You was glad of that deodorant,' Lenny says quietly. He pulls another dandelion out of the ground and eats its roots despondently, wiping dirt from his chin.

It's late afternoon and the few passing vehicles have dried up altogether. I must have been here three, maybe four hours. The boys are spread out on their backs in a place between sleeping and waking. We have spent our time in and out of silence. Lenny has been attempting to trap grasshoppers in my matchbox, each one leaping out as he tries to get another in, but now he's defeated. We all are.

Suddenly he lifts his head, cocking his ear to a sound. 'What's that?'

It's an engine. A small silver car comes slowly along the road. All three of us leap to our feet and I'm at the kerb-side with my thumb out. The man in the passenger seat scrutinises us as the car goes past, viewing the boys with disdain and me with too much interest.

Lenny can't believe he didn't stop. 'How come he just drove past? Fucking bastard. How long have we fucking waited and he just drives past?'

He is crestfallen, sinking back onto his haunches.

Mawkin has other things on his mind. 'Did you see that; did you see the way that chap looked at us? Did he know you Lenny? He looked like he knew us.'

'How could he know us? How could a bloke in a silver car just going past know us?'

'I don't know, but he looked like he did.'

Mawkin is panting. It's as though he can see everything he's planned and prepared for slipping away. He looks at us accusingly. It's either my fault because I materialised out of nowhere or it's Lenny's fault for being so useless.

'We need a fucking lift,' he says with an air of finality.

Lenny doesn't seem to believe what he's hearing, 'I know that, don't I? Tell me something I don't know, you wazzock!'

No other traffic comes down the road and the light fades as dusk approaches. A slight wind has risen and it blows through my hair. Mawkin pulls his thin denim jacket tight and buttons it. His face has lost all its earlier hardness. His eyes are pale brown and he has long ginger lashes. I'm surprised to see he is silently weeping, keeping his head turned away so Lenny can't see.

'I'm bone tired, Lenny.' He rubs his face with the heels of his hands, smearing dirt, tears and sweat across his cheeks. 'Head-aching, bone-aching, bone tired.' His voice is barely audible.

Lenny has a hard edge to his voice. 'Me too, big man, only we can't give up. We've no choice.'

They've come to the end of their resources. There's a chill

in the wind and I don't fancy being here all night. I get to my feet.

'There's got to be a café at the Services up the road,' I say decisively. 'We should go and maybe get some food. We'll never get a lift from here.'

'We can't go there, people will see us, we'll stand out like tits on a bull.'

'Come on Mawkin,' I say. 'Let's stick together and do what we can. Anything's better than here.'

Mawkin is thinking hard. I see it in the way his eyes flick from side to side. 'Aye, well, I suppose it's better for all of us if we *do* stick together. We won't stand out so much like escaped borstal boys if we've got a lass wi' us. And you'll be safer with us than hitching on your own, won't you? What with that murderer what's out there, taking lasses off and strangling them.'

'It's a deal, then.' I put out my hand to help him to his feet. 'Let's stick together for a while.'

Already on his feet, and dusting himself down, Lenny is ready to go. 'I'm ready to take our chances at the Services. I can't eat no more fucking dandelions. I need a cup of tea and some nice burger and chips.'

24

Nel

Viktor views me intently from his chair. Whisky bottle in one hand and tumbler in the other, he says, 'You should wait before you make all these decisions Nel. He'll be back.'

'I don't want him back,' I say.

'Nel, sweetheart,' Gen intervenes as Viktor wonders what to do with the information that I have no interest in being reunited with his friend. 'Vik just wants things to work out, that's all. We care about both of you,' she says, 'but what we've decided is Vik's looking after Si, and I'm looking after you.'

I try to be generous, but I can't do it. 'Does he need looking after by Vik? I can't imagine it. He's got his new fucking girlfriend now. I can't think he wants for anything.'

I can't help the irritable look I give Vik. It's not fair, because this is clearly distressing for him. He's gone quiet, staring at his glass, chewing words at the front of his mouth. It takes him a while to spit them out. 'I stopped with them over the weekend.' He takes a sip of his whisky. 'She doesn't seem all that much to me. I don't know what he sees in her. I don't think she's all that smitten either. He's cut his hair to look like David Bowie. It makes him look a bit podgy around the face. She's . . . you know . . . how would you describe it?'

He looks at Gen for help.

'Don't know. Never met her.'

Searching for the words, it takes him a while to find what he's looking for. 'Very *southern*. I'm thinking they'll not last.'

'She can keep him or dump him, I don't give a fuck,' I say shortly.

Gen says, 'OK, that's that sorted then. Let's have some food.'

Now that I'm single, everyone wants to keep feeding me all the time. They keep trying to make me eat because they think I'm unhappy and that sorrow needs to be fed. But I'm not sad. I'm just seeing ugly things for what they are. Accepting they're shit. Glad to give them their real name and turn my back on them. Getting a bit happier every day because I'm starting to realise what I actually want. I won't pretend anymore.

I drink wine while they eat soup. It's quiet here; all the lodgers have been banished so that we don't get bothered. Gen is trying to make me feel coddled, which is nice of her, but it's like being inside of a felt-lined box. Muffled and silent except for the sound of eating and breathing. The dynamic is odd with just the three of us, like there's a piece of the jigsaw missing. If I was on my own with Gen, or if Sid and Michael were home, it would be fine. But now there's us two women and Viktor. It's quieter than we're used to. It would be better if Vik would go to his studio. I can tell he wants to, but he can't think of a reason.

'Right,' I say. 'Give me your dishes, I'm washing up.'

Vik leaps to his feet. 'I think I'll just go for a smoke in the studio.'

Neither of us protests as he heads back to his big black drawing with nothing but his cigarette and whisky to keep him company.

As I wash up, Gen wipes the dishes dry. 'So,' she says, 'you're really packing it all in?'

I nod and feel a guilty flush of happiness. I let myself hold on to it, allow it to grow bigger.

'Aye, I am, and I'll tell you something: it's like this huge bloody weight has just fallen off me.' I take my soapy hands out of the water because I need to gesticulate as I look for the right way to express it, 'D'you know what, Gen? I'm supposed to be devastated. But I'm really not.'

Her eyes widen, 'Aren't you?'

Washing-up foam runs off my wrists. 'I'm rid of Simon. It's been a massive thing to do. But it's good.'

Gen's whole demeanour changes. Her shoulders relax, like she's relieved.

I drop a handful of cutlery into the sink. 'You know, since we split up, I haven't cried about him once. I've grieted for everything else, but not once have I cried over him.'

Gen dries the small soup bowl for a long time, polishing it until it shines, considering what she says next. 'You've always been a better artist than him. You know that, don't you?'

'What?'

'He's ambitious, but . . . don't tell Vik I said this. Who's ever heard of a famous printmaker? Printmaking is something good artists do as a second string, you know, like David Hockney and Picasso. I know *you* make prints, but you're really a water-colourist. I print too, but I'm a designer. Simon is just a middle of the road, please everybody, silk-screen printer. I've never known why you thought you should play second fiddle to him.'

Her assessment comes as a complete shock. It has never occurred to me that I might be the one with talent or that Simon might be mediocre. 'Do you mean that?'

'I wouldn't say it if wasn't true.' She dries a knife, puts it in the drawer and starts on a glass. 'What will you do for work if you move back to Sheffield?'

'Lauren said there's a job like hers coming up at the City Museum. I might try for it.'

'Or here's an idea,' she says. 'You could work for me. Nick won't be able to do it much longer, what with his final show coming up. I've been wondering how I'd replace him. You're a good printer, *and* you're better at maths than me. I need help with the books, and with the shop. I'll pay the going rate. You could live on it.'

I stop in the middle of scrubbing out the soup pan. 'Would I do the printing as well?'

'That's what I need help with most. We can't keep up with the demand. You could print for me and do your own stuff too if you want.'

'You're not kidding me? You really mean it?'

'Of course, I do. I need the bloody help, don't I?'

'That would be incredible. Oh my God, thanks! It would suit me so much better than working at Lauren's place.'

Gen seems happy about it. 'That one at the City Museum would suit Toto, don't you think? All that stuff with paints and everything.'

I laugh. 'Aye, and if I knew where she was, I'd tell her so.'

'Well, who knows what she'll do next?' Gen folds up the teacloth. 'I'd be surprised if she goes back to Callie. I think that's well and truly over.'

'Thank fucking God,' I say a little too angrily. 'I hope she's just hitched back to Chapeltown to lick her wounds. Silly wee bugger.'

'She won't stay in Leeds without you.'

'I know.'

Genevieve pauses thoughtfully and touches my arm for a moment. 'You two are good together.'

I stare at her. Gen has known me and Toto for so long. She shared a flat with us. She's seen us drunk and sober and stoned and tripping and happy and sad. She knows everything about us.

'It's OK,' she says.

I stare back tentatively. 'Is it?'

'Yes.'

25

Toto

The service station rises in the distance like a fairy-tale city built on a bridge spanning the motorway. Dark gathers but the lights are warm and orange. We peer through the windows like Dickensian waifs. Waitresses in cheery sailor suits lean over smart couples drinking cocktails. I feel like I'm in a film. A really bad one.

I remember this place now. We broke our journey here a couple of times on our way back from our summer seaside holidays in Devon. We wondered about the Jamaican jambalaya on the menu but were too shy to ask what it was. Dad always settled on something familiar like fish and chips, Mum would have steak, and me and my brother and sister ate burgers to the sound of traffic passing underneath us. There are four restaurants, ranging from an upmarket one called The Captain's Table, to a common transport café serving bacon butties and mugs of tea.

That's the one we head to. Maybe we'll find lorry drivers.

They're always good for a ride. Right now, none of us cares where they take us, anywhere will be better than this.

Mawkin is drawn and worried. Lenny is alert and upright, monitoring his surroundings more and more keenly with every step. We walk into the neon light of the café, and the cloying smell of old food greets us. I find it slightly disgusting, but Lenny sniffs like a hungry animal and heads towards the counter. Mawkin hangs back and scans the people seated at the tables. They are not interested in us. They're eating greasy food off orange plastic trays. None of them looks like a lorry driver. They're families and travelling salesmen.

Mawkin blends into the edges of the room. He checks out the open kitchen doors, clocking its layout, equipment and people before nipping almost invisibly through an exit marked 'staff only'. Lenny scavenges cold chips from an abandoned table and shoves them in his mouth. He is as deft as a thief should be, and quickly drinks the dregs out of a lipstick-stained cup. When I get to the counter, the grubby glass cabinets are full of dry-looking pies and sausage rolls on paper plates. Small change plays through my fingers. I consider what I can afford. If I'm careful, maybe I can get tobacco too. I decide on a Cornish pasty and a small carton of milk.

Carrying my food, I look for somewhere to sit as Lenny strolls next to me with studied innocence. We pull out some plastic chairs but before we can seat ourselves, Mawkin reappears. He beckons to us from the door and, pasty in hand, I follow him and Lenny outside, around the car park and through a gate. There are big bins there, full of leftovers and stale pies and sandwiches.

'Pig food,' Mawkin says succinctly, 'and we're the bloody pigs.'

Flies swarm, and the smell is rank, but they sort through and find some sandwiches that aren't too stale or mouldy. I can't bring myself to eat any of it, so I stand to one side and have my pasty and milk. They wolf down the sandwiches. Afterwards they share a bottle of coke, which Lenny pinched from the counter. Once we've finished, he looks up brightly, his faith in life restored.

The place is busy with travellers coming and going. Coach loads spilling out into the car park to use the toilets and buy hot dogs. Some of them wander the terrace on the outside of the bridge, stopping to inspect the cars below, and dropping lolly sticks over the edge.

We find an obscure corner in a grubby passageway where the lights are not buzzing, and no one notices us when we give in to our exhaustion and lay down to sleep. Lenny has pulled chairs in front to keep us hidden. I lie with him at my back, his arms around me, sleeping with his cheek on my head. Mawkin is somewhere on the other side. His breathing deepening as sleep overcomes him.

I try to count all the times I've woken up on floors after parties. I used to like it. I remember the delight of carrying my boots through Whetheridge Common in the early morning. I remember the sound of a record player coming through a window playing a song about water and wine and happiness. And in my mind, I'm waving at the people in the window. They've been awake all night, like me, and even though we've never met before, we agree silently that life is more fun than a crate of crackerjacks.

But this is not like that. This is cold and hard.

Lenny rolls onto his back in his sleep. He's muttering

something. His voice is small and distressed. 'Mam, where's me dog. Where's she gone? Someone's killed me dog.'

In front of a dirty mirror in the service station toilets the lights flicker unpleasantly, and even disinfectant doesn't conceal the stink of stale urine. I'm combing my hair with my fingers, washing my face and armpits, using Lenny's deodorant, which he's gallantly lent me.

I wash my hands once again to try to rid them of grime. A toilet flushes. Reflected in the mirror, a door opens and a girl about my age comes out. She's wearing a grubby Afghan coat and a floor-length Indian dress. Her long mousey hair is tied back under a spotted bandana, and she has dark stains under her eyes. When she catches me looking at her through the mirror, we silently salute each other.

'Hey,' I say quietly. 'Everything cool with you?'

She responds with a nod, turns on the tap and proceeds to wash. She looks at me again through the mirror. She has a long, thin face and her skin is scabby around her bottom lip.

She considers something for a moment and blurts out, 'Are you in a car? I need a lift out of here.'

When I shake my head, she is only slightly crestfallen, as though it's the answer she expected. 'I've been here for so long, man. This place is shit. I never knew that the truckers don't stop here much. A bloke in the shop told me that Newport Pagnell services has a much better transport café and all the lorry drivers go there. And have you seen the exit ramp? It's too short; the cars have got no time to see you. This chick and this guy who were there before us, they said they'd been here for four days. Four bloody days, man!'

Now I'm concerned on at least two counts. I'm concerned for me, because I desperately want to get out of this place, and I'm concerned for her because she looks so worn down.

'Are you on your own?'

'No, me and my old man are trying to get to Bedford.' She shivers. 'We were robbed by these bastards pretending to give us a lift. Pulled knives on us, took all our stuff and chucked us out on the hard shoulder . . . haven't even got any smokes anymore.'

I end up giving her a couple of Rizla papers and a scrap of tobacco and we part quietly.

On the way back, I notice the phone booth on the wall between the toilets and the café. Ten pence for a national call. Every penny I've got counts. But I want to speak to Nel. She needs me after all that shit that's happened with Simon. I want her to know that I haven't forgotten her. I've lost count of days, but I think it's the weekend now and that's when she said she'd be at Gen's. Even if she isn't there, I could leave a message so at least she knows where I am. Unlike Jo and Hank, Gen's had a phone for so long that I know the number off by heart. I feel for a coin in the depths of my pocket and twirl it in my fingers.

The coin clicks into the slot as Gen answers.

'Gen,' I say, 'it's Toto.'

She squeals with pleasure and I laugh, holding the handset away from my ear until she finishes.

'It's got to be quick . . . is Nel there?'

'She is, and we were just talking about you. Nel, quick, it's Toto.'

There's barely a breath before I hear Nel's voice. 'Where are you?'

'On the road. I finished with Callie.'

'I know. Gen told me, and I'm glad, Toto. Really fucking glad. You two weren't meant to be together. She wasn't doing you any good.' I can tell that she's genuinely relieved, which makes me happy. Before I can reply she continues, 'Where the hell are you?'

'I've got a bit stuck at Leicester Forrest East. It's a bitch to get out of, apparently. I just want you to know I'm all right.'

'What are you doing there? That's the wrong way.'

'I know. I was really fucked off when I left Callie's. I wasn't thinking straight. It was a mistake. I'm heading for Leeds now, if I ever get a lift, that is. Are you heading back there soon?'

'OK, now. . . have you got another coin?'

'No.'

'Then listen. I'm moving back to Sheffield to work for Gen.'

'You're leaving.'

Abandonment swells up and I can't speak.

She doesn't give me time to dwell on it. 'Now don't get mardy, you're coming with me. I've sorted loads of things out since I last saw you. I'm going to get us a flat, Genevieve says Susan Rilsdon has converted her attic and she's looking for tenants. It's the whole top floor. Big enough for both of us and a studio as well. Gen said it has great light.'

'Move back to Sheffield with you?'

'And there might be a job you'd like. Lauren says there's more trainee posts coming up at the museum. She's already told them about you and they said you sound great for it. Would you do that? Would you want to do painting conservation?'

'And we'd have a studio in our flat?'

'Yes. I'm going to get my own loom. You can get an easel and everything. A proper one. Do you want to do this?'

I struggle for words. None of it seems real. I'm dirty and sleep deprived in an inescapable service station on the Highway to Hell. Yes, I want it, but part of me thinks I'll be stranded here forever.

'Yes. Fuck yes.'

'All right then, get yourself back to Leeds and we'll sort things out from there.'

There is a silence as we both ponder this.

'I love you, you annoying wee bugger,' she says suddenly.

And as the phone goes dead, I hear myself replying into thin air, 'And I fucking love you too.'

I try not to read anything into it. Try not to hope. Telling the air that I love Nel.

The boys are seated in the only one of the cafés that they haven't yet stolen from. On my return, I take a diversion to the window, and prop my forehead against it, staring onto the darkened highway. Her words are in my head, *I love you, you annoying wee bugger*. I can't help my smile. I think about being with her and having a job that lets me paint. A job that helps me learn more about pigment and oil and varnishes. I feel almost crushed by my hope. I don't know if that could even be true, but I want it so bad. I need to get back to Leeds now. I have a purpose. I've been so lost for so long; I barely know who I am. At the cusp between the road and the hard shoulder are shadowy figures. Some have their thumbs out, others aren't even bothering, and they're indistinct shadows. They look like lost souls waiting for the boatman at the side of the Styx. I really don't have a good feeling about our chances of getting out of here.

The dull café light distorts Lenny and Mawkin lounging at their table, making them seem older than they are. They're like characters from a German Expressionist painting. I sort of feel responsible for them. It's stupid, but I do. A little earlier, I was struggling with myself, weighing up whether to stay here with the boys, or to risk hitching the motorway by myself, braving the possibilities of soldiers, or other carrion-eaters cruising the highway. I don't know. I'm good at this shit, but I'm getting tired and the view from this window tells me that it makes no difference whether we hitch together or separately. No one's getting out of here, so I might as well stick with what I know.

There are three cups of tea steaming on the table when I get back to the boys. Mawkin is triumphant.

'Who bought those?' I ask.

He jerks his thumb towards his chest. 'There's coats hung in the kitchen area,' he says. 'Lots of loose change in their pockets.'

He winks as he gulps his tea. He is a revelation in his happiness, a newer, lighter man. We are fed and warm. It makes us much less driven to get back on the road. Lenny lolls on to the table. He has stolen two packets of tobacco, and a new plastic lighter lies on the table next to him. He slides a pack of Golden Virginia towards me without a word. I glance at him gratefully as I secrete it in my pocket.

The girl in the afghan coat gives me a feeble wave as she adjusts her dress and squeezes closer to her bearded boyfriend who is asleep with his head on the table.

Lenny gesticulates in her direction. 'Do you know her?'

'We chatted in the toilets. She's been stuck here for ages; her and her boyfriend. This place is hopeless. I reckon we need to go back out and walk across the fields or something. Get to a proper road with cars that bloody stop for you.'

Mawkin sighs and spreads his arms along the top of the seat. 'It's good here, though. I could get used to this place.'

His response agitates me. I push the tea out in front of me, and stare into it to see the distorted reflection of the tubular light above us.

Lenny smiles his best boyish smile and agrees with Mawkin. 'We could stay here a while, eh, Mawk? Easy pickings, warm, don't have to eat raw spuds and dandelions. Pinch stuff from one café and move on to another before they clock you. Easy, got it made.'

I'm adamant. 'No. Better to move on.'

He twirls his new lighter between his fingers. The shake of his shaggy head charms me. 'Why would we? I'm happy as a fucking pig in shit. You know what'll happen when they catch us?'

'They'll take you back to that Young Offenders place.'

'No, me duck, after they've given us a leathering, they'll take us to Wormwood Scrubs and reassign us. Only this time it won't be some nice soft place like Glen Parva, not somewhere like Gaynes Hall, or one of them other open units. They'll send us to some fucking hard place like Portland. So, this is probably it. This is as free as we're going to get. I'm not going to get to see Lizzie, and he won't see his grandad. Not this time. We can go out there and stand by some fucking road again, or we can stay here and be warm and fed and dry, at least for a while.'

There's nothing sad or angry in his declaration. He's amiably matter-of-fact, but Mawkin's face has fallen. 'I am going to see my fucking grandad. I didn't plan all this just to end up in fucking Portland.'

He rips a cigarette out of a new packet, jams it into his mouth and lights it as though he bears it a grudge.

There's an awkward pause as Lenny takes in the effect he's had on Mawkin. He softly punches his friend's shoulder. 'OK, OK, we'll keep trying. Don't worry, me old marra, we'll keep trying.'

As I reach to stub out my fag, the hem of my sleeve knocks my tea onto the floor. The cup smashes and spills tea onto my boots. The boys laugh and I swear. I pick up the pieces and deposit them on another table. I'm so tired and sore and fucked off. The image of the road below us winding interminably into the dark comes into my mind. I feel like I'm stuck at the side of the River Styx sitting under a sign that says ABANDON HOPE.

26

Nel

Hank is testing the plumbing by flushing the toilet and running taps. Jo is fingering cotton curtains.

'New,' she says. 'That Susan Rilsdon's done this place up nice.' The loft conversion is white walled. Windows have been inserted in the roof-shaped ceiling. Low enough to see through, high enough to flood with light. The tops of tall elms are visible outside, the movement of their leaves gently audible in the gaps in our conversation.

'It's nice,' Hank approves. 'Good choice. Can you afford it?'

'We can once the wages start coming in. I've got a wee bit put by that my granny left me. I was kind of saving for when me and Simon got married.' I laugh at the stupidity of that, and I'm pleased that laughing is getting easier. 'It's paid for the deposit and it'll keep us going for a while.'

'You'll need to furnish it.' Jo is going from room to room,

her shoe heels clicking on the wooden floors, her voice resonating through the emptiness. 'We've got a few bits and pieces you can have.'

'There's a great junk shop down the road. Some nice old furniture in the window.' Hank opens and closes a kitchen cabinet and randomly taps a wall. 'This area's good for stuff like that.'

I'm quietly happy that this part of town is further away from the art school than where we used to live. The population is a mix of working-class families, students and freaks like us, lively and full of brightly painted vegetarian cafés and artist-run galleries. Better still, we're not likely to bump into the Reynards or any of their ilk.

'I don't think we'll need much,' I say. 'A few chairs. A table . . .' My head drops, and I run out of words.

Jo rubs my shoulders. 'It'll be good, petal, don't you worry.'

I move away from her touch and look out of the window into the vast municipal park below. Green slopes roll down to a lake in front of the City Museum. A solitary swan loiters at the edge as a boat is rowed slowly over the rippled brown surface. Where's the other one? Swans mate for life.

'Right, then.' Hank rubs his hands together. 'Are we off up to Leeds or not?'

'Aye.' I'm decisive. Jo is going back into her last term at university. I'm going to tie up loose ends and start the process of moving out. 'I'll go down and see Susan,' I say, 'get everything sorted, and then we can be on our way.'

I think about Toto a lot on our journey, as I sit cross-legged on cushions behind Jo and Hank in the van. I harbour this hope that we'll walk into a house resonating with her joyful chaos. When Jo opens the front door, Hank and I are close behind. A radio is playing in the kitchen.

Jo says, 'Oh, the light's left on,' and instinctively switches it off.

'Is she here?' I look hopefully into her bedroom as Hank takes the groceries to the kitchen. 'Toto?' I raise my voice and listen. Nothing.

'Anyone home?' Jo calls.

'She's not in here,' Hank responds from the kitchen. 'No sign she's been here, no dirty pots. Nothing.' He comes back down the passageway with his hands in his pockets, 'Has she she's been in her room?'

'No, it's like the bloody *Marie Celeste*,' Jo says. 'She must have forgotten to turn everything off when she left. I don't think she's been here for a while.'

'No. I don't think she has,' I say. We exchange a quick glance.

'Where was she when you spoke to her?' Jo never worries about Toto. But now I can see it in her, and it freaks me out.

'At the services in Leicester. I mean, she did say she was having trouble getting a lift.'

I see Jo's mind working. She's thinking through all the possibilities, trying to find one that reassures. 'Oh, you know what she's like.' Her joviality is unconvincing. 'The bugger's probably gone to her mam and dad's for a few days.'

'She was heading straight here. That's what she said.'

We stare at each other, not wanting to name our fears, and we peel away to our separate rooms. As soon as I open the door, I'm greeted by the sight of a forgotten jar of flowers. The stalks are brown and mushy, like they're melting into the stinking water. Petals have fallen across my drawings and into my watercolours. They look like curled-up cream beetles lying on their backs. I brush them up, rolling them into spongey tubes in my palms. In the bin they unfurl back into petal shapes.

As I tighten the latch of the rattling window to quieten it, I scrutinise the street below. The contrast with the view from our new Sheffield flat is stark. The road is as dirty and as unfriendly as when I last saw it. The street walkers are up and about. My Uncle Fergus always referred to them as 'ladies of the night', and I always thought it meant that they were ghosts or something. The blonde one with the greying roots has always seemed rather ghostly to me, being so pale and bony. She sets off in the direction of the corner shop with a stooped man exiting the door of the brothel after her. He does up his coat, hides behind his collar, and scurries off towards the main road.

The young prostitute, Janice, is perched on their low garden wall talking to a couple of the local lads. Her hair is red and for a split second my heart leaps because I think it's Toto. But no, nothing else about this girl is a match for Jude Totton. She has a thin presence, like she wants to disappear, which is the opposite of Toto. She does, however, look more animated than I've ever seen her before.

The lads can't be more than fourteen or fifteen and they're acting out a story that's making her laugh. One is dramatically cowering with his hands over his head, and the other is strutting about like he's Al Capone. The first boy gesticulates as though telling a punchline, and they all fall about laughing. The tomfoolery subsides and the lads settle themselves down on the wall. One of them whispers in Janice's ear. In the blink of an eye, the mood changes. She checks up and down the street and reaches into her cleavage, retrieving something small for each of the hands now putting money into hers.

The exchange is so quick that I almost miss it. Secreting whatever it is into their pockets, they seem intent on getting to the park. That's got to be drugs. Probably dexies. That would explain why all the kids are so crazy around here. Speeding their tiny little minds off.

I sink into the dark brown armchair by the window, my favourite books stacked on the wonky wee table I got from the market. The chair settles its sagginess around me as I search the room for evidence of Simon. What has he left me with? I want to dispose of all traces of him. I tick things off on a mental list. He bought my shoulder bag, but I need that and I don't really associate it with him these days. Better keep it. There's the perfume he gave me: *Charlie*. It's the only posh perfume I've got. No, won't chuck that out. Simon's flowery bastard shirt hangs forgotten on the wardrobe door. It incenses me. That can bloody go for a start. I reach for a rubbish bag to stuff it into, thinking about his Ziggy Stardust haircut that Vik says makes his face look podgy, his new Bryan Ferry jacket and that fucking bangle. I think about all those wee bruises building, one jab at a time. I ram the shirt into the bag so hard that it splits.

'Fuck you!' I'm surprised to hear myself saying it out loud.

'Y'all right petal?' Jo's at the door. Half in, half out, half surprised, half amused.

I'm kneeling on the floor, struggling to fit everything into another plastic carrier, 'Never been better.'

Jo nods at the flowery sleeve that's still visible. 'Is that Simon's stuff you're chucking out?'

'Aye. It's going out into the garbage right now. I'll check

Toto's room while I'm at it. God knows what she might have left lying around.'

'You might need a bigger bag if you're going in there.'

All Toto's things are strewn around as though she's only just left. There's a T-shirt on the floor. I pick it up and absently stroke it with my thumb, like it's a part of her that remains here. What if this is all that I'll ever have of her? What if she doesn't want me, or she never comes back? I can't stand that thought. It makes my hands shake, so I push the notion away as hard as I can.

Her wooden chair is a makeshift easel, and a palette balances amongst the paints on the triangular, plastic-topped coffee table. All the bottles and tubes are open. I screw the tops on to her precious paints, starting with an oversized tube of Flake White, which is rolled from the bottom and splitting at the sides. It extrudes a paste of drying paint that I wipe off on to Simon's shirt. Thick colour. So hard to clean off.

Once I've tidied everything up, I notice the picture she's been working on.

A small canvas is part-painted in her characteristic style. In it, volcanoes erupt on a vast plain where a naked girl flees a band of howling monkeys. Toto has blocked in most of the forms on a black background. The monkeys are blurred shapes, whereas the girl and the volcanic fires are wholly realised. The running girl casts a long shadow in the gleam of the eruptions. Her palely painted face is filled with dread.

27

Toto

Lenny and Mawkin have found another fly-buzzing skip. It's bigger than the others, and they're inside it, picking out enough stale sandwiches and discarded sausage rolls to fill two plastic bags, also sourced from the skip. We're getting ready to go. I've finally convinced them that the only way out of here is over the fields to a road we can hitch on. They're knee-deep in rotting food, gravy stains seeping up their trouser legs.

'Fucking *pie*! Look at that . . .' Lenny twists the cellophane-wrapped article to see the label. 'Steak and mushroom. Top!'

Mawkin is focusing on a pile of stale loaves like he's trying to decide if they're made of gold or shit. He sniffs at one and inspects each side. 'Bastard mouldy,' he says, and tosses it against the container's metal-ridged side.

Suddenly he's happy. 'Mandarin yoghurt!' Two leaking plastic pots go into his bag.

Lenny is pushing the pie into his mouth until his cheeks

bulge. Mawkin shakes his head at him. 'Can't you even put one fucking thing in your bag? You're just bloody eating everything.'

'I've got some rolls, haven't I?' He opens his carrier to reveal the mushed-up pile of bread and cheese that were once sandwiches.

I can't believe the things they're willing to eat. It looks like a heaving pit of salmonella to me.

'Come on, we better get going, someone's going to see us.'

'What's the plan, chief?' Lenny clambers out of the skip to join me on the tarmac. To my surprise Mawkin looks over at me enquiringly.

Seems like I'm in charge.

'We've got to get to an *actual* road, with *actual* cars on it. If we go through the fields, we're bound to come to one.' I gesture at the farmland behind us. 'I mean, you guys can do what you want, but I'm going to find another way out.'

Bits of stodgy pastry are stuck around Lenny's mouth. 'What, back towards the unit? I'm not doing that.'

I shrug as though it makes no difference to me, but in my heart, I want us to stick together. There's adventure in being with them. They know and do things I've never thought of. They find food, steal cars, and have nothing to lose in ways I've never considered. More than that. I've grown to like them. I come up with another thought. 'The other way then? Over the other side of the motorway?'

Mawkin considers my suggestion.

'Aye, all right.' He thinks for a moment. 'We'll be going south. Wrong way like, but at least it will be away from here.'

Lenny and Mawkin have stolen coats from the kitchen workers. A beige mackintosh covers Mawkin to his knees. Lenny is sporting a motorcycle jacket. They think it makes them look less conspicuous, but it's the opposite. The mac looks like it belongs to a woman, and the leather jacket is too classy for Lenny, especially when you compare it with the state of his shoes and trousers.

As we make our way through the car park on the southbound side, Lenny quietly tries the door handle of every car he passes. Looks like second nature to him. 'Locked,' he murmurs after each attempt. Mawkin does the same, inspecting each vehicle's interior with a quick dip of the head.

A bald man, with epaulets on his dark grey uniform, is monitoring the boys from the walkway with his arms folded. He doesn't seem to have noticed me yet, and I want to keep it that way. It won't do me any good to be associated with these two borstal boys that he's observing so intently.

Moving away to the side, I manoeuvre through two rows of cars to walk a little ahead of them. From here I can monitor both the man and Lenny and Mawkin. I hiss a warning at the boys but I'm not sure if they can hear me and I don't want to draw attention to myself by speaking any louder.

The bald man's jacket is undone and he seems to be on a break. Without taking his eyes off the lads, he picks up a mug sat on the handrail dividing the pavement from the carpark, and drains it of its contents. Slowly buttoning up his jacket, he retrieves a peaked cap from the railing and steps towards an open door in an office building on the corner of the car park. Lenny hasn't noticed him, but Mawkin has. 'Come away from the cars, Len. He's on to us.'

'Who is?' Lenny stiffens like he's come out of a dream.

Mawkin points soundlessly, as I nip through the cars to draw alongside them.

'Is he police or something?' I whisper.

'No,' Lenny's attention is fixed on the man as he disappears inside.

Another thought occurs to me. 'Is he a borstal officer?'

'They don't wear uniforms, and they always have a long keychain looped on their trousers.' Lenny steps away from the row of cars, making sure there's clear space between them. 'He's probably security or something.'

Mawkin walks very fast towards a fence. 'Don't run,' he says, 'but get the fuck out of here as fast as you can. That bastard's going to call the cops. I'm fucking sure of it.'

We climb through the wire fence into a field of brussels sprouts and run. I don't know why I'm running alongside them. I haven't done anything. I'm not a fugitive, but I've thrown my lot in with them and I run as hard as they do.

The acrid smell of sprout follows us as we clamber through bushes of thorns and startled birds. Scratches on my hands. Stumbling breathless all the way through another field and through another hedge. We can't run anymore and we're walking through a meadow of grass, gradually breathing less loudly.

Lenny stops. He leans carefully into the thick of the hedge we've just pushed through. Cradling a small turquoise egg in the centre of his hand, he gently holds it out towards me.

'Look,' he says, 'I never found one of these before. It were in that nest.'

'Oh, that's so lovely.' I barely touch it, one finger stretched out to feel its chalky texture. The grey-brown speckles make the turquoise sing, and I want to paint those colours. Mawkin is impatient to go, but when he sees what we're doing, he stomps back.

'Blackbird egg,' he says like an expert.

Lenny's eyes are soft as they catch mine. 'Blackbird!'

'Was there more?' Mawkin is intent on finding the nest, pushing branches back and looking under leaves.

'There's three, if you count this one.' Lenny cups his other hand over the top of the egg.

'We can eat them.' Mawkin is matter of fact.

'Fuck off. There might be baby birds in them. I'm not eating raw baby birds. What the fuck's the matter with you?'

'It's good protein.' Mawkin looks to me for support, but he's not getting it.

I once knew a kid that collected bird eggs. I was there when he found a robin's nest. He took a thorn, pierced a hole in each end of the shell and blew into it to remove the contents. A monstrous embryo, with beak, feathers and huge yellow eye, spilled out. I never went collecting with him again.

'You don't need it, Mawkin. Look at all that stuff you scrounged before.' I point at the bag of manky food hanging from his hand.

Lenny carefully puts the egg back in its nest. 'Stop trying to fucking eat everything, Mawk. I'll eat dandelions when I have to, but I'm not eating raw fucking baby birds.'

Mawkin inspects his bag of spoils. 'Aye, I suppose there's enough there. We *could* eat them, though. That's all I'm saying.'

We reach a farm track made of tractor-marked yellow clay, tall weeds growing between the ridges. I stumble in one of the ruts and Lenny grabs hold of me. 'All right, me duck?' he puts his arm around my waist, pulling me into his side to keep me steady. I put my arm around him in return.

Mawkin touches my elbow fleetingly. 'Is your ankle OK? You haven't turned it or owt?'

I reassure him with a headshake and a smile, and look up and down the track, trying to decide which way to go.

We turn toward a copse of poplar trees by a metal gate. Getting closer, I smell a mixture of cow shit and boiling potatoes. Lenny runs ahead, vaults the gate, and is gone from sight behind trees and shrubs. I hear a radio playing somewhere and a woman's voice calling to a child, or a cat or something. Wind blows the words away.

'Farmyard,' Mawkin says to himself. 'Best not go too near the house. Find the sheds. There's always stuff in sheds.'

Lenny comes back running. He motions us to the left of the track and disappears through a hole in the hedge. We find him crouching in shadows as we clamber through undergrowth. He puts his finger across his lips.

'The wife's home. Sheds and stuff around this way . . .' he whispers and points to his left. 'Hay barn, tool shed, tractor shed. Loads of good stuff.'

As we circumnavigate the farmyard, following Lenny through the wind-swaying poplars, the sounds of life get louder. Pop music accompanies the sounds of someone sweeping with a hard-bristle broom.

Lenny leads us to the back of an asbestos outhouse. Mawkin looks at the closed window with the measured eye of a housebreaker.

'Hold on to these,' he says, hands me his food bag, slips off his coat and heads off around the side.

Lenny settles on his haunches to wait. 'He'll get us in. He can get into anything.'

Sunlight dapples him. His eyelids close, and I realise he can sleep anywhere, in any position. I crouch down and stroke his head. He opens one eye.

'You're full of bits of tree, ginger.' His fingers untangle a twig complete with tiny green leaves from my wild hair. 'Look at the fucking state of us!' He's joyous and incredulous. 'You'll never get a lift looking like that. I better nick a car – only chance we got.'

The sound of movement inside the building brings him to his feet. He stands on tiptoe so that he can see better through the head-high window.

'He's in. Through the skylight.'

Mawkin pushes the window above us open, and with a combination of pulling from Mawkin and lifting from Lenny, I get myself inside. Lenny tumbles through behind me.

The denseness of the cobwebs across the inside of the doors tell us that no one has been in here for a long time. Light is green-filtered through dried algae on windowpanes. The broken skylight that Mawkin used to gain entry rattles with each gust of wind. We're in a garage or a workshop: double doors to the front, piles of junk and worn-out machines throughout. Beetles and oily grime cover a workbench piled with dented paint tins, rags and old tools. It smells of engines and the walls are thick and soundproof. It feels safe in here.

Mawkin heads over to a thick ceramic sink with a cold-water tap. There's a brief rattling noise, then the water spouts brown and thick. When it clears, he cups his hand to drink and pronounces it clean. We slake our thirst.

A dried-up, industrial-sized block of grit-pocked green soap sits next to the tap. He massages it under the running water until it releases a paltry amount of foam. First, he washes his hands, then he strips his shirt off to lather his body.

'Don't look,' he says, 'I don't like no one looking at me,' and he strips off his trousers to attend to other regions. When it's my turn to wash, they look away and busy themselves sorting through junk as quietly as they can. I'm not sure whether they'll steal glances or not, so I pull an old door between us and prop it up against the workbench.

The soap is harsh on my skin and abrasive on my blue clothes, which are now starting to fall apart, no substance to them. I'm left smelling like a hospital and much colder than I was before I started.

'What do you think?' I point at the back window. 'If we come in and out of there, we could stop here the night. Go in the morning? If that bloke has called the coppers, I bet they won't be looking around here tomorrow. They'll think we're long gone.'

Mawkin nods. 'Aye, good idea.'

'All right, chief.' Lenny pulls out a couple of old stepladders and fixes them up as stairs on both sides of the rear window, as Mawkin sets food out on the workbench he's cleared for a table. I don't know whether we're more like the three bears having breakfast or the Mad Hatter's tea party as we sit around a pile of food from a skip and drink water out of three cleaned-out jam jars.

After we've eaten, I notice the state of my coat and make a feeble attempt to get it clean by sponging it down with a wet rag. I wish I could wash my hair. No shampoo though, and god knows what that hard green soap would do to it.

I play my harmonica quietly, so that it can hardly be heard at all. The feel and sound of it makes me feel safe. Makes any place I stay into my home.

Mawkin settles down to go through all the tools. He is paying special attention to a pair of pliers and a roll of wire. He cuts lengths and fashions them into loops and hooks. He is very meticulous about it. Every piece of wire eventually becomes a burglar's key, which he handles with the reverence of a master craftsman.

Lenny has taken off through the window and I make up my mind to follow. I've tucked my too-bright hair under a black woollen hat found amongst the rags. I imagine myself as a commando as I climb out down the stepladder.

The farmer's garden is edged with jungled rhododendron bushes. In their interior it's like a spacious, foliage-covered tent. I rub dirt on my face and, picking my position carefully, I lie on the leaf mould to peer out from under the big leathery leaves.

The radio sounds the pips that mark the hour and the announcer intones in a clear, upper-class accent, 'The body of a young woman, suspected to be that of Jennifer Curtis-Pope who went missing after last being seen hitch-hiking towards Derby, has been found in a lay-by near Cheltenham.'

It is switched off abruptly and a youngish woman in an apron emerges out of the door to prop a broom against the whitewashed house. Two cats yowl and wind around each other, whilst a chained German Shepherd sleeps on the flag-stones near the door. The dog doesn't stir as a man in overalls appears around the edge of the building.

'All right today, missus?' he says. 'Gaffer says he'll be back for his snap soon, but he can't get the cows across because of the police on the road.'

She wipes her hands with her floral apron. 'It's soup,' she says, 'it'll keep. Enough for y'sen too, if you want.'

'Aye. Won't say no.'

'What's the police doing out there?'

'Looking for some lads run off from the borstal. Two of them: tall one and a short one, they said.'

She follows him into the house. 'Again!' she says. 'They need to do something about that place. Hot, in't it?' She props the door open. The dog shifts and opens his eyes for a moment.

From inside, the man says, 'Them lads was seen at the motorway services. Looked like they were coming this way, the cops said.'

'How long before he can get the beasts across?'

I hear dishes and plates being set down.

'Shouldn't be long. They don't seem that interested. Wasn't only coppers though, there were a vanload of other chaps: plainclothes and long keychains. Tough-looking buggers.'

'From the borstal probably,' the woman says. 'I've seen them catch lads before. I pity those boys when they find them.'

'Serve the little sods right. You're too sentimental, missus.'

Pulling back from the overhanging leaves, I retreat into the shrubbery. Trying to move fast without making any noise, I stumble through soft leaf loam and ankle-deep humus. I almost bump into Lenny who is coming back to the outhouse just as fast as I am.

'We've got to get the fuck out of here!' His pupils are pinpricks of darkness.

Mawkin is surprisingly calm when we tell him.

'No,' he says, 'we'll wait. They'll not look in here. Calm down, Lenny. They won't think to come here. We're not escaped murderers or nothing. We're just two lads absconded from borstal. The cops won't waste time on it. The screws might keep looking, but they're bloody thick, and they can't go on private property unless they're invited. We just need to stay here tonight like we said. Wait till they're proper sleeping like, pinch their car and leg it.' He turns to me and his voice gets gentler. 'Are you up for it?'

I nod. There doesn't seem any other way out of this situation.

'We can't head north though, not at first,' he says. 'When they report the car missing, the cops'll be looking all the way to Nottingham. We got to go south, dump it, and get another one with a different number plate before we head back. All right? All agreed?'

Lenny thinks about it. 'Aye, suppose so,' he says eventually. 'Might as well kip for a while, then.'

28

Nel

The university corridors are quiet and I'm glad, because I don't want to talk to anyone. Clearing out my locker, I feel the elation of an escaping prisoner. Gathering up an armful of terrible paintings, done by children I never liked, I head along the corridor to heave them into a big black bin marked *University of Leeds*. It gives me the same satisfaction I had when I chucked Simon's things away. Feeling I should mark the import of the occasion, I give myself a moment to stare quietly into the bin, lapsing into a kind of peaceful contentment.

It's spoiled by the sound of coughing. Mira is on her own at the coffee vending machine. I greet her as we are the only two people here. She's the last one I want to have a conversation with, but I try to be polite.

'Hello Mira, how are you?'

She whirls tea dregs in the bottom of her plastic cup, glowering at them. Glancing up, she attempts something like a smile.

'What's up?' I ask tentatively.

'Didn't get that job at that grammar school in Sussex.' She looks defeated. 'I think it's because I've got a Sunderland accent. I tried not to let it show, but I think they heard it.'

I pat her arm because I can't think what else to do. 'Have you got something else lined up?'

'A comprehensive in Stockton-on-Tees.' She looks on the verge of tears. 'Things aren't working out like I wanted. Philip says there's no way he'll ever live up north. So that's another blow. He's saying I should go for it though. Use it as a stepping-stone to something better.'

'If that's what you want, do it,' I say, 'It's you who should decide.'

She composes herself, scrunches up her plastic cup and aims at the bin by the coffee machine. It misses and rolls under the table. Making no attempt to retrieve it, she looks at me sidelong. 'I overheard Barry and some of the other tutors saying you didn't even go for your interview at that girl's school.'

I shrug. 'I've got a job in a textile workshop with my friend in Sheffield. There's a possibility of Jude getting a job in the museum there as well. We're going to get a flat together. Just me and her.'

There must have been something in my voice, because Mira looks at me oddly.

Has she guessed at what I've only just come to understand and accept?

Something that my family will reject me for.

Something that might get me fired from jobs or beaten up outside nightclubs.

Something that's fine amongst arty elites from proper

middle-class backgrounds, but the wickedest of sins for the daughter of a Presbyterian bank clerk.

Where is Toto? Getting off the bus at the top of our road, I'm trying to ignore the feeling in the pit of my stomach. Stupid scenarios run through my mind. What if she's dead? What will I do? Who would tell her family? Would I have to pack all her possessions up? Would I have to throw things away? I couldn't do that. I couldn't discard even one tiny part of her.

I laugh at my stupid fears. She'll be fine. Stop thinking about it. She's probably at the Alternative School, larking about.

Mrs Silvera and her daughter, Pearline, step out onto the street just as I'm approaching our front door. I often see them after they've had lunch together at home. Both wear crisply laundered uniforms. One is on the way to work at the hospital and the other is going back to school. They're an oasis of normality.

'Good afternoon, Nel.' Mrs Silvera is gracious. She didn't use to acknowledge us, but now she greets us like friends.

'How are you young ladies getting along? It's been a bit quiet. I haven't heard Jude playing on her mouth organ for a while. I suppose you're all working too hard for your exams?'

'It's nearly all done now,' I say. 'You'll probably be having new neighbours soon.'

'Oh dear,' she says brightly as she pulls the door tight and double locks it. 'Never mind. Things never stay the same, do they?'

'Mrs Silvera?' I call her as she turns to depart.

She looks at me patiently, 'Yes?'

'You haven't seen Jude over the past couple of days, have you? She's been away, and we were expecting her back sooner.'

Mrs Silvera shakes her head. 'No, not for a while.' As she observes my face, she becomes pensive, 'Oh dear, Nel, I hope nothing's happened to her. There have been terrible things happening to girls around here, and on the news . . . that poor student who was strangled.' She remembers Pearline's presence and backtracks. 'No, I'm sure she's fine. Now don't worry yourself.'

29

Toto

I feel a deep sense of foreboding as the night darkens into patterns of stars through the skylight. Half-awake, half-asleep, I have the sensation of falling through the concrete floor into a crimson place swimming with eels and the scent of geraniums. I'm plummeting like Alice. I twist and wake up with a jolt.

Lenny is huddled under his jacket on the mattress next to me, his breathing soft and rhythmic as he sleeps, but Mawkin is bolt upright in a broken-backed wooden chair. He rubs his growing beard as though testing its unfamiliarity. Awake now, and uncomfortable, I have this feeling deep in my guts, a nagging disquiet that I don't understand.

'What's that sound, Mawk?' I whisper, and he shifts his position a little as he listens. It's like a frog or a cricket, whirring like a ratchet, churring continuously in the darkness.

'It's a nightjar. Have you ever seen one?'

'No. Is it like an owl?'

'A bit, but really ugly. They're brown and they've got huge

wide mouths, but they look like big fat swifts. They lie flat on the ground in the day like an old duster, and only fly at night. They used to be on my grandad's farm. I saw one once, looking at me from a pile of leaves like a fucking ugly toad-bird.'

'What do they eat?'

'Moths and that. Me grandad used to call it a moth owl. He said they drank milk from the goats too.'

'I'd like to see a moth owl that drinks goat's milk.'

Mawkin laughs and the moonlight glints off his teeth through the skylight. 'They don't drink goat's milk, that's all bollocks that me grandad heard when he was a kid.'

Lenny has woken to the sound of our voices. 'Who drinks goat's milk? That sounds fucking disgusting.'

'No one does.' Mawkin gets up and rubs dusts off his trousers. 'Thank Christ you're finally awake. Let's get this car nicked before they get up.'

I'm cold, so I'm happy to get moving. I've got my coat on and my bag slung across my chest. Lenny puts on his shoes and jacket, eats one last dried-up sandwich and takes a long drink with his mouth pressed to the cold tap. Mawkin has found a pop bottle from somewhere. He's washed it out, and he fills it with tap water for our journey.

'Right,' says Lenny. 'I'm after string. Did you see any?'

'Over here: thick stuff; rough stuff; thin stuff.' Mawkin pulls a drawer open in the workbench. Lenny assesses each roll and selects some lightweight twine. Using a blunt-bladed penknife from the same drawer, he cuts a length and ties a small loop in the middle.

The farmer has two cars, a Land Rover and a Cortina. Lenny

positions himself by the driver's door of the Cortina, holding the ends of the piece of string in each hand. Starting at the top corner, he hooks the twine over the doorframe, and works the knotted loop through into the interior. His brow is furrowed as he manoeuvres the loop over the lock-button, pulls it tight, then yanks on it.

It unlocks.

In a flash, he has the door open. 'Get in the car. You in the front, Jude, they won't be suspicious about a girl.'

He disappears beneath the bonnet to do something with the engine. It shudders to life and he jumps in, settling behind the wheel with a look of pure joy. 'Come on you little beauty!'

Behind us, Mawkin laughs exultantly and we creep the car down the track to freedom.

The road is ghostly as we head southwest. It's the time between dark and light. An owl made of snow feathers swoops into meadow grass, blurred like a poorly developed photograph, a smudge of white in a field of charcoal.

'Shit,' says Lenny. 'What were that?'

'Barn owl,' Mawkin says matter-of-factly. 'Caught himself breakfast.'

Lenny taps the glove box, taking his eyes from the road for a moment. 'Look in there, Jude. Might be summat useful'

As I reach in, I realise that, without even thinking about it, I've become a thief. I'm in a stolen car. I've got stolen tobacco in my pocket as well as my lump of dope. I hesitate.

'Go on.' Mawkin nudges me.

There's a book of roadmaps, and a tin of travel sweets that rattles when I shake it.

'We'll have them,' Lenny says cheerfully. 'Owt else? Fags? Sunglasses?' He gropes around in the glove compartment, keeping his eyes straight ahead. As he pulls out a pair of yellow tinted spectacles, he cracks a smile. They're aviator style and he looks quite cool in them.

'Night-vision glasses,' he says. 'Bloody perfect! Give us one of them sweets.'

Dispensing stolen confectionary feels like another step along the road to hell. I pass the tin to Mawkin. He gives the lid a twist and proffers the contents. Green sweets nestle in a pile of icing sugar. Lenny takes three and eats them in one go. A trail of white powder transfers from his fingers to his chin and marks the end of his nose.

'Quiet, isn't it?' Mawkin says. 'Nobody about this time of day. Them farmers will only now be realising their car's pinched. It'll give us a chance to get this one dumped and another one nicked. They won't look on the M5, either. They're never going to think we're going this way.'

Lenny is jubilant. 'Aye, I know. We'll get to Gloucester – get a nice car down there, bound to.'

In the driver's mirror Mawkin is lounging against the window as the day gets lighter.

'What would you know? You've never been there.'

Red creeps into the sky behind us as we go west. A vehicle speeds along the other side of the road. As the sun rises, there are a couple more cars. A lorry. The boys strain their heads to follow a police car cruising in the opposite direction. Lenny takes off his glasses as though that will give him a better view. I'm nervous about the police, as nervous as the boys are.

'They're not bothered about us,' Mawkin settles back down to eat another travel sweet. We fall into silence.

Soon I'll go my own way. I think about being warm. I think about clean clothes and washed hair. I hope the boys get to do the things they've planned before the cops catch up with them.

'Fuck,' Lenny says simply.

'What?' Mawkin and I respond simultaneously.

'Out of petrol.'

'Shit. How far can we get?'

'Don't fucking know.' Lenny's voice is strained. 'You'd have thought they'd keep the bastard thing filled up.'

'Pull over, maybe there's a petrol can in the boot.'

Lenny takes the car up the hard shoulder and partially onto the verge. We get out and feel the early chill. Our breath is like steam. It's too still.

Lenny jerks the boot handle.

'Locked.'

'No problem,' Mawkin takes out his wire tools.

Up the bank are some bushes and a set of silver birch. I'm busting for a piss, and I don't want to be hanging around with them while they're breaking into the car boot. There still aren't many vehicles on the road, but this is stupid. People are looking at us already.

'I'm going up behind those trees for a pee,' I say.

They're hunched over the back of the car, intent on getting the boot open.

'Aye, all right, me duck.' Lenny doesn't look up as Mawkin tries another piece of wire in the lock.

Behind the trees and the cover of the bushes, the grass is wet with dew and thick with clover. The sun is up over the low hills and the boys sound a long way away.

My bag keeps getting in the way as I try not to pee on my boots. It's really difficult when you've got trousers on. It takes a while for me to get myself sorted out, and as I'm finally buttoning myself up, I become aware that something has changed. The sounds are different. The boys have stopped talking. Slow rolling of tyres crushing gravel. Sounds of car doors opening.

I crouch down.

A police car: two policemen.

A deep voice with a West Country accent: 'Is this your car?'

I'm hidden by the lowest branches of a silver birch. The boys are sat facing outward in the open doors of the Cortina, one in the back, one in the front, feet on the tarmac. Two uniformed policemen stand over them. Mawkin is smoking with affected indifference, whilst Lenny shoots a glance up the hill towards me and shakes his head. The police don't seem to notice. They're eyeing the boys' clothes.

'Well, look at you two in your smart borstal buffs,' one says, reaching for handcuffs on the back of his belt. 'Couple of runaways?'

I've got my fingers around the wrap of dope in my pocket, thinking about throwing it away. Two to five years in jail if they find it. I'm holding it tight, ready to chuck it if they see me.

Lenny jumps up to make off, but the bigger of the two officers pushes him back into his seat. With an easy movement, he cuffs one of Lenny's wrist to the door handle. 'You're not going nowhere, sunshine.'

The other cuffs Mawkin, who hasn't put up any fight at all.

'Right, you little bastards, sit tight while I radio in about you.'

The bigger cop goes to their patrol car, and as he turns to face in my direction, I duck down. Tinny voices and radio crackling.

When it feels safe, I take another look. Lenny is grinding out his cigarette under his boot. He stretches his head up to talk to Mawkin over the door dividing them. 'Fancy a singsong while we're waiting? Beatles, I like the Beatles.'

Before there's a reply, he's started singing 'Hey Jude'. Telling me not to be afraid.

'Shut your mouth,' the cop interrupts. 'No one wants to listen to an off-tune little twat like you. Sounds like a bloody scalded cat.'

'Fair enough, chief,' Lenny says and aims a grin up the hill in my general direction. 'What about some mouth organ though? I've got one I took from a bird I know . . . to remember her by.'

Mawkin widens his eyes as Lenny reaches his free hand deep into his trouser pocket to bring it out. 'Fuck, pal,' Mawkin says, but Lenny just laughs.

He's stolen my bloody harmonica. He just wanted it, that's all. He can't play it. He can't sell it, but he just wanted it. I bet the police take it off him, too. Some bloody pig's kid will be wandering around filling my precious harp with noise and snot. For fuck's sake, Lenny, is there nothing you won't steal?

'Let me see that,' the cop gives it a cursory inspection, rolling it in his hand contemptuously. 'Not much to write home about, looks rusty. That'll get confiscated down the nick.'

Lenny takes it back. 'You're right. Not much point holding on to it,' and with that he flings it onto the hard shoulder. 'No use to me now.'

He's given it back to me. I bet that's the first time he's willingly returned anything in his whole life.

The cop adjusts his stance as he waits for his colleague to return. 'Which borstal did you abscond from, lads?'

'Glen Parva.' Lenny looks like he's trying to stare him down. 'Which one's that?'

They don't need to answer. The other policeman comes back looking pleased with himself. 'Leicestershire: one of them open borstals. We've to take them back to the nick in central Gloucester. They'll ship them off to Wormwood Scrubs.'

He turns to the boys. 'You're going to have a lovely time at the Scrubs, lads. I bet they'll throw a party for you. What do you think? Some nice jelly and cake? Or maybe you'll just get a good hiding.'

'Get stuffed.' Lenny says as though he can't endure the boredom any longer.

Up on the hill I hold my breath.

'What did you say?' The big cop leans over him.

'Stick it up your arse.'

The swift backhander across his face only makes Lenny sneer. The coppers act in one accord. Both boys are uncuffed and hauled into the back of the police car. Doors are slammed on them. The car turns on its flashing light and reverses briskly onto the motorway.

And they're gone.

I stay where I am. Trembling like a leaf and suddenly, alone. I try to make a cigarette, but I can't hold the paper straight. My hands are sweating. The tobacco goes everywhere. I bundle it all back into my tin and look hard at the wrap of cannabis. Two years in jail for possession. Close fucking call.

Houdini, that's what they should call me. No such luck for the boys, though. I feel their absence like the whole world's gone quiet. They've put them in the back of their car and driven them away. Just like that. Gone.

30

Nel

The sky through my window never goes completely dark. Here, on my back, in this bed that now belongs only to me, the house feels wrong. It feels morose. Jude's absence is like a hole in me. I feel the lack of her in these empty rooms. When she's here, it's like she touches me through the walls. We talk without speaking. We're the same.

Jude, I'm crouching by the fire, with handfuls of rosemary and thyme and scatterings of bark from the moors at Windgather Rocks. I'm throwing them in. I'm watching you. You, with that look that you get before you need to run. Up above me on that ridge, you rush at the upward draft where the wind gathers. Face upward, arms out, you run. So fierce, and shouting like your lungs will break.

*

Your heart is a compass. Follow it back to me. To my fixed point, that place that never moves or changes.

31

Toto

I'm standing at the side of the motorway with Lenny's voice ringing in my head, telling me not to be afraid. But I am. All last night and ever since I woke up today, I've had this feeling that something bad is happening, and I can't shake it. It's like some dreadful thing is walking towards me. It's been there, under everything all morning. The sky is still, waiting for thunder to break. My skin prickles like it does when you feel someone looking at you. But there's no one there. Nowhere for them to observe me from. Except the road. Someone in those cars going slowly by. Someone looking at me like a tiger stalks its prey.

My harmonica got stepped on in the scuffle. The top's caved in and it's unplayable, a mashed-up lump of metal and cracked wood. That cost me nearly as much as a week's rent. I can't bear to look at it in that state. What's the point in keeping a harp you can't play? It would be torture, so I send it twirling through the air into the grass up the bank. I love that bloody harp, my lucky charm.

Bloody Lenny.

Mawk won't see his grandad. Lenny won't get his pint, nor see his Lizzie. They went through all that just to get a beating and sent to a tougher borstal. It's weird to be without them now.

The stolen car sits as though waiting for something. The policemen closed the doors, but they didn't lock them. I make a quick check of the interior for things I could use or eat. The sweets are still in the glove box. I stuff two in my mouth and put the tin in my bag for later. I suppose someone will be coming to tow the car away soon, so it's probably best to get out of here as soon as possible.

Watching the cars stream past, I wonder what the best plan is. I could head towards Gloucester through the fields, hope I come to a road and try to hitch up north. That would mean trusting that the farmland up there is navigable. That seems too exhausting. I could get lost again and I can't face that.

A battered petrol can is lying empty by the back wheel. As I pick it up and screw its cap back on, I have an idea. Someone walking along the motorway with a petrol can would look completely legitimate. They might even get a sympathy ride. If the boys were here, they'd think that was a *top plan*. Lenny has rubbed off on me. Mawkin's thinking has got lodged in my brain.

I'm nervous; those cops might come back, or a patrol car could turn up, and I wouldn't have a good answer for why I'm supposedly getting petrol for a stolen car. The canister makes hollow sounds as my coat knocks against it. Even though it's empty, it smells of gasoline. Maybe the boys managed to use it to refill the tank. I feel guilty. If they hadn't had to wait for me, would we have been on our way before the cops turned up? Can't think like that. No one can help needing to pee. It's not my fault that the police came. I'm sorry though. Sorry it happened. Sad, because I miss them.

It's a long, seemingly endless walk along the hard shoulder. I notice all the things that wash up on the shore of a motorway. The strangest flotsam and jetsam. An oil-bruised doll's head in a pile of twigs, a shredded pyjama top caught in brambles, a Sherlock Holmes pipe full of charred tobacco. Things flung out of windows or carelessly dropped on those sunny days when arms trail out to feel warm air.

Trudging with the direction of the traffic, I carry the bruised doll's head. I'm absorbed by it. Sprouts of plastic hair punched into its rubbery head. Squeezy like a tennis ball. Little pouting lips. Spiky eyelashes like a row of spider's legs. One eyeball like a blue-glass bead, the other socket empty and stained with oil. What happened to the body? Did somebody rip off the head and chuck it out of a car window? It's the sort of thing my dad used to do to our toys when we pissed him off. Mawkin's bottle of tap water is in my bag. Dropping the doll's head, I watch it roll to the kerb whilst I drink. The water tastes disgusting: peaty and lukewarm. I arrange the bottle on the verge with the doll's head on top. It's a bizarre little totem. Maybe it will protect me.

The constant drone of passing cars is as claustrophobic as silence. If time stopped now, I would be forever frozen as a reckless ne'er-do-well, a grubby, hungry lost girl, listening for the ticking of an unseen crocodile.

Eventually I reach a feeder road that leads down to an inter-section. A sign points into Gloucester in one direction and the M1 North in the other. This is where I need to be. I hurl the redundant petrol can over the tall hedge behind me and cross the road to face the northbound traffic.

My calf muscles contract with weariness. I stretch, overwhelmed with exhaustion. I need a real bed. Ahead of me the highway is momentarily obscured by a pollen cloud that disappears like steam.

A man is standing on the hard shoulder, but when I blink there's nobody there.

Today is eerie. So still. Like the moment before catastrophe.

Nothing untoward is happening, but I want to run away.

Something coming closer.

Its breath on my neck.

A pale-grey car speeds past. My thumb's not even out, but about fifty yards beyond me, it pulls to an abrupt halt. Pausing, the car suddenly reverses at high velocity. Alongside me, it slams to a stop.

A very ordinary-looking woman rolls down the window on the passenger side. Round face, glasses, pasty skin. Her hair is parted unfashionably on the side and cut to rest on her shoulders. Her cold eyes flit over me. She has the most insincere smile I've ever seen.

'All right sweetheart? You waiting for a lift?'

Her expression is at odds with the words, but nevertheless I move closer. It's not the kind of car I've seen much on motorways; it's small and outdated. Travelling salesmen would never drive one of these. In fact, it doesn't seem like a car that does long journeys. It belongs in a village.

Her eyes are hard and brown behind her glasses. She is

dressed like a forty-year old, but without the unfashionable clothes and hairstyle she could be twenty or even younger.

She says, 'Get in, why don't you get in?'

There's a smell like biscuits and baked beans. Something else too: something like the layer of dirt just under the topsoil, or the damp earth at the edges of ponds.

'Look, I'm a woman, how am I going to hurt you?'

Weird thing to say.

She sees my doubt and makes a big play of a bright reassuring smile. I can see the legs of the male driver, but not his face. He is silent and still. I don't like anything about this. I don't like the way they reversed the car. I don't like the way they stopped even though my thumb wasn't out. I don't like the way she single-mindedly wants me to get into the car. There's something wrong about this, but I can't work out what. She's ordinary. So bright and cheerful with her high-pitched West Country accent.

'Don't be frightened of us,' she indicates her belly. 'Look, I'm pregnant, how's a pregnant woman going to hurt you? You haven't got nothing to worry about with us.'

I can't speak. My mind races. It's true. She's pregnant. There's a small tight bump under her cream blouse. My reason struggles with my instincts. She's right. What is a pregnant woman going to do to me? Pregnant women are not dangerous. I'm being offered a lift. I should take it. But the hairs on the back of my neck are prickling.

I don't take my eyes off her. I'll get into the car. I reach for the back-door handle. There isn't one, which disconcerts me. I examine the car meticulously. It's an old Ford Popular, like the one Dad had, which got too small for us kids. He upgraded to a Zodiac with bigger back seats and four doors, but I still recall the claustrophobia of that first car: the tiny space in the back, the small windows, the mock leather sticking to my thighs.

It was difficult to get out of. The front seat had to be lifted and we had to clamber over bent metal legs through a tiny gap.

If I get in this car, I'll be trapped.

As I give the interior the once over, I feel the woman watching me closely.

There is no rear door, so it breaks one of my rules: I have to be able to get out as easily as I got in.

I step back and shake my head politely. 'No, it's OK. Thanks anyway'.

She readjusts her approach and a soothing tone emerges in her high-pitched voice. Singsong like a little girl, she says, 'Where you going, my love?'

Why didn't she ask that first? Why did she ask me to get in before she knew where I was going?

'Leeds.'

'Come with us and have a cup of tea.' Her voice is honeyed, motherly, as though she's talking to a tired child. 'You can stay with us or we'll bring you back later, come on . . . Nice cup of tea and a biscuit. You must be hungry.'

Weird offer. Breaks another of my rules: *never leave the main highway*. But yes, I am hungry. Well, more thirsty than hungry. I don't even like tea, but it's true; I'm tired and thirsty, and I feel like I haven't been inside a house for ages. I eye the interior again. This tiny hesitation prompts a wheedling invitation.

'Go on, just get in, why not? Come on home with us and we'll feed you.'

I'm thinking of a deep forest where a woodcutter's daughter is eating the walls of a candy house. The Gingerbread Witch, with small red eyes, smiles from behind a sugar window. She sniffs the dank air. In the house is a cage. Inside the cage are finger bones in a neat little pile.

Bringing my attention back to the car, I look at the woman's pallid face. She's waiting with the crooked expression of a child who is about to pull a trick. Her breathing is audible, her eyes are fixed on mine and there's tension in her jaw.

But she's harmless because she's pregnant. I'm thirsty and she's offered me a drink.

The driver lunges into view.

A man with curly hair and a mouth full of chipped teeth. His eyes are depthless. He trawls them over me.

It's a physical assault. I step back, and back again, gasping for air.

I'm so far away from their car. How did I get this far away?

What's that smell? Is it phlegm? Is it spunk? Is it blood?

There is no fucking way in the world I am getting in that car.

When I was eight there was a man in the quarry pit behind our house who killed children. Gillian Preece at school told me. She said he climbed up the drainpipe and stole children away to his hut. It was always at night, when their parents were watching television. Her brother Glen agreed it was true.

Once inside that hut, he killed each child, flayed it and stashed the skin in a big wooden box. Every night I slept with a penknife under my pillow, waiting for him to come and get me, terrified of going to sleep, my heart pounding.

He's here. He's here now.

*

The Childskinner and the Gingerbread Witch sit in their car and weigh up their chances of bagging me. A car comes past, and then another. I'm right against the tall hedge surrounding the exposed grass verge. Waiting. He'll have to drag me back and push me through that tiny door. It's all too exposed. He won't do it. Too many cars at this time of day. Stay here. Don't move.

They are observing me, calculating. A clock is ticking in my head.

She makes a decision, turns her head into the car and screams at him. 'You put her off, you prick. What's the fucking matter with you, Fred? Don't look at them. I keep telling you!'

Her face reappears at the window and she glowers at me, all pretence of care and concern gone. 'Fuck you then, you little bitch. It's your loss.'

She winds the window shut, the car revs up and shoots off as fast as it came.

My knees give way and I fall against the hedge. I need to get as low as I can. I need to dissolve into the ground. I push myself into the roots of the hedge. Branches tear the skin of my hands and twigs break off in my hair as I wriggle into the ditch. Pressed flat to the ground, my body has disappeared.

Waiting for them to come back. I see it in my mind. It's like I'm standing outside myself. Watching the Childskinner getting out of his car in slow motion, scanning treeline and verge. I wait and wait, lying on the cold wet ground.

Waiting for the hunters to come back.

*

How long have I been here? Maybe ten minutes, maybe twenty. Fear has made time pass strangely, stretching and slowing it. Grasses rustle at the edge of the road. Apart from this sound there is nothing but silence and stillness.

I have pissed myself. As I crawl out of the ditch a pigeon lands in the tree above and the violent clatter of its wings makes me catch my breath.

I need to get out of here.

No one's going to give me a ride in this state. Shaking, filthy, covered in piss, I crouch behind the hedge and change into my spare knickers. My trousers are a different matter. I wash them out in a puddle at the bottom of the ditch and put them on whilst they're still wet. The heaviness of the sky breaks and water covers me. Rain. For the first time, I'm thankful for it.

I walk into Gloucester along tree-lined roads, right up against hedges, blending into walls. Hands in pockets. Head down. This jaunt needs to be over. I've got to hitch home, but right now I feel paralysed. Too scared to be anywhere near the motorway.

Lost in streets I don't know, after hours of wandering, I stop to rest in a bus shelter. I'm trying to calm myself by sitting perfectly still and watching the moonrise. But nothing feels safe any more. The sickle-shaped moon looks bitten; like she got too close to a wolf, and it ate her cheek. Is that what I've been doing? Some stupid version of Red Riding Hood, searching for wolves to eat me? I've been busy looking for danger, now it's turned around and come hunting for me.

I check how much money I've got. I'm praying for enough to buy a coach ticket, but there's barely enough for a sandwich.

I will need to go back to that slip road to try again, but I can't. Not yet. Tomorrow. A girl on a bicycle comes into sharp focus, the pedals clicking rhythmically as she passes close to the kerb. Two middle-aged men smelling of beer look into the shelter and make remarks to one another that I can't quite hear. They linger too long. A grey car goes past. The glint of an eye in the dark.

    Everywhere.

    They're still everywhere.

As the streetlights come on, I find myself by a gated park. Fields and woods behind them. It's dark over the high fence. Dark and quiet. I climb up and over.

In the morning it doesn't seem odd to wake up on a bench in a park. It's becoming normal to awaken in cold uncomfortable places. But Lennie and Mawkin aren't here. I'm on my own now, and I have to work out how to get water and food for myself. There's no Mawkin to pull up roots or find eggs; there's no Lennie to steal tobacco and bread.

    Alone in the freezing dawn, I walk around the boating lake trying to unknot my head and my muscles. There's a toilet block next to rows of moored rowing boats, and outside is a public drinking fountain where clean water arcs from its spout into a metal hollow. As I quench my thirst, a feral cat is busy tearing at something down by the water. When it sees me it bolts into the trees.

    It would be easy to believe I'm the only person left alive in the world. I wouldn't mind that right now. If everybody disappeared that would be fine by me. All the running and hiding I've done over the past couple of days has left me exhausted.

Sunlight on my face feels like it's cleansing me.

Smile.

Fucking smile.

Smile and feel it.

Back out on the streets, that small grey car is everywhere. I never noticed cars like that before, but now they're wherever I look, insinuating their way through traffic or hiding in parking spots.

I see the Gingerbread Witch and the Childskinner everywhere too. I buy a sandwich in a café and catch a glimpse of him at the kitchen door. She is on a bench waiting for a bus, fondling her bump and watching me.

When I look again, she isn't there. But she is.

She's everywhere now. They both are.

Stalking me.

32

Nel

There's a letter on the door mat addressed to Miss Penelope Gale. I don't open it straightaway because I'm distracted by the postmark. It reads *Leeds – Motorway City of the Seventies*. It's ludicrous. It reminds me of a film we were shown in Freshers' Week at art school. As the camera rolled over a landscape of cranes and bulldozers, a man with a booming voice announced, *Sheffield – City on the Move*. I can't even work out what these slogans mean. It's very optimistic about something to do with transport, but I can't think what.

The handwriting on the envelope belongs to my tutor, Barry. I yawn and scrunch it in one hand as I wander into the kitchen. Jo is already at the table, churning her spoon through a bowl of cornflakes.

'Ey up, flower,' she says. 'You haven't seen the sugar, have you? These are horrible without it.'

I shake my head. It's drab and dark in here. 'Why are you sitting in the gloom?'

I try to open the curtains wider, but they don't budge. Jo looks around, as though considering the situation for the first time. 'Oh, I never noticed. Doesn't really bother me.'

Switching on the light, I'm depressed by what the forty-watt bulb reveals.

'Fuck, this place is shit.'

'Can't argue with that,' she concedes. 'What's the letter?'

I put the envelope on the table and reach down a mug to fill with tea.

'It's from Barry. I'll tell you once I've had a look.' I use a paring knife from the drawer to slice it open.

She watches me. 'Bet he's telling you not to give up on the teaching. He said he were going to do that.'

I barely read beyond the first line before it becomes apparent that she's right. I refold the page meticulously, slip it back into the thick envelope and chuck it in the bin. 'When you see him, tell him I'm sorry, but I'd rather have all my fingernails pulled out than become a teacher.'

I look at the time on the wall clock and notice she's not fully dressed yet. 'Are you not going in today?'

'No. There's nothing on. Thought I'd finish that essay.'

'So, you'll be stopping home?'

'Either that or go to the library,' she ponders.

'You don't like libraries. When we were kids, you'd run in, choose some books, get them stamped and then run straight back out.'

'I'm over that now. Back then libraries were bloody unnerving for a kid like me. Too big and too quiet and too clean. And them librarians didn't like me. Actually, nobody much liked me back then, what with me coming from Doncaster.'

'I liked you. God knows why.'

'Cheeky cow. You never had much choice in your pals anyway. Little Scottish freak. I was the only one what would put up with you.'

'Cheeky cow yourself.'

Down the passageway, the letterbox clatters in a gust of wind and draws my attention to the emptiness of the space leading to Toto's room.

Jo notices. 'Are you all right flower? Are you fretting about Toto?'

'A bit. Are you?'

'Aye. A bit.' She looks away, like she knows something she doesn't want to tell me. 'I didn't say last night because it was late and you were already asleep like. But I talked to Hank from the phone box on the corner. He got the Totton's number through directory enquiries and rang her dad. She's not there. She hasn't been back there since last November.'

That makes me bite the inside of my lip. 'Has she gone back to Sheffield?'

'Not according to Hank. He's rung Gen and everybody.'

'Fuck. Jo. Really? Fuck. Where is she?'

Jo puts her arm around my shoulder and lays her head against mine, 'She'll be all right. Stop fretting. There's other places she could have gone. She might even be back in Leeds already. You know . . . staying with those lasses she volunteers with. Last time she went to a party with one of them, didn't she? I tell you what I'm going to do,' she says quietly. 'Once I've been to the library I'll nip down to the Alternative School and ask those lasses if they've seen her.'

'I don't know, Jo. She seemed adamant she was coming straight here.'

'Nel. Flower. Just answer me this: when did Jude Totton ever turn up anywhere when she was supposed to? Ever since I've known her, she's been in the wrong place, on the wrong day, with the wrong stuff. Why would she be any different now?'

I know she's right about all of those things, but I feel like there's been a change. Something has altered in me and in Toto. I can't put words to it yet, or say it out loud. I can't answer Jo's question, because I don't know why Toto would be any different now. I only know she is. We're both changing shape from the inside out. I heard it in her voice on the phone, and I believed her when she said she'd come straight back. Jo is doing her best to reassure me, but nothing is comforting. Everything feels wrong. I don't know how to believe that it's all going to be all right.

After Jo leaves, I go into Toto's room and stand among her things. A sock lies balled up in the darkened corner by the window. I've been in and out a few times this morning, straightening the bedding, picking up clothes and throwing away a stray tobacco wrapper. Each time I visit this room, I search for more of her. Each time I tidy away, there's less. The sock is a red-and-black striped one that's escaped from a cupboard. It has a hole. All of the socks it's reunited with are also holed, either in the heel or the toe.

Everything she owns seems to be falling apart: a tattered paperback about politics; a book in a ripped dust jacket called *The Techniques and Materials of Oil Painting;* and a pile of dog-eared novels which are stacked across her mantelpiece. An empty blues-harp case, bearing the letter G on a yellow sticker, sits alongside them. Toto's mouth organ has gone with her on her journeys. That's comforting somehow.

I sit on the bed and remember her lying here with it cupped in her hands. She would play the blues late into the night, not stopping until Jo or I came down in our pyjamas to point out to her that it was two in the morning. I remember her surprised look the last time it happened, peering blearily at her clock and apologising. Toto has so few possessions and I like the thought of that familiar object travelling with her.

It's impossible to settle when I'm here without her. I get to my feet to study all the images stuck haphazardly to her wallpaper with Sellotape. Alongside her own drawings are pictures torn from magazines. Portraits of poets sit among highly coloured reproductions of works by contemporary painters and Renaissance masters. All the images are placed where she can study them from behind her makeshift easel. The easel itself has been positioned near the end of her bed. That way, she can fall asleep each night while contemplating the wee, improbable painting that she's worked on during the day. Every time I come in here, I spend more time with the picture she was painting before she left.

That girl is still running. The volcano still streams fire. Such delicate brushwork. Almost invisible blends and glazes. I pick it up to examine it more closely and as I do, another, smaller canvas topples out from behind.

Under the starless night sky, a dog nips the heels of a man fleeing the yellow hook of a moon. In the foreground, two girls are frozen in the moment before a kiss. They are leaning together, lips parting, eyes half-closed.

It's me and Toto.

Then I know it for certain. Just like I knew that Simon didn't love me, I know that she does.

It's so unexpected and beautiful, but I feel like a voyeur. No one should be looking at this without Toto's permission. I fumble with the larger painting of the running girl and place the canvases one behind the other, as I found them.

Hiding one secret with another, seeing the look of terror in that painted face as lava erupts around her, I think I hear a scream. Or maybe imagined it; perhaps it was a combination of my brain and this painting?

If I heard it at all, it was somewhere outside.

At the front door, I look both ways along the pavement. It's quiet. Almost deserted. Hardly anyone owns a car here, and these streets don't lead to anywhere important. It's too early in the day for kerb-crawlers to be looking for prostitutes. Far, far away, high in the sky, hot-air balloons are floating. They look the size of tennis balls and are coloured like children's toys. A faint and discontinuous grumble comes from them and I wonder if that was what I heard. But it's too muffled and too distant and it disappears completely when I return inside.

There's no point in going back into Toto's room just to mope and worry. It won't do any good. Down the dark passageway, our shared cooking and sitting room has never lost the smell of cats that we've tried so hard to eradicate with bleach and air freshener. As I open the cupboard, silver fish slither over the greaseproof paper that lines it. I survey the old tins of stew that were in there when we shifted here. They have rusted to the lining and the labels are brown. Twisting them off the paper, I think I might as well start cleaning things out. We'll all be gone from here soon.

There's some kind of commotion going on out the back.

Sounds like the kids kicking the trash cans over in the close. There are so many truants around here, and sometimes they run down the back alleys, throwing dustbins around and pulling washing off the lines. I've got some clothes hanging out there that I left to dry overnight. I need to check they're still there, or stop the kids messing with them. The last thing I need is to be washing my smalls all over again.

In the backyard, as the dampness chills me, I have the oddest sensation, like something is wrong.

Shouting and screaming.

A howl like an injured cat.

A raw wail of fear.

Against my better judgement I push through the back gate, out onto the cobbles to look. A little further down, a gaggle of kids are staring at something by one of the gates.

They are all strangely motionless, but one of them is screaming and screaming and screaming.

A man comes out of a gate, cursing the children for their noise and stops stock-still. He stares at whatever it is they're looking at on the ground.

I take a few steps towards them as though sleepwalking.

The kids run, scattering in all directions: away, just away, over fences and down the close. Their guttural sounds make my blood run cold. One pushes past me, and his eyes are full of terror. A woman comes out of another gate, and when she sees what is lying there, she covers her mouth and doubles over, retching.

Then I see it too. Lying partially buried under a discarded mattress, her face twisted away from me, is a girl.

The blood on the cobbles isn't liquid, it's a sound.

Thick with the buzz of flies. I can smell that smell, the smell from the back of a butcher's shop.

Long auburn hair matted with blood, coagulated like bitumen.

Oh Jesus Christ.

Toto.

I can't exhale. I put my hands on my knees and choke.

I turn away. There's nothing to hide behind.

I run back into the house and slam the door shut. I crawl under the table.

33

Toto

As I get close to Chapeltown, scruffy shops cluster and the smell of frying emanates from cafés. I've been walking for a while and my legs are tired, but near to Potternewtown Park I catch the scent of wet grass as a blackbird makes the chuck-chuck-chuck noise that warns of predators. I feel good. I almost feel safe. I hitched all the side roads to get here. Town by town, all the way from the West Country, never going near the motorway and finally climbing out of a truck in the centre of Leeds.

A lemon-striped hot-air balloon drifts low overhead. I've never seen one before and its presence above Chapeltown is strange and beautiful. Passengers peer from the basket and I'm taken by surprise by the sudden dragon-like roar of the burner. It's dropped way too close to the rooftops by my estimation. The pilot checks over the side, near enough for me to see his expression, and we acknowledge each other with a wave of the hand. Pulling on a rope, his attention suddenly shifts, as though he's seen something concerning over the roof behind our house. The passengers are all pointing in the same direction. Maybe they're worried about the balloon dropping any lower. Swaying in its slow traversal of our street, it fires up and climbs over chimneystacks to float away, its intermittent grumbling still audible in the distance.

When I arrive at the door to our house I search for my key, first in my coat, then in my trousers and bag. It isn't there. I check again more fervently. Then it dawns on me that the last time I remember seeing that key was on the dressing table in Callie's house.

I check every pocket again and it really isn't there. I rap on the door and wait. There is no response, so I do it again louder. Nothing.

'Shit.'

Cupping my hand over my brow, I press my nose against the dirty window to see if anyone is in my room. I rattle it, trying to wrench it up, but it's well secured. I pace up and down until I remember the loose latch on the kitchen window. I'm good at wriggling through windows. I'll give the back a try.

Sirens intrude as I walk down the street. They're coming this way. I stop to gawp in the direction of the squealing that's getting shriller as an ambulance turns down our road followed by a police van. The ambulance rattles past me towards the entry of our back alley, but the police van swerves to a stop outside the brothel.

A load of policemen jump out of the van wielding truncheons just as Tommy Strangman bursts out of the house and runs up the street, shirt unbuttoned and feet unshod, towards a parked car. A set of keys flies out of his hands as he is tackled to the ground by a young copper.

The pimp flails at his captor, 'Get the fuck off me!'

But more coppers pile on top of him, and only his head and his hands can be seen.

The street fills with onlookers, Mrs Silvera's front door opens and I find her by my side. 'What is it? What's happening?' she says breathlessly. 'Pearline, get back in the house!'

One of the local paperboys pushes in to get a better look and to share his knowledge.

'Tommy Strangman stabbed that Janice. She's lying around the back there. All in her blood.'

My heart lurches. A picture of the pearl-handled knife comes into my head.

I stare at Tommy and the word *butchered* keeps repeating in my brain on a loop. Has he cut her throat? I try to recall her face, but I can't. It's like the shock has turned her into a blur. It wasn't that long ago, but it feels like years. It was the first time I saw her, the day she asked me if I was in business and warned me off her patch. I remember lighting her cigarette. I remember she smiled, but somehow I can't picture what that looked like. I remember the writing on our door the day we moved in here. A curse in blood-red chalk.

I feel faint. Lowering myself onto our doorstep I hold my head in my hands.

'Is she dead?'

The boy is staring at me.

I ask him again.

'Has he killed her?'

He fixes his attention on Tommy, who is writhing on the ground with two coppers struggling to handcuff him.

'No, I don't think so,' he says. 'She were moving when the ambulance arrived. There's blood everywhere though.'

'She was moving?' Mrs Silvera interjects. 'Are you sure?'

'Oh aye,' he says in a matter-of-fact way. 'She were kind of waving her hands about.' He gives me a meaningful look. 'Bet that Tommy never expected the cops to turn up that quick. Someone must have got on the phone and grassed him up.'

As they lift him from the ground, Tommy Strangman swears and rages. It takes four of them to get him in the van, and he kicks and struggles every inch of the way. Even after the doors slam, his ranting can be heard, muffled and hoarse.

'Fucking pigs. You're dead. You're all fucking dead.' He bangs on the interior, making the whole vehicle shake. 'I'll kill every last one of you.'

I peel away from the growing crowd of spectators and run to the alley where a smaller band is gathered around the ambulance. Two medics lift a stretcher over the strewn rubbish and manoeuvre it to the back of the vehicle. I elbow between two teenage girls to get as close as I can. Janice is barely conscious but I think she sees me. Wan face, glassy eyes and just a glimmer of recognition as they hoist her into the ambulance.

The driver notices me as he climbs into his seat. 'Know her, do you?'

'Yes, will she be OK?'

'She's had a hell of a whack to the head and there's stab wounds on her hands and arms. Doesn't look like it hit an artery or anything important. She'll need stitches, that's for sure. Probably concussed as well.'

As the medics drive off through the scattered refuse, onlookers disperse and the ginnel becomes quiet. I tread around the blood stains, past a broken bottle and over a pile of abandoned clothes. Sparrows peck at a crust as though nothing has happened.

Our wooden back gate is slightly ajar. It creaks for lack of oil as I shoulder my way around it. The kitchen window is still not latched, but before committing to climbing in, I test the back door and find it unbolted.

It's dark inside. The sunlight never seems to reach our windows over the rooftops. I don't know why the door is open when nobody is at home. I remember Janice warning me that someone might break into the place while we were away. The room seems wrong, none of us would leave it like this. The doors to the food cupboard are wide open and there are tins set haphazardly on the counter. I'm alert like a fox, like I'm a vixen who knows how the hunter thinks. Ready to fight and ready to run.

There's something full of fear in here that isn't me. I listen for it.

Breathing comes from under the table.

Nel's arms are covering her head. She's curled tight like a thing inside a shell.

I crouch down. 'Hey, you.'

Her eyes flash open. She grabs me and pulls me under the table. As she tangles herself around my body, I hold on to her as though she's falling from a cliff.

'Oh, sweet Jesus,' she says, 'I thought you were dead.'

I bury my head into her. 'Fuck I've missed you.'

We crawl out of the dark and she leads me towards the door of my room. Her trembling stops as mine begins.

'It's OK,' she whispers. 'I'm not stealing your soul through your fingers.'

I don't care if she is. Something spiky and scaled falls away from me as she squeezes my hand. Something calloused softens inside me as I accept her touch.

34

Toto

In the days that have passed, sudden heat has turned spring into summer. Yesterday morning we were still in Leeds. I was lying in Nel's bed listening to the shuffling sounds of boxes being carried down the passageway and out into Hank's van. I shifted myself into the warm hollow that she had left, waiting for her return, hearing her tread on the stair. We drank coffee propped against each other. Our clothes lying intertwined on the floor.

This afternoon we're back in Sheffield's crumpled landscape. It's a town made of woodland, with trees in every street. Like Rome, it's built on seven peaks, and our new flat is right on top of one of those rises. Massive roots buckle the pavement just outside our gate, trunks so wide that you have to make a diversion around them. To one side we overlook strips of allotments spreading down the hillside, full of rows of DIY sheds and patches of cabbages and pea-flowers. On the other is the City Museum and its surrounding parkland.

Hank's van is parked on the footpath outside, back doors

open. An oak-leaved table stands on the pavement next to a set of matching chairs. He and I have just come back from collecting the stuff that Nel and I chose together in the local junk shop this morning. It was a mission getting that amount of furniture into the van. It made us slow, but I was insistent that we were extra careful with it all. It is precious already.

Hank pulls a double mattress out of the back in one determined movement and lays it next to the table.

'Are you all right with that?' he shouts after me down the path. 'Take a breather.'

'Yeah. I might. Good idea.' I labour for air as I lower the worn-out art deco armchair to the ground.

There's a sweet fragrance coming from somewhere. Honeysuckle, maybe, or perhaps it's jasmine. Park sounds wash in from the distance. Games being played. The shouts of swimmers in an outdoor pool. Purring traffic on an uphill road. In the park, two swans zigzag through the dinghies on the boating pond. Children chase balls across mown grass. A dog rolls in a flowerbed.

Hank's voice interrupts the moment. 'Do you want to get Jo and Nel? We'll need them to come down and give us a hand.'

The newly painted exterior door is studded with the number 24*a* in shiny brass. It doesn't shift when I give it a shove, so I beat on it with the flat of my hand. 'We're back,' I shout through the letterbox. 'We've got the furniture.'

Hank shakes his head at me. 'Where's your key?'

His reminder sends my hand into my pocket, and my fingers close over its smooth brass shape, still attached to the leather keyring it came on.

The door is our own private entrance. A wisteria vine forms

a natural portico and its flowers overhang the doorway. Nel has written our names, in her tiny, ink script, on a strip of her best cartridge paper and I've placed it in the slot above the bell. Seeing our names together like that brings me an involuntary smile and I brush my fingers over the words. *Totton and Gale.* Me and Nel. Pollen from the overhanging wisteria has left a barely visible film like powdered pigment. It makes my fingertips green, and when I brush my hands clean the stains on my T-shirt are leaf-like. Small and delicate. Hardly there at all.

I unlock the door, but it still doesn't move when I push.

Hank flips the mattress over to get it through the gate. 'You keep forgetting, don't you? Pull. It opens outward.'

The door swings ajar. Jo and Nel's voices drift down the stairs. Laughing lightly, words coming and going, half-heard and gentle. I stand perfectly still so that nothing will change. Close my eyes and let it all lap around me. Make it last for ever.

Acknowledgements

Thanks go to:

My agent, Jonathan Ruppin, without whose patient guidance nothing would have happened.

My editor, Becky Walsh, who pushed me to better writing with charm and humour.

All the people who helped along the journey, including Kristine Keir, Stephen May and Rachael Lowe.

But most of all, deep love and gratitude goes to my mentor and constant support – my *True North*, my wife, Jess Richards.